STATELINE

A DAN RENO NOVEL

DAVE STANTON

LaSalle Davis Books

This book is a work of fiction. Names, characters, places, and inci-
dences are products of the author's imagination or are used fictitiously.
Any resemblance to actual events or locales or persons, living or dead,
is entirely

LaSalle Davis Books

ALSO BY DAVE STANTON

Dying for the Highlife

Speed Metal Blues

Dark Ice

Hard Prejudice

For the late

Richard Nelson Salle

1

I KNEW WENGER WOULD be pissed I was bailing early, but he would have to live with that. Unfortunately, I had to live with it, too. It wasn't that I considered him a bad person, but as a boss, Rick Wenger was a tremendous pain in the ass. Besides being a chronic clock watcher, he was also the most obsessive tightwad I'd ever known. He always felt a three-dollar lunch tip could trigger financial disaster, and habitually pinched pennies to the point that the effort far outweighed the fiscal benefit. In the two years I worked for him he'd never bought me lunch, and after a couple of embarrassing restaurant incidents, I'd started picking up his share of the gratuity.

As an investigator, Wenger also left much to be desired. His latest fiasco was his interview with Lem Tuggle the day before up at San Quentin. Tuggle, a psychotic 250-pound ghetto thug, despised the white establishment and was well known in San Jose law enforcement circles for his history of violent offenses. Wenger had insisted I come with him to the interview in case things turned ugly.

"My schedule's packed, Rick," I told him.

"Rearrange your meetings, then."

"What do you think he's gonna do, leap over the table and attack you?"

"He's in prison for an unprovoked battery on two white businessmen in broad daylight. He didn't even try to rob them. They're still in the hospital."

"The jailers will have him cuffed. You got nothing to worry about."

"I still want you there."

Recently Wenger had begun ordering me to join him every time he had to interview anyone who posed a physical threat. I didn't think this was out of cowardice, but rather out of fear that an altercation resulting in injury would cause him to miss work, and he'd never recover the lost billable hours.

Since I relied on him for a paycheck, I tried my best to accommodate Wenger. But the previous morning found me wasting time with a street hustler who claimed he witnessed a robbery I was working. It took until noon to sift through his lies, and by then it was too late—Wenger had headed to San Quentin on his own.

I was at my desk when Wenger burst back into the office late that afternoon, his heels clicking with energy as he walked across the marble floor. "Tuggle was a piece of cake," he said. "I had a feeling it'd go well. He was totally cooperative and came clean with everything I needed."

"Sounds like they must have upped his dosage of Valium."

"Huh?"

"Nothing. Good job, Rick."

He shot me a slightly disgusted glance, then his smile returned. "Covie's gonna love this," he said, referring to Covie and Associates, one of San Jose's largest law firms and by far our biggest customer. Wenger looked giddy—the scent of money always did that to him. I knew he was probably consumed with plotting how the information he gained from Tuggle might justify a healthy rate hike to Covie. Maybe he could even parlay this into some higher profile cases; Covie generally only used us for chickenshit stuff that other investigators didn't have time for.

Wenger pulled out his Sony portable recorder and said, "Dan, you want to see what a real professional investigator does? Maybe you can learn from this." He grinned as he pushed the play button. I waited for the interview to begin, but the tape was silent. He hit stop, clicked play again, then once more. His forehead wrinkled. Nothing but silence.

"What the…" he muttered as he popped the eject button. He held the tape up close to his face and squinted, as if trying to read it. Then he put the tape back in and spent the next half hour jabbing the play, fast forward, and rewind buttons, until he finally accepted the fact that somehow, he, Rick Wenger, PI, had not recorded the interview with Lem Tuggle.

Without the recording, the interview was worthless. Wenger snatched up the tape and heaved it across the office, then smashed it into oblivion with the heel of his cordovan wingtips.

"Tough break," I said, biting my lip to hide the smile spreading across my face, but Wenger caught my contortions. Then I really did it—I pulled open my bottom desk drawer, grabbed the bottle of whiskey I kept handy, poured myself a slug in a Styrofoam coffee cup, and toasted him.

• • •

It was a few minutes past eight-thirty the next morning when I walked into the office. Wenger sat behind his desk, wearing his suit coat, studying his computer screen. His curly dark hair was freshly cut, and it made his ears stick out and his face look fleshier than usual. He glanced up at me.

"Glad you could make it," he said. "I trust you can do some meaningful work today."

"Morning, Rick."

His eyes narrowed, then he tossed a file across the desk. "I hope you enjoyed your imbibing last night. But you're on the clock now."

I felt my eyebrows rise. "Imbibing?"

"Do you really think you're impressing anyone with your drunken private eye act?"

"I had one drink yesterday."

He rolled his eyes, which looked particularly watery. Wenger had a chronic allergy problem. "I want a diagram of AJ's Saloon and write a complete report on the mugging," he said, then his gaze returned to his computer screen. "Make it chronological—describe everything that happened."

"It's almost finished, you'll have it by noon when I take off," I said.

His head snapped up. "What?"

"I told you before—I'm heading to Tahoe today."

"What? You never said a damn thing about leaving early."

"Yeah, I did. Anyway, look at the bright side—you get some extra time off from managing me. Consider it a bonus."

"Ha, ha," Wenger grumbled under his breath. He stood and paced around the office. "You know, maybe we should have you punch a time card."

"Gee, Rick, that sounds fun. Would I get to punch out when I go take a leak?"

"You better watch it, mister, or I'll write you up."

"Write me up?"

"That's right—it's what they do in corporate America. When an employee screws up, they write up an incident report and put it in your permanent file. It's how managers document subpar performance, and justify terminating an employee."

"Wow," I said. "Here, let me help you out." I grabbed a pen and paper and scrawled: *Dan Reno left early Friday to go to Tahoe. What an asshole.*

"Here you go," I said.

Wenger's face reddened, then he crumpled the paper and tossed it at the trash can, but missed. "I've got more important things to do than have this conversation," he said. "I've got a meeting with Steenebeck Trotter. I'm gonna win some business." He grabbed his briefcase and walked out the door, then popped his head back in.

"Make sure you leave your report on my desk and please show up sober and on time Monday, eight A.M. sharp," he said, tapping his watch. I gave him a mock salute as he left, but he was already gone, hunched forward and hurrying down Second Street in the cold February drizzle, a man with figures, decimal points, and high dreams of billable hours at inflated rates on his mind.

•   •   •

By eleven-thirty I had finished my report and Wenger hadn't returned yet, so I dropped it on his desk and jogged across the street through what had turned into a heavy rainstorm. I would have liked to pick up a sandwich from the lunch joint down the street, but I was getting soaked and had at least a four-hour drive in front of me, so I peeled off over to the half-flooded lot where I was parked.

I climbed into my car and relaxed as she fired up without a hitch and idled smoothly, despite the clatter from a muffler that needed replacement. My white Nissan Maxima had served me faithfully since I picked it up brand new ten years ago. I bought it with my fiancée the day before we married, and when she left me five years later, I lost our savings, the furniture, the appliances, and just about everything else of value, but I kept the goddamned car. It was a great car for an investigator; a Japanese four-door sedan, white, sporty for its time, but mundane enough to not create undue notice in a stakeout.

When Wenger did surveillance, he used his late-model BMW, and I used to think he was foolish, but BMWs and other expensive cars had become so common in Santa Clara County that they just faded into the street scene. It was all the money generated from the exploding computer and technology industries that paid for these cars. A lot of people here were getting rich. I wasn't one of them. I just hoped the Nissan could hold up and give me another couple years of reliable service before it faded into the ranks of a beater, a piece of shit, a heap, and then I could drive around Silicon Valley and clearly be identified as a member of the underclass.

I pulled out onto Second Street and turned the wipers to full speed to keep up with the heavy splatter of rain on my cracked windshield. I was anxious to get out of town; the traffic out of the Santa Clara Valley would be hell if it got too late. I blew through a yellow light on Guadalupe Parkway, blasting through the rain and onto the freeway like a man on a serious mission. My driving was typical of the traffic-weary commuters in San Jose; when presented with a rare space of open road, I'd always gun it in revenge for the gridlock that inevitably lurked ahead.

I had received the invitation to the wedding in Lake Tahoe four weeks ago. It was addressed to Mr. Daniel Reno, and I noted that my last name was spelled correctly—this was often not the case. My father was born Richard Reynolds, but when I was in high school he started researching our family tree, and found out his true surname was Renolowski. My grandfather was half Polish and half Hungarian and emigrated from Poland to America in 1916, but evidently the immigration officers at Ellis Island couldn't understand his broken English or decipher his crappy penmanship, so they penciled in Reynolds on his citizenship papers. The name had suited us well until my dad got a wild hair up his ass and decided it was high time to recognize our heritage and assume the proper family name.

To my family's dismay, he was utterly insistent, but in a bizarre twist of logic he decided to assume a shortened version of the name and had our name legally changed to Reno. My mother, 100-percent Irish and a very practical woman, wept out of frustration, but the old man never wavered. Eventually my younger brother and sister and I accepted the name and got on with our lives. It took a little longer for my mother—it wasn't until my father died that she forgave him.

I was invited to the wedding of my ex-wife's niece, Desiree McGee, who was marrying a man named Sylvester Bascom on Saturday at Caesar's in South Lake Tahoe. I was surprised to be invited, and my first inclination had been to decline, but the prospect of a day of skiing in Tahoe won me over. The night before, Julia, my ex, had called to instruct me on proper behavior.

"Do you have a decent-looking sports coat?" she asked.

"Sure."

"Well, this is a fancy wedding. Don't try showing up in jeans."

"Of course not."

"And getting drunk would be totally uncalled for."

"Don't worry, I'm not drinking anymore," I said.

"Or any less, I'm sure."

I cleared my throat. "So, who's the lucky groom?"

"Sylvester Bascom. Desiree's been going out with him for years. Haven't you ever met him?"

"I don't remember."

"You'd remember if you did," she said. "His family is one of the richest in California. The wedding's going to be fantastic."

"I'm still wondering why I'm invited in the first place."

"My family still likes you, Dan."

"Oh."

"Anyway, I helped Desiree with a lot of the arrangements. It's going to be the largest wedding ceremony they've ever had at Caesar's."

"Jesus, how many people are going?"

"Over five hundred," she said.

"No shit, huh?"

"Mmm-hmm," she hummed. Julia was a huge fan of weddings. "It will be something else. The Bascoms are paying for the whole thing. The wedding party's been up at Tahoe all week, living it up, skiing, the nicest restaurants every night, staying at the best hotels, all on the Bascoms' tab. The rehearsal dinner is at the Mountainside Mine. They've reserved the entire restaurant on a Friday night for a private party of two hundred. Can you believe that?"

"No kidding," I said, properly impressed. The restaurant was probably the most exclusive steakhouse between Sacramento and Salt Lake City. I'd never eaten there, but I'd occasionally stopped by the adjoining Midnight Tavern to enjoy a cocktail in their funky old-West-style barroom.

"It's true," Julia said. "John Bascom, Sylvester's dad, is mega-rich. He's the president of the Bascom Lumber empire. Listen to what Desiree told me about how he arranged the Mountainside Mine."

As might be expected, Julia explained, John Bascom had some difficulty convincing the restaurant's management to close the facility to the public and host his son's pre-wedding party on a Friday night during the peak of the ski season. The majority owner, a severe-looking man who was also the head chef, had treated Bascom with disdain, as if Bascom were a typical commoner trying to finagle a table without a reservation. Bascom had offered two hundred dollars a head, or forty grand total, and when the owner refused, Bascom asked him to name his price.

"You can't afford it," the man said, his assistant manager smirking behind him. Bascom stepped back, instructed his personal clerk to write a check, then handed it to the chef. "I assume that will do," Bascom said. The man nodded, holding the $100,000-check in front of him with both hands, an uncertain smile on his face.

"In the future, don't ever tell me what I can or cannot afford," Bascom said, then walked back to his limousine, his aide hurrying to keep up.

Julia also went into detail about the lavish arrangements for the wedding ceremony and reception. Desiree, a sleek, blond, twenty-four-year-old, was grateful for Julia's help with the wedding plans. Since so many people were invited, there was a number of challenging logistical issues. For instance, the chapel at Caesar's was much too small, so the grand ballroom was converted into a makeshift church, complete with portable stained-glass façades and an elaborate multi-tier pulpit. I found myself wondering if Desiree's father, Jerry McGee, felt awkward about his daughter's wedding being paid for by the groom's parents. Jerry was a dentist and was still recovering from personal bankruptcy. Julia said Jerry insisted on paying for the flowers, but had no idea they would cost upward of $10,000. John Bascom's wife, Nora, sent him a dummied invoice for $900.

I'd met Jerry a number of times, and I knew Desiree casually, so I guess that was good enough to make the invite list. It wasn't much to be proud of, but at least I still had a friendly relationship with my ex-wife's family. It was more than I could say for most of the divorced men I knew.

• • •

The rain slackened outside of Stockton as I headed north on Interstate 5. I pulled into a fast-food joint, ordered a chicken sandwich, and ate in my car as I drove. An hour later it started raining hard again. I was in the foothills, nearly to Placerville, and thought about stopping for a whiskey at the old Liars Bench Bar and maybe having one for Wenger, who despised liquor and did not even tolerate a glass of wine with dinner. He had gotten drunk a couple times in college, and made such an ass of himself he swore off alcohol for life. But I resisted the temptation and drove on through the wet gloom. Ten miles up the grade, the rain turned to snow, slowing my progress until a man in a yellow slicker and a cap with a Caltrans insignia flagged me over to the side of the road. "You got to chain up," he said.

I pulled on my coat and stepped into the flurries. The temperature was in that indeterminate range where it was cold enough to snow but not quite freezing. I lugged my chains out of the trunk, along with a tarp, channel locks, and a pair of canvas gloves, and went to work on my front tires. I finished without too much trouble and was congratulating myself when I noticed the late-model Ford station wagon that had pulled in behind me.

A man lay on his back in the muddy slush, struggling with a set of chains. He wore an Indiana Jones brown leather jacket that looked a size too small, and his hands were red with cold. He pulled himself out of the muck, looking around in despair. I could see a woman in the passenger seat of the station wagon, trying to calm two crying toddlers in the back.

"Trouble?" I asked.

The man threw up his arms. "I thought there would be some of those guys who install chains for twenty bucks," he said, shaking his head. He was chubby and balding, his face flushed from his efforts.

"Let me take a look." I laid out my tarp next to his car. Cable-style chains hung off his front tire.

"Hey, you don't have to. I'll pay you." He pulled his soggy wallet from his back pocket.

"Naw, that's all right," I said. I finished his first tire quickly and was moving the tarp to the other side of the car when a white Chevy four-by-four truck came roaring around the bend, its oversize, off-road tires spitting chunks of ice and gravel. The driver set the truck up in a four-wheel drift and came within six feet of where we stood, spraying slush and dirt all over both of us and our cars. A dude with dirty blond hair stuck his head out the passenger window. "Get a four-by-four, losers!" he yelled, and backhanded a partially full Coors can in our direction. It skipped off the hood of the station wagon and skidded through the scree and into the pine trees. I wiped my face and stared, hoping to get a license plate number, but my view was cut off by the chubby man sprinting after the truck.

"Lousy punks!" he screamed, hurling a handful of slush in their direction.

• • •

By the time I cleared Echo Summit and dropped into Tahoe Valley, it was dark. My visions of early happy hour had turned into a soggy two-hour drive over the pass at twenty-five miles an hour. I took the chains off and drove down Highway 50, South Lake Tahoe's main drag. Most of the businesses had left their Christmas lights on for the winter, and the colorful patterns reflected off the deep banks of snow lining the roadway. The brightly lit casino hotels loomed ahead at the Nevada border, dominating the skyline and overlooking the splendor of the lake. I'd spent plenty of long nights in those casinos, throwing away money and slurping free casino drinks.

Nora Bascom had arranged for a block of rooms to be reserved for the wedding guests at the Lakeside Inn, which was a step up from the cheap hotels I was used to. I walked into the lobby and smiled. The hotel was on the Nevada side of the border, in the city of Stateline, Nevada. You always knew you were in Nevada when you smelled the cigarette smoke and heard the clanging of slot machines. It was like walking into a different world, or like stepping back in time, to a place where bars never closed, gambling and prostitution were respected industries, and drunk driving was still treated as a minor offense.

· · ·

I chucked my bag on the bed and unpacked, hanging my sports coat and slacks. The wedding would be a swank affair, and I wanted to look presentable in front of my ex and her family, most of who would be there.

Although Julia and I were on friendly terms now, our divorce five years ago had been ugly. Julia had accused me of being a drunken loser, and despite what I thought was a reasonable excuse for my drinking, she was uncompromising. I'd been hitting the bottle hard during a depressing investigation involving a child pornography ring, and in the end I learned the hard way that women generally do not find excessive drinking an endearing trait.

The porno case culminated when the ringleader, a pedophile named Elrod Bradley, tried to slit my throat in the parking lot of the Y-Not Lounge in San Jose. I had left the bar after last call and was walking out to my car when Bradley emerged from the shadows behind me and got his arm around my neck. After a brief struggle, I managed to pull my Beretta .40-caliber pistol and stick it against his ribs. He had me in a chokehold from behind and was trying to crank my head back to cut my jugular with the razor knife in his left hand. Once I had my gun out, I gave him one warning, told him to drop the knife, then I felt a stinging pain as the blade nicked my ear, and I jerked the trigger. The hollow-point bullet entered the side of his ribcage and blew a fist-sized chunk of his spine and guts into the open window of a blue Corvette that belonged to the late-shift bartender at the Y-Not.

My recollection of what happened after that is disjointed. I remember holding my ear as Elrod Bradley gurgled his last bloody breaths into the broken glass and dirty gravel coating the parking lot. The blood dripped steadily from the deep slice in my ear, running through my fingers and soaking my sleeve. The bartender and three or four of the local drunks came out after they heard the gunshot, and a minute later the San Jose PD showed up, their sirens wailing, their lights turning the night into a carnival. A detective led me aside and started questioning me, but I had a damp bar towel clutched to the side of my head and didn't hear much of what he said. Eventually a uniformed cop took me by the arm. I stood under the kaleidoscope of blue and red lights while he cuffed me, drunk and disoriented and wondering what the next chapter of my life held in store.

2

IT WAS PAST SIX o'clock, and when I looked out the hotel window toward Lake Tahoe, the snow was falling steadily against the dark silhouettes of the pines. I showered and put on dry clothes, resisting the urge to first go downstairs for a drink. I had spent three years dead sober before I started working for Wenger, but I fell off the wagon the day he hired me, somehow already knowing I would need to drink to tolerate him. This time though, I had figured, I'd manage my drinking with the maturity befitting a man who had survived himself into his thirties. That's what I kept on telling myself.

The alarm on the clock radio must have gone off while I was in the shower—country-western music blared through the cheap speaker. I switched it off when I saw the message light blinking on the phone. I stared at it for a minute, hoping it wasn't Wenger. It would be like him to leave a message on my hotel room phone instead of just calling my cell. It was Wenger's way of trying to be unorthodox or unpredictable. I never quite understood his motivations in this regard. His voice came over the phone, and I frowned, as if battling a persistent case of diarrhea.

I listened to Wenger prattle on about a few spelling mistakes in my report, his need for me to arrange a second meeting with Lem Tuggle, and his expectation that I'd be in the office early on Monday. He was still talking when he exceeded the time limit and was cut off. I made a mental note to not tell Wenger where I was staying in the future, and deleted the message.

Through my window I could see the snow was now falling in a thick curtain. I stared, mesmerized by the random patterns of the snowflakes. If the storm let up by Sunday morning, there would be epic skiing conditions at South Lake Tahoe's massive resort. I ran my fingers down the edges of my skis, which I had propped up in a corner of the room. A good day on the slopes might be just the thing to put me in a positive mood come Monday morning.

•   •   •

It wasn't until I pulled into the Midnight Tavern and began futilely searching for a parking spot that I remembered the rehearsal dinner. Sylvester Bascom and Desiree McGee's dinner was being held that night at the adjoining Mountainside Mine restaurant. The parking lot was crammed full with the cars of the two hundred guests attending the event. I found a spot down the street and hiked through the snowfall back to the bar.

As I was passing the restaurant, I noticed a white Chevy truck parked in a handicapped spot. It was maxed out with off-road gear, including a lift kit that made it sit high above its thirty-eight-inch mud tires. The front grill, headlight guards, and steel step bars were polished chrome, as was the six-point roll cage mounted behind the extended cab. I looked through the windshield and saw a handicap permit hanging from the rearview mirror.

The permit looked bogus; the color seemed wrong. I walked around to the tailgate and checked out the license. The customized California plate under the steel bumper said "PSYCHIC." It looked suspiciously like the truck that rooster-tailed me with road snow earlier in the day, and I had a hard time believing the driver of this vehicle had handicapped parking privileges.

I climbed the four wooden stairs to the main entrance and pushed through the bar's heavy saloon-style doors. The restaurant was to the right, and was well known for its expensive menu and celebrity clientele. The Midnight Tavern, on the other hand, was targeted at less-discerning customers. It was popular with the local crowd, which, in Lake Tahoe, meant hard-partying snowboarders, timeshare salespeople, blackjack dealers, and miscellaneous loadies. But it also attracted its fair share of tourists looking for a real drink, hot pub food, and a break from the casinos.

The bar was about forty feet long, and the floor was made up of what looked to be ancient wood planks, but they felt solid and didn't bow when I walked across the room. I took a seat on the far side of the bar, near a wood-burning stove. There were about a dozen cocktail tables on the floor, set up to view a small, raised stage with a drum set and a pair of guitar amps. Three old-fashioned Western-style chandeliers hung from heavy beams that sectioned the ceiling.

About half the seats in the bar were full, mostly on one side where a group of locals were laughing and talking loudly. The bartender, a brown-haired girl with tight jeans and a white half shirt, finished pouring them a round and walked over to me.

"Do you still have beef stew on the menu?" I asked.

"Sure do," she said, pointing it out on the menu with a purple designer fingernail. She smiled, showing teeth that were a little too small for her mouth. But that didn't distract me—she had smooth skin, long, shiny hair, and her outfit was the type that suggested she was proud of what she looked like when she took it off. The type of woman that made for good, idle, bar fantasies.

A worker threw some split wood in the stove. I relaxed in the heat of the fire and watched the joint begin to grow more crowded. I ordered a beer and a shot of Canadian Club when the bartender brought out my dinner, and then a couple of men pulled up seats next to me. One of them, a blond dude with a three-inch billy-goat beard, said, "I'd like a Beam on the rocks, and get my date here a Shirley Temple."

"No, no, a double Jack and Coke!" the other guy exclaimed, while his buddy grinned. I tried to mind my own business, but the blond guy leaned forward and said to me, "Don't worry about my friend here. He's gay, but I've trained him to keep his hands to himself." I laughed, and the poor guy who was the butt of the joke looked over at me, sputtering, searching for a remark to save face. Then his eyes widened, and he said, "Dan!"

"Brad-o-Boy?" I had to look at him for a moment before I was sure. It was Brad Turner, my old next-door neighbor from San Jose.

"What the hell, buddy?" Brad said, standing and embracing me in an awkward hug.

"Good to see you, Brad," I said. "It's been too long."

Brad sat down and ran his hand through his thick mane of dark hair. He was about six years younger than me, and when we were kids I felt like I was the older brother he never had, which was unseemly considering the relationship I had at one point with his sister. Ahh, fun-loving Lana Turner. My teenage first.

"Is that you, Whitey?" I said, looking around Brad at the other man.

"You're goddamn right it is," Brad said. "You're looking at The Cheeseball himself."

Derrick Whitehouse and Brad had been best friends since elementary school. Brad had referred to him as The Cheeseball for as long as I could remember. Whitey was a gregarious, round-headed guy with an ample beer gut. I remembered he used to drink imported beer and smoke pot profusely. Looking at him, I got the impression not much had changed.

I shook hands with Whitey. "How have you been, man?" I said.

"Dude, I am insane," he replied.

"What you been up to, Dan?" Brad said, clubbing me on the shoulder with his open hand, looking at me with watery eyes. His complexion was ruddy, he needed a shave, and he smelled like cigarette smoke. It had been some years since I'd seen Brad, and he didn't look like the innocent, happy-go-lucky kid I remembered. I'd heard he'd been in and out of rehab a few times, had gone through a court-mandated twelve-step program, and had a failed marriage with a couple of kids behind him.

"Same stuff, Brado, just workin'."

"You know, I was in the Y-Not a couple weeks ago, and they still got a chunk of that guy's spine on the shelf."

"What?" I said, my fork hovering in front of my mouth.

"It's in a jar of vodka behind the bar. And you know what? They put up a sign next to it that says 'No Preverts.'" Brad started laughing and took a long swig from his drink. "Fuckin' classic," he said.

"His spine?"

"You knew about that, right? When you shot him, it blew one of his vertebras into the Corvette the bartender used to drive. Right? So the bartender cleaned it up and put it behind the bar."

I'd never been back to the Y-Not Lounge after the night of the shooting. It had been more than five years. I threw back my shot of whiskey. That night had caused me a heap of grief.

"Well, I guess that is classic," I said.

"Damn right it is. So, you just up here on a ski vacation?"

"Yeah, but I'm going to a wedding tomorrow."

"No shit? At Caesar's?" Brad looked at me in surprise.

"How'd you know?"

"Because that's why I'm here, buddy! Osterlund's in the wedding." Brad smiled and sucked on his drink.

"Sven Osterlund?"

"Yeah. He's in there at the rehearsal dinner." Brad pointed toward the hallway that led to the fancy restaurant. "As soon as it's over we're heading back to Caesar's for the bachelor party."

"You're still buddies with Osterlund, huh?" I said. Sven Osterlund had gone to the same high school as I did, but was a few years younger. He and Brad had become friends sometime after I left home, and I had never met him, but I'd seen him on TV doing commercials with his mother, Zelda Thomas, a popular psychic in San Jose. Osterlund always had his shirt off in the commercials, for no reason other than to show off his steroid-enhanced physique. Brad had told me stories of wild parties in hotel rooms with unlimited cocaine and expensive strippers, all funded by Osterlund. According to Brad, Whitey had pissed off Osterlund at one of those parties by suggesting that Osterlund didn't really work but was supported fully by his mother. Osterlund gave Whitey the option to fight him or jump from the hotel room's second-story balcony. Whitey jumped, and nearly bit his tongue off when his knee slammed into his chin on impact.

"Osterlund's all right," Brad said. "He's not a bad guy–"

"For a douchebag," Whitey interjected.

"Anyway, he offered to drive us up here, and he's got a righteous new truck," Brad continued. "It's a totally maxed out, brand-new Chevy four-by-four. Cost fifty grand."

"Must be some truck," I said.

"Dan, why don't you stop by the bachelor party? I'm sure it'd be cool," Whitey said. Then Brad leaned toward me. "If you need anything for the nose, let me know."

I looked at Brad, hoping he wasn't dealing. He'd always had a compulsive personality, and was the type who would probably snort himself out of business in a hurry and maybe end up owing some serious people a lot of money.

"You holding, Brado?" I asked.

He shook his head. "No. But Osterlund is. He's got a connection in Placerville, and he picked up a pack earlier today. Dan, this shit's da kine. You ever have core?"

"Core? Never heard of it."

"It's like half coke and half crank with ecstasy mixed in. It's the best junk I've ever had."

"I'm just going to take it easy tonight, Brad," I said, and excused myself to go to the head.

·　·　·

The door to the men's room at the Midnight Tavern was locked, so I walked down the hallway to find the restaurant bathroom. A waiter balancing a large tray of desserts hurried by me, and I followed him down the hall to the entrance of the main dining area, where the rehearsal dinner was being held. I heard the tinkling of silverware against glass, and the din from the large gathering subsided. A man in a steel-gray business suit stood at a podium on the far side of the room. His head was bald and his taut features were offset by a neatly trimmed gray mustache beneath a hawk-shaped nose.

I turned to continue down the hall, but when the man started speaking, I found his voice arresting. Despite feeling like an intruder, I stopped and listened.

"I'd like to thank everyone for being here in Lake Tahoe for this momentous event, the wedding of my son, Sylvester, to Desiree." The speaker was John Bascom. His voice came over the PA system with perfect clarity.

"Many of you, both family members and my good friends, have traveled great distances to be here, and I especially appreciate that. This is a major event for me personally. Those of you who know me well know how strongly I feel about family. A strong marriage is the basis for a strong family, and behind every successful man stands a strong woman. I can attest to that." He gestured toward a demure, sophisticated-looking woman sitting in the front, who stood and waved to a scattering of light laughter. "I've seen Sylvester develop over the last five years," he continued, "since he graduated from college, into a fine business executive. I'd like to feel I taught him well, and I believe I have, but all the teaching in the world is meaningless unless the student has ability. And instincts." He paused, leaned forward, and tapped his temple with his index finger.

"Sylvester," he said, "when you return from your honeymoon and walk into the offices of Bascom Lumber, you'll do so as our new vice president of operations."

A number of people in the front stood and clapped, and eventually half the room rose to their feet. John Bascom stepped down from the podium and shook hands with his son, then picked up a glass of wine and returned to the microphone.

"I'd like to propose a toast to the success, prosperity, and happiness of my son and his new wife, Desiree." Everybody clapped again and drank.

I found the restroom, but as I was walking out I nearly tripped over my ex-wife and her husband, Parkash Singh.

"Watch where you're going, you doofus!" Julia said, her eyes twinkling in amusement at having caught me off guard.

"Oh, hi," I said.

"What are you doing here?" The freckles on her cheekbones danced under her brown eyes.

"I was having dinner over in the bar." I turned to her husband and stuck out my hand. "What's happening, Parkash?" I said, feeling a grin spread across my face.

"Very good of course, Dan," he said. "And you are well?"

"Yeah, I'm good."

Julia had married Parkash Singh two years after we divorced, and despite occasional pangs of remorse over my failed marriage, I found it impossible not to like him. He came to America from India ten years ago and had established himself as a successful pediatrician. He seemed to be continually amazed and delighted with American culture, but after getting to know him, I saw through it. His naïve tourist persona was genuinely part of his charm, but Parkash was a shrewd, tough man. He had spent some difficult years in India, had seen two of his sisters disappear, and did three months in a squalid jail in Bombay when he complained too loudly. Despite his background, he was a naturally effervescent individual; he exuded good humor, laughter, and optimism.

"Why don't you come join us for an after-dinner drink?" he said.

I looked at Julie. "Come on, say hello to the gang," she said.

"Okay, just one drink."

"Excellent," Parkash said. He had an affinity for sweet drinks. I'd seen him swill copious amounts of Grand Marnier, peppermint schnapps, Yukon Jack, and the like.

People were milling around the plush dining room as the waiters served coffee and the last of the desserts. We sat at an empty table.

"My god, I would be so pissed if I was Desiree," Julie said.

"Why?"

"You should have heard all the speeches before dinner. Nobody hardly said a word about Desiree, it's all about how amazing Sylvester is. Then, to top it off, John Bascom announces the great Sylvester is getting a big promotion."

"Didn't Jerry get up and say something?" I said, referring to Jerry McGee, Desiree's father.

"I don't think they even gave him a chance," Julia said. "I think if the Bascoms had any class they would have said something nice about Desiree themselves."

"Sounds a bit self-centered on their part," I offered.

"That's an understatement. I think they're a bunch of snobs."

Jerry McGee saw us and walked over, preventing Julia from elaborating further. Jerry was a handsome man, but even for an event like tonight's, he hadn't deviated from his typical dress code. His blue Dockers were rumpled, and his old pink oxford shirt looked like it had been pulled out of a laundry hamper. His sleeves were rolled to the elbows, and his worn, brown belt was too long—the end hung halfway down his pocket. I looked down and was relieved to see he was wearing shoes; Jerry's habit was always to take off his shoes when indoors.

I shook hands with him and said, "Congratulations, Jerry."

"Thanks...I think," he replied, but then he laughed. "The Bascoms are nice people. I'm very happy for Desiree."

"I hear they are famously wealthy," Parkash commented.

"Well, I suppose that's true," Jerry said.

The guests were beginning to disperse. John Bascom, his wife, and the rest of the group at the head table stood and began making their way toward the exit. I spotted Desiree, looking quite slender and chic, and her husband-to-be, Sylvester Bascom, a well-built, balding man of medium height. They went their separate ways; Sylvester joined a cluster of fellows I assumed were the groomsmen, and Desiree was gathered up by the bridesmaids.

In my peripheral vision I noticed a curvy female figure in black walking toward us. The tantalizing shape of her body was clearly visible through her sheer gown. It was Mandy McGee, Desiree's voluptuous sister.

"Hello, Dan," Mandy said, peeking at me from under her thick eyelashes. The bangs of her dirty blond hair hung in a straight line over her eyebrows. An electric jolt charged through my groin, and immediately my heart rate picked up. She gave me a sly little smile, leaned down, and brushed her lips against my cheek, affording me an unavoidable, close-up view of her large breasts, which were barely restrained by the lacy bra beneath her low-cut dress. I averted my eyes, embarrassed by the provocative gesture, especially because it was in plain view of her father and my ex-wife. But Mandy didn't seem to care—I'd known her since she was sixteen, and she'd always loved to tease. I suspected she'd been doing so since she first reached puberty and realized the power she held over men.

"Hi, Mandy," I said, and took a long sip from a cognac that had appeared in front of me. "How are you?"

"Just peachy."

"Mandy, where's Renaldo, your boyfriend?" Julia said.

Mandy pursed her lips in a mock pout. "Oh, him. He got upset about something and drove back to San Jose. Can you believe that?"

Jerry dropped his eyes. "Time for me to get some rest," he said. "Goodnight, folks."

"Goodnight, Daddy," Mandy said. "I'm going to have a cigarette, Dan. Care to join me?"

"Sure," I said. As I left with Mandy, I felt Julia's eyes burning a hole in my back.

3

SHE LED ME DEEP into the building to a lounge I'd never been to. The room, dark and elegant, had the unmistakable aura of old money. The bar's ornate brass fixtures shined with a dull luster, like polished silver, and the woodwork looked carved from jade. Antique cocktail tables, glowing dimly under yellow mining lanterns, beckoned from the shadows. Between the tables, framed sepia photographs hung from the walls, depicting images of tycoons from the gold-rush era. I had a quick vision that maybe their ghosts would emerge from the pictures in the wee hours after closing time, to get drunk and relive the glory days of the boomtowns.

Mandy sat with her legs crossed, a Menthol 100 between her fingers, the smoke drifting into the shaft of yellow light above our table. Her black gown had a deep slit, and it fell open to reveal her shapely calf and tanned thigh.

"How long have you been up here?" I asked.

"Since Wednesday. We skied yesterday, before the storm came in."

"How was the snow?"

"There was tons of fresh powder, it was awesome. But unfortunately my date didn't think so."

"Why not?"

"Because he told me he was a great skier, which was a lie. We went to the summit and he threw a total yard sale and never found one of his rental skis."

"How did he get down the mountain?"

"They took him down on a stretcher sled. Can you believe that? He wasn't even injured, and Renaldo goes down on a stretcher."

"I guess it was either that or walk," I said.

"He's a big pussy, and I'm tired of his whining Chihuahua act. We got in a huge fight and when I got back to our room, all his stuff was gone. We drove up in his car and he left me. So, I'm here all alone." She paused. "What have you got planned tonight?"

"Are you in the wedding tomorrow?" I asked. I assumed she was.

"Nope." She blew a stream of smoke into the hazy lighting. "Desiree has a lot of friends. They just headed over to Nero's for her bachelorette party."

"Aren't you going?"

"I might. Unless something more interesting comes up, Dan." She tilted her head and looked up at me from under her bangs. I didn't know if she did it instinctively or if it was rehearsed, but her brown eyes conveyed her offer as clearly as if she had spoken it outright. I'd also been around long enough to know she probably meant a boatload of trouble and heartache.

"Maybe another time, Mandy."

She didn't say anything, but leaned forward and put her hand on my chest, then glided her lips over the ridge of my ear. "That's too bad," she whispered. She moved back and took a sip from her drink, her eyes silently considering me.

"I guess I'll go hang out with my sister and her friends," she said after a moment. She excused herself to go the ladies' room, and I headed back to the Midnight Tavern, glad to have resisted her, despite my body declaring otherwise.

•   •   •

Brad and Whitey were no longer at the bar, which was now nearly full. I sat alone near the end, drinking a cup of coffee. I was considering one more shot of whiskey before heading back to my hotel.

Two women at a nearby table were having an animated conversation. They looked to be in their thirties, and their dress seemed more appropriate for a nightclub than a casual bar. I couldn't help overhearing as one said loudly, "My god, I went to the bridal shower last month, and I blacked out!"

"Tell me about it," her friend said. "You know how some people are chain smokers? I'm a chain drinker."

I finished my coffee and relaxed for a minute, wishing I had a cigarette. I turned around to the two ladies. "Excuse me, are you two by any chance in town for a wedding?"

"Why, yes," giggled one with blond hair and dark eyebrows. "And you are?" She held out her hand, which looked like a junkyard of costume jewelry.

"Dan Reno." I shook her hand while taking a good look at her. She might have still been in her thirties, but if she was, those were some hard years.

"Say, could I bum a smoke from you?" I asked. There was a pack of Marlboros on the table.

"Absolutely," said the other one. She had straight red hair parted in the middle and was wearing a low-cut blouse that showed a good four inches of freckly cleavage. She pulled a cigarette from the pack, but just before my hand reached hers she dropped it between her legs, and the cigarette tumbled to the floorboards.

"Oops," I said automatically, bending to pick it up. I felt her hand on the back of my head and she held it down for a moment, near her lap. "While you're down there," she said, loud enough to make people look. She and her friend howled as I walked away, trying to hide an embarrassed grin.

It had stopped snowing and the cold outside was bone-numbing. The night air was still, but the high clouds were moving quickly against the thin moon, which meant the wind was probably whipping over the ridges. Patches of stars were becoming visible, twinkling above the black peaks. I smoked for a minute, then put the cigarette out in the snow and dropped the damp butt in a trashcan.

When I went back inside, a large man was leaning over the two ladies, his hands planted on their table. He was blocking my way to the bar. I said, "Excuse me," and when he didn't move I wedged my way past him and sat down. A slight man with stringy brown hair was also mixing drinks now, and I caught his eye. "What'll it be?" he said, licking his lips and wiping his hands on his apron.

"CC straight up," I said. The new bartender looked like a definite speed freak, like a rat that had spent too much time on the wheel.

Someone poked my shoulder. It was Julia, standing behind me with Parkash.

"I cannot believe her," she said, and pointed across the room, where Mandy McGee had suddenly appeared. She was talking to a man I didn't recognize. She looked to be in an intense conversation with the guy, who had bleached-blond hair cut in a flattop and a deep bronze tan that looked a little silly in the dead of winter. He leaned close to her ear, speaking rapidly with his brow furrowed. He stood about six-foot-three and was wearing tan slacks, tasseled loafers, and a light blue polo shirt stretched tight across his chest. The sleeves of the shirt clung halfway up his oversize biceps, and his forearms rippled with veins.

"She may be my niece, but that little sleaze is nothing but bad news, Dan," Julia said.

Mandy glanced in our direction then turned back to her conversation. The man looked up, and our eyes clicked for an instant. It was Sven Osterlund.

"I'll see you two tomorrow at the wedding," I said.

Julia and Parkash left, and when I looked a minute later, Mandy was gone. Then a commotion caught my attention.

"I'm sorry, we're leaving *now*," the redhead who gave me the cigarette said. Her voice was shrill. She was standing, and the man at their table was holding her arm at the elbow. She tried to move away, but he pulled her toward him.

"Come on, why don't we all go to my room and do some blow?" he said. I put my shot glass down and turned all the way around on my barstool. The man had one foot hiked up on a chair, and the sole of his boot was worn almost slick. He wore a brown Pendleton shirt with the sleeves rolled, showing light hair on his forearms that was kinky, like it had been singed by heat. His mug was framed by a choppy haircut, or maybe he just hadn't bothered with a comb recently. He was probably a little over six feet, and I guessed his weight at 220. His pale blue eyes caught mine, and in that instant I knew it was trouble. I'd seen the look plenty of times, a bully's insolent glare, one that was meant to demean through physical intimidation. Being whacked on coke or crank added fuel to the attitude, and this dude was chewing his cud like he hadn't eaten in three days.

I stood up. "Take your hands off her," I said. He curled his lip at me, then shoved her away. She tripped and fell to the floor.

"Who died and left you in charge, motherfucker?" he rasped. Before I could respond, he took two quick steps, cocked his shoulder, and threw a roundhouse punch at my head. I ducked, and a rush of rank air swept over my face, the stench like damp, unwashed clothes. I sprang forward and drilled him flush in the face with a straight left. His nose cracked like a chicken bone, and blood and white snot burst from his nostrils. He was stunned for only a second, then his eyes went wild and he came at me again with another right. I blocked the punch and hit him with a solid uppercut to the jaw. As he fell over a table, the back of his boot caught the scrawny bartender in the stomach. The bartender had foolishly come over the bar to break it up—now he lay gasping in the fetal position, tangled amid the legs of the tables and chairs.

The crowd was scrambling to get clear, but I thought the dude was done. I was wrong. He climbed back up, spit out a mouthful of blood, then threw a table out of the way and bull-rushed me. I grabbed a barstool, jabbed it at his knees and felt his shin crack against it. Then I shoved it in his midsection and ran forward, driving him into the double doors of the saloon's entrance.

He grunted as his back slammed into the heavy wood, but he was still holding on to the barstool and trying to take it from me. The doors gave way, and I gave him one final shove, then let go as he fell outside. He tumbled backward down the steps, flailing wildly while clutching the barstool with one hand. The back of his head smacked hard against the steel bumper of an old Dodge pickup, and his body thudded to a stop in the snow. I'd seen men die from lesser blows to the back of the head, but the bastard must have had a thick skull, because he came to a moment later, groaning, and puked up a belly full of liquid.

I stood on the steps as the patrons spilled out the entrance. The two women came out, the redhead crying and holding a bloodied elbow. The crowd clustered around, chattering in stunned tones and watching intently. They formed a loose circle around the injured man, but most stayed far enough away to avoid catching a whiff of his vomit.

After a minute, two Ford Explorer sheriff's vehicles with their bubble lights on bounced up the ice berm and skidded to a stop in the slush of the parking lot. A beefy black man climbed out of his rig and surveyed the scene. His striped Silverado County Sheriff's Department pants were too short and looked too tight, and his gun belt rested on the paunch above his crotch. His thick upper body looked like it would split the seams of his green shirt if he moved too suddenly.

"Officer, I'm Dan Reno," I said, sticking out my hand. He hesitated, then shook it briefly.

"Are you the one who called?" he said.

"No, I'm the one involved here." I gestured at the man, who was on all fours over the contents of his stomach. Blood dripped out of his nose into the puddle. Three other deputies walked up. One of them stood with his palm resting on the butt of his service revolver. He wore aviator-style sunglasses, even though the sun had gone down hours ago. He looked to be in his early twenties.

The sheriff led me over to his vehicle. "Tell me what happened," he said, looking past me at the other officers, who were talking to the spectators. The young cop was leaning down, speaking quietly to the man who was still on his hands and knees.

"The guy was bothering these ladies. I told him to knock it off, and he shoved one of them to the ground and took a swing at me. I hit him a couple times and pushed him out into the parking lot."

"Looks like you beat the hell out of him."

"He had it coming."

"And you had no problem obliging, huh?"

"It was self-defense, Sheriff. The guy was looking for trouble, and if I hadn't shoved him outside, people might have been hurt."

"Sounds like you're an A-number-one citizen. Let me see your ID, please." I pulled my wallet out and was handing him my driver's license when the cop in the sunglasses walked up and unclipped his cuffs from his belt.

"Put your hands on the car and spread 'em," he said.

"No need, Fingsten," the sheriff said. "Did you call the ambulance?"

"No need, my butt," the man named Fingsten said, and put his hand on my arm and tried to push me into position against the sheriff's car. I leaned my weight against him and didn't budge.

Fingsten's lips quivered and he sneered under a mustache that looked like an undernourished caterpillar. He continued trying to force me against the car, but he was giving away about fifty pounds, and I'd tussled with stronger women.

"Move it, you son of a bitch," he said, and unsnapped the steel button on his holster.

"Goddammit, Fingsten," the sheriff said, "I told you to call an ambulance. Now."

"You're not gonna let this guy walk?"

The sheriff's eyes flashed, and he took a quick step toward Fingsten. "Move," he ordered. Fingsten smirked and sauntered away slowly, his shoulders back and his thumbs hooked in his belt loops. "Stupid…" he muttered, and I swore I heard him say "nigger." I looked at the sheriff, but he'd already gone to his car to radio in my ID.

Fingsten bent down and put his hand on the injured man's shoulder, as if reassuring him. I walked around and sat on the back bumper of the sheriff's vehicle. Another deputy was taking a statement from the two gals, who were gesturing vigorously, waving their arms about and throwing punches in the air.

"Then he says, 'I wouldn't mind giving an older broad like you the high hard one,'" said the redhead. "Yeah," the blonde said, "and he asked me if I take it up the ass!"

The redhead looked like she was doing a drunken imitation of a kung fu movie, when suddenly she ran over to the injured man, who was still on his knees, and hooked him in the nuts from behind, as if she were kicking a field goal. The dude jerked upright, screaming the way a man only does when his testicles are grievously injured, and fell over onto his side, knocking Fingsten's legs out from under him.

Fingsten swung his arms desperately, his clipboard in one hand and his pen in the other. But his weight was already committed, and he fell over the man into the steaming puddle of vomit. He dropped his clipboard and broke his fall with his hands, but the puke splashed into his face, and then his sunglasses and cap fell into the puddle.

The crowd was stunned for a second, until a voice said, "Yo, nice moon glasses!" A couple of guys began laughing, then more joined in. The other two deputies started rousting folks, telling them to either go inside or split. A minute later the parking lot was empty, except for the cops, me, the two ladies, and the dude with the busted head and nuts. I sat on the sheriff's bumper, taking in the spectacle.

"Mr. Reno," said the sheriff, looking like he was repressing a smile. "I understand you have a license to carry a concealed weapon. I assume you're not tonight."

"It's *Reno*," I said, correcting his pronunciation. "As in 'no problemo'. My piece is locked in my trunk."

"Are you here on business or pleasure, Mr. Reno?"

"Pleasure, although what happened tonight wasn't exactly what I had in mind."

"I hope not. I'm Marcus Grier, sheriff," he said, smiling briefly and showing a big gap between his front teeth. He handed back my license. "I'd like you to stop by my office tomorrow and register. It's required of anyone with a license to carry a firearm."

"No problem. Am I free to go?"

"For the time being you are. I don't believe Jake there will be pressing charges. But he is the son of one of the big shots who runs Pistol Pete's, and we don't condone fighting in this town."

I looked at him, trying to figure his meaning, but he wouldn't meet my eye. He took the clipboard from his hood and began writing.

"Sheriff, I believe he's under the influence of coke or probably crank. You may want to search him."

Marcus Grier looked up and sighed. "I'm familiar with the habits of Jake Tuma, I assure you." An ambulance pulled into the parking lot, and two paramedics stepped out and pulled a wheeled gurney out the back doors. The man named Jake Tuma was still on the ground but was sitting upright. They began to help him onto the gurney, but he pushed them away and tried to climb on himself, lost his balance, fell down, and tipped the gurney on its side. Two deputies came over to help, and they finally loaded him into the ambulance. It drove away slowly, its tires spinning on the ice. I looked around for Fingsten, but he was nowhere in sight.

4

O N THE WAY BACK to the Lakeside, I hit the red light at the intersection across from Caesar's. Near the entrance to the casino I saw the white Chevy four-by-four truck. I pulled in, and, sure enough, it was parked in a handicapped spot. I dialed the number on Marcus Grier's card, and a female officer answered. I reported that a vehicle I believed had a phony permit was parked illegally. The woman said they'd send a car to check it out.

When I walked back into the Lakeside, it was eleven P.M. The casino was packed, and the noise level sounded like a television turned up too loud. I went straight to my room, drank a tall glass of water, and lay on the bed.

The fight at the bar had evolved so quickly that there was no way to defuse the situation before it turned violent. Not that it bothered me—there wasn't much doubt Jake Tuma deserved whatever unhappy fate he brought upon himself. He was sadly typical of most of the criminals I dealt with in my career. I rubbed the bruised knuckle on my right hand and thought briefly about icing it. "Typical," I muttered out loud. Then I reminded myself to let it go and not let others randomly impose their problems on my life.

But the conversation with Sheriff Marcus Grier kept nagging at me. It had been too quick, too easy. I expected to be in that parking lot for a lot longer, possibly even end up down at the station. But when Grier and his deputies saw Jake Tuma, they seemed to draw conclusions on their own. The remark Grier made about Jake being the son of a Pistol Pete's casino executive left me with the distinct impression he was afforded special privileges. Grier also said he was "familiar with the habits" of Jake Tuma, which I assume meant drug abuse and other related troubles, but I didn't get the idea the Silverado County Sheriff's Department intended to charge him with any offense.

I figured there was more to it, but it was none of my business, I told myself.

• • •

I'd been asleep for only five or ten minutes when someone knocked on my door. I sat up for a second and made sure I wasn't dreaming, then threw back the blankets and walked through the darkness. The chain latch wasn't attached, so I hooked it and opened the door a couple inches.

Mandy McGee's gold-flecked eyes stared in at me. "Hi," she said. "Can I come in?"

My mouth wouldn't say no, and I opened the door. She was still wearing her evening gown, and she stepped in, closed the door behind her, then pressed her body against mine in the pitch-blackness. I felt her hands on my bare chest as she kissed me lightly, holding me against the hallway wall. My heart thudded in my throat at her touch.

"You thought you could resist me," she whispered.

I could feel her soft contours and smell her perfume. She reached out and flipped on the light switch, a sly smile on her face. Standing in her heels, she turned so I could unzip her dress. I moved the length of her silky blond hair over her shoulder and kissed her neck, and then, my hands almost trembling, I unzipped her down to the where her back curved and the swell of her ass began. Then I moved my hands to her breasts, but she stopped me, took my hand, and led me to the bed. "Sit here," she said. I did, and she slowly undressed for me. It wasn't until she was naked that she let me touch her.

I closed my eyes and became immersed in the shape and scent of Mandy's body. We started slowly, almost timidly, and it was surprisingly romantic. But before long I caught a mischievous glint in her eyes, and we quickly became entangled in positions I'd only imagined. Then she took control, climbing on top of me, her eyes half shut, her hips gyrating and her breasts bouncing in rhythm, until I exploded into her sweet softness. As I lay panting beneath her, the conflicts, challenges, and uncertainties of my life all seemed a million miles away.

•   •   •

The light of dawn filtered through the curtains, and we finally fell back exhausted and slept. We'd been up all night, and our couplings had grown progressively more athletic, to the point I felt strangely outside myself, like I was watching us in a pornographic movie. Mandy certainly would have no problem getting a part. She made love like a woman with an abundance of sexual instinct and a lifetime of promiscuity to back it up.

It was going on noon when I woke, bleary-eyed and feeling like a king. Mandy was still there, curled in the sheets, sleeping soundly. I called room service and ordered the works, pancakes, scrambled eggs, bacon, sausage, hash browns, orange juice, and a pot of coffee. I shaved, and was in the shower when Mandy peeked her head around the shower curtain.

"Hi." She smiled and stepped in.

"Oh," I said, fearing the worst. My genitals were sore after last night's workout, and I doubted I was up to any more activity. Mandy put her arms around me from behind and soaped up my chest, slowly working lower and lower.

"Be careful," I whispered, cringing. She was, and I surprised myself. After a few minutes, we heard a banging on the door. "It's room service," I said.

"Mmmm." She jumped out of the shower, naked and wet. I heard her tell the waiter to leave it in the hall, then she was back next to me. We completed our lovemaking, leaving me thoroughly spent. I felt like I'd be limping for the rest of the day.

We sat at the table near the window, and I opened the curtains to let the sun in. It was a bright day, and I hoped no one could see in our window because Mandy hadn't bothered putting anything on except for a white towel neatly wrapped around her head. I watched her breasts jiggle while she ate breakfast.

"I'm starving," she murmured. Her nipples were dark and her tan line plunged low, highlighting the shape of her breasts with sharp contrast where her skin turned from white to copper. I forked a couple of pancakes and a sausage link onto my plate.

"My god, what time is it?" she asked between bites.

"Quarter after twelve," I said, sipping coffee. "The wedding's at three, right?"

"Mm-hmm. It will be a full Catholic ceremony, about an hour and a half." She sat with her legs crossed and leaned back.

"What do you think of Sylvester?" I asked.

"I think Desiree's gonna live the lifestyle of the rich and famous. Lucky her. They've already picked out a mansion in Monte Sereno, and Sly's been shopping for a Ferrari."

"How does Desiree feel about marrying into all that money? Do you think that's part of the reason they're together?"

"I think that any time somebody is that rich it has a lot to do with everything," she said, dabbing her mouth with a napkin.

"How do your folks feel about it?"

Her eyes narrowed. "My dad's too freaking stupid to run a business, and my mom's just hoping maybe some extra money will float her way."

I sat there silently. As usual, I had no idea what to say to an angry woman. I tried anyway.

"Money's not everything," I offered. She reached over and patted my hand, like she was reassuring a child who was trying very hard to understand an adult conversation. Then she stood and said, "I better go."

She walked to the bathroom, and I stared after her nude body. I couldn't guess what kind of head trips Mandy was into, and I didn't really want to find out. She had the type of outrageous physical presence that could make rational men do things that were stupid or insane, or both. So when she emerged from the bathroom in jeans and a sweater and coolly asked me to call her a cab, part of me was disappointed, but I was mostly relieved at the distant tone in her voice.

5

THE NISSAN'S FRONT-WHEEL DRIVE bit into the ice as I left my hotel to head to Caesar's for the wedding. I swung onto Highway 50, driving slowly past the t-shirt shops, restaurants, liquor stores, small hotels, and the big casinos: Harvey's, Harrah's, Buffalo Bill's, and Pistol Pete's. The entrance to Caesar's was the next turn-off, when I remembered the sheriff. For a minute I considered his request that I stop by his office, but the prospect of a beer and a few hands of video poker before the wedding was too tempting; the visit to Marcus Grier could wait.

• • •

I hit a lucky streak, and after drawing a full house I was up a hundred bucks. But I had lost track of time, and by the time I found the grand ballroom it was ten past three. I was ready to quietly slip in the back, but when I peeked in, the wedding hadn't started. The room was loud with the conversations of the huge audience; the makeshift chapel was packed. I looked around for a minute before I spotted an empty seat in the middle of the back row. I sat there waiting for the ceremony to begin, squished between a large woman and a couple of little boys playing with Legos.

"I like *Star Wars*. Do you?" one of the youngsters asked me. He was a chunky kid with a buzz cut and a jack o' lantern smile.

"Sure I do," I said, though I'd never seen any of the movies. I felt an odd pang of sadness when I looked at the kid. Julia had talked about having a family and we considered it many times, but by the time I decided I liked the idea, our marriage was going bad.

The minutes ticked away, and by a quarter to four the crowd was restless and impatient. Folks were standing, talking in the aisles, shrugging their shoulders. I spotted a clergyman striding from a side door. He disappeared behind a thick curtain, then I saw the groomsmen, in black and lime-green tuxedos, come from behind the curtain and look around briefly.

I went out to the hallway, where John Bascom stood in his tuxedo, talking on a cell phone. Then I saw Marcus Grier and two deputies come around the corner. I looked at Grier in surprise, wondering if he was looking for me. But they blew past me as if I weren't there.

The wedding still hadn't started when I looked back in. At least half the people were now standing in the ballroom, and thirty or forty people were in the hallway, smoking cigarettes and wandering in and out of the restrooms. Everyone was talking about the delay and the cops who had just shown up. I spied Brad and Whitey off to the side and went over to them.

"Hey, dude, where you been hiding?" Whitey said. He was wearing a pair of dark blue Levi's and a pressed, long-sleeve button-down shirt with a purple, red, and yellow pattern. His lank blond hair hung almost to his shoulders. He looked like a combination hippie, hillbilly, and beatnik.

"What's goin' on, Whitey?" I said. "Hey, Brad."

"Fuck, man, we've been getting blasted," Whitey said. His eyes were red and glazed, and he sucked deeply on his cigarette. Brad nodded, looking shaky and disheveled, like maybe he had just survived a horrible car wreck.

"What'd you boys do last night?"

"Shit," Brad said, shaking his head, walking around in little circles.

"The core, dude, to the core," Whitey said. "We went to the bachelor party in the penthouse suite," he went on, pointing upward. "You should have seen these three strippers, they were incredible." He lowered his voice. "Osterlund kept trying to offer them money for a blow job, but none of them would go for it. Finally this hot blonde says to him, 'Why don't you go outside and play hide and go fuck yourself?' He freaked out, I'm surprised he didn't punch her in the head."

"I think he took off with Bascom to try to get laid after that," Brad said.

"You guys look like you could use some sleep," I said, remembering the cocaine blues—the sunrise shows, chain smoking, trying to drink enough to come down, and not being able to sleep until hours after the blow ran out.

"Exactly," Brad said. "I'm toast."

"You just need another rip, dude," Whitey said.

Marcus Grier's voice boomed into the hallway. "May I have your attention, please?" The PA system was turned way up, and everybody crowded back into the ballroom. Grier stood to the side of the priest's podium, holding a microphone. His two deputies, plus two Douglas County officers from Nevada, were with him.

"I'm Deputy Sheriff Marcus Grier of the Silverado Sheriff's Department, City of South Lake Tahoe." The ballroom was deathly still.

"I have some terrible news to report. There's been a tragic accident, and the wedding is canceled. I'm afraid that's all I can say now. Please exit the ballroom in an orderly fashion, for your own safety."

Grier stepped down from the stage. A stunned silence engulfed the room; the moment was so abrupt and so utterly inconceivable that I thought it might be some kind of morbid practical joke. A hushed murmur rose from the crowd and built into a crescendo as people near the front surrounded the cops and besieged them with questions. More people surged forward, a man fell and cried out in pain, and one officer pulled his billy club as he was pushed back against the pulpit. Another cop grabbed a bullhorn and told the crowd to stand back.

Then a tormented female voice from the front cried out, "Sylvester is dead!" The crowd froze for a moment. And then chaos ensued.

All around people were round-eyed, muttering "my god" and "it can't be." A middle-aged woman wandered by, saying, "What? What?" as if in a trance. Moans and cries of grief from the front of the ballroom rose distinctively above the noise level.

"Whoa, dude, what a rat fuck," Whitey said behind me, adding his own emotional perspective.

Some ladies nearby were crying, two men in their fifties started arguing loudly, and the kids who were sitting next to me began flying their Lego planes in a dog fight. The ballroom dissolved into a scene of confused bedlam, with hundreds of people milling around with their heads cocked and their eyes glazed in bewilderment. I scanned the crowd for Julia and Parkash, then I saw Brad stumble toward me, his legs crumbling, his mug pasty white. He let out a distressed groan and collapsed at my feet.

"Brado!" I bent and saw his eyes rolling back in their sockets. He was pouring sweat.

"Water," he mumbled with a thick tongue.

"Whitey, stay with him," I said, and ran out to the hallway to where a portable bar had been set up. I grabbed a plastic water bottle and a glass of ice and came back to Brad, who was barely conscious. I held his head and poured a little water into his mouth. He tilted the bottle and drank it down and fumbled a few ice cubes out of the cup. He ran the ice over his forehead, and his color gradually started to return. A group of people had formed a circle around us, and then Parkash was there, taking Brad's pulse, shining a penlight in his eyes.

"I'll be all right, I'm feeling a little better," Brad said.

"Lie and rest there for a minute," Parkash said. Brad lay on his back with his knees raised. His thick black hair was plastered against his forehead. Parkash and I stood and he pulled me aside.

"Do you know him?"

"We grew up in the same neighborhood."

"His pulse is racing. I think he's on drugs, probably of the methamphet-amine variety. He's young and strong, but those drugs will make you old before your time."

"I believe you," I said.

"He needs fluids and rest."

"I'll see if I can get him a wheelchair and get him to his hotel."

He patted me on the back. "Yes, good idea, Daniel."

Julia appeared at my shoulder. "Nice friends," she said.

I turned to her. "Sylvester? What the hell? How could he die?"

"My god, I'm sure Desiree is freaking out. I think the McGees are with the sheriff." Julia walked away abruptly, and Parkash dutifully followed.

Brad was sitting up. I found a white courtesy phone, and a few minutes later a security guard arrived with a wheelchair. We loaded Brad in and took him to a side exit. I left him with Whitey and the guard, walked out to my car and drove around to the door. Brad was able to get up on his own and climbed into the backseat. Whitey sat in front.

"Where you guys staying, Whitey?"

"Over at the Lazy Eight, it's right next to Harvey's."

"How'd you get here?"

"We walked," he said. "Did you hear, Osterlund's truck got ripped off."

"Really?"

"Yeah, somebody freakin' heisted it from Caesar's parking lot. Can you believe that?"

"Did Osterlund report it to the cops?"

"Shit, I dunno. We've been so fried this trip, I got no idea."

"You think maybe Sylvester OD'ed last night?" I said.

"He wasn't too messed up. At least not when I saw him."

I looked at Whitey. He was a likable guy, but I wondered what his future held in store. I knew guys I went to school with who were thirty-three, thirty-four years old, and hopelessly addicted to alcohol and drugs. They lived with their parents and worked occasionally at menial odd jobs. Their worlds revolved around the daily challenge of coming up with enough scratch for a cheap twelve-pack and a pack of hacks. In times of prosperity they'd splurge on a bag of crank or maybe find some Ritalin or ecstasy. Eventually, I imagined they'd either become successful twelve-steppers or end up on the street and probably die prematurely of liver disease or exposure.

I looked in the rearview mirror. Brad was leaning back with his eyes closed and his mouth open. I could hear him breathing.

"Hey, Whitey," I said, "check it out. I'm driving up 50 yesterday afternoon, I'm chaining up about ten miles past Placerville, and this big white Chevy truck comes power sliding around the curve and sprays me with a bunch of snow. Then a guy sticks his head out the passenger window and yells some shit and flings a half empty can of Coors at me. I see the license plate on the truck. It says 'PSYCHIC.'"

Whitey's mouth opened and his eyes widened. He looked like he'd just been caught in a ladies' locker room.

"Hey, man," I said. "I'm not pissed anymore. I just want to know who did it."

"Dude, I can't say for sure, but it was probably me," he blurted. "I mean, yeah, I was with Osterlund in his truck, we were drunk, and we did a couple fat rips right after we scored, and we were screwin' off on the drive back. I'm sorry, dude. I didn't know it was you."

"It's cool, Whitey. But I was pissed at the time, you know?"

"I'm sorry, dude."

"Osterlund's a good buddy of yours?"

"Yeah, he's all right. He just goes a little psycho at times."

"When he's too messed up?"

"Shit, sometimes even when he's straight. It's like he's got demons in his head or something."

I turned into the Lazy 8 and parked in front of their room. Brad was snoring. I pulled him out of the backseat and lifted him over my shoulder. Whitey opened the door, and I dropped Brad on one of the beds.

"I think I'll take a bong hit and pass out too," Whitey said.

"When you see Osterlund, tell him he should check to see if his truck was towed by the police."

"Towed?"

"Happens all the time around here."

I went to my car, thinking I'd head back over to Caesar's and offer my condolences to the families, but I didn't know the Bascoms, and the McGees would be surrounded by relatives and close friends. Maybe I'd just send a card to Julia's family, although I wasn't sure what kind of card would be appropriate.

I looked down at my fancy shirt and slacks, and it occurred to me my plans for dinner and the rest of the evening were shot. It was a few minutes past five when I drove from the Lazy 8 back toward the Lakeside. I hadn't slept much the night before, and the prospect of a slow night started sounding pretty good. There was an off-the-beaten-path bar and grill a little ways up 50 in Nevada that served good, old-fashioned greasy chow, burgers, tacos, pizza—the kind of food that made you feel warm and content when it hit your stomach. I could sit at the bar, drink a couple of margaritas on the rocks, play some video poker and mellow out, maybe crash around ten or so. But first I wanted to change clothes, so I pulled into my hotel.

I hung up my jacket and slacks and put on my Levi's and my old, comfortable, rust-colored cowboy boots. I was just walking out the door when my cell rang.

"Is this Dan Reno?"

"Yes, who's calling?"

"This is Edward Cutlip, personal assistant to John Bascom, president of Bascom Lumber. I'm calling because Mr. Bascom wants to speak to you regarding investigating his son's death. He'd like to see you immediately. Can you come to our suite at Caesar's right now?"

"Actually, I was just heading out to get a bite."

"Mr. Bascom views this situation with tremendous gravity, as you might imagine. He also pays very well, but he insists on timeliness. I think you'll find it worthwhile to delay your dinner plans."

I looked down and watched the toe of my boot tap the floor a few times. "Okay, I'll come over. What room number?"

"Suite four hundred. It's five-seventeen. Can you make it by five-thirty?"

"No problem."

"Good. I'll tell Mr. Bascom. Please don't be late."

6

THE SUN WAS SETTING over the snow-capped ridges above the west shores of Lake Tahoe. A strong wind had kicked up, dropping the temperature below freezing. The lake was twinkling with the sun's last reflections, and the trees were fading to black. I had to park at the outer edge of Caesar's crowded lot, and I zipped my ski jacket while I made the hike to the lobby.

I took the elevator to the fourth floor. A slightly built, brown-haired man in a dark business suit stood outside suite 400.

"Dan Reno?"

"*Reno*," I said. "As in Reynolds."

"I'm Edward Cutlip," he said in a hushed tone. "This way, please." I followed him into the suite, a large room lined with couches and padded chairs. On a small conference table in the center was a phone, some coffee cups, and a bottle of Wild Turkey. Two notebook computers and a printer sat on a credenza against the back wall, where a small group of people huddled together, talking in whispers. A woman with a tear-stained face came out of the bathroom; her puffy eyes met mine for a moment before she left the suite.

We went through a side door I assumed was to a bedroom, but instead of a bed there was a large wood veneer desk. Behind the desk sat a man in his late fifties: John Bascom.

Cutlip closed the door behind us and motioned for me to sit in a chair facing the desk. He took a seat at a small table off to the side.

Bascom had changed out of his tuxedo into slacks and a black polo shirt. An oversized vein pulsated on the side of his forehead, and he looked at me with small, darting eyes. His lips were pressed against his teeth, and his jaw quivered in the last of the day's sunlight, which weakly lit the room from a large window looking over the street.

"Do you have a business card?" he asked. I pulled one out of my wallet and handed it to him. He looked at it long enough to read every word twice.

"Okay, Reno, here's my situation," he said. "My son was beaten, robbed, stabbed to death. He died of his wounds, probably bled to death, in a suite at the Crown Ambassador Hotel. I just got back from there, and now I need to go formally identify his body at the coroner's office." He stopped talking and turned and gazed out the window. I waited, and the silence grew awkward, but he just sat and stared, for a minute, then two, until finally he regained his composure and continued.

"I just met with the two local detectives assigned to investigate my son's murder. I don't have a great deal of faith in small-town police agencies, and these two are a good example why. I question their commitment and competency—let's leave it at that. And I won't even go into my opinions about the state of our courts." He stood, sighed deeply, and walked over to the window.

"I lost my first son when he was twenty-one. My remaining son has just been murdered…" His voice cracked, and I thought he might break into tears, but instead he whipped around so quickly I almost put up my hands. His eyes were red-rimmed, his teeth clenched in a snarl. "And I want the lousy scum who did it." He stood looming over me, shaking with anger. "Am I clear?" he hissed. "I want who did it! I don't give a flying fuck about anything else! I don't want the murdering bastard on the streets or even sitting in a cozy little jail and getting butt-rammed all day long! I want him!" His words exploded from deep in his chest, his face purple, spittle flying from his lips.

He took a couple of long breaths, then snapped his fingers at Edward Cutlip and said, "Turkey." Cutlip scrambled out the door and returned with the fifth of whiskey. Bascom splashed a few ounces in his coffee cup, drained it, and sat back down heavily.

"Reno, I've checked your background. I know your history. The only thing that concerns me is you've never been in the service," he said.

"How did you access my background?"

"I'm connected, believe me."

I wondered to what extent. "What does the service have to do with it?" I asked.

"I did two tours in 'Nam, Reno, and spent six months in a POW camp. It gives one a certain perspective on crime and punishment."

"I'm not sure what you want from me," I said. "The police are just beginning their investigation, and there's a good chance they'll make arrests within a couple days. Why do you need a private investigator?"

"And if they don't make arrests quickly?" Bascom said.

"Why not give them a chance?"

"Yes, and wait for them to flounder and let the trail grow cold. And then I wait for them to commit more time and resources they don't have to the investigation. And eventually the case gets old and stagnant, and that's it." He paused, and we looked at each other for a long moment.

"Answer me this, Reno," he said. "In most cases that get solved, an arrest is made in the first seventy-two hours. Am I right?"

"Maybe," I said.

"Let me clarify a few things for you," he continued. "I'll make this very simple. I will pay you to drop everything and focus entirely on finding who killed my son. Take a leave of absence or quit your job at…" he picked up my card from his desk. "Wenger Associates. Understand, I don't want a large, accredited detective agency involved. This is under the table. I do not want it publicized. The bottom line is I want you to identify and bring me the person responsible for…" He paused, and the room became quiet, then his shoulders hunched and he looked deflated and much older. "For the murder of my son."

I looked away from Bascom, unable to resist a weird but profound sense that in some dark corner of my psyche, I shared his loss. I shook my head, trying to ignore the random emotion, and glanced over at Cutlip, who was eyeing the whiskey. I stood, poured myself a jolt in a plastic cup, then poured one for Cutlip, but he wouldn't take it from my hand so I set it in front of him. Bascom held out his cup, and I measured him a shot. The sky was dark outside, and the casino lights reflected into the room.

"You're asking me to leave my job and undertake a secret investigation without the knowledge of any police agency," I said.

"I didn't say 'secret.' I want low profile." Bascom leaned back in his chair. "If the police learn of your involvement, so be it. Your job will be to do what they can't, or won't do, if that's what it takes."

I tasted the whiskey. A slew of issues and pros and cons jumbled around in my head, and finally I went to the bottom line. My old man had told me years ago to never lead with your chin in a negotiation; get the other party to the name the price first.

"How much are you willing to pay?" I said. My sympathy for John Bascom did not extend to his bank account.

"Name your price," he shot back. So much for my strategy. I decided to start wildly high—from what I'd heard, he could afford it.

"One hundred thousand up front."

He didn't blink. "I'll give you fifty thousand up front and the remaining fifty K for delivering the killer."

"Delivering a person constitutes kidnapping, and my bounty hunting license is expired," I said.

"Get it renewed."

"It's not an overnight process."

"You're not the right man for the job then. I'll find someone else."

I looked at Bascom warily. "You're asking me to stretch the law," I said. "But for a hundred K, I'll deliver your man."

"Dead or alive," Bascom said flatly.

"I'm a private investigator, not a hit man. I'll deliver the killer. You want him dead, that's your business."

"Yes. It is," he said slowly. Then his eyes snapped back on mine, once again addressing me as a subordinate. "I'll want daily reports," he said. There was a light knock on the door, and Nora Bascom stuck her head in. "Edward will take care of the paperwork and details," Bascom said. "I need you to call him with a progress report daily." He stood without further comment, went to his wife, and left me with Cutlip.

"Give me a minute," Cutlip said as he typed on a notebook computer. I went over to the window and gazed out at the neon lights of Pistol Pete's casino. A thirty-foot-tall cowboy was in a fast-draw stance, the sign underneath him boasting, "Loosest slots in Nevada." The sidewalks were crowded with tourists pouring in and out of the casinos, and the road was a solid line of cars. For a moment I felt strangely removed, like I was down on the street, not here in a room watching the masses from above. It was an odd feeling—fifty grand. More money than I made working for Wenger the year before. I had under five hundred dollars in my checking account at the moment. What the hell would I say to Wenger? He'd probably want in on the deal; I smiled at the thought. I'd have to ask him for vacation time, or maybe a leave of absence. He'd have a shit hemorrhage.

It took fifteen minutes for Cutlip to create the paperwork detailing our arrangement. When I read it I saw a provision for expenses, including travel, meals, and entertainment. That gave me moment for pause—Wenger reimbursed me for nothing. If I wanted to loosen someone's lips with a few cocktails, I did it on my own dime. I finished reading the contract, signed it, and Edward made me a copy. Then he wrote and handed me a check for $50,000. I looked at him, and his face was impassive. I stared at the Bascom Lumber Enterprises check, carefully folded it, and put it in my wallet.

"You realize if the police make the arrest first, the remaining payment becomes null and void," he said.

"Right," I said. And there was the catch. If the cops solved the case quickly, I'd walk away with the fifty thousand, but wouldn't collect the balance. If they didn't make an arrest within a week or so, I might have a reasonable shot at the bounty. I wondered what the odds were of my being able to identify the killer before the police. Hell, they could wrap the case up in twenty-four hours.

"Mr. Bascom is a stickler for detail," Cutlip said. "Make sure you call me every day with an update." He searched his pockets. "Shoot, I've left my cards in my car. Come with me."

On our way outside, we passed a lounge where the groomsmen and bridesmaids, still in their wedding clothes, had congregated, along with a number of the McGee family members. Jerry and Shelly were there, as well as Mandy, who was wearing a burgundy gown and holding a martini glass in her hand.

We walked through the icy lot to Cutlip's car, a dark Ford Crown Victoria. He reached in the glove box and handed me his card.

"Gad, it's cold out here," he said, rubbing his arms through his suit jacket.

I looked at my watch. "Have you eaten yet?"

"No, but I need to–"

"Come on, let's go down the road, get a beer and something to eat. You look like you've had a long day."

"No kidding," he sighed, rubbing his eyes with his palms. "All right, a beer sounds good. Where do you want to go?"

I climbed into his car. "Go out on 50 and hang a right. There's a good place a couple miles up the road."

Edward accelerated into the stream of traffic on the highway, heading out of town. I stared through his windshield across the road, out to the dark waters of Lake Tahoe. I had to resist the urge to pull the check out, look at it again, make sure it was real. A financial windfall was the last thing I expected to walk into. Some people were born into their money, others dedicated their lives to chasing it. I fell in neither category. I'd always had just enough to get by, and never much more. Carrying a $50,000 check in my wallet seemed absurd. The money would completely change my financial situation.

But maybe the idea wouldn't be so hard to get used to. I let my mind wander to what I might spend the dough on, thinking easily, not really concentrating, just indulging myself for a moment or two. Then I added in the additional fifty K and started figuring a little harder. And it was then that I felt the workings of greed seeping in from the corners of my mind. I was surprised at how quickly a small hit of wealth could launch a covetous thought process. It made me feel an odd psychic connection to Wenger, like I was seeing out of his eyes.

A couple of minutes later we pulled into a small bar and grill called Chuck's Pit. Inside, it was warm and dark, like a cave. We took a seat at the bar, and Edward asked for a bottle of Heineken, which he drained in long swallows. The bar maid took our dinner orders, and Edward ordered another beer and a shot of Patron. He leaned his head back and shot the cognac-like tequila, then sat hunched over the bar on his elbows. He kept shaking his head.

"It's unbelievable, absolutely unbelievable," he said. "You wouldn't believe the preparations that went into the wedding. And the impact this has on Bascom Lumber and the Bascom family. It's monumental. I'm in a state of shock." His brown hair was parted on the side—it looked like it had been hair sprayed in place, but the wind had messed it up. I noticed one of his front teeth was bigger than the other, which made him look boyish, like a child whose adult teeth were still growing in. But he had to be close to forty.

"How well did you know Sylvester?" I asked.

"Fairly well, I guess. Understand, he's a lot younger than me. We didn't socialize outside of work, but he seemed to be pretty typical."

"Typical? How so?"

"Well, here's a twenty-seven-year-old son of an extremely wealthy and powerful man. He's got everything going for him; his career is in place, he's got a beautiful new fiancée, he's got enough money to live however he wants. He's got it made. All he needed to do is go with it and not do anything stupid. I guess that was too much to ask."

"How do you know he did something stupid?"

"Well, I…" Edward shrugged. "Just an assumption, I guess."

"Was Sylvester intense and committed to the business, like his dad?"

Edward waved at the bartender, ordered another tequila, and gunned it with a quick flip of the head. I could see him start to unwind as the booze hit him. The lines around his eyes and forehead lightened, and he smiled for no reason. The tension seemed to leave his body like steam rising off wet concrete under a hot sun.

"I don't usually drink much," he said. "But this situation…"

"I understand," I said.

"Let me give you a little Bascom Lumber empire history," he said, beginning to slur a little. "The original founder was Leland Bascom, who started a small timber business back in the early eighteen hundreds on the East Coast. He built it into a pretty good company, and then in the eighteen-fifties his son, Hamilton, came out west to expand the business during the gold rush boom days. Hamilton Bascom was very successful in California and extended the company's timber rights into Oregon. He was known as a ruthless, uncompromising businessman and was shot to death in eighteen-eighty. He's become kind of a symbol to the Bascoms, representing toughness and tenacity. They like to bring him up in meetings.

"Anyway, after he died, his son William inherited the business, which by now was well established and very profitable. William was a competent executive but had a notorious record of philandering. He died in the nineteen-twenties—had a heart attack while in bed with a prostitute. His son Stephen then became the top executive." Edward paused, holding up his fingers and counting them off. "And he was in charge until after World War Two, at which time Stephen's son Samuel returned home from Germany as a decorated war hero. Stephen retired, and Samuel took over. Samuel was at the wedding; he made a speech at the rehearsal dinner. He just turned eighty-two."

I nodded, and the waitress brought our food and took orders for another round. We ate in silence for a minute, then Edward started again.

"Samuel retired about twenty years ago, and that's when John Bascom became president—John Bascom is Samuel's oldest son. I started working for the company ten years ago, right after Seth Bascom was killed. This whole situation kind of seems like déjà vu."

"How did Seth Bascom get killed?" I asked.

"He was crushed when a cable snapped while loading a trailer with redwoods in Southern Oregon."

"Ouch. Back to Sylvester, tell me how he compared to his dad."

Edward sat for a moment, chewing his food while he stared at the bottles behind the bar. "I was getting to that. I never knew Seth Bascom, but from what I hear he was a tough kid, a fighter, stubborn as a mule—very similar to his father. Now, this is just my opinion; I haven't worked directly with Sylvester very much, I'm sure I would have in the future if he, uh, was still with us. But I got a feeling he was too young, too green, not intense enough. He seemed to spend a lot of time running around house shopping, taking Desiree on exotic vacations, and partying with his friends. I never got the impression he was that interested in the business."

"Why did John Bascom want to promote him?" I said, thinking that it didn't sound like Sylvester would have been the right guy to run his father's business. But that didn't mean he deserved to die.

"Because he's his son," Edward said. "It's a family business."

"I see."

"Think about it," Edward said, resting his forehead on his fingers as he looked at me. "For every man like John Bascom, there's a thousand ordinary types that maybe are somewhat ambitious, but don't view business as life and death. I think Sylvester was smart enough to know he had it good, but as far as him being driven, I never sensed that."

I considered his remarks while I dosed a taco with Tabasco sauce.

"What about Sylvester's friends, the guys in his wedding? Do you know them?"

"Not really," he said. "His best man's a guy named Chris Dickerson, they went to school together, like back in grade school. The Asian guy is Rod Yamato, he's another old school buddy. I don't know the other ones."

"How about the big guy with the flattop, Sven Osterlund?"

"Oh, the bodybuilder?" Edward shook his head. "I never met him. But listen to this: last Thursday night Sylvester and all his guys are out at the casinos living it up. They end up back in Sylvester's room at Caesar's about two or three in the morning and completely wreck the place. I mean, there's a couple holes in the sheetrock, they were throwing furniture around, the TV gets busted up, there's food flung all over the place, and this guy Osterlund heaves a table off the balcony into the pool. From what I hear, he was the ringleader and was really going crazy. Anyway, I had to go fix things with the hotel manager—he wanted to kick the whole group out. I finally soothed it over, and Sylvester told me not to tell Mr. Bascom."

"What did you say?"

"Not much. It kind of put me between a rock and a hard place, you know? I just wrote it off as a boys-will-be-boys thing and let it drop."

We finished our drinks, and the bartender took our plates and left the check.

"I'll get it," I said, the new high roller on the block, ready to give my fresh expense account a workout.

7

WHEN EDWARD DROPPED ME off back at my car, he gave me the room number at the Crown Ambassador where a maid had found Sylvester's body. I watched Edward walk across Caesar's parking lot toward the entrance to the casino. He appeared to be a straight shooter, an intelligent guy, a regular guy. But what type of person allows himself to be a personal errand boy for an arrogant, high-powered executive? When John Bascom snapped his fingers, Edward jumped. It seemed to be a demeaning existence, and my impression of Edward was that he had more going for him. Maybe he didn't mind the work, but something didn't seem right about it, and I wondered if perhaps his situation was due to some unfortunate circumstance.

I started the Nissan, and the bad muffler rattled like mad. Maybe now that I could afford it, I'd get it fixed. If I had the time. Or made the time. Hell, maybe I'd just get used to the noise and drive the car until the god-damned muffler fell off. I revved the motor a couple times, challenging the racket to outlast my patience. Then I stuck the car in gear and drove across the border into California, to the Crown Ambassador.

The hotel was one of Tahoe's largest, rising sixteen stories on prime real estate right at the state line. I stared up at the green and gold structure, then traded my ski jacket for a black cotton coat. I pulled a small forensics case and a roll of yellow crime-scene tape from the suitcase I kept in my trunk, and grabbed my generic gold badge, which was mounted on a black leather backing attached to a thin neck cord. Then I strapped on my shoulder holster with the Beretta and went into the hotel lobby.

I walked around the perimeter, checked the restaurant, the lounge, and the men's room, scouting for uniformed or plainclothes cops. It was almost nine o'clock on a Saturday night, and I hoped the detectives, forensics squad, and coroner would have already cleared out. I didn't see anyone suspicious around, so I took the elevator to the sixth floor. The hallway was empty, and the door to 672 was sealed with three bands of yellow tape.

I went back down to the registration counter. I waited there for a minute until a pretty Asian girl stepped out from a side door.

"Hi, I'm Rich Conrad, Douglas County Sheriff's Office," I said. My coat was unzipped, the badge resting on my chest. "I need to go up to six seventy-two."

"Oh, yes," she said, looking around. "My manager should talk to you, but I think he's on break."

"I'll only be a couple minutes, it's standard procedure. My wife is waiting at home with a movie, so I'd like to get back soon." I gave her my best "ah, shucks" smile. She glanced around again, then ran a plastic card through an electronic box. "I guess it's okay. Here you go."

I went back to the sixth floor. After snapping on a pair of rubber gloves, I used a razor blade to slice the crime-scene tape crisscrossed over the doorjamb of room 672. Then I ran the card key through the reader and went in. It was nine-fifteen. I wanted to be in the room for no more than ten minutes.

I avoided touching anything as I surveyed the crime scene. At the foot of the bed, a large bloodstain on the carpet spread past the boundaries of a taped silhouette of a body. The bedspread was pulled partially off the mattress, revealing a smeared streak of blood on the white sheets. A dried pool of vomit lay near the window, the sickly odor hanging in the air.

I looked underneath the bed and saw nothing. I studied the pillows with my magnifying glass, but it was probably pointless. Forensic evidence can make a case if one has access to a lab, and the time to wait for results. Neither applied to me.

I checked the bathroom and went through the dresser drawers, careful not to touch the white fingerprint powder. I didn't really expect to find anything, but I felt it was important to check, to get a feel for the room, if nothing else. There was a large walk-in closet next to the bathroom. It was empty except for the non-removable hangers and ironing board. The closet floor had a few muddy scuffmarks, and I knelt down to see if I could make out a footprint. I couldn't, but I did notice some lighter-color dirt, and I pinched some between my fingers. It was sawdust. I took a small flashlight from my forensics case and studied the floor carefully. There appeared to be a light coat of dust mixed with some fine sawdust, and then some heavier shoe dirt was scattered about. The sawdust could mean anything but was probably meaningless, I thought, and I was about to get up when I noticed an inch-long curlicue of wood shaving hiding in the crevice where the cedar floor butted up to the carpet.

I picked up the shaving, then stood and took a better look at it, and when I raised my head I found myself looking at a neat little hole that had been drilled in the closet door.

"Son of a bitch," I whispered. The hole was an inch or so above my eye line and about a half-inch in diameter. I stood on my tiptoes, looking through it, then closed myself in the closet and peered out. I could see the bed pretty well, but not much else. I stepped back out, taking a look at the hole from the outside. It was right above a mirror mounted to the wood-grain closet door, and although the hole was visible, it wasn't obvious. It was a damn peephole—but for what purpose?

I heard voices and footsteps in the hallway. I pressed my ear against the door and listened to the voices pass. It was time to boogie. I opened the door and the hallway was clear. I ripped the three strips of tape from the door, replaced them with new ones, and moved swiftly to the stairwell. A minute later I was walking through the dark parking lot to my car, congratulating myself on a smooth operation but eager to get out of there. Tampering with crime-scene evidence, especially in a murder case, would definitely piss off the locals.

•   •   •

I sat at the bar at the Lakeside and considered the peephole in the closet door. It was a perplexing find. Possibly it had been there for quite some time, but the sawdust seemed fresh; it wasn't ground into the floor and pressed into the corners. The hole was probably something a guest or a maid would notice before long, then it would be repaired. My suspicion was it had been drilled recently, maybe even the previous night.

I called the Crown on my cell, identifying myself again as a cop from Douglas County, and asked for the most recent registration records for room 672. The clerk told me Sylvester Bascom had checked in last night at ten-thirty. Brad had said Sylvester and Sven Osterlund left the bachelor party last night to try to get laid, which I assumed meant hookers. Did they bring a hooker to the room at the Crown? Had the Lake Tahoe police talked to Osterlund yet?

I sipped on my drink and decided to call my old buddy Cody Gibbons, a detective with San Jose PD. It had been a couple weeks since we'd talked, but he'd had the same phone number in San Jose for years. I dialed it from memory, and he answered on the second ring, his voice gruff and loud.

"What? What? Dirty Double-Crossin' Dan? Thanks for returning my call."

"What call?"

"I left you a message at your house."

"I've been in Tahoe since yesterday. You should have called my cell."

"Oh," he said. "Hey, they gave me another paid vacation. Can you believe it?"

"I hate to say so, but yes. What happened?"

"What? I was in pursuit of a car-jacking suspect over near King and Story. This asshole's driving like a complete maniac, he's blowing through red lights in crowded intersections, he's driving on the sidewalk and takes out a hotdog cart, it's amazing he didn't kill anyone. So he finally loses it around a corner and slams into a curb and breaks both axles and folds the tires under the car. By the time he gets out of the car we're right on him, but he takes off anyway. My new partner—I call him Fast Eddie, he's a black dude who used to run the hundred in college—he catches him, but this dude is jacked up on PCP, and it's like he's Superman. He knocked out Eddie with his first punch then grabbed his piece."

"Sounds like trouble."

"Fuckin' A. I was caught in the middle of the street with no cover. Lucky for me the guy couldn't shoot straight. He got off two shots before I drew on him. I hit him between the eyes with my first shot. I'm serious, can you believe that? Right between the eyes."

"DOA, I imagine."

"And then some. It took the top of his head off and splattered his brains all over the street. I'm suspended with pay for the time being, pending the investigation."

"What is there to investigate?"

"They suspect my ammunition might have been non-regulation, but shit, half the force is packing hollow-point cutters."

"It never occurs to you to play it by the book, does it, Cody?"

"Play it by the book? That gets you nowhere except dead, maybe. Come on, Dirt. Anyway, it's not uncommon to go SWP after a killing. They won't give me too much heat unless it gets political. He would have bought it no matter what kind of bullet I used. It may have been the greatest shot of my career."

"In the meantime you're on vacation with a pay check coming in."

"You got that right, Dirt. So, what the hell are you doing?"

Cody Gibson and I had known each other since we played football together in high school. Cody was our star defensive lineman. Sometime after high school, he began calling me Dirty Double-Crossing Dan, the result of a forgotten, drunken episode at a pick-up bar. The nickname had survived the years. Cody was like that—on impulse he would nickname people, and the names tended to stick for life. His mom was Old Glory, he called his dad The Big Guy, and one of our old running buddies was No-Morals Andrew. He called Wenger "The Sniveler."

I quit football after I blew out my knee in my junior year and took up wrestling, but Cody went on to play on the defensive line for Utah State, despite being expelled from high school for throwing his coach in a Dumpster. By that time Cody was six-foot-five, 270, and still growing, and was wearing the trademark red beard he grew every winter since. He came back to San Jose after college and worked for a private security firm for a few years before hiring on with the San Jose Police Department. They promoted him to plainclothes detective three years ago.

"I'm working a case up here freelance," I said.

"Yeah? You going to be up there for a while?"

"Could be."

"What's The Sniveler have to say about that?"

"I haven't told him yet."

Cody laughed. "You think you could run a couple names through the system for me?" I asked.

"Shouldn't be a problem. Fast Eddie owes me."

"Right. The names are Sylvester Bascom and Sven Osterlund. Bascom's a murder victim, and Osterlund's a suspect."

"I'll have their records pulled. Call me in twenty-four hours," Cody said, still chuckling.

"Thanks, buddy."

I left my drink half-finished and walked out of the casino. If Osterlund wasn't already being held as a witness, I wanted to talk to him. But first I needed to sit down with Whitey and Brad. I drove back down 50, to the Lazy 8 Hotel. The light was on in their room. It had been about five hours since I dropped them off, and I imagined they were sitting around watching TV before revving up for another long night of partying. Hopefully they had got some sleep. Whitey parted the drapes and looked out the window when I knocked.

"Dan, what's up?" he said, opening the door. He was wearing boxer shorts and a t-shirt.

"You guys rested up?" I said. "You ready to go do some drinking?"

"Shit, I'm dying for a beer," Whitey said. The room smelled like pot, and his bong was smoldering on the nightstand. "Brado's in the shower, he just woke up. I've been up for about half an hour. I'm freakin' starving, I'm ready to split and get some fast food. You want a bong hit, man?"

"No, thanks. But let's go out and I'll buy you guys dinner."

"No way!" Brad yelled, walking out of the bathroom with a towel around his waist.

"Yup," I said. "I'm up a hundred at the casinos. Come on, get your asses dressed. I'm buying."

"Right on," Whitey said. They threw on their clothes and we were on the street in two minutes flat. The Lazy 8 was one of a number of cheap hotels on the California side of the state line, across from the casinos. We crossed the street over to Buffalo Bill's Casino, which had a good all-night restaurant. The joint was raging with a rowdy Saturday night crowd. Rock n' roll blared from the speakers, blending with the ring of slot machines, the clatter of dice, and the buzz of cards being shuffled. A couple of girls in tight jeans were trying to dance at the craps table and knocked a guy's beer all over him. We wedged our way through the masses over to the restaurant. I steered us to a table toward the back, away from the noise.

"Brad, you're looking a little better than you did earlier today," I said.

"Shit, man, I felt my temperature shoot up, and I was pouring sweat, and then it started going black all around the edges." He waved his hands around his head. "I felt like I was gonna freakin' die."

"That's because you're a pansy," Whitey said.

"But that sleep did me right," he went on. "I'm fine now, just a little hung over, and I need to eat. But give me a few beers, and I'll be a hundred percent."

The waitress came by, and I ordered a pitcher of beer and a round of tequila. Brad ordered a bacon cheeseburger with fries and onion rings, and Whitey went for a pepperoni pizza with a Mexican fiesta plate as an appetizer.

"No food for you, Dan?" Brad said.

"I'm just drinking. You ever catch up with your buddy Osterlund?"

"No. He's probably still at Caesar's. He had a room there," Whitey said. "I haven't heard from him. Shit, can you believe Bascom's dead? I mean, on his freaking wedding day? I wonder how he croaked."

"Bascom took off with Osterlund from the bachelor party last night, huh?"

"They split after that stripper told Osterlund to fuck off," Brad said. "Osterlund got it in his brain he wanted a blow job, and if he didn't get one last night he's either still looking or blowing himself."

"What about Bascom? Did he want to get laid too, the night before his wedding?"

"I think Osterlund gave him a couple lines, and Bascom was probably into it after that," Whitey said.

"That core can make you freakin' horny," Brad added. "I had a rod the whole time the strippers were there."

"Osterlund was probably looking for one whore for him and Bascom to tag team," Whitey said. "He's into that kind of shit."

"What, you mean two on ones?"

"Yeah, that, and also he likes to watch and jerk off. I'm serious, he's perverted. Did you ever hear the story about him and Wayne Majors?"

"Yeah, yeah, check it out," Brad interjected. He was on his second beer, and his shot glass was empty. His eyes were bright, his voice energetic.

"Dude, it's my story," Whitey protested.

"No, come on, let me tell him," Brad said. The waitress brought the appetizers and Whitey started eating, so Brad jumped into the story.

"Get this. Remember Wayne had that girlfriend with the big tits? She wasn't that good-looking, but she had a nice body and a pair of jugs that wouldn't quit. I don't remember her name, this was maybe a year ago, but Osterlund and Wayne and this chick are sitting around one afternoon getting wasted, and Wayne and her decide they wanna screw. So Osterlund begs them to let him watch, but she won't go for it." Brad grabbed a *quesadilla* from Whitey's plate, folded it in half, and shoved it in his mouth. I waited for him to continue.

"So anyway, they finally agree to let Osterlund watch from outside, in the backyard. So he goes outside, and Wayne's banging her like a screen door in a hurricane, and Osterlund's looking in the window, spanking his monkey in the backyard in broad daylight, and then…" He paused to finish his beer.

"And then, Osterlund disappears all the sudden, and the next thing you know he bursts into the bedroom! He's stark naked with a hard-on, and they're yelling at him to get out, but he goes right up to them and shoots his load all over her. And some of it even gets on Majors!" Brad laughed loudly, pounding the table.

"It's true," Whitey said between mouthfuls. "Remember Hanna? She was this chick I used to go out with. She was totally cool, she was a nurse.

And Osterlund is trying to convince me to let him video us in the rack. I'm like, 'You gotta be kidding, there's no way.' But, dude, I'm telling ya, he gets off on shit like that."

"Yeah, Whitey, I'd really get off seeing your big white ass humping away in a porno," Brad said. Whitey flipped him the bird, but upside down, waving his middle finger back and forth limply.

"Osterlund sounds like a real piece of work," I said. "I wonder where he'd go looking for hookers."

"He'd probably call one of those escort services. Those broads will polish your helmet if you can afford it," Brad said.

The waitress brought out their main courses and another pitcher. They dug in, eating and drinking like medieval lords. I didn't want Brad or Whitey to get the impression I had more than a casual curiosity about Bascom's death. I wanted to talk to Osterlund as soon as I could find him, and my goal was to catch him off guard. I had no doubt the police were looking for him as well, as he was the most obvious potential witness; everyone at the bachelor party saw him leave with Bascom. But I thought there was a good chance he was either lying low or on the run, so maybe the cops hadn't interrogated him yet. I imagined he would have already left town if his truck weren't impounded. He was probably cursing his bad luck at having it towed. *Bad luck by your own design, dude.*

I tried to imagine different scenarios of what might have happened in the hotel room the night Sylvester Bascom was murdered. Suppose Bascom and Osterlund had been there with a hooker or two, and maybe Bascom was getting laid and Osterlund was watching. Then she pulls out a knife for some reason, say she's a nut case, and stabs him. But John Bascom said Sylvester had been beaten as well as stabbed, so that didn't make sense. If he was beaten, I assumed it was by a man, possibly Osterlund. Maybe Osterlund beat him and stabbed him because they were arguing about who was going to do what to the prostitute. But what about the peephole?

If Osterlund drilled it, he probably planned on watching Bascom get laid. Maybe Bascom didn't want him to watch. Would Osterlund stab him to death for that?

My thinking was all based on the assumption there were actually one or more hookers in the room. I needed to see the coroner's report on Sylvester Bascom. It would help to know if he had sex that night. Also, I wanted to know the extent of his injuries, including the specifics on the knife wounds.

The waitress started clearing the plates and asked if we wanted anything else. I handed her my credit card.

"Thanks for dinner, buddy. That's totally cool," Brad said.

I signed the bill when the waitress returned, then left Brad and Whitey at the table. Outside, the cold night air was harsh compared to the warmth of the casino. I shoved my hands deep in my pockets and walked back across the street to the Lazy 8, where my car waited patiently in the dark parking lot, like a faithful old dog.

8

IT WAS PAST ELEVEN when I dialed Caesar's and asked for the room of Sven Osterlund. They connected me, but there was no answer. I dialed Edward Cutlip next. He sounded groggy when he answered, and I thought I may have woken him.

"Edward, I need to see the coroner's report," I said. "Did you talk to Bascom after he got back from the coroner?"

"Yes, I did. He looks like he's aged ten years. Obviously this whole thing is hard on him beyond description. The coroner did a preliminary exam on the body, but I don't know any details. He's going to come in tomorrow afternoon and do the formal autopsy."

"It's important for me to get a copy of his report right away. Actually, it'd be better for me to just go to the autopsy and get the facts on the spot."

"You, you want to go to the autopsy?" Edward asked. "Why would you want to do that?"

"The sooner I know what I'm working with, the better. I need you to arrange it so I can be there."

"It sounds highly irregular," he said. "I'll have to ask Mr. Bascom to use his influence."

"Fine, if that's what it takes. Have you heard anything on Sven Osterlund?"

"Osterlund? No, why?"

"Do you have any idea if the police are talking to him, or holding him?"

"No, not to my knowledge."

"Okay. Look, I'll talk to you in the morning. You can come to the autopsy with me after lunch if you'd like. I'll take you out for Italian food."

"Very funny."

We hung up, and I thought for a minute about Edward Cutlip. Could he stand to benefit by Sylvester's death? With Sylvester out of the way, might Cutlip improve his position at Bascom Lumber? He didn't seem to be the scheming type, but I couldn't rule it out.

I called Caesar's and again asked for the room of Sven Osterlund. There was no answer. I tried Chris Dickerson and Ron Yamoto, the two grooms-men Edward knew by name. Dickerson didn't answer, but Yamoto did.

I introduced myself and asked if he knew Osterlund's whereabouts. He said he didn't and referred to Osterlund as "that weird guy."

I sighed, headed to 7-Eleven, and bought a twenty-ounce coffee and a copy of the *Reno Gazette*. Then I drove back to the Lazy 8 and found a dark spot across the street in another hotel parking lot that had a clear view of Brad and Whitey's room. I backed into the spot, grabbed my sleeping bag out of the trunk, and made myself comfortable in the Nissan's passenger seat. My theory was Osterlund would likely reconnect with his pals sooner rather than later.

Around two in the morning I dozed off, then woke at 3:00 A.M., shivering, and drove out for another coffee. I returned and continued watching. By eight the sun was shining, and people were coming out of their rooms. It looked like it would be a nice day to ski, I thought fleetingly. I moved my car onto the side street off the main highway. Though I could no longer see Brad's room, if Osterlund were to show up at the Lazy 8, he'd have to drive, or walk, past me.

I called Caesar's on my cell and once more asked for Osterlund's room, but there was no answer. My eyes were sore and my mouth felt gritty. I was just about ready to head to my room at the Lakeside when I decided to try something. I dialed San Jose directory service and asked for Zelda Thomas, Osterlund's mother's name. There was no listing. I tried Zelda Osterlund, with no success. I asked if any Osterlunds were listed in the San Jose area; the operator gave me the names and numbers of four listings. I called each number asking for Zelda, and on the third try, to the residence of Jane Osterlund, a woman's voice said, "Who's calling?"

"Ma'am, this is the Silverado County Sheriff's Office. We have a white Chevy truck with license plate 'PSYCHIC' in our impound lot, and we're trying to locate the owner."

"That's my son's, goddammit," she said. "Why are you calling so early?"

"We charge for storage by the day, ma'am. If he picks it up this morning he'll save himself the daily lot fee."

"Well, I talked to him yesterday, and I'm wiring him the money later today, but he probably won't get it until tomorrow."

"We also take checks and credit cards," I said.

"Listen to me," she said, her voice rising. "Do not, I repeat, do not take a check from him. If he's stupid enough to write the cops a bad check, and you're stupid enough to take it, then god help us all. And he better not be using a credit card. He just declared personal bankruptcy in January."

"Okay, thanks for your help. We'll look for him tomorrow."

"If he doesn't show up, please call me," she said.

"Why wouldn't he show up?"

"Who knows?" she said, exasperated. "He's unpredictable."

She hung up, and I drove back up 50 to the Lakeside. I was getting the impression Osterlund was a son only a mother could love, and maybe even that was a stretch. I mentally ticked off what I knew about him: drug problems, reckless driver, falsified handicapped parking permit, sexually perverted, violent tendencies, and bankrupt. His life sounded like ten pounds of shit stuffed in a five-pound bag.

I rubbed my eyes. It was typical behavior for criminals to keep close ties to their mothers. When everyone else they knew abandoned them, they'd always go back to dear old mom for money. It was a pathetic but predictable tendency. I frowned as I remembered I hadn't talked to my mother for a month or so. She was probably disappointed; I'd try to call her later, when I had time.

I lay down on my hotel bed and slept for an hour, clearing some of the cobwebs from the long, uncomfortable night in my car. In the back of my mind I knew I had to call Wenger, but I decided to put it off until later in the day. It was nine A.M. I punched in Edward's number on my cell phone and told him I wanted to talk to him and Bascom in person. He sounded distracted, but agreed and said to come on up to their suite.

When I arrived, John Bascom himself opened the door. There were dark circles under his eyes, and his shoulders were slumped. His voice was barely audible when he told me to come in. We went into the connected room, where Edward was typing on a computer.

"We're making arrangements for the funeral," Bascom said. "What have you found out so far?"

"Sylvester left the bachelor party around ten o'clock with Sven Osterlund. Sylvester checked into the room at the Crown at ten-thirty. I spent all last night trying to find Osterlund. I'll try to track him down today."

"The reason you couldn't find him is he spent most of the night at the police station," Bascom said.

"We just found out ourselves," Edward added before I could say anything. "The detectives picked him up and took him in for questioning and grilled him most of the night. They think he knows more than he's saying, but they don't have enough to charge him with anything."

I opened my notebook. "Who are detectives on the case?"

Edward handed me two cards, and I jotted down the names: Don Raneswich and Paul Iverson.

"What's Osterlund's story?" I said.

Edward and Bascom looked at each other. "You tell him," Bascom mumbled.

"Osterlund admits he and Sylvester went to the Crown. But he claims Sylvester called a hooker and went to the room by himself to wait for her. Osterlund said he left the Crown at that time and went back to his room at Caesar's."

"It sounds like bullshit," I said. "I learned a lot about Osterlund last night. He's a guy with a lot of bad habits, to put it lightly. Mr. Bascom, I'm curious about how Sylvester became friends with Osterlund. It seems like an unlikely match."

"That's a good question. I think they'd only known each other for a year, maybe less. The only thing I ever heard was Osterlund's mother is Zelda Thomas, that nutty psychic. Other than that, I don't know."

"If the cops find Osterlund's prints in the room, they can charge him with obstruction and hold him, and maybe he'll talk," I said.

"It doesn't look good," Edward said. "They have a couple smudged, partial prints, but it's not much."

"Do the detectives have any leads on the hooker?"

"They're working on it," Bascom said, "but if Osterlund's full of shit, who knows if there even was a hooker?"

We were all silent for a moment. "I'm gonna find Osterlund and see what I can get out of him," I said. "Obviously he knows more than he's admitting. He may even be your son's murderer. But he didn't break under the police interrogation, so I'll have to see what I can do to get him to talk."

"That's what I'm paying you for," Bascom said.

"Edward, am I set to go with the coroner?"

"The autopsy is at two o'clock," he said. "The coroner wasn't particularly happy about it, but agreed you could be there after certain influences were applied."

"Certain influences?"

"I told you I'm well connected, Reno," Bascom said.

"I see. How long do you plan to stay here in Tahoe?"

"At least another couple days, maybe longer depending on how the case goes," he said, his voice drifting away.

I paused, then said, "Mr. Bascom, I'm sorry I haven't already said so, but I want to extend my sympathies for your loss."

Bascom's eyes met mine briefly. "Thank you," he said.

Edward followed me out into the hall. "These detectives don't know about your involvement. Are you planning on telling them?"

"Not unless I have a reason to."

"Okay," he said. "I hope you don't mind if I pass on your invitation for lunch and the autopsy." He smiled weakly.

"Yeah, you're missing out on memories that could last a lifetime." I was trying to kid him, but he didn't laugh.

I took the elevator down to the lobby, almost walked outside, then turned around and picked up the courtesy phone on the wall. I called the front desk and asked for Julia's room. She answered promptly.

"You're investigating Sylvester's death?" she said, her voice incredulous.

"That's right. I'm down in the lobby. Can you spare a few minutes?"

"What for?"

"I'd like to talk to you about what you're hearing from your side of the family."

"Really? Okay, Parkash and me are on our way down. We're gonna get a bite at the coffee shop on the far side of the casino, on the opposite side from the lobby. We'll be there in ten minutes. Why don't you meet us?"

They showed up right on time. Parkash looked as rotund and happy as ever when they approached my table.

"I hear you're tracking the murder case of the unfortunate Sylvester Bascom," he said.

"Yes, Parkash, and I suspect some very bad people were involved."

"Make sure they receive justice."

I nodded and turned to Julia. "So, how's your family taking it in general?"

"You know," she said, "it's funny. Some people are very emotional and are acting like a close family member died, and other people seem like it really doesn't affect them. It's interesting to stand back and watch the varieties of behavior." Julia, the psychology major.

"I mean, Shelly is totally freaked out, she's crying and running around hugging everyone. I guess she feels that, as Desiree's mother, it's appropriate for her to act like that, more out of sadness for Desiree than grief over Sylvester. On the other hand, Jerry seems totally stoic and unemotional, like it's just another event in life. He's been like that ever since his bankruptcy."

"How's Desiree holding up?"

"At first she was completely hysterical, but then she came down to the casino about nine o'clock, and she was pretty composed. By the way, there was a rumor going around that some really perverted stuff happened at the bachelor party, involving whores. Were you there?"

"No, I didn't go," I said, not adding that I spent the night exercising my own perversions with Desiree's sister.

"How about Mandy?" I said.

"Speaking of whores, you mean? She didn't seem to have any reaction one way or another. I think she's too self-centered to care about other people's problems."

"I need to talk to Desiree. Do you think she's up to it?"

Julia's eyes jumped. "I think it's too early, Dan. It's inappropriate."

We chatted for a few more minutes, and when Julia and Parkash ordered breakfast, I excused myself and went back to the courtesy phone and asked for the room of Desiree McGee.

"Hello, Desiree?" I said.

"No, this is Desiree's mother. Who's this?"

"It's Dan Reno, Shelly. Is Desiree available?"

"I'll see if she can talk," she said. A minute later, Desiree picked up.

"Hello?"

"Hi, Desiree. I'm sorry for your loss," I said, feeling the awkwardness of the words hover in the line between us. "Are you okay?"

"Sort of."

"Desiree, I've been hired by John Bascom to investigate Sylvester's death. I'd like to sit down with you for a few minutes and talk about some things, ask some questions. It's something I need to do right away."

"Like, now?"

"Yes."

I heard muffled voices, then Shelly came back on the phone.

"Dan, I'm sorry," she said, "But this is really not a good time."

"I see. I understand this is difficult. But whoever stabbed Sylvester to death is still at large." The line was silent for a moment, then I heard muffled voices.

"Okay, where do you want to do this?" Shelly said.

"I'm in the lobby downstairs. It would be best to come up to your room."

"I suppose that's okay," she sighed, "as long as you make it quick. We're in room five-oh-eight."

I went out to my car and strapped on my shoulder holster. Then I took the elevator to the fifth floor and knocked on their door. Shelly let me into the room, where Desiree was sitting on the bed in gray sweats and a black sweatshirt. She wasn't wearing makeup, and I was surprised at how different she looked. But even in her loose-fitting clothes, her body looked toned and slinky. I guess I never noticed before—maybe because I was too distracted by her sister.

There was a bunch of crumpled tissues scattered about the bed and the floor. I stood in the room silently, holding my coat.

"Why are you carrying that gun?" Shelly said in a brittle voice. She was plump and had nice features but was way past her prime. Some women stayed sexy into their fifties. Shelly wasn't one of them.

"There's a killer on the loose. There's a chance he's here at Caesar's. I intend to find him, and I don't expect he'll surrender easily."

"Here? In this hotel?"

"I need to talk to you alone, Shelly. Do you have a separate room?"

"Yes, next door."

"Let's go," I said bluntly.

"Des, will you be all right? I'll be right back."

We went to Shelly's room. I had guessed Shelly would be intimidated by the gun and a little B-movie tough talk. It didn't take much.

I asked Shelly about her perception of the Bascoms and Sylvester and his friends—it became obvious she didn't know them very well. She said Sylvester was a nice man with a bright future and made some other meaningless remarks that were the type of things people say out of habitual politeness. I listened to her for a couple of minutes then went back to Desiree's room, after telling Shelly not to disturb us.

She was smoking when she answered the door. She had put on lipstick and had done something with her hair. Her feet were bare, and her toenails were painted red. She sat down at the round table near the window, and I took a seat across from her.

"I want to apologize in advance if any of my questions make you uncomfortable, Desiree. Have the police questioned you yet?"

"Only briefly, yesterday. I talked to the black guy, the sheriff."

"Not the detectives?"

"No."

"Hmm. Let's talk about Sylvester's friends. I assume the groomsmen were his best friends?"

"Well, basically, yeah," she said, then gave me a brief rundown on each of them. There was an old high-school buddy who was an accountant at a real estate firm. Another one was married with four kids and worked at Bascom Lumber as a crew supervisor. Next, a Japanese guy, an engineer for Intel Corporation. The fourth was a divorced computer salesman.

She paused, took a final drag off her cigarette, and stamped it out in an ashtray.

"The other one is Sven Osterlund. He and Sly had been friends for about a year, and I've only met him a couple times. He's a real partier."

"A real partier, huh?" I said. "How so?"

"Well…" she looked down, then glanced at me briefly.

"Don't worry, this conversation is confidential."

"Okay. We used to do a little coke, and Sven was the connection," she said.

I looked out the window. The sky was bright, but there was a dark layer of clouds hanging low over the mountains.

"So you and Sylvester would do coke with Sven?"

"Yes."

"How often?"

"Not that much," she said. "Maybe twice a month. Sven always seemed to have it, but I'm not that into it. Sly liked to do it when he was drunk."

"Did you ever think Sven was weird sexually?" I said.

"Oh, you know about that? Yeah."

"Yeah, what?"

"Yeah, he was into some kinky stuff. Like, he was really into porno movies. He wanted to film them, and he had a big collection. One time he asked Sly and me if we'd be interested in being filmed, and of course we said no way."

"What else?"

"He was on some kind of voyeurism trip. Sly told me he got off on playing with himself while watching other people have sex. Is this really important?"

"Yes, it could be very important," I said. "Do you think he influenced Sly with his, uh, preferences?"

Desiree's dark skin flushed deeper, and she fumbled for another cigarette.

"Desiree?"

"I don't see how Sly's and my sex life is of any importance or any of your business," she said, her eyes flashing. She glared at me like I was a lecherous drunk making an obscene suggestion.

"Look," I said quietly, "I don't give a damn what you two did in the privacy of your own home. Movies, group sex, coke, it's all pretty routine. So don't think I'm gonna be shocked. But we're talking about murder. Someone stabbed your fiancé to death, so I need you to get past your embarrassment and answer my questions."

Desiree looked like she was going to burst into tears, but she dragged off her cigarette until the moment passed. I'd always thought of her as the beautiful, innocent debutante, but she looked like she aged five years before my eyes. The cheerful naïveté of her youth seemed to fade into a past life that was becoming a bitter memory. Her eyes grew hard and defiant, and the smooth skin around her jawline tightened like a clenched fist.

"Fine," she said. "Sylvester was also into movies. And yes, we have private films of me and of each other. But that's the extent of it, so don't cum in your pants. Sven was never involved with us sexually. I would never allow that, not even when we were whacked out on coke. He never filmed us or watched us or anything."

We sat across from each other in the stillness of the room.

"Look, my life just got flushed down the toilet," she said. "Are you done with your questions?"

"Just one more. Do you think Sylvester was cheating on you?"

"Yes," she whispered.

•   •   •

I returned my pistol to my trunk and went back into Caesar's to call Osterlund's room again. There was no answer after a half dozen rings, but then I looked up and saw him at the registration counter. He had his bags with him and kept glancing around like he was looking for somebody. His upper back muscles flexed against his white t-shirt, which was tucked into jeans that looked form-fitted to his legs. I waited for him to finish at the desk, then fell in beside him as he walked toward the exit.

"Hey, man," I said. "You need a lift?"

"Huh? Do I know you?"

"Dan Reno. I went to Oakbrook. You're Sven, right?"

When he didn't respond, I said, "I think you were a freshman when I was a senior. I grew up next door to Brad Turner."

He stopped and peered at me with half-lidded eyes that seemed dead and void of emotion. He looked down on me slightly; he had me by an inch and maybe twenty pounds.

"How'd you know I need a ride?"

"Well, I was drinking with Brad and Whitey last night. They said your truck got ripped off."

"It didn't get ripped off, it got fuckin' towed," he said. "I could use a ride over to the Lazy Eight. It's the fleabag they're staying at."

"Come on," I said, leading him outside to my car. He threw his luggage into my backseat, and we drove across the street to the cheap hotel. As soon as we stopped, Osterlund grabbed his bag out of the Nissan and walked to Brad and Whitey's room. He left my car door open. I walked around and closed it.

He tried to open the door to their room, but it was locked. He pounded on it hard with the meat of his fist. "Open up," he said. Brad swung the door open, and his jaw dropped.

"Sven, buddy, what the hell, man? Dan? What's goin' on?"

"Bong hit, Sven?" Whitey said, his voice a rasp, holding a hit deep in his lungs.

"I saw him over at Caesar's and brought him over," I said, following Osterlund in.

Whitey blew out his hit. "Dude, any word on your truck?"

Osterlund loaded himself a bowl out of Whitey's plastic baggie and lit it. He held it in for about thirty seconds, and when he exhaled there was no smoke.

"Yeah, it's in the sheriff's impound lot. They towed it."

"Those motherfuckers," Brad said.

"Dude, what's up with Bascom kickin' the bucket? Did the cops talk to you about it?" Whitey's eyes were red and glassy.

Osterlund glanced at me. "Talk about it later," he mumbled.

"Christ, Sven, what happened last night?" Brad said.

"You got any beers in this dump?" Osterlund said.

"No, we finished our twelve-pack."

Osterlund pulled a ten out of his wallet, crumpled it up, and threw it in Brad's direction. "Why don't you go get us a half rack?"

Brad picked up the ten and smoothed it out. "Okay," he said, looking at the bill.

"Dude, what about Bascom?" Whitey said. Osterlund cut his eyes toward him, but Whitey was obliviously stoned. "Hey, maybe Dan can help figure out who killed him, he's a private eye!" Whitey smiled, his jaw hanging stupidly, nodding his head as if it were attached to a spring. Osterlund turned toward me, and I could see the suspicion glowing behind his reptilian eyes.

"How nice, a private investigator," Osterlund said. "You been messing around with Mandy McGee?"

I felt my brow crease. "What?"

"She told me you short-stroked her the other night. Hope you enjoyed it, but she's off limits from now on, you got it?"

I shrugged. "Sure."

"So, did you fuck her?"

"Is that what she told you?"

"I'm asking *you*, bitch," he said, the cords in his neck like taut rope beneath his skin. I was leaning against the windowsill with my arms crossed, and he was on the other side of the room. He stared at me hard.

"Whitey, why don't you load Sven another bong hit?" I said.

"You got a real smart mouth on you, buddy."

"What happened at the Crown Ambassador last night?" I said.

"That's a good question. Why don't you stick your head up your hole and ask around?"

He took a step in my direction. Brad and Whitey were silent and frozen.

"You and Mandy might consider a future in Mexico," I said. "I'd say it will take about forty-eight hours for the cops to gather enough evidence to arrest you. If you head south quick, you might make it."

He shook his head. "Unbelievable," he said. Then he pointed at me with two fingers. "It's time for you to leave, fuckwad." He came forward and opened the door. No more than four feet separated us. We stood staring at each other.

"Fuckwad, huh?" I said. "I haven't heard that one in a while."

"Hit the road, pal, before I rip your throat out."

"You're one badass son of a bitch, aren't you?"

A tight smile formed on his face. He moved his arm in an underhanded motion, gesturing toward the door. I decided I'd split—there was no point in sticking around now, unless I wanted to try to beat a confession out of him. I doubted I could, but for a long moment I was tempted to try.

"You're welcome for the ride," I said finally, and as soon as I walked out he kicked me hard in the ass. I whirled around, but he was already in position, and his leg shot out, the sole of his shoe aimed at my chin. But his kick wasn't quite high enough, and I took the blow in the meat of my chest. Before he could snap his leg back I grabbed his ankle and jerked it upward. He fell back on his neck, bucked his legs and was on his feet like a cat, but not quick enough. I jumped forward and hit him in the jaw with a straight left. His skull snapped back, and I threw a roundhouse right, going for the knockout, but he blocked it neatly, then his fist came out of nowhere and slammed me hard on the side of the face.

The blow sent me reeling out the door and into a maid's housekeeping cart. The maid screamed as it fell over into the parking lot with a loud crash. Various cleaning supplies and rolls of toilet paper spilled across the pavement and into a snow bank. I scrambled to my feet while Osterlund eyed me from the doorway, with blood on his mouth and the beginnings of a nice fat lip.

"Go fuck yourself," he said hoarsely, and spat a stream of bloody saliva in my direction. He slammed the door and I heard him lock the bolt. I stood there, and after a moment I helped the maid pick up her cart, then I drove back to the Lakeside.

9

I LAY ON MY bed for half an hour with an ice pack on my jaw. The adrenaline lump in my stomach had subsided, leaving me with a slight headache. My attempt to get any meaningful information out of Osterlund had backfired miserably, but considering his frame of reference, I couldn't imagine what would have worked, short of torturing him. I smiled at the thought. If I caught him in his room I could have jolted him with my stun baton, but instead I had hoped to sit around with him, Whitey, and Brad, maybe have a few beers, and if he felt relaxed he might start talking. But he was wound tight as a winch, and now I had lost the element of surprise.

I adjusted the ice pack. The mention of Mandy had come out of left field and caught me off guard—by telling me to stay away from her, was Osterlund insinuating he had plans to win her heart? If so, he could add her to his growing list of problems. But obviously Mandy had told him we'd been together, for what reason I had no idea. I decided I'd talk to Mandy soon. If she was involved with him, she was inviting trouble.

The ice was melting, and cold water began to run off my face and onto the sheet. I pushed myself off the bed, checked the address for the coroner's office, and saw it was in the same complex as the sheriff's office. If I moved quickly I could fill my obligation to register my handgun with Marcus Grier before meeting the coroner. If I was skiing and then heading back home today, I would have blown him off. But given the events of the last twenty-four hours, I thought it would be a good idea to comply with his request.

It had warmed up outside and little rivers of water were flowing everywhere, off the icicles that hung from the roofs and eves, across parking lots, around dirt banks and into the street. At night, when the temperature dropped, the runoff would freeze and turn to black ice.

I parked under a grove of immense, old-growth ponderosa that seemed to reach to the boundaries of the sky, and popped my trunk. My gear was stashed in an old suitcase I had secured to one side of the trunk with bungee cords. I opened the suitcase, reached under my bulletproof vest and pulled out the shoulder holster that held my Beretta, then went through the glass doors and into the small lobby of the sheriff's office.

"Marcus Grier asked to see me about registering my handgun," I told the receptionist, and set my piece on the counter. We were separated by a thick glass window with a speaker installed in the middle.

"I don't know any specific form we use for that. I'll have to call the sheriff."

A few minutes later Marcus Grier opened the door and motioned for me to follow him.

"I didn't expect I'd be seeing you, Mr. Reno," he said as I walked down the hallway behind him. He pronounced my name correctly.

"I've been distracted, but I always cooperate with the police, Sheriff."

We sat in his office. One of the walls was glass, overlooking a dozen or so desks in the main squad room. A few deputies were doing paperwork; among them was the young cop who tried to hassle me at the Midnight Tavern. Fingsten, if I remembered right.

"Yes, South Lake Tahoe can be a distracting town," Grier said. "Twenty-four-hour drinking and gambling, live titty shows, rock and roll, and all this beautiful scenery." His voice was deep and gravelly, and he spoke slowly and enunciated with unusual emphasis.

"And every weekend five to ten thousand people come to visit us. They come to enjoy themselves, to partake in all these wonderful activities. They get drunk on free casino liquor and drink in the streets, and then they walk in front of cars, or beat up their wives, or get pick-pocketed. And every so often, someone gets killed. Do you know why I'm telling you this, Mr. Reno?"

"I imagine the weekends are busy for you," I said.

"Yes, but here's my point." He smiled, showing a gold molar in the side of his mouth. "Some of my deputies refer to our visitors as 'tourons,' which is a combination of a tourist and a moron. They think they can't get in trouble or die because they're on vacation. What I'm getting at, Mr. Reno, is I have enough trouble without a PI from out of town, with a license to carry a concealed firearm, coming into one of our quaint little bars and causing trouble."

"It was unavoidable," I said, but he raised a hand to stop me.

"I understand it was self-defense. That's why no charges are being filed. But my point is this: watch yourself, don't look for trouble, and don't do anything stupid. Frankly, the thought of an armed citizen in my town gives me cause for concern. Are you leaving today?"

"No," I said. "I have some business that will keep me a few days."

"Oh?" he said, his wooly eyebrows rising on his forehead, his expression contemplative. I knew he had seen me the day before at the wedding.

"Please make sure there's no reason for us to talk again. Other than that, enjoy your stay." He stood and we walked out into the hallway.

"Fingsten," he said, and the deputy looked up from his desk.

"Make a copy of Mr. Reno's driver's license, his concealed weapon permit, and take down the serial number and make and model of his firearm." Grier walked away and left me with Fingsten. I gave him the Beretta and licenses, and we stood at the copy machine while he made copies and scribbled down the notes on my gun.

"Don't even spit on the sidewalk, man," he said.

"Huh?"

"You heard me, tough guy," he rasped. It sounded like he was doing a bad Clint Eastwood imitation.

"I have no idea what you're talking about," I said.

"Stick around, and you will." His muscles tensed and he slowly clenched and unclenched his fist. He looked barely old enough to shave, and his skinny body was the type any respectable man could snap like a pencil.

"Yes, sir, Officer," I said, standing at attention and saluting. I walked away and tried not to laugh. Evidently Sheriff Grier had a shallow talent pool to choose from.

• • •

The coroner's facility was next to the sheriff's office. I tried the door, but it was locked. I stuck my hands in my pockets and kicked at pebbles for a few minutes until I saw a man carrying a briefcase climb from a car and walk toward me. His shoulders were hunched against the cold, and his gait was bowlegged and hitched.

"Who the hell are you?" he said, his blue eyes glaring from under his bushy gray eyebrows.

"I'm Dan Reno. I'm here to witness Sylvester Bascom's autopsy."

"What? Do you have permission to do so?"

"I was told by the Bascom family it had been arranged."

"Arranged, my ass," he grumbled. "You need formal permission. From me." He opened the glass door and stepped inside, holding it open against his shoulder. "Come on out of the cold, goddammit," he said. I followed him in.

"That's the problem with your generation. You got no manners, no respect for your elders."

"I beg your pardon?"

"I ain't heard you say goddamn 'please' yet."

I sighed and straightened my posture. "Okay. Can I please have your permission?"

"Yeah, against my better judgment, you can. As long as you got the stomach for it. You puke on my floor, I'm gonna kick your ass. You got it?" When he looked at me I thought he winked, but then I saw that his right eye had a nervous twitch. He blinked hard four or five times, then he smiled and stuck out his hand, his eyes alive with mirth.

"I'm Jack Myers," he said. I followed him into his office. "Actually, I was called by an aide to the governor of California, telling me to expect you. You must be working for someone who's got some clout. You're Reynolds, right?"

"Reno."

"That Eye-talian?" he asked, but didn't give me a chance to answer. "Give me a minute. I need to pull the paperwork. You been to an autopsy before, right?" His voice was like a gravel pit.

"Yes."

"All right. This way." I followed him to a changing room. He pulled a white gown over his sweater, and over that a yellow apron.

"Let's see if we have an XL for you." He took a gown from a neat pile on a green counter top.

"These too." He handed me the gown, an apron, a white hair cap with an elastic band, and a mask that covered from my chin to just below my eyes.

"And also these," he said, dropping a pair of blue rubber gloves into my hands.

We finished suiting up then went into the autopsy room, which had a linoleum floor and green tiled walls. My gown and apron kept me comfortable in the room's lowered temperature. I wrinkled my nose at the chemical smell, but I welcomed it—the stronger, the better.

There was a stainless-steel counter in the center of the floor, which harbored two sinks with faucets. On the floor below the counter was a large grated drain. A set of knifes, scalpels, and surgical pliers lay in a metal pan between the sinks.

"Wait here while I get the body," Myers said. When he turned to leave, I picked up a scalpel and idly inspected the blade. "And don't touch anything," he said, looking back and shaking his head. I put the knife down and waited for him under the flat light from a powerful rectangular lamp that hung low from the ceiling. He came back through a separate door a minute later, wheeled the covered body over to the sinks, and latched the gurney securely to the counter with two steel clasps.

"Everything I say from this point will be recorded," he said, and pushed a button on a console next to the counter. He was now wearing glasses, but his face was covered by the mask from the eyes down.

He pulled the sheet down to the waist, and there on the aluminum slats of the gurney lay the whitish-gray body of Sylvester Bascom.

There was a cut and swelling above his left eye, a discoloration on his chin, and a large abrasion on the right side of his rib cage. A two-inch-wide entry wound above and to the left of his navel appeared to be the cause of death. Jack Myers started speaking for the recorder.

"Case seven-zero-zero-nine-five-six. Sylvester Bascom. Visual inspection of the body indicates Caucasian male, approximately late twenties." He pulled the sheet completely off the body.

"No visual tattoos or scars on front side. Approximate height five-foot-nine, weight around one seventy-five, muscular build." He went on to describe the injuries. My first impression was that Sylvester had been in a struggle or a fight, and I doubted it was with a woman. I didn't see any scratch marks, but someone had popped him a couple good ones in the face. I bent down to take a close look at his knuckles—his right hand was cut on the fore and middle fingers. I thought back to Osterlund. There were no visible marks on his face earlier, at least not before our encounter.

"Son, give me a hand. I got problems with my back. Turn the body over for me." I tipped the body, which felt like a cold bag of hardened rubber, onto its front side. To my amazement, there was an exit wound in the lower back, maybe half an inch wide. Whoever stabbed him used one hell of a knife and must have rammed it into him with great force. The knife had to have been at least a foot long, maybe fifteen inches. No way was it a woman, unless she was extraordinarily strong. Jack Myers finished his description of the backside, and I turned the body back over.

He began an inspection of the genital region and said there was "significant residue, appearing to be dried semen and/or female bodily fluids." He took some scrapings, sealed them in a shallow glass container, then reached over and shut off the recorder. I followed him away from the body to a pair of metal folding chairs against the wall. He pulled his mask down under his chin.

"Next, I need to cut the body open and inspect the wound. Also I'll cut open the testes to determine if the subject had ejaculated recently." He looked up at me over his glasses. "You're welcome to stay if you're interested, or we can talk later, and I'll tell you what I've found."

"Okay," I said. I'd seen what I needed to and had no desire to watch him take the knife to Sylvester's genitals. "I don't want to impose, I know it's Sunday, but could we get together later this afternoon and go over it?"

"We could, as long as you have no objection to meeting me at the local pub."

"Done," I said, and managed a smile. "As long as you let me buy."

"You got a deal, son." He looked at his watch, then lifted his mask back over his mouth. "The King's Head, off 50 on Fremont Street. Be there at five."

"Thank you," I said, careful to show the gruff old bastard the proper manners.

· · ·

The gambling crowds at the Lakeside had thinned out, and I found a quiet desk in the keno lounge. My jaw was throbbing. I ran my tongue over the series of cuts Osterlund's punch had left inside my mouth, closed my eyes, and tried to relax. I hadn't got enough sleep, and felt tired as hell. My head became heavy, and the jumble of sounds from the casino blended into a dim haze of bass notes. Colors began to take shape on the insides of my eyelids, which felt like they were weighted with lead. The shapes became images of John Bascom and Jack Myers, and then they were replaced, as if a page had turned in my subconscious, by the presence of my father. My head fell forward, and I floated back to when I was a child.

It had rained most of that day, until dusk when the gray clouds moved east and the skies lightened. It was colder than we were used to in San Jose. The rainwater flowed down the gutters below the branches of the willows and oaks that lined the sidewalks on my street, and I thought if I looked close enough I might see slivers of ice in the runoff. Our front yard was nearly flooded—pools of water covered the lawn, and the mud around the shrubs was so deep that if you stepped in the wrong place, it might take your shoe off. I was eating dinner with my family that evening when we were interrupted by a loud pounding on our front door. My father left the table, I heard the door open, and heard the rumble of men talking. I walked to the door and two men I'd never seen stood on the porch.

One was large and fat, wearing a dirty t-shirt and faded brown pants, his hair covering his head in sparse patches. The other man was much smaller, not much taller than me even though I was only ten years old. He had greasy black hair and strangely deformed lips that seemed locked in a continuous sneer. Their conversation grew louder, and ugly tones intruded into our home like a vile odor. My father closed the door behind him, but I went outside to the front steps. The men stood shouting in the driveway of our San Jose home, and then I remember my dad saying, "You want to settle it that way? Then let's settle it."

They squared off on the driveway, he and the big man, with the deformed one watching not five feet from where I stood. The fight lasted maybe sixty seconds but seemed at the time to go on forever. My mother and sister came outside and watched my dad beat the man bloody, but the man wouldn't quit until he reeled around, staggering like a drunk, and fell face down onto the wet, gravely street. "You're not only an evil man, you're also stupid," my father told him. "You'll go to jail for your crimes." His friend helped him into their truck, and they drove away.

My mother was crying back in the house, and my father put his thick arms around her shoulders. "He had the nerve to confront and insult me at my home," he said, wiping the tears from her face. "Would the Richard Reynolds you married take that lying down?" His shirt was ripped, and a thin trail of blood ran from his cheek into his black beard.

As a district attorney, Richard Reynolds was widely feared for his vehement approach. A number of men he'd prosecuted swore they'd get back at him, and at one point we had our phone number unlisted. But my father loved his work; he did it fearlessly, and his mind was as sharp as his physical presence was intimidating. He was a large man with hard, dark eyes, and I never remember him without a full, coal-black beard, but in our home he was as kind and patient as he was relentless as a prosecutor.

It was around that time he changed our family name from Reynolds to Reno, and he was labeled as an eccentric in Santa Clara County's legal ranks. He eventually left the DA's office, went into private practice in San Jose, and had a successful career as a trial lawyer until one late fall day.

He had come out of his downtown office later than usual that evening, on a windy, moonless night. The man, whose name I later learned was Hubert Sheridan, was hiding in the parking lot, lying in wait for the day he had promised himself for the last three years. My father never had a chance. He died instantly from the point-blank blast from Sheridan's ten-gauge shotgun.

Hubert Sheridan was arrested later that night as he crouched in the weeds down on the banks of the nearby Guadalupe River. He was a lifetime criminal, an unintelligent, bitter man who had lost any real hope of a normal life by his teen years, when he was convicted of rape and sentenced to a year in a juvenile detention center. Afterward, he took his place among the criminal element on the outskirts of society, until eventually he was arrested for a series of felonies. My father convicted him of armed robbery, kidnapping, and a number of lesser charges, but prison overcrowding and a paperwork glitch set him free after serving only three years of his twelve-year sentence. He had been out of jail for a week when he murdered my dad, and it wasn't until I went to his sentencing hearing that I realized he was the same man my father had fought in our driveway on that cold night, back when I was a young boy.

•   •   •

A waitress tapped me on the shoulder and I snapped awake. I ordered a coffee, called Caesar's, and asked for Mandy McGee. There was no answer. I sat around for a few minutes, filled out a five-dollar keno slip, and gave it to the runner when she came by. Then, as much as I didn't want to, I called Wenger's home number. He answered on the first ring.

"Hey, Rick—

"Enjoying your long vacation?" he interrupted.

"Rick, something's come up here in Lake Tahoe."

"Don't tell me—you're hung over, and you'll be late on Monday."

"No. You know the wedding I'm here for? The groom was murdered, and his father has hired me to investigate."

"Hired you to investigate?"

"That's right."

"What? You mean Wenger and Associates, right?"

"No, I'm going to do this freelance."

"*Freelance?* What does that mean?"

"It means I'll need to spend another couple days up here, maybe more."

"You're joking."

"I'm not."

"So, you're not coming in tomorrow?"

"That's right."

"Dan, what are you saying? You can't just drop your responsibilities. You have a job working for me."

"I understand that. I'll need to take some vacation time, or possibly a leave of absence."

"What? That's bullshit! You can't just call me up on a Sunday afternoon and say, 'Oh, by the way, I won't be coming in for a while.'"

"Sorry, this was unexpected."

"Unexpected, huh? Listen, buster, that doesn't cut it. That's not the way professional careers work. I've treated you fairly, paid you on time, and now you're completely disregarding that." His voice had risen about two notches higher, the way it always did when he was emotional. I didn't say anything for a moment. I could hear him breathing in the phone.

"Rick, I don't feel good about putting you in a bad spot. You've been a fair boss, and I don't take my job for granted. But depending on what happens here, I may or may not want to continue working for you."

"What? Now you're quitting without notice? You asshole!"

"Now, calm down—I didn't say I was quitting. Goddammit, Rick, here's the bottom line. I was paid a large amount of money up front to investigate this murder. There's no way I could pass it up."

"How much?" he said. I knew he would ask that.

"It doesn't matter," I said. "It's enough that I accepted the offer immediately."

"Tell me how much. You owe me that."

"What's the point, Rick?"

"The point is I may want to make a counter offer."

"There's no way you could offer me enough. I told you, it's a large amount of money."

"Dammit, Dan, I've treated you well for two years. You can't screw me over like this! I have the right to know what I'm up against."

"It's way more than what you're paying me."

"Dan, how much?"

"It wouldn't make sense for you to even consider–"

"How much?"

"I'm telling you, Rick–"

"How fucking much?" he screamed.

"Fifty thousand," I said.

"Stop lying."

"That's up front, plus another fifty K if I identify the murderer before the police."

"That's preposterous. No one would pay that kind of money."

"The guy's a rich executive."

"I don't believe it," he said.

"It's the truth."

"Fifty thousand for investigating one murder? What kind of idiot would pay that much? What if the cops close the case right away? Do you still get the money?"

"I already have the check."

"This is unbelievable. I think it's just wrong. And I think the right thing to do is bring this business to Wenger and Associates."

"Yeah, right. Look, I'll make you a deal, Rick. Don't jump to any quick decisions. This whole thing could be over in forty-eight hours. I'm asking you to cut me some slack, hang in there for a couple days, and I'll let you know how it's going."

"Bring the case to Wenger and Associates."

"Nope."

"Let's work it together. Me and you."

"Not gonna happen, Rick."

"That's it, huh? Just like that. Well, thanks a lot, Dan. It's all good. I'll be waiting to hear from you. Just call me at your convenience. Appreciate it, man. No problem."

"I'll be in touch."

"You better think long and hard about what you're doing here. What comes around goes around. Don't come running to me when you need work."

"Uh-huh."

"Don't forget, you're gonna have to pay taxes on that money."

"I know."

"You've got some growing up to do," he said, and started saying something else, but I hung up on him.

I pushed away the last of my lukewarm coffee, went to the bar, and ordered a CC Seven. My head was ringing from the effort of not telling Wenger to screw himself. All the months of tolerating his petty crap seemed to culminate in that phone call, as if our relationship was a festering boil that needed to be popped. That's what Wenger was, I decided: a festering boil on the ass of my life. *Fuck you, Wenger. Calling me a drunk, leaping to the conclusion last Thursday that I'd been boozing all night when I'd only had one drink. Sure, bring the case to Wenger and Associates. Right. Kiss my ass, you greedy son of a bitch. I'm done with you instructing me on the most basic elements of my job over and over, as if I were a fucking moron.*

I gunned my drink, and then an odd thing happened: I felt a silly grin take hold on my face, and I actually began chuckling. Ah, hell, Wenger was Wenger. I even felt a strange affection for him, probably because he was so predictable. I'm sure he was eating his liver over the fact I had run into such an unexpected bonanza. To him money meant everything: status, prestige, comfort, self-esteem, self-image—it was all tied to income and finances. Wenger would always find a way to determine how much money a person made, and then he assigned respect accordingly. If someone made less money than he did, he'd rejoice smugly, but if they out-earned him, he'd be bitter and jealous. I'd gone to pick-up bars with Wenger, and his usual tactic was to suggest to young ladies that he made more money than whomever they were mingling with. In the best-case scenario, women would ignore him, give him dirty looks, or tell him to beat it. In the worst case he'd get his ass kicked, and on a few occasions I'd saved him from a likely beating.

I called Mandy three more times, then I tried Jerry McGee, and he answered.

"How you holding up, Jerry?"

"Ah, jeez, I'm fine, but Shelly's going crazy, and Desiree is really freaked out."

"Man, that's too bad. I wanted to call to say I'm sorry."

"Appreciate it. After what I've been through in my life, this is just another test. But we'll be fine. It'll pass, and life goes on. Hey, Shelly tells me Bascom hired you to investigate the murder."

"Yeah, looks like I'll stay up here for a little while."

"You couldn't have picked a nicer place, except for the weather."

"Jerry, have you seen Mandy around?"

"I think she's downstairs playing slots. She's riding home with Shelly, me, and Desiree. Her boyfriend, Renaldo, deserted her. They had some fight or argument, and he left her up here. The guy's a real class act."

"No kidding, huh?"

"These damn kids. Like I don't have enough problems."

"Are you going to take off tomorrow?"

"No, I'm gonna load up the girls and go after dinner. Maybe I'll give them all a Valium, so I can drive home in peace."

We laughed. "Not a bad idea," I said.

I hustled out to my car and drove straight to Caesar's, hurrying because I only had forty-five minutes before my meeting with Jack Myers at the bar. Caesar's layout was typical of a large-scale casino. The carpet had a geometric pattern designed to cause disorientation, and the walls were mirrored in strategic places to confuse one's sense of direction. The walkways seemed to wind mazelike in all directions, and everywhere banks of slot machines beckoned, clanging loudly and luring in the distracted passerby. There were no clocks on the walls, and the bathrooms were infrequent and out of the way.

Fortunately it was late Sunday afternoon, and the casino wasn't particularly crowded. I started at the elevators to the hotel rooms, searching outward until I found Mandy about ten minutes later at a bank of quarter slots. I took a seat next to her and began playing a machine.

"Any luck?" I said.

"Hey, you," she said, and touched my shoulder. She was wearing jeans, black open-toed heels, and a white V-neck shirt cut just low enough to allow a tempting glimpse of cleavage. I burned through a few bucks then stopped and took a cigarette from her pack. She kept on playing her machine as if she were oblivious to my presence.

"You hear from Renaldo?" I said finally.

"No," she said. "What happened to your face?"

"Sven Osterlund hit me with a right cross." She blinked and her lips parted.

"I hear you know him," I said.

"And your point is?"

"Osterlund's a prime suspect in Sylvester Bascom's murder. He's also got more problems than a math book. He's trouble, Mandy. Don't let him drag you into his gig. It'll have an unhappy ending."

"Since when did you start seeing into the future? That's Sven's bag."

"I deal with criminals for a living. As a group, they're pretty predictable."

"Really? Well, tough guy, maybe next time you should try to predict when you're gonna get punched out."

"I've been hit harder, believe me," I said, but I could feel my patience eroding. "He said you and he are together now, and he warned me to stay away from you. Is that true?"

She bet the last of her credits, pulled the handle, and came up bust. "What we did the other night was fun, Dan. But don't get your hopes up for a repeat performance." With that she walked away and left me sitting there, feeling as manipulated and inadequate as a rookie gambler going broke on his first big night at the casino.

10

The King's Head was on a road I'd never heard of, but I thought it would be easy to find. I turned left off the highway, searching for the address, and found myself driving fruitlessly through a dark, older neighborhood. The houses were a mixture of ancient cabins, dilapidated pre-fab units, and trailer homes that had long ago sunk into their final resting place. Half the structures were boarded up, and some looked condemned. The other half appeared to be lived in—and badly. A child in soiled diapers sat crying on a sagging, rotted-out redwood porch, while in the driveway next door a man in a grease-smeared down vest wrenched on a rust-bucket Ford Bronco. He shot me a look as I drove by, his eyes black with aggression. Dead pine needles were matted on his deck, and the fresh snowfall in his yard was stained by soot and dirt, as if filth grew like weeds beneath the snow.

When I finally made my way back to Highway 50, I had to wait through a series of lights before I found the street I was looking for. The parking lot for the King's Head was small and the spots were narrow. I banged my knee on the corner of the car door as I climbed out and slammed it shut so hard the Nissan rocked on its springs. I felt my teeth grinding as I approached the entrance to the bar.

"Don't worry, be happy," said a man who was smoking on the steps to the entry. I looked him in the eye. "Fuck off," I said. He took a step back.

I strode into the building and glared around. The place was quiet; it was nearly empty.

I wanted strong drink at that moment, with an urgency I hadn't felt in years. I walked up to the bar, knowing myself too damn well to even hesitate. Had I been someone else, I might have chosen meditation, or yoga, or maybe Prozac or Valium. But I didn't subscribe to any new-age therapies; my medicine was of the old-fashioned variety, eighty proof, and readily available.

Have a drink, bring it on, and let the past few days dissolve into a hazy memory. Let the fight with Osterlund fade into a blur, have another and laugh off Mandy's involvement with him. Fuckin' right. Have a few more, and forget about the bullshit guilt trip Wenger was laying on me. Goddamn, I wanted to get blotto drunk, like I used to in the old days. I hooked my boot on the foot rail and motioned to the bartender, on a mission, ready to do it the way my buddy Cody Gibbons preached: drink, man, drink until you pass out, puke, go broke, or brawl.

I leaned on my elbows, ordered a double CC rocks, and drank it in two swallows. I pushed my glass to the bartender.

"Do it again," I said.

"What's the matter, you just lose your girlfriend?"

"Pour it," I said.

I raised the glass to my lips and let the smoky liquor slide down my throat, but then I slowly set the drink down in front of me, still half full, and listened to a small voice telling me to remember—and learn for once—how not to be a fool.

The night I shot the child pornographer had marked the beginning of a bleak year for me. In the months after killing Elrod Bradley, I was sued for divorce and lost my job as an investigator for Ortega, Davis, & Associates, a first-class detective agency. I also went through the nightmare of being prosecuted by a miserable bastard of a teetotaling district attorney, who felt the killing was my fault because I was carrying my piece while getting loaded at one of San Jose's numerous dive bars, which, despite the Valley's increasing affluence, still stubbornly spotted the city like venereal warts on a bad pecker. After the magnitude of Bradley's depravity became publicized, the DA eventually dropped the charges, but my permit to carry a concealed firearm was revoked, and it took me two years to get it back.

When Bill Ortega fired me a couple months after the shooting, I felt almost as bad for him as I did for myself. A friend of my father, Ortega had hired me fresh out of college and took me under his wing like a son. In the beginning, he brought me with him on interviews, and we spent countless hours on stakeouts, during which he discussed the myriad nuances of detective work, gleaned from over twenty-five years in the business. He also knew as much or more about criminal law than most attorneys and regularly lectured me on the legal aspects of different cases he had worked.

After five years with Bill Ortega, I considered myself a seasoned private investigator, a professional. But despite his good intentions, Ortega couldn't offer the perspective I needed most, which was how to come to terms with taking another man's life.

My life became unraveled, and to combat the guilt and despair I went to the only relief I knew, one where escape came in the form of double vodka tonics with lime, the ice cubes crackling merrily at the promise of blessed numbness. I was out on a $10,000-bond for a manslaughter charge, and that distraction, plus my worsening hangovers, caused me to become incapable of doing decent work, which made me feel stupid and incompetent.

I hit rock bottom on a Tuesday morning that July, when I woke at dawn in the dirt parking lot of the Corners Club, a seedy, lowlife wino bar in Campbell. I was huddled against the side of the building when the morning bartender arrived with his pal to open up at 6:00 A.M. They helped me up, and I went into the bar as if I had never left. My wallet was gone, but the bartender poured me a free one like my situation was a typical event.

During the next hour, the regulars arrived. At first they looked to be mostly older, in their sixties perhaps, but then I got in a blurry conversation with two men and realized that despite their stained and missing teeth, ruined skin, and overall wizened appearance, they were probably no older than I was. I went to the bathroom, and a tall man was standing at the urinal next to me, slowly letting his bladder drain while retching up his breakfast. I walked out into the sunlight, into a warm summer morning, a day that should have been full of promise. The sky was so blue I had to squint, and chirping of the birds in the trees pierced my head like hot wire.

When I staggered into my apartment that day, I looked in the mirror and didn't recognize the bloodshot eyes that stared back. I suffered through a horrible five-star hangover, shaking and dry heaving, feeling like I was looking over the edge into a dark chasm, a place where people go when all luck and hope has run out. I didn't want to go there and swore to myself I'd dry out. I did, but it was too late.

After I didn't show up to work or call in, Ortega called that evening and fired me. The next day Julia filed for divorce and left to live with her sister in Sacramento. I turned my phone off, closed the drapes, and lived like a hermit for a couple of days until Cody Gibbons showed up, body-slammed the door open, and set me up with a job as a skip tracer for Ray Lorretta Bail Bonds.

· · ·

By the time the coroner walked in a few minutes after five, I had managed to curb my desire to get blackout drunk. Two double whiskeys and a pint of stout English ale had calmed me sufficiently, for the moment.

"Starting without me, huh?" he said.

"Jack," I nodded, "appreciate you coming."

"Yeah, it's a big sacrifice. And you can call me Mr. Myers…" He grumbled something unintelligible, and I tried to read his expression, but it was hidden under his shaggy eyebrows. But then he smiled, like he held some aged secret. "Come on, buy an old man a goddamned drink," he said.

The King's Head was Tahoe's representative British pub, complete with soccer paraphernalia, English flags, and a large selection of British food and beers. The two men sitting at the bar had English accents, as did the bartender, who asked Myers if he wanted the usual, then brought him a draft and a shot. I handed the bartender my credit card.

"Hey, kid, I was only kidding. You don't need to pay for my drinks," Myers said.

"I'm buying," I said.

"If you insist, I ain't gonna argue."

"You lived here in Tahoe for long?" I asked.

He looked at me, his eye twitching, and I thought he might tell me it was none of my damn business. But instead he took a long hit off his beer and said, "Couple winters now. I was coroner in San Francisco for years, and before that I worked in Houston. I came up here to retire, and the bastards put me back to work."

"You like working in San Francisco?"

He didn't answer for a while, staring up into the heavy timbers supporting the peaked ceiling. "The politics of the job eventually drove me crazy," he said finally. "I spent more than forty years in the public sector…" he tailed off and mumbled something, then tilted his shot glass back.

"Our esteemed elected officials, they're supposed to be serving the people. That's the idea, right?" He looked at me directly, and when I didn't answer, he said, "It's bullshit. Let me tell you something—politics is all lies. It's all self-serving agendas and convenient ethics. Spent most of my life in that cesspool."

"I imagine up here you don't have those types of big-city issues."

"Catch glimpses of it here and there, though it's nothing like San Francisco. But actually the previous coroner left amid some controversy."

"Really?"

"I'm gonna order dinner. You hungry?"

"Is the food here good?"

"For British food."

Myers signaled the bartender for menus, and we ordered another round.

"You were talking about the previous coroner."

"Yeah. Supposedly he talked to some reporters at the local newspaper about the death of two casino employees. This was about a year ago. He told them the deaths were caused by drug overdose, and the paper published a story. The sheriff was unhappy about that, and one thing led to another."

"Sheriff Grier?"

"No," he growled. "Grier's a deputy sheriff for South Lake Tahoe. The county sheriff is Conrad Pace, based in Placerville. He was elected about a year ago. I think he thought the article was bad press for his office, though I really don't know what happened. It was all a bit hush-hush. Typical cover-up, seemed to me."

"What's the big deal about a drug overdose? Happens often enough."

"Sure it does. In San Francisco, OD cases are routine. But Silverado County has a tiny fraction of the population of San Francisco. Here, I only do a couple, at the most three or four, autopsies a month. So a double OD case was big news."

"The coroner was fired because he talked to the press?"

"That's my guess. Knowing Conrad Pace, it wouldn't surprise me. He's more of a self-serving prick than most. It was a sad day when he was elected sheriff."

"That right?" I said.

"Yeah, he's right up there with the worst of them. He's the type that would sell out his mama for a buck, you know? Son of a bitch got a mean streak a mile wide."

"Wouldn't be the first cop I met like that."

"I know him from way back," he said. "Steer clear of him."

"Somehow people like that get elected," I said, curious to hear what else he had to say about the local police.

"It's sad is what it is. We end up represented by the best liars, and some of the people we elect are ruthless behind closed doors. They'll do whatever it takes to maintain their domain. Get in their way, they'll find a way to fuck you. Bunch of assholes, for the most part. You ever notice how politicians tend to be wealthy? It ain't on the salaries they're getting paid, believe me." He coughed, then pulled reading glasses and a folded sheet of paper from his coat pocket. "Enough about that. Let me tell you what the results were on Sylvester Bascom.

"His death was in fact precipitated by the knife wound, but the official cause of death was loss of blood. The knife penetrated his midsection on the left side above his navel and exited in his back about five inches higher. He was stabbed right below the rib cage, and the blade sliced through his traverse colon and stomach and severed his splenic artery. The spleen holds a significant amount of blood, and that's why he bled to death."

"What kind of knife was used?"

"Join me for a smoke on the patio," Myers said. We took our beers out back to where a couple of redwood picnic tables sat under a sloped aluminum awning. The sun was getting low, and while it had been in the high forties during the afternoon, the temperature had dropped to twenty-seven degrees, according to the thermometer hanging on one of the overhang posts. A large rectangular barbecue covered in clear plastic was pushed in a corner, and two dirty white plastic chairs were set out to accommodate the smokers. Beyond the covered section, three feet of snow blanketed the beer garden.

Myers lit a stogie, and I smiled, thinking that every coroner I'd ever met smoked cigars. Something to do with blotting out the odor of a corpse, I figured. He propped one leg up on a plastic chair and rested his elbow on his knee. "The knife had to be a minimum of fourteen inches. It was serrated on one side and razor sharp on the other, like an oversize survival knife. I've seen plenty of stabbings, the majority done with common blades, like jackknifes or switchblades or kitchen or steak knives. But I've also seen people die of wounds from screwdrivers, scratch awls, chisels, and even machetes. I think the first thing you need to consider is the killer is carrying an unusual and possibly a specialized weapon." He hit off his cigar and blew a puff of smoke into the twilight. "Second, the man who did this, and I assume it was a man and not a woman, was very strong. Imagine the leverage it took to drive the blade in like that." He took a pen out of his pocket and held it in his right fist. "I'm sure Bascom was standing when he was stabbed. It would be pretty difficult to get the right upward angle if he was sitting." He put his left hand on my shoulder, then stepped toward me and brought the pen upward to my stomach.

"You see, for a right-handed man this is a motion that can generate a lot of power, especially if the man was taller than the victim."

We headed back inside, and the bartender brought out our dinner. Myers stuck a fork in his entree, which was steak and kidney pie. "It's the coroner's special," he said with a dry laugh. Then his face went serious. "I think you're looking for a man who knows how to kill, and kill brutally, with a knife. He very well could be ex-military."

"Maybe two people were involved," I said. "Someone could have been holding his arms from behind when he was stabbed. Did you notice any bruises on his arms?"

"No, but he looked like he had been in a pretty good scuffle. You saw the marks on his face and knuckles?"

"Yeah. Did it look like he had sex before he died?" I asked.

"He did indeed, shortly before. He died a happy man."

A group of about a dozen men came through the front door, loud and ruddy-faced. Some still wore ski pants or had lift tickets attached to their jackets. They crowded up to the bar, yelling in thick English accents for schnapps and buckets of piss.

"You like living up here, Jack?"

"I'm not a big fan of the cold, if that's what you're getting at. But my daughter and her husband moved here, and I like to be near my grand-kids. Here," Myers said, pulling pictures from his wallet. Four little devils grinned back at me.

"Still married?" I asked.

"Divorced years ago."

I ate about half my meal and pushed it away. It was an old habit, not wanting to fill up on food when I was more interested in drinking. I had the bartender bring me a whiskey.

"Did you find any evidence of drug use?"

"No outward indication, but we'll have to wait a couple days for the toxicology results."

The two men who had been at the bar since we came in asked us to roll dice for drinks. We played liars and boss dice for a few quick rounds. I felt a numbing euphoria as the whiskey loosened the band of tightness that had been cranked around my skull. I opened my eyes wide and felt the tension in my brow recede. The details of the case became blurred and unimportant. We began playing darts, then Myers ran the pool table against the gang of Brits, who actually were from Australia. They started up a game of quarters, bouncing coins off their table into beer mugs, and every time someone made it everybody drank. The night became a rowdy, boozy party, we were all drunken friends, and they started calling me "Yank." At one point I thanked Myers for being supportive and told him I wouldn't mention his name if I ever met Conrad Pace.

"Fuck him. What's he gonna do, fire me? I don't need his money," he said, and I shot the rail, buying a round for the house to celebrate his attitude.

Somewhere in the night I vaguely wandered out to the Nissan and carefully locked my wallet with the $50,000-check in the glove box. Then I went back into the bar and turned it up a notch, hitting the whiskey and keg beer like an alcoholic fraternity brother. Around midnight Myers stumbled out to take a cab home, a couple of the Australians were puking in the bathroom, and I went out into the cold and started walking to the Lakeside. I staggered about twenty yards down the street before returning to my car. I drove slowly, carefully in my lane, one eye closed so I wouldn't see two of everything.

11

EVEN THOUGH MY FATHER was sitting ten feet across from me, I could feel his hand on my shoulder. He was telling me about the case he was trying as district attorney. I started to ask him a question, but it didn't seem he could hear me. I walked toward him, but I was moving in slow motion, and with every step I took he seemed to move back an equal distance. Somehow we both understood he was dead, and our conversation was temporary and unreal, but I didn't want that to be. I strained and searched for some logic that would reverse his death.

The dream faded, and my transition from drunken slumber to consciousness was slow and confused. When I finally came to, I was aware the knocking on my door had been going on for some time. I was fully clothed except for my shoes, and I had slept on top of the bedspread. My eyelids creaked open, feeling like rusty hinges on a saloon door, and the ceiling moved in a wavy pattern. As I rolled off the bed, it occurred to me the reason I didn't feel so bad was because I was still drunk.

I put the chain on the door and opened it two inches. A stocky man holding a badge peered in at me. I saw a uniformed deputy from the sheriff's department behind him.

"Dan Reno?"

"*Reno,*" I croaked.

"I'm Don Raneswich, detective, Lake Tahoe Police. We need to speak with you."

I opened the door. Raneswich was not a tall man, but his shoulders were wide, as were his waist and hips. He looked like a short refrigerator.

"Make yourself comfortable, men. You woke me up," I said thickly, and went into the bathroom. I splashed water on my face and hair, brushed my teeth, and drank three glasses of water out of the little plastic cup next to the sink. Through the fog in my head, a basic conclusion emerged: they had found out I was investigating the Bascom murder and wanted to speak to me about it. I came out, and they were sitting in the two chairs in the room, so I sat on the bed and leaned against the headboard.

"Where were you last night?" Raneswich said.

I laughed. "Actually, Detective, I spent the entire evening at the King's Head."

"I believe it. Your room smells like a freaking distillery," said the deputy, whose name I would later learn was Louis Perdie. Raneswich shot him a look.

"You can check it out. I was there the whole night."

"We will, you can count on it," Raneswich said.

"Why, what happened last night?" I said.

"The guy you got in a fight with yesterday afternoon, Sven Osterlund? We fished him out of Emerald Bay this morning. Someone put three bullets in him."

• • •

Osterlund, dead? I had to tell myself to close my mouth, and my eyes felt as round and dumb as a bloodshot Saint Bernard's. The prime suspect, or at least the most likely witness, found floating in the waters of Lake Tahoe. I imagined him lying on the surface of the cold, blue-green water, face down and half submerged, like a snorkeler scanning the bottom. Except when they turned him over, his face would be white and bloated, his lifeless eyes locked forever on their final vision. I wondered if in his last moments he regretted what he'd done with his life. Somehow, I doubted it.

I stared out the window past the cops into the dark, overcast morning. Raneswich wanted to check out my gun, so I put my boots on, and we went out to the parking lot. I opened my trunk and let him inspect the Beretta.

"It hasn't been fired since the last time I went to the range, about a month ago," I said.

"What was your fight with Osterlund about?"

"Uh, it's a long story. Meet me in the diner in fifteen minutes, and I'll tell you about it."

"Good, I'm hungry," said Louis Perdie, who was taller and skinnier than Raneswich, except for his midsection, which hung over his belt like a sack of flour.

"All right, don't make us wait," Raneswich said. We walked back into the Lakeside, and they went toward the restaurant.

I would have loved to sleep until noon, but I put my brain on autopilot, ordered a double Bloody Mary from room service, and was brushing my teeth again when the drink arrived. I drank it straight down, in a hurry to keep my buzz going and postpone what I knew would be a grueling hangover. I gobbled four aspirin and sat down heavily. In my surly state, the same thought kept running through my mind: *Osterlund went and got himself killed before I had a chance to kick his ass.* I sat there with my head hanging, my chin on my chest, saying it over and over to myself until I started laughing like a madman. Then I lit a cigarette and went downstairs.

Raneswich and Perdie stared at me as I walked through the tables toward them. It seemed rude, but I didn't care—I was toxic. I slowed at the coffee shop's aquarium, and I swear the fish started turning belly up.

"Enjoying your breakfast, gentlemen?" I said, sitting at their table. Raneswich only had a cup of coffee, but Perdie was eating from a plate stacked with pancakes, scrambled eggs, bacon, and sausage links. The waitress handed me a menu, and I asked her to bring me a Bloody Mary, a coffee, and the same thing Perdie was having.

"How did you know Osterlund?" Raneswich said. He put his mug down and opened a notebook.

"We went to the same high school."

"Okay. Tell me about the fight you got in with him."

"Detective," I said. "Can I call you Don?" I felt the alcohol coursing through my veins. I was shaky but happy. I wasn't quite sure what I was going to say, but I felt confident. He nodded, and I smiled.

"It was basically over a woman. He came after me, and we threw a couple blows. That was about it."

"Do you have any idea why someone might want to kill him?"

"Hell, yeah. He was an asshole. By the way, Don, who did you get my name from?"

"I'll ask the questions here."

"Okay, fine," I said with a shrug. "I'm on your side, man."

Raneswich blew his breath through his teeth and rolled his eyes.

"Did you talk to Brad and Whitey?"

He didn't say a word, and the waitress brought me a coffee. "How about the Bloody?" I asked her.

Raneswich sat still as a potted plant, staring at me with bland eyes. I looked back at him, and when he didn't respond I said, "What is this, a stare down?" He didn't answer, so I turned to the other cop. "How's the grub, Deputy?"

"Good," Perdie said around a mouthful of food.

"We can do this here or down at the station," Raneswich finally said.

"Sure, why not? I was there the other day, talking to Marcus Grier and some dipshit of a cop who looked like he was still wearing diapers."

Perdie started laughing and blew some eggs out the corner of his mouth. "I know who you're talking about," he said, wiping his lips.

Raneswich shook his head slowly, almost imperceptibly, and stared at the spoon in his hand. He tapped it twice on the table.

"Again, why would somebody want to kill him? Come on, give me your expert opinion."

"From what I gather," I said, trying to pick my words carefully, "Osterlund was a guy who went through life looking for trouble. He could have had any number of enemies."

I could see him weighing the issues as he watched the waitress serve me my Bloody Mary.

"All right," he said, once she left. "Let's make sure we're clear on this. I know you're investigating Sylvester Bascom's murder. We believe Osterlund did it, and now he's dead. So there's really nothing left for you to investigate."

I sipped my cocktail and studied Raneswich, as his real agenda slowly dawned on me.

"No kidding, huh? Do you have any solid evidence that Osterlund killed Bascom?"

"That's police business, not yours."

"So I should just pack my bags and leave town?"

"That's right," he said.

"Here's my point of view on this, Detective," I said, trying for a businesslike tone. "If the South Lake Tahoe PD formally concludes Osterlund stabbed Bascom to death, and John Bascom agrees with your findings, I suppose there's no reason for me to hang around. But until then, I'm willing to work with you and cooperate. Hopefully my involvement can be of some help. Keep in mind I'll be working full time on this case. Consider me a resource."

Raneswich's face betrayed no opinion, but I was pleased with how I phrased it. Not bad, considering my disheveled state. It was bullshit, of course, but I thought it sounded very diplomatic.

"Consider you a resource?" he retorted. "I consider you a liability. If you do anything to impede or otherwise get in the way of a formal police investigation, it's a major problem."

"And what if you run into dead ends, and the case stalls? What then?"

"You know, I love you PIs. You're mostly drunks, one step up from a minimum-wage security guard, but you love to treat the police like we're a bunch of bumbling bureaucrats. I want to make sure we're clear on this. If you create problems for me, you'll cool your jets in our jail. So don't put a target on your back. I could have you arrested for drunk in public right now, but I'll give you a break. But get my meaning."

I almost snapped back at Raneswich, but I kept my mouth shut and tried to think calmly. The synapses in my brain felt like they were short-circuited, snapping and sizzling like downed power lines on wet pavement. I suddenly became very thirsty and guzzled my ice water in one long pull.

"I'm sorry you feel that way," I said slowly. "But I'm not a criminal, and I resent being treated like one. I'm a licensed investigator, employed by a legitimate company, and I have a job to do." I paused, and his fleshy face turned a deeper color. I noticed he had a big mole under his eye and some smaller ones on his cheek.

"Now, I've offered nothing but a respectful attitude and the willingness to cooperate," I continued, telling myself to shut up but getting on a roll, giving in to the drunken tendency to babble. "And you give me this hard-ass stuff. How do you expect me to respond to that? You think I'm just gonna go away? That ain't gonna happen."

"Louis, thanks, you can go back on patrol now," Raneswich said to Perdie, who had seemingly ignored us while he ate his breakfast. He mopped up the last of his eggs with a crust of toast.

"Good enough, Don. You ought to get some sleep, buddy," Perdie said to me as he stood. Then he leaned down, put his hand on my shoulder, and his mouth near my ear. "Your eyes look like two piss holes in the snow." I felt his hot breath on my neck, and he kept his head near mine for a long moment. I finally turned and looked up at him, and his face was blunt and cold. Then he tipped his cap, winked, and walked away.

"Where'd you find that guy?" I said.

"Don't ask," Raneswich said. He motioned at the waitress for the check, and I pulled out my wallet but couldn't find my credit card. With a shock I realized I must have left it with the bartender at the King's Head.

"It's good for me to know what to expect from you," he said. He threw down some singles to cover his coffee and the deputy's breakfast, then walked away without another word. As I watched him leave the restaurant, I tilted back my drink, but it was empty.

"Nice going, that was well done," I muttered. Goddammit, I should have played it more low key, humored Raneswich a little, been more agreeable. That's what I tried to do, at first anyway, but clearly he wasn't buying it. Fuck him, then. Still, the last thing I needed was some cop with an axe to grind on my back. But he dealt the play, not me. Could I have been more cooperative? Sure, if I was willing to quit the job, which would mean screwing John Bascom and foregoing the shot at another fifty thousand dollars.

I stared at the remains of my Bloody Mary and wondered what was motivating Raneswich. As a general rule, most police departments understand and tolerate the rights of private investigators. Raneswich's effort to make me back off was atypical. Maybe he sorely needed to solve the case to further his career and viewed my involvement as a threat. Or maybe he had some reason to not want Sylvester Bascom's murderer caught.

I pushed my plate away and started doodling on a cocktail napkin. In the center I wrote "Sylvester," circled it, and beneath it I wrote "Osterlund" in smaller letters, then connected the two with a line. I started trying to write all the things I knew about them, their friends, backgrounds, hobbies, anything that came to mind, and the napkin was soon too messy to make sense of. "Fuck it," I said, and balled it up and dropped it in Raneswich's half-full coffee cup. Then I left a ten-dollar bill on the table, walked out to the Nissan, and drove out onto the highway, toward the Lazy 8.

12

UNBEKNOWNST TO ME AT the time, as I was driving down 50, Deputy Louis Perdie was five miles further on the same road, heading to the county sheriff's complex in Placerville. When he arrived forty-five minutes later, he eased himself out of the car, yawned and stretched, passed gas loudly, and hitched his pants up. A crooked smile creased one side of his face as he walked into the building.

A tall, shirtless man with a scraggly blond beard was struggling with two deputies in the lobby. The deputies were red-faced and straining mightily to cuff the bigger man, whose eyes were dilated and wild with adrenaline. "Get your dirty hands off me, pigs," he shouted, as the trio spun around the lobby area, banging against the walls, knocking a potted plant off a table. Two more uniformed cops jumped into the fray, and one was kicked hard in the knee and went down with a yelp of pain.

Perdie removed his baton from its holder, waited for the right moment, then swung with a quick chopping motion across the blond man's jaw. The man's eyes rolled back, and he dropped to the floor, jerked momentarily, then lay still as a corpse. The deputies stood panting over him.

"My god, Louis," said one cop.

"This man's seriously injured," said another. "That was unnecessary. He's a paranoid schizophrenic. We would have restrained him in a minute."

The shirtless man lay in a pile, a pool of blood forming under his mouth, which looked oddly deformed.

"Probably got a broken jaw," Perdie said. "Teach him to mess with Placerville's finest. Clean up the mess, boys." Perdie smiled again and walked through a glass door into the interior of the building.

Sheriff Conrad Pace sat at his desk, idly considering a local neighborhood petition for increased patrol at a park that had been overrun by truant teenagers. He tossed the paperwork aside when Perdie knocked and let himself in.

"What's shakin', Cuz?" Perdie said.

"The usual, Louis," Pace said. "Mothers Against Drunk Drivers want checkpoints set up nightly in front of the bars on Main Street, a twenty-year-old woman claims she got raped at a house party last night, a senile old man took a chainsaw to a hundred-year-old pine in his front yard and dropped it on his neighbor's garage, and we busted some hippies running a meth lab in a shack up in the hills behind Adler Street."

Perdie laughed. "These mountain folk just know how to party, huh?"

"Damn hippies up here are just as bad as the blackies back home, Louis." Pace stood and lit a cigar.

"Another year then we heads back South?" Perdie said.

"Sooner than that. This climate ain't to my liking. I don't aim on spending another winter here."

"That's music to my ears, Cuz."

"You catch up to that private eye this morning?"

"Yes sir. I do believe he's an ornery one."

"You played it the way I said, right?"

Perdie leaned back in his chair and stretched his legs out. "Sure did. I just had me some breakfast and let Raneswich do the talking. But the private eye didn't seem too interested in backing off."

"Well, we ain't done much to discourage him."

"Not so far," Perdie said. He shrugged, his eyes widened, and his lips seemed to purse and smile at the same time. It was an innocent expression, as if he was saying, "Who, me?" and it created the impression he was a slightly confused country boy. It was a look Pace knew well. Pace remembered seeing the same expression when Perdie was twelve years old, when the Pace family adopted him and brought him into their home.

When Pace's father had let Perdie sleep in their barn that rainy night forty years ago, Conrad was perplexed. Vernon Pace was a ruthless sharecropper, and he treated the people in his life, including his family, not much differently than his livestock. But he had seemingly taken pity on the soaking-wet, skinny boy, who was trying to fashion a shelter under a pecan tree on the boundary of the property. Louis Perdie was fed, given dry clothes, and put to work on the Pace farm. And he worked hard, happy to escape the horrors of his past, horrors that eventually Conrad would learn about, and then he would grow to understand why Louis Perdie could smile harmlessly and a moment later inflict physical damage on a human being that would leave scars for life.

"Let's just watch him for now, Louis."

"You're the boss, Cuz," Perdie said, smiling crookedly, but his eyes were as hard and flat as iron rivets.

Back in Louisiana all those years ago, Pace realized Perdie could easily outwork him in the field. It took a special kind of person who needed so little and accepted the grueling hours of labor as a perfectly acceptable condition. Pace wasn't like that himself. He wanted more out of life. He wanted to be like the wealthy men he'd see in New Orleans on the occasions his father took him to town in their old Packard truck. They'd pick up goods that weren't available in the parish's general store, and then Vernon Pace would typically spend a couple hours in a saloon on Bourbon Street, while Conrad waited outside, a sixteen-year-old kid in overalls and an old straw hat. He'd stand and watch the people of the city while his father drank. He saw men in fine suits of silk and wool, sporting gold pocket watches and driving shiny sedans. These men were finely groomed and manicured, and they walked with their shoulders back while people on the sidewalk made way for them. Conrad watched them and knew that he would have everything they had some day. It was just a matter of taking it from them.

One afternoon Vernon Pace came out of the bar, and Conrad knew something wasn't right. His father's face was unnaturally red, and his eyes were hot and bulbous, as if a furnace roared beneath the sockets. A man with slicked-back hair and a white shirt stumbled out from the saloon behind him. He held a towel to his mouth, and there was blood flecked on his shirt.

"You'll pay what you owe all right," he yelled. His lip was bleeding and swollen. Vernon Pace turned back and strode toward the man as if powered by an inner storm.

"You say another word, you won't have any teeth left."

"Pox on you, Pace. You're a welsher and a crook," the man said, but he moved back into the doorway.

Vernon sprung forward and kicked the man in the stomach, as if he were kicking a door down. Conrad stood on the sidewalk and saw the man fly back into the saloon. Inside there was a crash and loud voices. A moment later two large men walked out of the bar. One had thick arms covered with tattoos, and the other had a chest like a barrel and an ugly scar under his eye. They moved toward Vernon with a steady purpose.

"Peckerwood shit like you thinks he can make his own rules, eh?" said the one with the tattoos. The second man didn't break stride. He put his hand on Conrad's face and shoved him away, then snorted like a bull and threw a quick right jab at Vernon Pace. Conrad watched from the gutter as his father ducked the punch and moved laterally, a blade now gleaming in his hand.

The tattooed man stepped up, suddenly holding a two-foot piece of dowel stock. He swung it rapidly with one hand, back and forth, forcing Vernon Pace to the middle of the street. People stopped and stared from the sidewalks as Pace and the man circled each other. Conrad rushed toward the man wielding the stick, but the barrel-chested man stopped him with a fist to the side of the head. Stunned, Conrad dropped to his knees, and watched his father move in close and take a hard shot to the ribs, then lash out viciously with his knife. The freshly sharpened blade whipped across the tattooed man's eyes, and he staggered back holding his face, blood streaming down his fingers. Then Vernon drove the knife up to the hilt in the man's side, beneath the rib cage.

The street was silent. The barrel-chested man held out his hands and slowly retreated. Vernon stood in the street, holding the bloody knife over the dying tattooed man. Then Vernon and Conrad Pace ran for their truck.

Conrad never forgot the drive home that day. The sights from the window of the truck were the same ones he'd seen so often they'd become as mundane as a dirty plate. But now he stared out the window in wonder; everything seemed fresh and new, as if the landscape had been reborn. The thick grasses that rose beside the highway, the rotted timber littering the swamplands, the wisps of pink clouds in the soft hue of the sky—it was all brand new and sharp as a fresh razor. He felt as if his senses were tuned to a dimension he never knew existed.

He looked at his father, amazed at the pride bursting in his heart. His father stared out the windshield, his gnarled fingers clamped like vices on the wheel. "Dad," Conrad said, "that was truly…" The words died in Conrad's mouth when Vernon Pace hit the brakes and yanked the truck to the side of the road. "You think there's something to smile about?" Vernon said. Then he got out of the truck and walked around to the passenger side. "Get out," he said. Conrad climbed halfway out of the seat before his father grabbed his forearm and flung him into the soggy weeds that lined the road. Conrad stared mutely as his father got in the truck and spun the tires back out onto the highway. A hot blast of sand and grit rose to Conrad's face. He stared at the truck, watching it become smaller and smaller.

• • •

The black car arrived at the Pace house early that night, shortly after Conrad had made it home, his feet blistered from the ten mile walk. The sun hung just over the horizon, and the night air was dense with humidity. It was the type of evening that offered no respite from the heat of the day.

"He's gone," Conrad told the man who climbed out of the sedan, which had come to a stop in the dirt between the house and the Pace's barn. The man was huge, his fat hanging off his body in slabs. He leaned against the car, his thumbs hitched in his belt, and looked down at Conrad Pace. Two Negro men sat in the backseat of the car, staring forward, their eyes pale as milk against their skin.

"You wouldn't lie to me, now would you, boy?" the man said.

"How in hell would I know where he is?" Conrad said.

The man rolled a toothpick around his mouth on his tongue, which looked red and obscene against the white of his face. "He's your daddy," he said, his smile tiny, like a half moon punched into a ball of dough.

"My pa's gone, I told you."

The man sighed, and when he spoke he looked away from Conrad and gazed out over the farmland, as if he was enjoying the scenery. "That's very noble of you, defending your father, boy. I suppose I'd do the same. Now I'm gonna make this real simple for you. We can do this the easy way or the hard way. It's your choice. Where is he?" His eyes fell back to Conrad.

"And you're full of shit too," said Louis Perdie, who had quietly walked up behind Conrad. At thirteen years old, he was close to six feet already, with veined forearms and scarred hands. He held a pitchfork at his side.

"Well, lookee here," the man said.

"Get off my property, mister," Conrad said. He stared hard at the man's face.

The man swung his arm lazily backward and rapped his knuckles against the car window.

The two black men climbed out, wearing blank expressions.

"This boy needs some learnin'," the man said, pointing at Louis Perdie. "Take him to the barn."

"My ass," Perdie said, gripping the pitchfork.

"You catch on quick," the man said. One of the black men, stout and blunt as an ox, feinted to the right, and the second Negro rushed at Perdie from the left, and a moment later the pitchfork was clattering across the dirt, and the men had Perdie's arms pinned behind his back.

"He ain't involved in this. Let him go. He's just a farmhand," Conrad said.

"It ain't too late to stop what's gonna happen to him in that barn," the fat man said. "You just tell me where to find Vernon Pace."

"I already told you, mister, I got no idea where he's gone."

"Well, that's a shame, it really is," the fat man said, and waved his arm at the Negros, who lifted Perdie, swearing and writhing like a snake, and carried him to the barn. Conrad scrambled toward the pitchfork but froze when a shot rang out, dust exploding at his feet.

"Might as well make yourself comfortable," the man said, the black revolver shining in his bloated hand. "We got all night here." Conrad sat on the ground, and a minute later the screams from the barn began. "You want it to stop, you just say when," the man said, leaning against his car, the gun hanging from his fingers. "Just remember, you're next."

Conrad looked up at the man, let his eyebrows droop, and slowly stood up. "I'll tell you where he is," he said, his voice resigned, his head hanging.

"Out with it then," the man said.

Conrad shuffled forward, his shoulders slumped, his arms limp. But he kept his eyes on the gun. "He's gone to Baton Rouge. He's…" The fat man's eyes gleamed in expectation. Then Conrad leapt forward like a coiled spring, his foot kicking out at the man's hand. He felt the man's fingers crumble, and the revolver flew over the hood of the car like a wounded bird. "Sonofabitch," the man shouted. He started after the gun, but Conrad leaped past him and pounced on it in an instant. The man tried to get back into the car, but his girth hampered him, then he felt his shoulder explode in a flash of white-hot pain. He fell over, moaning, and looked up from the ground at Conrad Pace.

"You shot me, boy," the man rasped, his fleshy face wet with perspiration. "You done it now. I'm the law—I'm Sheriff Bode. Call an ambulance."

"Sheriff, huh?" Conrad said. He opened the door to the black sedan and found a set of handcuffs on the passenger seat. "Maybe you are," he said, and snapped a cuff around the man's injured arm. He yelped in pain as Conrad yanked the cuffs, and blood was soaking all down the front of his shirt, making it cling to his belly like wet paint. "You done it now, boy," the man said again. "But you call the ambulance and—"

"Sit up, you sack of pus," Conrad said, and leveled the gun at his head. The man pushed himself up, and Conrad pulled the handcuffs through the car door handle and closed a cuff around the man's other wrist. "You can sit here and bleed for a while," Conrad said, then he grabbed the pitchfork and ran for the barn.

Inside, Conrad Pace froze at the sight of his friend, his pants around his ankles, and what one Negro was doing to him while the other held his arms stretched over the low railing of a horse stall. The one holding Louis Perdie looked up, his eyes met Conrad Pace's, and then the revolver bucked in Conrad's hand. The Negro's face jolted, blood pumping from his forehead, and he fell over as if his legs had been kicked out beneath him. The second man stepped back, his face startled, his genitals glistening and engorged.

Conrad pulled the trigger, and a hole no larger than a penny appeared on the man's stomach. The Negro stood and watched the blood flow from the wound, and looked up at Conrad with a quizzical expression. Conrad smiled at him and handed the pitchfork to Louis. And then Conrad had to cover his ears and leave the barn, and even the horses recoiled when Louis Perdie started in on his rapist with the pitchfork.

The early evening had given way to darkness by the time Conrad returned to the car. The fat man sat soaked in blood, his face pale and shaking. Conrad read through the man's wallet and tossed it to Perdie. "He's a sheriff all right, I guess," Conrad said.

Louis Perdie squatted down on his haunches and lifted the man's head by the hair. "You think because you're a lawman you got the right to put those niggers on me?"

"You boys are in so deep, I can't tell you. But it ain't too late. If I die, you'll fry in the chair at Angola."

Perdie laughed. "Hey, Sheriff, when I was in school, I heard about what they did in medieval times, back when they had knights and castles. They'd tie ropes to some poor sucker's arms and legs and tie each rope to a horse. Then the horses would take off. People used to bet on what would come off first, right arm, left leg, whatever. And then, when the man was just a stump but still alive, the knights would piss on his face. I always wondered about that." The sheriff looked up, his face trembling, and saw a grinning Conrad Pace drop a coil of rope in his lap. "I'll go fetch the horses, Louis," he said. "You keep the sheriff company until I get back."

13

THE DRAPES WERE HALF open in the room at the Lazy 8. I looked in and saw Whitey, in a pair of stained gray sweatpants, lying on the bed next to the window, one hand scratching his ass cheek, the other holding a bong. I knocked on the window, startling him. He rolled off the bed and let me in.

"Good morning, boys," I said. Brad was sitting on the other bed, drinking coffee and watching TV.

"Dude, dude, dude," Whitey said.

"Dan, Osterlund's freaking dead!" Brad said, jumping up and waving his arms around. "He was shot dead! And the cops think you did it!"

"I know, Brado. Relax, man," I said. His yelling was making my head hurt. Their room looked like a garbage dump hit by a tornado. Taco Bell wrappers were strewn about the floor, along with Styrofoam cups, beer cans, clothes, and scattered newspapers. A large, dried tomato slice was stuck to the wall above the TV.

"What's the matter, don't you guys like tomatoes?" I said.

"Not that one," Whitey said.

"Sorry this place smells like a bag of assholes," Brad said. "Whitey got into the pintos and gassed me out all night."

"Kinda makes you homesick, don't it, Brad?" Whitey said, as his ass barked out a short cadence.

"I'm taking you off the beans," Brad said, fanning his hand in front of his face.

"Boys, I need your help," I said, moving away from Whitey. "I've been hired by the Bascoms to investigate Sylvester's murder, and I suspect Osterlund's murder is connected."

"Whoa," Whitey said.

"But what about Sven?" Brad said. "Did you…"

"What, did I have something to do with him getting killed?"

"No, I didn't mean–"

"Relax, Brad, I never saw him after I left here. But I am curious why Osterlund had such an attitude. I need to ask you some questions. Maybe you can help me figure some stuff out."

"Hell, yes, Dan, anything," Brad said. "Um, does that mean you're not going home today?"

"No, I'm gonna have to stay up here for the time being. Do you guys have any other way to get home?"

"We'll figure something out."

"It's no biggie. We'll take the shame train if we have to," Whitey said.

"Try calling the casinos. You can get a bus from there."

"Dan, the cops were already here this morning for about an hour. They woke us up at about six-thirty and grilled us about Sven. It's like they think we're involved. This one dick wanted to bust us for the bong."

"Did they leave their cards?"

"Here," Brad said, taking them from the nightstand. It was Raneswich and a Detective Paul Iverson.

"Yeah, one guy was pretty mellow," Whitey said, "but the other cop was a Penisaurus Rex. He kept on threatening to take us to the station."

"Sounds like a typical good-cop/bad-cop routine. What did the bad cop look like?" I walked through the trash to a folding chair.

"He was, like, stocky with a big round head."

"How about the other one?" I asked, wondering why Raneswich visited me with a deputy instead of Detective Iverson.

"He almost looked like an albino. But at least he wasn't being an asshole," Brad said.

"Let's go over everything that was said."

"Okay," Brad said, and I could see his body language change as he prepared to go into the story. Brad was a natural bullshitter. For as long as I'd known him, he habitually embellished and exaggerated everything. He stood tall, his hands poised like he was ready to play the piano.

"Whitey and me are sleepin', and the cops are bangin' on the door at freaking *six-thirty*. I'm like all, 'Who the bone-smoke is it?' So I get the door because The Cheeseball won't get up, and it's the cops, and they come in and start askin' us all these questions about what we were doin' last night. And we're all, 'Whoa, we didn't do anything, *why are you here?* But we tell them what we were doin', which was me, Whitey, and Sven had dinner at Taco Bore-hole." He gestured at Whitey and added, "And that's why this room smells like an un-flushed toilet. After that we went and drank some beers at Zeke's Pit and watched the band for a while, and then we went over to Pistol Pete's around midnight and sat and played some slots and keno and tried to milk as many free drinks as we could." Brad paused and blew his nose and tossed the crumbled tissue over his shoulder.

"So, it's getting pretty late, and actually me and Whitey wanted to leave for San Jose yesterday afternoon 'cause we're both supposed to be working today, but Osterlund hadn't gotten his truck yet. He was gonna pick it up today."

"Why didn't he pick it up yesterday?" I said, curious if Osterlund had told them he had to wait for his mother to wire him the money.

"Who the hell knows?" Whitey said. "I've known the guy for years, and he used to be pretty normal, but like every year he'd get a little more screwed up in the brain. It got to the point where being around him was pretty sketchy. He was doing a lot of coke, and there was some weird shit goin' on with his mom and her psychic business. They used to be swimming in dough, but I think they lost some money in the stock market or something, I dunno."

Brad nodded, then said, "Dan, by the way, that was pretty awesome the way you went after Sven. His lip was cut to hell and puffed up like a balloon." He pulled his lower lip down to demonstrate.

"I guess he wanted to get into it," I said. "Was he always like that?"

"Dude," Whitey said, "ever since he got into the steroids and the kick-boxing thing, it's like he went through life trying to prove he could kick anybody's ass. It was getting pretty old."

"Okay," I said, "so you're at Pistol Pete's. Then what?"

"He disappeared," Brad said. "I think he went to take a leak, and after about half an hour we start looking for him, and he's nowhere. We spent a while searching around the casino, but we couldn't find him, so we walked back here, and that's it."

"And that's what you told the cops?"

"Yeah, and they kept on asking us if we saw him talking to anyone, or if there was anybody hanging around, and I finally said, 'Look, go check with the freaking casino. They got all those guys watching everything from up in the ceilings, they got video cameras, all that shit. And then the guy tells us Sven was killed last night, like he has no respect for our feelings. He doesn't give a shit our buddy's dead, he's here at six-fuckin'-thirty, giving us the business."

"This is the round-headed cop, right?"

"Yeah, him. The other guy at least said something nice. What was it, Whitey?"

"'I'm sorry your friend got killed,' or 'I'm sorry for your loss,' or some phony shit like that," Whitey said.

"At least he tried. That's better than nothing," Brad said. His eyes turned red and watery, and his voice sounded like it was ready to crack. "I'll tell you, personally, I'm pretty damn sad about it. I've known Sven since before I could jerk off."

"When was that, about two weeks ago?" Whitey said.

"Ah, blow me, Cheeseball. You got no feelings," Brad said. "Why don't you make yourself useful and load me a goddamn bong hit?"

"Brad, you told the cops about my fight with Osterlund, right?" I saw his body twitch, and his head looked like it was vibrating. He hesitated a long moment before answering.

"Yeah, I did." He sounded like he was admitting to his wife he got the clap from a street whore.

"Don't sweat it, Brado, it was the right thing to do. I got nothing to hide."

"Did they come talk to you yet?"

"Yeah, they woke me up."

"Is everything cool?"

"Sure, they're just doing their job. Now, Osterlund didn't say anything about taking off last night, maybe to meet a call girl or for any other reason?" Both Brad and Whitey shrugged and said no.

"What about Osterlund and Sylvester Bascom? I get the idea they hadn't known each other for that long, and it seems kind of odd Osterlund would be in the wedding. What do you guys think about that?"

"I'll tell you what," Whitey said. "Sven always had money, and that was a big part of him. It's like, if he was paying for the party, he could be a total prick and people would tolerate it. But I'm pretty sure he was running low on bucks. He'd never admit it or talk about it, but it was pretty obvious his mom was turning off the faucet."

"Yup, definitely," Brad said. "My opinion is he was hoping some of Bascom's money would rub off on him one way or another."

"Yeah, but why would Bascom want to be friends with *him?*" I said.

We were all silent for a moment.

"Maybe drugs?" Whitey said.

• • •

The visibility had dropped dramatically by the time I left the Lazy 8. Thick gunmetal-gray clouds hung low over the valley, covering the choppy lake and surrounding mountains in a dense winter haze. Light flurries were falling from the heavy sky, and the town seemed deserted and quiet, except for the eerie roar of the wind sweeping down off the peaks and across the lake.

I drove slowly down Highway 50, fighting to think clearly through my hangover, which was emerging through my drunken state like an unstoppable illness. I felt Brad and Whitey were telling me everything they knew, but none of it pointed me in any particular direction.

Horns blared, and I looked up to see myself rolling through a red light. I pulled into the local bank, opened a checking account with the $50,000-check from Bascom, then drove over to the King's Head to pick up my credit card. The daytime bartender found it and I signed the slip for the tab, but I was in such a daze I couldn't calculate the tip, so I told the bartender I'd trust him to do the math. I sat at the bar alone, drank two pints, then went to the head and threw up. On the way back to my hotel I picked up one of the free local papers, but when I got to my room my eyes wouldn't focus, and I fell asleep.

It was midafternoon when I woke. I felt like dirt, but I'd be functional, whereas I'd have been useless without the sleep. The curtains were open and I could see the snow falling while I brewed a pot of coffee. I poured myself a cup, then sat down at the small table with the local phone book.

There were at least a dozen ads for escort services advertising dancers for bachelor parties and the like. Some had low-key names, like Top Shelf

Entertainment or Hourglass Escorts, but others were more obvious in their marketing. Starting with the largest ads first, I began calling the numbers. SchoolGirl Playmates had a recording, and no one answered at Ecstasy Phase, but I did get an answer at Fantasies Unlimited. They claimed to have no record of sending anyone to the Crown Ambassador on Friday night.

I spent half an hour calling the remaining numbers and got nowhere. I was considering laying down again when my cell rang.

"Hey, what's going on?" Edward Cutlip said.

"All sorts of shit. Have you talked to the police today?"

"No, I left them a message but haven't heard back."

"Sven Osterlund was murdered sometime last night. They found his body over toward the west shore of the lake, in Emerald Bay."

"My god," Edward exclaimed. "Do you…do you think his murder is connected in some way to Sylvester's?"

"I'd say it's likely."

"Are there any suspects?"

"Osterlund was the primary suspect in Sylvester's murder and also the best potential witness. I think he was killed for that reason; because he either witnessed Sylvester's murder or at least knew who did it and why. I suspect he was involved in some sort of scheme with Sylvester, possibly involving drugs, probably cocaine or meth."

"Drugs? Sylvester? He seemed to function well at work, I never saw him miss a day. I don't think he was on drugs."

"He didn't necessarily have to be using. He may have been financing a dealing operation for Osterlund."

"But Sylvester had it made! It would be sheer idiocy for him to get involved in something like that. He would have no reason."

"That you know of," I said. "Edward, I'd like you to get Sylvester's bank records for the last twelve months. Whoever is executor of his estate has legal access. You can get copies of canceled checks too. We may find something."

"Okay, I'll work on it. It just seems crazy."

"Look, everything I've learned about Osterlund points to him being a world-class asshole. Besides being a coke head and a steroid freak, he'd go around looking for fights to prove how tough he was. His truck was towed by the sheriff because he had a phony handicapped parking pass, and he also declared bankruptcy last month."

"Jesus, what in the world was Sylvester doing hanging around him?"

"That's what I'd like to know. Also, I need to know where the strippers at Sylvester's bachelor party came from."

"I can tell you that, I arranged it. The company is called Dancing Babes. Their office is in Stateline, up on Kingsbury Grade."

"Thanks," I said, mentally kicking myself for not calling Edward in the first place. "Hey, you know this detective on the case, Don Raneswich?"

"Yes, what about him?"

"He and I didn't exactly hit it off. Don't be surprised if he brings my name up."

"Why, what happened?"

"He tried to convince me that the police have evidence Sven Osterlund killed Sylvester, so there's nothing left for me to investigate. Have the detectives said anything to you about this?"

"No, nothing."

"That's what I figured. Anyway, Raneswich gave me a bunch of shit about staying out of his way. I basically told him I'm going after the case all gas, no brakes, and he had a problem with that."

"Will that affect your ability to investigate the murder?"

"No. But it might make it interesting at some point."

"Keep me posted," he said.

We hung up, and I called the number for Dancing Babes. A male voice answered and put me on hold. I set the phone back in its cradle, looked out the window into the snowy twilight, then headed downstairs.

Highway 50 was plowed, but I had to chain up at Kingsbury Grade. I found the address about a mile up the road in a little strip mall housing a pizza joint, a snowboard shop, and a few business offices. I walked through the glass door into a hallway and found suite B.

A guy in his twenties was on the phone in the small office, and he motioned for me to sit. His foot was up on the edge of the desk, and he was wearing a very hip and funky white satin V-neck shirt. There were two small silver hoops in his right ear, a stud below his lip, and two more hoops in his left eyebrow.

I took a seat and listened to his conversation. He had a cigarette lit, which he tapped constantly in a marble ashtray.

"Yeah, man, these chicks are cool, they got a good attitude. Huh? Yeah, but they basically work for tips, that's how it works. Yeah, they do the two-girl number, the double-ended dildo show, all that. You'll be happy with them, they're the bomb. What do you mean, anything else? They're dancers, man. Yeah, they do more the more you tip. Huh? Look, like I said, the gig is dancing, the two-girl show, for tips, okay? All right, lemme know."

"What can I do ya for?" he said, turning toward me. He was a good-looking guy with a square jaw and even features, but he looked like a walking fashion trend magazine. I guessed he was ten years younger than me. I handed him my card, and he glanced at it briefly before flipping it onto his desk.

"I'm investigating a murder that happened last Friday night," I said. "Three of your girls were in a suite at Caesar's that night, and I need to talk to them."

His eyes clicked, and his lips turned downward. I felt a stab of irritation at his expression.

"Harsh, man. Who got killed?" he said.

"Guy named Sylvester Bascom."

"The ultimate bad trip, huh?" He held his smoke between his thumb and forefinger and took a couple quick puffs.

"Are these your girls?" I pointed toward a large white binder on his desk.

"That's our talent book," he said. I thumbed through a couple of pages and looked at the different promotional photos of the strippers.

"I'm sorry, I didn't get your name," I said.

"I didn't offer it."

Okay, tough guy, I thought. I picked up a card from a holder on his desk. It read "Dust—Talent Agent."

"You're Dust, huh?"

He nodded blithely.

"Dustin?"

"Nope, just Dust."

I wondered what his mother really named him. I looked at a couple more of the pictures, then closed the binder and set it neatly on the corner of the desk.

"Maybe you can help me out here. I really don't feel like chasing down your girls and questioning them."

He lit another cigarette. "I'm a busy man," he said.

"I'm sure you are, so I'll make it quick. I imagine guys are always calling and trying to figure out if your dancers will hook on the side. Like your last call, right?"

"If you say so."

"Let me tell you first, some guys were trying to solicit your girls at Caesar's for sex, and they shut them down. Not that it matters to me, Dust, but I imagine you run a clean operation."

"As clean as they come, man."

"So suppose a guy is looking for a local hooker. Who does he call?"

"The Mustang Ranch," he said in a bored voice, referring to the infamous whorehouse outside of Reno that had shut down years ago.

"No, I mean, he wants a woman to come up to his room, and he's–"

"I heard what you said," he interrupted. The phone rang and he picked it up. I waited for about five minutes while he talked to another potential customer. When he hung up, he pulled a file from his drawer and started writing something.

"Excuse me," I said.

"Like I said, I'm busy, man. Sorry I can't help you." After a moment, he leaned back in his chair and pointed toward the door with his pen. "You still here?" he said. The phone rang again, and I watched him reach for it.

I took a deep breath, but suddenly my mind felt like a cassette tape switched to fast forward, and I shot out of the chair like a piston under full load. I grabbed Dust's wrist just as his fingers touched the phone, his mouth in mid-syllable. I snatched the phone with my other hand and flung it against the wall, the plastic and metal crashing and busting apart. Then I jumped over the desk.

His eyes were wide in disbelief as he tried to push me away. I slapped his arms aside, grabbed him by the throat, and shook him like a rag doll. He put one arm over my wrists and tried to pop me in the nose with his other fist, but I threw him against the wall before he could hit me, and when he bounced off I punched him with two short rights across the head, my fist ripping out his eyebrow rings and leaving watery trails of blood running down his face. His foot kicked out at my crotch, but I turned sideways, undercut him in the gut with enough power to make his feet come off the ground, then I grabbed him by the shoulders and slammed him down on the desktop.

"Answer my fucking questions," I yelled, holding him down by the neck. "A man's son is dead, you piece of shit!" I could feel my eyes rolling around like a lunatic's, but the adrenaline rush felt wonderful, as the tension of the last couple days exploded to the surface. I bounced his head off the desk and swore at him for another minute until I regained control. Dust was white as a sheet and hadn't yet caught his breath from the gut shot. I finally backed off and paced around a little.

"Whew, that felt good," I said, a crazed grin on my face. "Now, where were we?"

"I think I'm gonna puke," Dust moaned. He rolled off the desk and vomited in his trashcan. I went over, patted him on the back and helped him into his chair.

"Two places," he said in a small voice. "Try Dana's Escorts or Erotic Striptease. They're both in Reno."

"They run call girls?"

He nodded. "The cops seem to lay off them. Erotic has been busted once, but I don't think Dana's ever has. Dana's is owned by the same people who run Pistol Pete's."

"I need their addresses."

"Here," he said, pushing his Rolodex to me with shaky fingers.

14

I LEFT DUST TO clean his office and tend to his wounds as I drove back down the grade. The snow had let up, and I took my chains off at 50, then headed east over Spooner Summit. The roads were icy, the visibility obscured behind a heavy mist that had settled over the pass.

I kept my speed at about thirty-five, climbing the pass toward the high desert and Carson City. Reno lay thirty miles north of Carson City, and in clear weather the drive from South Lake Tahoe to Reno could be done in an hour. Given the night's conditions, it would take close to two. I had plenty of time to think as I drove through the swirling snowfall, up into the shrouded desolation of the Sierra's eastern ridge.

Toward the end of our marriage, Julia had once called me a no-good, drunken, brawling son of a bitch. I laughed out loud when she said it—I *was* drunk at the time—but her words stuck in the back of my mind like a bent nail buried in a fencepost. After I sobered up, and during my three dry years, I tried to develop a more cerebral approach to my job. My goal was to convince people to cooperate through the leverage and persuasiveness of my words. Sometimes that worked, but often it didn't. In the event of the latter, I returned to the old tried-and-true methods: when in doubt, put your hands on someone.

In a business where information is a vital commodity, it often can only be bought with threats or violence. The ability to gain real intelligence is the difference between success and failure in an investigation. Problem is, people have endless reasons to not cooperate. Most criminals share one thing in common—they are habitual liars out of necessity, as a practical means of sustaining.

But what about supposedly law-abiding citizens like Mandy, or Desiree, or even borderline crooks like Dust? I asked Mandy to talk to me about Osterlund, and she blew me off. Desiree didn't want to talk about her sex life because she was embarrassed, which was understandable. Dust made the mistake of blatantly not cooperating, probably just the result of a philosophical resentment of authority. If he had been a little more responsive or polite, I might have let it go. But the punk had picked a bad time to be disrespectful.

What about Edward Cutlip? I was a little wary of him, although nothing in his behavior indicated he was hiding anything. Still, I had to consider him a possible suspect, maybe as an envious aide working some sort of scam on his boss's spoiled son. I hoped this wasn't the case; I'd not held back in my communication with him.

One thing I knew for sure was that Osterlund knew a lot more than he told the police. Unfortunately, he took the knowledge to his grave.

I dialed Cody Gibbons as I drove over the dark summit, to ask if he'd been able to get copies of the police files I'd requested. The cellular reception was scratchy, but I was able to hear the gist of his message: Sylvester had no criminal record to speak of; his worst offense was open container. Sven Osterlund's case file was littered with alcohol, drug, and battery charges, but he had never done any real time. Cody was saying something about high-priced defense lawyers when I asked him to run Edward Cutlip, but we were disconnected before he could answer.

The cloud cover broke up as I dropped into Carson Valley. Light patches of snow spotted the desert floor, reflecting the distant glow of stars sparkling like cut diamonds against the black sky. I turned north toward Reno and drove the length of the main drag of Carson City, past old bars in brick buildings that had been doing business since the late 1800s, past second-rate casinos, cheap hotels, fast-food joints, auto dealerships, and discount gas stations. I went by the state capitol building in the center of town and decided to get dinner, but I felt overdosed on greasy chow, and Carson City wasn't the type of town that would offer much in the way of healthier fare. Eventually I found a small restaurant that was closing up even though it was only eight o'clock. I convinced the cook to make me a garden burger and ate leaning against my car in the parking lot. Then I drove another couple miles until the RV centers and convenience markets faded in my rearview mirror, and the commercial strip gave way to State Highway 395.

The four-lane highway through the desert was straight and flat, and the road seemed to pull the Nissan along, as if the pavement was charged with an energy it drew from the earth below. I cruised along at ninety, making time, my headlights flashing against the sagebrush and scrub that dotted the landscape. A few miles outside of Reno I stopped, filled my tank at a Terrible Herbst gas station, and bought a city map. The address for Erotic Striptease was on Fourth Street.

I took the Virginia Street exit, driving under the archway proclaiming Reno "The Biggest Little City in the World." The town was lit up by the neon brightness of the casinos. I drove past The Silver Legacy, The El Dorado, The Nugget, and others, but it was a Monday night and the streets were mostly empty. I hung a right on Fourth, couldn't find the address, and had to double back, driving slowly until I pulled over in front of an old Victorian-style home set back off the road next to an apartment complex. The house was dark, with a "For Rent" sign in the front window. I walked to the front door, jiggled the locked doorknob, then returned to my car and dialed the phone number for Erotic Striptease. It was disconnected. I rubbed my brow and studied the map until I found the street for Dana's Escorts. It was on Taylor, on the south side of town.

Dana's Escorts' address was for a well-lit office building with floor-to-ceiling glass walls facing the street, but the sign on the door said Diamond Talent Agency. Velour shades hung from the top of the windows, and a few of the blinds were partially open. I opened the door and stepped inside.

"Hi," a quite large woman said to me from behind her desk. She had bright eyes, red lipstick, and a pretty face framed by long curls of blond hair. Her bosom was huge, and her arms were bigger than mine. Despite her girth, she bounced up lightly and stuck out a chubby hand.

"I'm Gloria Damone. May I help you?"

"I'm not sure I'm in the right place," I said. "This is a talent agency?"

"Yes. We specialize in musical acts, dancers, comedians, and the like."

"I see. How about magicians?"

"Yes, we place magicians occasionally. Are you a magician?"

"No, but sometimes I wish I were. I'm a private investigator."

Gloria sat down, and while she still smiled, she looked a little unsettled. I tried to think of something witty to put her at ease.

"Actually, I'm trying to solve a mysterious case, and a little magic might go a long way." It sounded lame, and I regretted it as I said it. *Christ, how many brain cells did I fry last night?*

"I see," she said. Her voice confirmed my hokey attempt at charm wasn't working. "And what can I do for you?"

"Do you also manage Dana's Escorts?"

"Yes," she said slowly. "That is one of our businesses."

She seemed an unlikely madam, running a call-girl service behind the front of a talent agency. I wondered how tough she was beneath her cheerful demeanor.

"Last Friday night, probably around midnight, I believe one or two of your escorts may have gone to the Crown Ambassador in South Lake Tahoe. Did you send any girls there?"

"I'm sorry, I can't disclose that."

"Why not?"

"The nature of our escort business is confidential. Our clients like it that way."

"Your client at the Crown wouldn't care."

"And how would you know that?"

"He's dead."

"That's too bad," she said after a long pause. She had not invited me to sit, but I did so anyway.

"How did it happen?" she asked.

"He was murdered."

Her mouth opened and closed silently, and her eyes darted. Then she excused herself and went to the ladies' room.

The office walls were decorated with framed pictures of famous casino acts. Liberace and Siegfried and Roy were on one wall, and David Copperfield, Wayne Newton, and a troop of bikini-clad dancing girls were on another. I looked at the pictures for a few minutes until she returned and stood beside her desk.

"I'm sorry, I can't help you," she said, her painted lips a tight line.

"Whatever you tell me will be kept confidential."

"Even still, I'm bound by our policy."

"Look, lady," I sighed, "I'm not a vice cop. I don't care what kind of business you run. But if you sent a girl there, she may have witnessed a man stabbed to death. That means she's in danger. Am I getting through to you?"

"I don't think it's in my best interest to get involved," she said.

"You're involved whether you like it or not."

Gloria was trying to stay composed, but she was frowning deeply, as if weighing a great moral dilemma. She studied her desk, shuffled a few papers, then rested her eyes on mine.

"I can't help you, and I'd like you to leave," she said. I stood, taking note of the stout bolt lock on the metal frame of the glass door.

"Wait for me outside," she whispered.

When I reached my car, the lights behind me clicked off, and the parking lot went dark. I zipped my jacket and hiked a foot up on my bumper. After a minute she came out, wearing a thick fur-lined coat over her dress.

"Follow me in your car," she said.

I swung in behind her white Cadillac. We drove around the back streets of Reno, then onto Interstate 80, took the first exit, and drove another few miles before she finally pulled over on a dark residential street. I parked behind her and walked to her window. She motioned for me to get in the passenger seat.

"Why all the driving around?" I said.

"I didn't feel comfortable talking to you in the office. I wanted to go somewhere else."

"All right."

"Whatever I tell you, I want your word this conversation never happened."

"What conversation?"

She drew a breath, set her hands in her lap, and looked at me. "First, I don't know anything about what happened in that room. Understand?"

"Yeah."

"Here's what I do know. I got a call around eleven on Friday, and a guy wanted two escorts for the night at the Crown Ambassador. I tell him it's five hundred minimum per girl. That scares a lot of the lowlifes away, but this guy says no problem, and he says to send our hottest talent—he's a generous tipper. So I set it up, send two girls over to Tahoe. High roller comes to town, has a streak of luck, wants the company of some sexy ladies. Not unusual."

"Right."

"Yeah, well, that's what I thought. The next thing I know it's nine in the morning, I'm still in bed, and Samantha calls, says she quits and wants me to mail her check to a P.O. box. Very sudden, like that. I asked her, 'Why, what's up?' She says, for my safety, I don't want to know. Samantha's tough, she's seen it all, so I figure something pretty heavy went down. But I had no idea anyone got killed."

"What else did she say?"

"She said she'd be off the air for a while. Then she hung up."

"What about the second girl?"

"Beverly. She's young and inexperienced, and I left her a couple messages, but she hasn't called back. Here," she said, handing me two file folders. "This is their employment applications and some photos. You can copy down the information, but you can't keep the pictures."

"Did either of them have boyfriends?"

"Samantha ran around with this biker, a tall guy, dirty gray-blond hair and a long goatee and a bunch of tattoos. I have no idea who he is, but I saw Sam on the back of his Harley once."

"How about Beverly?"

"No one that I know of. She's only been in town for a few months."

It took me ten minutes to copy every word off both the applications. When I was finished, I took a look at their pictures. Samantha had dark hair, an olive complexion, and looked Hispanic or maybe part Asian. There was a full body shot in lingerie showing off her curvaceous figure and huge breasts I assumed were implants. I studied her pictures closely, looking for moles, scars, tattoos, or any other distinguishing features that could identify her.

Beverly was a marked contrast to Samantha. She had short red hair cut in a feathered pixie style and had a nice body to match her pretty face. She looked more like a country girl than a hooker.

I handed the files back to Gloria.

"You have any idea where they might be?"

She shrugged. "Who knows with Samantha? She could be halfway around the planet or over at the Silver Legacy playing cards. As far as

Beverly, I don't know. She wasn't from around here. Maybe she went back home."

I looked at the notes I'd taken from Beverly's application. Her previous address was in Salina, Utah.

"I appreciate your help," I said.

"Do you think the police will contact me?"

"It's possible. You never met me, right?"

"You got it," she said, and started her car. I climbed out with my scribbled notes and watched her drive away.

•   •   •

I suppose I should have been happy with the progress I'd made. Identifying the hookers at this stage in the game was a result of good, hard, nose-to-the-grindstone detective work. Make your own luck, I told myself, stay focused and ignore the distractions. But I kept sensing Don Raneswich in my blind spot. Unless he was grossly incompetent or lazy, the detective would be making progress, probably have a line on Dana's Escorts and Samantha and Beverly, or maybe he had other leads I was unaware of. The police had the tactical advantage of access to phone records, video camera tapes, and forensic evidence, plus it was a lot easier to coerce witnesses with a badge. My advantage was speed and stealth, and the willingness to break the law when necessary.

I stopped at a small all-night restaurant on the corner of Virginia and Fifth, drank a cup of coffee, and reviewed my notes on Samantha Nunez. She was thirty-two, and her background seemed as sad and wasted as an empty bottle of whiskey discarded in the weeds of a vacant lot. She had gone to high school in Los Angeles and did not check the box for "graduated." Her last three jobs were waitress, erotic dancer, and "escort" at the defunct Mustang Ranch. I went out the front door of the restaurant to a payphone, checked the phone book, and, to my amazement, there was a listing for Nunez, initial S, complete with phone number and address. Hell, maybe the bodacious Miss Nunez would even be home on a Monday night.

The address was in west Reno. I turned onto her street in a slummy, rundown section of town. Half the streetlights were blown out, and the curbs were jammed with a junkyard fleet of derelict vehicles, with enough bald tires, cracked windshields, and trashed interiors to keep an auto shop in business for a decade. On the corner, a group of black teenagers huddled under a streetlamp, beanies low on their heads, their hands thrust in their coat pockets. They eyed me sullenly as I made a U-turn.

I found a spot to park around the corner, strapped on my bulletproof vest, and tightened my holster across my chest. Then I walked back up the apartment-lined street toward the address I had written on the inside of a matchbook.

The Prairie Rose apartments looked like they may have bloomed years ago, then were left to shrivel and die in the cold desert air. The black wrought-iron gate screeched loudly when I entered the courtyard, and I walked around a large pool that, in better days, may have been sparkling and turquoise, but it had been drained and was caked with dirt, the bottom littered with beer cans, broken glass, a tricycle, and a plastic lounge chair.

I climbed the concrete stairs up to the second-floor balcony and went down a walkway crammed with weather-faded lawn chairs, soiled couches, and miscellaneous junk. I double-checked the address, then stopped at unit 216. Light was shining from around the curtains. I heard music, but I couldn't tell if it was coming from 216 or 215. I knocked, waited, then knocked again louder, peeking through the curtains, and when there was no answer I knocked so hard it bruised my knuckles.

The door to 215 flew open and rap music blared obnoxiously. A black kid with cornrows and a missing front tooth stuck his head out.

"Yo, man, yo' ho' ain't home, John, so save yo' money and go home and wax yo' own jimmy."

"Huh?" I said. He shot me a look that made it clear my presence on the balcony was an imposition, and slammed the door shut. I shuffled around for a moment, then knocked on his window.

"You deaf an' dumb, man?" he said, jutting his head out the door. He couldn't have been older than fourteen, but he had jailhouse tattoos on the fronts of his fingers, and had put on a red doo-rag to show his gang colors.

"You want to make an easy twenty?" I asked.

"Fuck you, faggot."

"Just looking for information," I said. I folded a twenty-dollar bill between two fingers and held it up.

"Inside," he said, tugging me by the sleeve and closing the door behind us. He grabbed at the twenty, but I held it out of his reach. Two preschool-age kids sat on the floor up close to the TV, so they could hear it over the music.

"Who lives next door?" I said.

"Mexican ho' with big tits, man."

"When was the last time you saw her?"

"I got better things to do than keep track a' her." I put the twenty in my pocket.

"Awright, a couple days ago she was here and left with Mr. One Eight Seven on his bike."

"Mr. One Eight Seven?"

"Yeh. He 'bout the only white man got the balls to come out here after sundown, you know what I'm sayin'?"

"Who is he?"

"He's her old man, jack. If it wasn't for him, I'd already been next door, pumpin' that fine bitch."

"You think so?" I said, and he glared up at me suspiciously, trying to figure if it was an insult.

"Whatchu sayin', man?"

"Forget it. Describe Mr. One Eight Seven."

"He's white, about yo' size, got a big, long mustache and beard." He ran his thumb and forefinger down from above his lip to below his jaw. "He got tats all over him. Rumor is he just did ten years in Soledad for homicide. That's why he called One Eight Seven. Now gimme the Jackson."

I held him off. "What's his real name?"

"Hell if I know, man."

"How do I find him?"

"Beat the fuck outa me. Go look around town for a ugly white motherfucker on a chopper."

"You want the twenty, you gotta give me more to go on," I said, and I could see the impatient aggression in his eyes.

"I dunno whatchu want, man, know what I'm sayin'? I never talked to him. I just seen him around. When she left with him, she had a suitcase."

"Tell me more about him."

He hesitated, and I could see the lies forming behind his eyes.

"Don't bullshit me," I said, moving in close and grabbing his arm around the biceps. I squeezed, and my fingers overlapped to the first joint. He squirmed and pushed at me, but I forced him down to his knees.

"What else?" I said.

He swore, slapping at my arm, his face twisted in pain.

"He got the good rock, man. Let go!"

"He sells to you?"

"Yeah, now let go," he pleaded. I eased my grip slightly.

"Is he big time? Supplying the neighborhood?"

He didn't answer, but I could see the fear in his face. I let him go, and he sat on the carpet, rubbing his bruised arm. I pulled an extra twenty from my wallet and dropped the two bills in his lap. "Buy the kids some healthy food," I said as I opened the door. The children never took their eyes off the TV.

It was nearing midnight when I drove away. I considered my options, none which were particularly promising. Samantha Nunez and her supposed biker boyfriend, Mr. 187, could be anywhere. Mr. 187 himself was now a suspect in my mind, based on the fact that he was a friend of Samantha and his name was a reference to the California penal code for homicide. I thought about driving around Reno and scouting bar parking lots for Harleys, but it was a long shot.

If I were a cop, I'd check to see where Samantha used a credit card last, or if she flew out of Reno, and I'd also check with Soledad and the other prisons in California and Nevada to see if anyone matching Mr. 187's description had been released in the last year. But none of those options were available to me at the moment, and I wanted to make progress now, while Officer Raneswich was at home with his head on a pillow.

I went back to the all-night restaurant, drank coffee, and tried to think clearly. It felt like it had been days since the cops woke me up in the morning. I reread the information from Samantha's application until I memorized it, and considered flying down to LA to try to find her parents. But when I called directory service, the operator told me there were ninety-two listings for Nunez in Southern California.

Staking out her apartment was an idea, but Gloria told me Samantha said she was going "off the air," and the gangbanger said she left with a suitcase. My face felt gritty, I hadn't shaved since the day before, and when I looked in the mirror in the men's room, my eyes were bleary and bloodshot. But I was wired, so I decided, *Fuck it, let's take it to another level*, but first I wanted to kill some time. I had a piece of apple pie and read the paper until one in the morning, then I drove back to Samantha's apartment.

I wore my black coat and an old ski beanie pulled low over my ears, and stayed in the shadows as I made my way to the gate of the Prairie Rose complex. I opened it with a quick jerk, not wanting a prolonged squeak. The night was still, the courtyard dimly lit. A couple of apartments across the way showed light through their drapes, but my timing wouldn't get any better than one-thirty on a Tuesday morning. Hopefully the crack addicts were sleeping off their weekend binges. The last thing I needed was some paranoid pipe-head spotting me and making a scene.

I stayed on the balls of my feet, climbing the stairs, gliding carefully around the clutter to apartment 216. A cheap outdoor light fixture between 215 and 216 illuminated the area, and I burned my fingertips unscrewing the bulb. When the light went out, I knelt down in the dark and waited, letting myself relax, scanning the courtyard. Then I went to work on the door with my lock-pick tools. It was a process that required patience and focus; I was never successful if I tried to hurry. I had been pretty good at it when I was doing a lot of bounty hunting, but I was rusty. It took a couple of minutes, though it seemed longer, then the tumblers fell into place and the lock clicked open. I went through the door in a crouch, my automatic in my hand.

I quickly checked the small kitchen, the bedroom, and bathroom. No one was home.

I started in the bathroom, where an *Easy Rider* and *High Times* magazine lay next to the toilet. On top of the tank, a box of anti-lice shampoo was proudly displayed. I went through her medicine cabinet and pocketed two small prescription bottles, one for codeine, the other for some medicine I didn't recognize. Both contained pills, but they were over two years old.

An unmade king-size bed took up most of the bedroom. The closets and dresser drawers were conspicuously empty—there wasn't a stitch of clothing left in the place. Two pillows lay on the bed, and I ran my finger over one and snagged a few long black hairs. The other one had a number of shorter blond and gray hairs on it. *Looks like Mr. 187 is losing his hair.*

I rifled the nightstand drawer, found a box of condoms, a vibrator, half a joint in a plastic bag, a paperback-size mirror smeared with white-powder residue, and two packs of matches. One of the matchbooks was from the old Mustang Ranch whorehouse. Before I left the room, I checked under the bed, finding only a dog-eared porno magazine and some crumpled tissues.

I quickly tossed the dingy mess of a kitchen and surmised that Samantha Nunez wasn't much of a housekeeper and also must have left in a hurry. A half-gallon carton of milk was left out on the counter, and a TV dinner was in the microwave. She must have really been in a rush to pack her clothes and split because she'd left two bottles of wine and a six-pack of Budweiser in the refrigerator.

I went back to the main room and pulled the cushions off the couch and easy chair. There was nothing but crumbs and pennies. Under an end table, an open phone book lay face down. I picked it up, and it was opened to the yellow pages under the letter "E" for entertainers. The two pages were filled with ads for the legal brothels in the Reno area, which were all on the outskirts of Carson City. I was scanning through the next few pages, reading the smaller miscellaneous ads for the sex trade, when I heard the heavy clump of boots on the balcony. I listened intently for a moment with my breath caught in my throat—it sounded like more than one person. I quickly retreated to the back bedroom. A few seconds later, they were knocking on the door as I slid open the window.

"Samantha Nunez," a deep voice, probably a cop's voice, called out. I climbed up on the sill and lowered myself down to arm's length, my boots skidding against the stucco wall for traction, and they were still knocking and calling her name when I let go. I hit the hard sand of the back alley in good position, felt the shock of the second-story drop jolt my bones, rolled over, and came up on my feet. My ankle twisted a bit as I landed, and my knees complained, but it didn't prevent me from moving away quickly.

I went through a missing slat in an old wooden fence and into the back parking lot of the adjacent apartment complex. I sprinted down the rows the best I could, limping a bit, staying out of the light. The lot ended in a narrow driveway leading out to the street. A sheriff's cruiser was double-parked down the road. I moved across the street under the darkness of a blown-out streetlamp and made it around the corner to my car.

Despite the cold, I had broken a sweat, and I drove back toward downtown with my window open. I took a roundabout way, staying carefully at the speed limit, and checked into a small hotel on Virginia Street.

I lay on the bed with my hands behind my head, but every time I closed my eyes they blinked open like a ping-pong ball bouncing off a hard surface. I stood up and began pacing around the room. It was critical to locate Samantha Nunez quickly, although I wasn't sure if the cops came to her apartment because someone reported me breaking and entering, or maybe they'd just learned Samantha was a likely witness to Sylvester Bascom's murder. I hoped it wasn't the latter. If the police were on to her already, any lead I might have in the race to solve the case would be precarious.

The prescription bottles were still in my jacket pocket. I tossed them on the bed, then flipped the hotel's phone book to the same page it was opened to at the apartment. I set the phone book on the bed next to the bottles, laid down my handwritten transcription of Samantha's employment application, and let my eyes wander over the words. The obvious connection was her stint at the Mustang Ranch and the phone book open to the page with the brothel's ads, but I wasn't sure what to do with it.

It was past two-thirty in the morning. I lay down again, but a minute later I was back up and wearing a path in the room's cheap carpeting. It had been a long day, beginning with being woken out of a dead, boozy slumber by a cop with a bad attitude. My teeth grinded, my jaw swollen and sore where Osterlund had punched me. I took some deep breaths, tried to relax, and stood very still in the center of the room. Then I reached down and abruptly tore the pages out of the phone book and went to my car.

. . .

Conrad Pace pushed himself up on his elbow and snatched up the phone. "Whoever is calling me at three in the fucking morning, this better be good," he croaked.

"Sorry, Cuz," Louis Perdie said. "Our friend in Reno just called me."

"What the hell about?"

"Someone just tossed Samantha Nunez's apartment."

"Samantha Nunez? Oh, yeah, Stiles' broad." Pace's voice came down a notch.

"You remember her."

"Some parts more than others, Louis," Pace said.

Perdie chuckled briefly, then the humor went out of his voice, "Could have been the PI we tried to get to back off. He may know she was in the room when the guy was stuck in the gut."

Pace yawned. "We got nothing to worry about unless he finds her. I don't see that happening."

"Depends how he goes about things, I guess."

"What's that supposed to mean?"

"I don't know, Cuz, just a feeling I got on this guy. I think he's in it for the long haul."

Pace laid his head back on the pillow. "Perhaps he needs some additional discouragement."

"Usually that's all it takes, Cuz," Perdie said.

"See to it, then." Pace yawned and went back to sleep.

15

THINGS FEEL MIGHTY LONELY at three A.M. in the desert, I thought as I headed east on Interstate 80, out of Reno and into the quiet solitude of the Great Basin Desert. The land seemed particularly suited for death—cold, endless, void of water or shelter, and unnaturally dark at night. If you wanted to kill someone and hide the body in a shallow grave…yeah, this would be the place.

I watched closely for the signs, and five miles outside Carson City a small billboard advertising Darla's Cathouse, The Velvet Ranch, and Tumbleweed Parlor Ranch appeared out of the blackness like a dream. I took the exit and navigated a narrow, unlit road that seemed to lead nowhere, until I came around the bend to a large gravel parking lot that served the brothels. I had a vague memory of being here years ago with a group of men, maybe it was a last hurrah before someone got married, and I remember driving around the desert wildly drunk in the middle of the night before we found the complex.

I idled slowly around the parking lot, past Darla's, The Velvet, Tumbleweed 1, and Tumbleweed 2, which was a sad pile of sodden ashes and charred debris. A large sign on a steel post still remained, but apparently Tumbleweed 2 had burned down, and the unsightly aftermath looked like it was left as is, like a stoic testament to life's inevitable disappointments. Whatever the case, it reduced my prospects to three. I started at Darla's.

Two long mobile trailers set in a V met at a peaked façade that served as the main entrance. I pushed a button at the front gate, waiting in the still light. The buzzer on the gate rang and the lock released. I hurried out of the cold and into the lobby. A group of about ten prostitutes stood in a lineup in front of the bar and introduced themselves while I stood there awkwardly.

"Need a drink," I mumbled, and they dispersed quickly.

There was no bartender, and one of the hookers walked around to fill her coffee mug. I asked her for a cup.

"It'll be three dollars," she said. "Okay?"

I checked my reflection in the bar mirror, wondering if I looked like someone who wouldn't want to pay for an overpriced cup of stale coffee. My mug didn't look indignant, just tired. Still, I probably looked better than the prostitute, a sour-faced thing who looked as bored and weary as an assembly-line worker. She had a sagging chest and bony legs and was probably barely out of her teens—twenty years old going on thirty-eight, I decided. I described Samantha Nunez and asked if she knew her.

"Nope," she said, blowing a hit off her cigarette into the cloud of stale smoke above the bar.

I took my coffee and walked into the adjoining room, where most of the prostitutes had retreated to a circular couch. I knelt down and started talking to them one by one. They were definitely the B team. One woman had a body like a skinny man, her shoulder disfigured by the blurry remains of a tattoo that looked like it had survived an attempt at removal. Another was a pretty brunette with a tempting cleavage, but her hips and ass spread out massively. A third had a pleasant face but a vacant stare, and when she opened her mouth I saw she was missing a number of teeth. I talked to them all, and none had heard of Samantha Nunez.

As I was going out, three Mexican dudes pulled up in an old red work truck, and I could smell their sweat and the liquor on their breath when we passed on the walkway.

"How are the *señoritas* in there, *amigo*?" one asked.

"Muy bonita," I replied, and walked out into the empty night, away from a sordid haven banished to the lost hills.

Across the gravel and sand, down a four-foot ridge in the terrain, was Tumbleweed 1. When I entered the building, the interior surprised me. If the other ranch was a greasy-spoon diner, the Tumbleweed was a luxurious five-star restaurant. A long mahogany bar overlooked the main parlor, where yellow lamps flickered faintly against the red walls. Dark velour sofas were grouped strategically in the shadows to the right and left, creating the impression that there were two separate, intimate rooms. About a dozen men sat scattered about the bar and the sofas, drinking and talking to the hookers. A few girls made a halfhearted attempt at forming a lineup as I came in, but they retreated when I walked up to the bar.

The bartender was busy mixing drinks, so I took in the scene while I waited. I tried to count the prostitutes, but different ones kept appearing from the hallways, and I lost track at fifteen. For the most part, they looked like strippers at a first-rate men's club. There were blondes, brunettes, Asian women, a few black girls, and a tall, stunning redhead in a leopard bikini. The bartender made his way over to me and asked what I was having. I ordered a Coke, then requested to talk with the madam.

"She's in the back. She should be out in a bit. Why don't you relax and partake in the fun?" He gestured with a sweeping motion.

"It's tempting, but I'm here on business."

He gave me a doubtful look. "Suit yourself," he said.

I sipped at my soft drink and after a minute a woman with long blond hair falling down her back approached me. She had a big nose but nice eyes and an open smile, along with a body that looked like it walked off the pages of *Playboy*. Her leotard was split down to her belly button, showing off a smooth, suntanned stomach.

"Hi, I'm Joanna. Why don't you and I go get naked?" she said.

"You're so gorgeous I doubt I could afford you."

She stuck out her lower lip in a mock frown and sat next to me. I smelled her perfume and felt her body's warmth as she leaned toward me, putting her lips up to my ear.

"I'll give you a blow job that will change your life," she whispered.

"That's certainly something to consider," I said. "But maybe you can help me with something else. I've been hired by a family to find their daughter. There's a serious illness in the family, and they'd like to reach her, to let her know."

"I see," she said, her eyes wandering out to the parlor.

"Her name is Samantha Nunez. She's thirty-two, dark hair, dark complexion, looks part Hispanic maybe, and had breast enlargement. Does that ring a bell?"

"Hmm," she snorted. "Sounds like that tough bitch Tina who used to work here. She got fired 'cause she's got a real gutter mouth and doesn't know how to treat customers."

"Did you know her?"

"Not really. She left about two weeks after I started. I stayed away from her."

"Why?"

"She was the ultimate hard-ass chick. Nothing but trouble."

"Do you have any idea where she is?"

"No, but I know who probably does."

"Who?" I said.

"Come to my room, and I'll tell you afterward."

"Hold on," I said. "Is this person here tonight?"

"Yeah, she's here." She looked down the bar and around the room. "I don't see her now, but she'll be around."

"It's important that I talk to her. I'll wait here until she comes out. Could you just point her out for me?"

"Honey, I'm working. You come to my room, and I'll find her for you when we're done."

"I'd rather wait for her," I said. Just then a man in blue jeans and a yellow polo shirt sat down on the barstool next to her. He had glassy eyes, a smarmy smile, and his hair hung in his face. She turned toward him, and I touched her arm.

"Okay, Joanna, let's go," I said. "You just promise you'll take me to her."

She took my hand and led me down a long hallway to her room.

· · ·

I walked back to the bar a half hour later and $150 lighter in the wallet. Joanna brought an Asian woman to where I sat. "This is Connie," Joanna said, then she winked and fluttered her fingers at me as she strutted away.

"Hi, Connie, I'm Dan."

"Actually, I just changed my name," she said. "I'm Sasha today. But you can call me Con, or Lola, or Sue Lin, or your little minky fuck toy. I don't care as long as you buy me a drink."

I ordered her a vodka Collins and decided to have a drink myself.

"Two cherries," Sasha yelled at the bartender. She looked about thirty. Her figure was slight, her chest relatively modest, but she had bedroom legs and perfect skin.

"Sasha, I'm working for a family that wants to find their daughter. There's been a sudden illness in the family, and they'd like her to know. I'm looking for Samantha Nunez. Do you know her?"

"Sure, we're buds," she said. Her features were a little too pronounced to be Asian—maybe she'd had plastic surgery or was part European. Her eyes were dark diamonds, and she had a wide smile and great teeth.

"When was the last time you talked to her?"

"I didn't know she had family." She put a cherry in her mouth and pulled on the stem until it popped off, then rolled the cherry around with her tongue and licked her lips. She smiled at me like we were sharing an inside joke.

"They're in LA," I said.

"Really. So one of Samantha's relatives is sick?"

"That's right. They want to reach her before it's too late."

"Why don't you tell me, and I'll call her?" She smiled again.

"I don't know Samantha. But my guess is if someone in her family is dying, it'd be best for her to hear it from her family."

She tilted her head. "I guess that's logical. Okay, she called me a couple days ago and said she's gonna go work a six-week shift at the Cat's Meow Ranch down near Vegas. Said she was tired of the cold up here."

Or more likely running from the heat, I thought. It was the break I needed—at this point I felt it was a given that Samantha Nunez was the key to the case. I thanked Sasha and walked out into the morning, but the sky was still black, and the distant glare of the moon shined in my eyes as if it was mocking me.

16

A WHILE AGO, I think it was in a bar, someone asked me if I believed in god. I don't remember what I said—the conversation probably shifted before I could come up with an answer. The truth is I'm not a religious man; it's been years since I've even gone through the pretense of attending church. But I don't reject the possibility that god, in one form or another, probably exists. I'm open-minded on the subject, and I consider that a victory of sorts.

As I drove back north toward Reno, I wondered if god would approve of the expansive sex trade in Nevada. I decided he would; my half hour with the blond vixen Joanna had certainly been heavenly.

• • •

It was dawn when I pulled into my cheap hotel in Reno and fell into bed with my clothes on for the second straight night. But this time I didn't even bother taking my boots off. I slept like a lodged stone for a few hours, and when I woke I called the airlines from bed and booked a three o'clock Southwest flight to Las Vegas.

I left the hotel at noon, hurrying out to the nearest shopping mall in my rumpled, dirty clothes, and bought two new pairs of Levi's, a long-sleeve plaid button-up shirt, some t-shirts, and a six-pack of underwear and socks.

I made it back to the hotel by quarter after one and called Edward Cutlip. He answered on the first ring and asked for a progress report.

"I was up until dawn chasing down leads," I said. "I'm getting on a plane and flying to Las Vegas this afternoon."

"What for?"

"I'm pretty sure I've identified a call girl who was in Sylvester's room. She's gone underground and is hiding out in Vegas."

"Do you know exactly where?"

"I'm pretty sure."

"Where?"

"I'll let you know when I find her."

"Ah, okay. I need to tell you that Raneswich and Iverson just left here. Raneswich tried to discourage Mr. Bascom from sending a PI after their case."

"What did Bascom say?"

"Well, he asked them if they had any leads or if they were near making an arrest. Iverson said they were still waiting for toxicology and forensics results, and they were interviewing a number of potential witnesses, but it didn't sound like they had anything solid. Bascom told them flat out that he hired you because he isn't convinced they know what they're doing. You should have seen Raneswich's face. He turned red as a tomato. They left in a huff a couple of minutes ago."

I laughed. "Bascom doesn't mince words, does he?"

"He'd tell the president of the United States he was doing a crappy job if that's what he thought. He's a straight shooter, all right. Anyway, it's going to take some time to get those bank records you asked for. Sylvester's bank is telling me standard processing time is two weeks."

"Typical. Turn the heat up on them. Use John Bascom's influence; tell them it's a murder case."

"Got it," he said. "I'll try again. Have you made any more progress on the drug-dealing angle?"

"Maybe. I think it's still possible Sylvester's murder was drug-related, but I haven't got a clear direction on it yet. Once I talk to this hooker in Vegas, I should know more. By the way, Edward, my expense report is getting up there. I had to spend a hundred fifty last night on, well, a kind of irregular expense."

"Do you have a receipt?"

"No, it wouldn't be that kind of thing."

"What was it, a bribe?"

"Yeah, sort of. It was the price of a piece of, ah, information."

"I'll need more detail to get it through accounting," Edward said.

"Oh, I see. Well, you'll see it on my expense report."

"You might as well tell me now so I can talk to accounting, or your check might be delayed."

"Right, then," I said. "I had to pay the money to a prostitute."

"A prostitute?"

"Yeah. She gave me the link to the witness, but she wouldn't talk unless I went with her. I'm serious."

"God, our controller's going to love this. Where did you find her?"

"One of the cathouses out in the desert."

"No kidding, huh? I've never been to one. What did she look like?"

"Blond with a body that wouldn't quit," I said, deciding to test Edward's character. I still wasn't a hundred percent sure I could trust him.

"You know, I think I'd be interested in visiting one of those places. Not that I would partake. I'd just be interested in observing."

"Uh-huh," I said.

"So, when will you be back from Las Vegas?" he said.

"Hopefully tomorrow."

"Well, maybe we can go when you get back."

"I promise I'll hurry," I said. We hung up, and I decided he passed the test. If nothing else, it meant he was a regular guy. I lay back on the bed, smiling at the casual camaraderie between men. The best times always involved the most basic common denominators: loose women and booze.

• • •

I spent the packed flight to Vegas crammed in a seat next to a fat, drunken man who complained incessantly about the lack of room. Halfway through the flight, he passed out and began snoring loudly, embarrassing his wife and teenage son. When we landed, he woke and started babbling about how he was going to break the bank at the casinos. *This is why I like to drive*, I thought.

I rented a new four-door Cadillac and decided to check into a first-class hotel. If Edward had a problem with the expense, I'd blame it on Sin City's decadent influence. Las Vegas had rapidly expanded in the last decade to accommodate the growing hordes of gamblers, conventioneers, and sightseers. Half a dozen new hotels had opened recently, each of them immense productions with over two thousand rooms, gigantic casinos, shopping malls, numerous restaurants, and extensive children's fun centers. Apparently the inexhaustible flood of gambling money was driving the city's expansion.

The black glass of the pyramid-shaped Luxor hotel and casino danced in the late-afternoon sun, but when I pulled in, the valet parking attendant told me they were sold out. I drove across the street and tried the mammoth MGM Grand, and they also were full, so I headed over to the Excalibur, which had vacancies, and checked into a room. The hotel had a medieval castle theme but inside it looked a lot like every other casino. The clerk pointed me across the gambling floor, and I lugged my bag for the length of a football field over to the elevators, then went up to my room on the twelfth floor.

I found the Cat's Meow Ranch in the phone book and called for directions. I didn't want to show up there until later in the evening, when they would most likely have a full shift working. That left me with a couple of hours to kill, so I went downstairs and found a small Italian eatery. I ordered a meatball sandwich and washed it down with a glass of cheap Chianti, then I walked out to the main floor of the casino, checked out the action, and almost stopped at a bar. Instead I decided to head outside and see the sights. On my way out I saw the same family that had been on the airplane. The man appeared to be arguing with his wife, then he turned away and sat at a blackjack table. The teenage son looked over at me, his face as sad and resigned as a beaten dog's.

I made my way down the crowded sidewalk on the Strip, walking through the cold, dry air. I zipped up my old red ski jacket and impulsively ducked into a small neighborhood lounge that had somehow survived the recent development.

The locals were enjoying the Wednesday twilight happy hour, sipping cocktails and munching popcorn in the mellow hideaway. A middle-aged couple was shooting pool while the bartender stood on a crate and fiddled with the TV set. I took a seat at a small table, ordered a whiskey highball, and watched the bartender pour a real drink—a relief after too many crappy casino highballs. I pulled my cell phone out and thought about calling Wenger, or maybe Jack Myers, to ask if he'd seen Sylvester's toxicology reports yet. And then I thought of Mandy.

I guzzled my drink and ordered another. An image of Mandy walking away from me naked stuck in my mind, like a slow-motion fantasy. I could see her toes sink into the carpet and her golden hair swish back and forth against her bare back. I shook the thought from my head, and the image was replaced by one of her leaning back at the breakfast table with her arms crossed under her breasts. My god, the woman was something else, she had a power that, if harnessed, could have limitless potential—*to manipulate and control*, I thought darkly. What the hell was her involvement with Osterlund? It occurred to me I should talk again to Zelda

Thomas, Osterlund's mom. It might be an interesting conversation. But it would have to wait.

I left the bar at eight o'clock, picked up the Cadillac from the valet, and drove west into the black abyss of the Mojave Desert. The Caddy's high beams pierced the night, and the narrow two-lane highway unfolded like a thin ribbon across the bleak terrain. My foot rested heavily on the pedal, barbed wire boundary fences raced past in a blur, and old wooden telephone poles flashed by every few seconds, like ancient signposts marking the pathway through an uninhabitable wasteland. The road turned north toward Death Valley, led over a modest rise then fell back, and I brought the Caddy up to 110. There wasn't another car in sight, and once the tripometer showed I'd gone a hundred miles, I slowed, watching for the Welcome to Pahrump sign. I passed it three miles later, took the second right, and drove another five miles into the desolate hills. I had a good suspicion I was lost when I saw a small, weather-beaten sign for the Cat's Meow Ranch.

There were about twenty cars in the dirt and gravel parking lot. The whorehouse stood lonely and forlorn against a shallow hillside, its windows barred, the paint peeling and colorless. A white lamp over the chain-link gate flickered weakly, as if it was the last beacon of hope in a dying land. The wind blew a tumbleweed off the hillside, and it rolled out of the blackness and moved silently across the parking lot, like a ghost in the night. Somewhere in the darkness a solitary coyote howled at the stars, its sad wail echoing thinly in the cold.

I rang the buzzer and went through the gate and into the foyer, which was well heated and larger than I expected. My footsteps thumped loudly on the wooden floorboards, and then I stepped onto the thick red carpet of the parlor, where six prostitutes stood in a lineup.

A buxom blonde introduced herself as Sheri, a young dark-haired girl was Melissa, and a younger blonde in a bikini stared me down with a big smile and said, "Hi, I'm Wild."

I'm sure you are, I thought, and reminded myself I was there on business.

Two very black hookers went as Randi and Brandi, and at the end of the line stood a tall, slender woman with long black hair falling over her shoulders. She had light-brown skin and wide-set, almond-shaped eyes. Her cheekbones were high and looked carved from marble, but there was a noticeable discoloration along her left jawline. I let my eyes wander up and down her body like an appraising customer. Her legs weren't quite full, but they looked muscular. A narrow scar running a couple inches up from her belly button marred her stomach below her primary attributes, a pair of huge double-D-cup breasts that stood out straight from her chest in a classic conical shape. She wore skimpy lingerie that barely covered her nipples.

"Tina," she said.

I asked if she'd like a drink. She nodded, and I followed her to the bar, where two men were sitting with prostitutes, grinning like jackals and talking in loud, drunken voices. The bartender wore tan pants with a black stripe down the side, and carried a holstered .38 revolver on a black gun belt. Armed security guard, doubling as bartender at a cathouse in the middle of nowhere. Seemed like a novel gig, but he just looked bored.

"A Bombay up," she said, then shifted her eyes to me. "What's your name?"

"Does it matter?"

"It doesn't to me if it doesn't to you." She lit a cigarette, letting the smoke drift out of her mouth. Her voice didn't sound jaded or disinterested; instead it was cool, aloof.

"Are you in Vegas with a convention or a gambling trip?" she asked.

I turned on my barstool, looking at her directly. Her eyes were a pretty dark brown, and she met my stare, our eyes locking long enough for both of us to consider who would look away first, and when I didn't she finally did, with the beginning a smile, or maybe a smirk, on the corner of her mouth.

"Do you like my eyes?" she asked.

"Yeah, I do," I said. I was aroused and felt stupid about it, but I let myself be drawn in. She mirrored my gaze, and after a moment she narrowed her expression, then stamped her cigarette out in the ashtray.

"I think we'd better go to my room," she said. "You look like you're ready to party."

I followed her down the hallway to a door toward the end. Her room was just big enough for business: a queen-sized bed, a small lamp on a night table, a portable boom box set up on the dresser.

"Take a seat," she said. "How much are you interested in spending?"

"Uh, I've got a hundred bucks."

She made a clicking sound with her tongue. "That's the house minimum, and I don't work for that. I'll show you a good time, but my rates start at four hundred."

We bargained back and forth, and I finally agreed to two hundred. She told me to take off my clothes and wait, said she'd be back in a minute, then left the room.

I quickly went through her dresser. Only the top two drawers were filled, mostly with assorted lingerie and undergarments. I opened the drawer to her nightstand, saw a tube of lubricant, a box of condoms, and a small makeup bag lying on top of a *People* magazine. I looked under the magazine, and found a black, pocket-size address book. I zipped it into my coat pocket and sat waiting on the bed. A half minute later, she came back through the door.

"You're supposed to take your clothes off," she said, pulling her shoulder straps down.

"How about if we talk a while first, Samantha?" I said.

She froze—her exposed breasts looked plastic and unforgiving. Her brown nipples extended before my eyes, like a dog's fur rising on the back of its neck. She pulled her top back up.

"Who are you?" she said.

"I came from South Lake Tahoe just to see you. The shit's really hit the fan back there."

"I have no idea what you're talking about."

"Yeah, you do. Your gig last Friday at the Crown Ambassador. Somehow it went bad, real bad, and your trick ended up stabbed to death. I went to the autopsy and checked out the knife wound. Pretty damn gruesome."

"You have the wrong person. I haven't been—"

"What happened in that room?"

She stared at me silently, her cheeks hollow, the skin tight on the bone. "Hey, Samantha," I said, stepping toward her. "You think you can hide out here and this thing's gonna go away? If you're an accessory, you'll be a hell of a lot better off if you cooperate. Worst case, you can probably cut yourself a good deal with the DA, maybe—"

"Shut the fuck up," she said.

"What?"

"You think I'm fucking stupid? I don't know who you are or how you found me, but you have no right to come to where I work and start accusing me of whatever this bullshit is you're talking about."

"Listen to me," I said. "The second guy in the room? The big dude with the flattop? He was fished out of Lake Tahoe Sunday with three bullets in his back. They say he was paralyzed but still alive when he was thrown in the lake. He drowned. Whoever's responsible is dead serious, and I'd say as a witness you're next on the list. You really want to live your life looking over one shoulder for the cops and the other for a murderer? That's a lousy existence."

"You know, you'd be funny if you didn't have your head so far up your ass," she said. The eyes I'd been so enthralled with were no longer pretty. Her brow furrowed and crow's feet etched the side of her face.

"You're a pretty tough broad, Samantha. But you're being stupid. What do you think the cops are doing right now? They're testing forensic evidence, and all they need is a person to match it with. I make a quick phone call, and the sheriff from Pahrump will be here in twenty minutes."

She flinched at that, then opened the curtains, stared out the window, and dragged deeply on a fresh cigarette. She stood with her hand on her hip, her back to me, and after a few minutes she glanced at her watch.

"Your time's going to be up soon," she said.

"Look," I said, making my voice quiet, "I'm not the heat. I just want to find out who killed him. Tell me what I need to know, and I can forget I was here. You don't have to let this thing destroy your life."

She turned toward me deliberately. "You gonna call the sheriff?"

"That depends on you."

"You promise not to call, or let anyone know I'm here, I'll tell you who to look for. No details, no questions, but I'll tell you who stabbed him."

"That's pretty thin," I said. "How do I know you won't bullshit me?"

"How do I know you won't walk out of here and call the cops?"

I could hear the heater start blowing warm air through the duct in the ceiling. "You have a name?" I said.

"Nope, just a description. But I'll tell you where to find him."

"That's not enough."

"Then hit the road, because we're done here."

I studied her for a moment, and said, "All right, go ahead."

"You promise not to fuck me?" she said.

"Hey, I paid two hundred."

She laughed, but it was more like a quick snort. "You chose how to spend your time, not me."

"Okay. If your information's good, I won't rat you out."

She sat on the bed and brushed ashes off her bare thigh, and paused just long enough to concern me. Then she said, "He's a big, dark man, not black but maybe Samoan or something. He's not as tall as you, but he's a lot bigger. His body is shaped like a fat torpedo. You'll know him when you see him. He's one *ugly* motherfucker."

"Why did he stab him?" When she shook her head, I said, "Where do I find him?"

"Go hang out at Pistol Pete's in Tahoe."

"Does he work there?"

"I said no questions. That's the deal. You go spend some time at Pistol Pete's, you'll find him."

I moved toward the door, but she stepped in front of me. "What happened to your ear?" she said, eyeing the damaged ridge of cartilage.

"An old knife wound."

She rose on her toes and leaned in close, her voice a throaty whisper. "When you find him, you'll have to kill him. Be ready, he's psycho. Even if you put a gun to his head, he won't back down." She pulled back, and my hand was on the door handle, but before I could leave she grabbed my arm and said, "Kill him, then come back and I'll give you a night of sex you'll never forget."

• • •

Back out at the bar, a group of college kids had taken over, happily drinking and horsing around, teasing the girls, arm wrestling, and playing the jukebox up loud. I felt a twinge of nostalgia, like I was looking back at a scene out of my youth, and for a moment I was tempted to have a drink with the boys. But my ski jacket was heavy with the weight of Samantha's address book, so I went out into the night like a grown man with obligations, and drove through the desert badlands back to Las Vegas.

17

I WAS DEAD SOBER when I pulled into the Excalibur at one in the morning, and I fell into bed and slept straight through to nine o'clock. When I woke I tried to figure my next move, but my head danced with visions of Samantha's body, and I had to take a cold shower so I could think without the distraction.

The fact that Samantha had fled from Reno to work a six-week stint at a remote brothel in southern Nevada suggested she was hiding from the law, or the killer, or both. Actually, it was an ideal place to lie low, hide out, and make money. She could live there and never leave the building, or use a credit card, or leave a phone trail. It was a good place to turn invisible.

But if she wasn't somehow involved in the murder as a knowing accomplice, why wouldn't she go to the police? Was she that scared of the man she thought might be Samoan? Or had she become implicated by an unwitting circumstance, and felt she could be accused of a crime she didn't commit? She could possibly even be the murderer, although I couldn't imagine her having the strength to ram a knife all the way through Sylvester Bascom.

One thing I didn't doubt was she knew a lot more than she told me. I began to feel increasingly uneasy about her story of the ugly man at Pistol Pete's. It could be a complete lie—he could be anyone, maybe someone she despised for different reasons—assuming he actually even existed. She could have made up the story on the spot to buy time and get me out of there.

I cut myself shaving and threw down the razor in disgust. What about her boyfriend, Mr. 187? What was his involvement, and what did he know? If he drove Samantha to Vegas, he'd probably be in violation of his parole. I might be able to use that as leverage to get him to talk.

The coffee shop downstairs was still crowded for breakfast at ten o'clock. I sat at a small table, drinking coffee, waiting for the waitress to bring my order. A keno runner came by, and I filled out three four-spot cards for two bucks each. Then I opened my notepad and started working on a list of things to do.

After none of my keno numbers hit, I went back to my room and called Gloria Damone at Dana's Escorts. Ten rings later I hung up and called directory service for her home number. She was listed and answered promptly. She didn't sound happy to hear from me.

"How'd you get my number?" she said.

"You're listed."

"That doesn't give you the right to call me at home."

"I apologize for the imposition."

"Well, please don't call me here. Or anywhere, for that matter."

"Can you tell me if you've heard from Beverly Howitt?"

"Not a word."

"Do you have any idea where she is?

"None whatsoever," she said, and the line went dead.

My next call was to directory service in Utah. There were six listings for Howitt, and one was in Salina. I called the number, and the woman who answered had a tired, impatient voice.

"Is Beverly there?"

"No, she's not."

"I'm calling from payroll services, and we have a check for her. Do you know how I can contact her?"

"I don't know. I heard she's back in town, but I haven't seen her. I suppose you can mail it here."

"Are you her mother?" I asked.

"No, her aunt."

I took down the address, then booked a one o'clock Delta flight to Salt Lake City. Salina was a small town about 140 miles south of Salt Lake, nestled in a five-mile-wide valley between the ten-thousand-foot peaks of the Fishlake National Forest. I had spent a night there about fifteen years ago with Cody Gibbons. I was visiting him in Salt Lake, and we decided to road trip to the Grand Canyon after a boring night of trying to get drunk on 3.2 Utah beer. It was springtime, and I remembered the country as clean and verdant. Cody had insisted we stay in Salina because he wanted to check out a well-known country-western bar called Stigs. I wondered if it was still there.

I checked out of the Excalibur, and on the way out I saw the family from the airplane in the hotel's bus terminal. The teenage boy sat close to his mother and away from his father, who was slumped over asleep at the other end of a long bench. There was a big group of older folks waiting in the crowded area, and some stood rather than sit near him, as if he had a communicable disease.

I dropped off the Caddy, found a bar in the airport, and dialed Wenger's office number. I got his answering machine as I'd hoped, and left a brief message telling him I'd be away at least through the end of the week. Then I called Edward Cutlip.

"Mr. Bascom's pissed," he said nervously.

"At who?"

"Me, you, the world. Actually, he's mad because the Tahoe detectives haven't returned his calls. He's making life miserable for everyone around here."

"Maybe my news will put him in a better mood."

"Yeah?"

"I found one of the call girls who was in Sylvester's room. She's a hard-core hooker who's probably been riding around on the back of a Harley since she had pigtails. She claims to know who stabbed Sylvester and gave me a description and told me where to find him. Says he's an easy guy to find, stands out like a chicken at a dog show."

"So you're on your way back here?"

"No, I'm flying to Salt Lake City."

"Why?"

"I think there were two girls in the room. I want to talk to the second one and get her story before I do anything."

"Okay. It sounds like you're making progress. That's good news, Mr. Bascom should be glad to hear it. How soon you think it'll be until you crack the case?"

"I don't know. Did you make any progress on the bank records?"

"Yeah, I'll have them next Monday. They put a rush on it."

"Good. Have you heard anything more from Raneswich and Iverson?"

"Nope, they've gone incommunicado since Mr. Bascom dressed them down yesterday."

"Raneswich strikes me as so uptight you couldn't pull a needle out of his ass with a tractor."

Edward laughed. "Call me tomorrow," he said.

I ordered a sandwich at the bar and declined a six dollar beer. Then I called Cody Gibbons.

"You'll never guess where I'm headed right now," I said.

"Gimme a clue."

"Stigs."

"What? You got to be kidding, you're going to Salina?"

"You got it. I'll be getting drunk at Stigs tonight."

"Good luck. They closed that joint years ago. Remember I pulled that babe out of there and you ended up sleeping in the car?"

"You'd never let me forget it," I said.

"She was good-looking too."

"My ass."

"What? You still sound bitter, Dirty."

"Damn right. I froze my ass that night."

"You're going to Salina for your case?"

"Yeah," I said, and gave him a short version of Bascom's murder and my findings.

"I got the records you asked for," he said after I finished. "Edward Cutlip has nothing but a few traffic violations, and the same for Sylvester Bascom. But Sven Osterlund is a different story: shoplifting and a couple busts for assault and battery, two DUI arrests and one conviction, a cocaine possession that was dropped, and an indecent exposure for pissing on the street in front of a bar. He's been represented by Lawrence Stein on his last couple arrests, and Stein's made a fortune defending wealthy lowlifes. It looks likes Osterlund's managed to avoid any serious jail time."

"Tell Stein he won't be representing Osterlund again, if you see him around the courthouse."

"Why's that?"

"Because dead men don't pay their bills too well."

"Osterlund's dead?"

"Yeah. Somebody shot him and dumped him in Lake Tahoe."

"Well, fuckin'-A. Hey, man, why don't I meet you in Tahoe when you get back? It sounds like you might need some backup." Then he lowered his voice. "I got to get out of here. Being home all the time is causing problems with my wife."

"I don't know if that would work. I've been busy as hell, Cody."

"So? Come on, I'll watch your back. Maybe I can help you, run license plates, you know? I got people who owe me favors at the precinct."

It sounded like a bad idea. I wanted to keep a low profile, and Cody's style was about as subtle as a buffalo stampede at a tea party.

"I don't even know when I'll be back in Tahoe," I said, but I knew I didn't sound convincing.

"How about if I call you Friday morning and drive up? You should be back by then, huh? Really, man, I got to split. Debbie and I had just patched things up, and now it's going bad again. Our relationship is better when I'm not around so much. I'm serious."

"Cody, I can't afford a shit storm in Tahoe. I got too much at stake to let things get out of control."

"What? What? Hey, you got my word I'll be mellow. Just easy times and slow beers. You know me."

"Yeah, I do know you. That's what scares me. All right, give me a call Friday, and we'll talk."

"We'll have a hell of a time, Dirt. Just like the old days!"

• • •

The wind was gusting when my flight took off, which made for a rough ride to Salt Lake. I sat in a row by myself in the half-full plane, watching the features of Las Vegas grow small and fall away. I reached into my pocket for Samantha's address book and slowly went through the pages, trying to read life into the anonymous names and numbers. The book wasn't very full. I counted sixteen female and nine male names, one of which could belong to Mr. 187. Toward the back, under X, Y and Z, were a number of sketches, mostly faces, of both men and women. They were well drawn, and I studied them for a while, then put the book away and closed my eyes. But I found the faces strangely compelling, as if perhaps they told a story, and I took the book out and was still staring at the drawings when the plane touched down.

18

SALT LAKE CITY LOOKED an ugly gray, as it always did in winter. The mountains that loomed over the city were snowcapped and foreboding and seemed to cast a pall over the uniformly dull and lifeless downtown buildings. Even the trees were bare and without color. You could film a movie here in black and white, and no one would know the difference.

I rented a Ford sedan and headed south. Once I'd been on the road for half an hour, the country opened up and the landscape turned green and picturesque. I turned off the interstate south of Nephi and drove a few miles down Highway 28 before pulling over at a small country market for a can of beer. A mountain range studded with fir and pine bordered the highway on the right, and a broad meadow lay to the left. A stream babbled faintly in the distance, and the wind made a rushing sound through the trees. The air felt cold and fresh on my face, in contrast to the smoggy grit of the city.

It was twilight when I rolled into Salina. The main drag of the small town was quiet, almost deserted, leaving the impression it was always silent and still here, as if the local population had long ago given up any hope of exuberance.

I spotted a state liquor store and picked up two pints of booze. A small hotel at the end of the street advertised color TV and cable. I checked in, and while the clerk did the paperwork, I read a thin brochure describing activities in Salina and the city's history.

Salina, the Spanish word for "salt," was named for the large salt deposits in the area. The primary recreation was fishing and hunting in the nearby Fishlake area, and the biggest employer was the coal mine thirty miles east of town in Salina Canyon. The town had been abandoned in 1872 because of Indian troubles, but was resettled in 1886, and today has a population of slightly over two thousand. It made for good reading to pass the time, but didn't give me any hint where Beverly Howitt might be found.

I stayed in my room long enough to brush my teeth and drag a comb through my hair, then I drove around town for a few minutes until I found the address on Third Street where Beverly's aunt lived. It was a small green home with a tar driveway and a shake roof so old it looked like a strong breeze would blow the shingles into the street. But the house was dark, the driveway empty, and no one answered when I knocked. I considered waiting in my car across the street, but I hadn't had dinner, and the pint of whiskey on my passenger seat kept whispering my name. So I drove back to Main Street and found a bar toward the end of town in a crumbling stucco structure with an old Western-style wood plank façade.

When I went in, every eye in the place turned to me, like they hadn't seen a new face for years. A couple of grizzled ranch hands sat at the battle-scared bar, drinking Coors bottles, their faces set with hard expressions and bleak eyes. Next to them was a middle-aged woman who looked like she might have been a schoolteacher or maybe worked at a general store. She wore her hair pinned up, and her dress had gone out of style decades ago. At the end of the bar, an old hippie wearing a green fatigue jacket and tattered blue jeans sat holding a bottle in a brown paper bag. He had long, dirty hair, a scraggly beard, and was smoking Pall Mall non-filters.

I took a seat on a rickety bar stool. The bar top was marred by hundreds of cigarette burns, and half of the lacquer had peeled off. In the back of the joint was a kitchen with a pass-through window cut out of the wall. The bartender was talking to someone; after a minute he took his foot off the sinks and came my way, flipping a coaster neatly in front of me.

"What you d-d-drinkin', buddy?" he said.

"Seven-Up." I pulled a pint of whiskey from my coat and set it on the bar, leaving it in the brown paper bag, as was the custom.

He served my drink and lit a smoke. "Where you from? We don't g-g-get a lot of out-of-towners." His eyes were green and wide, and he looked at me with frank interest, as he smoothed down his long Yosemite Sam mustache.

"Reno."

"D-d-d-did you drive across the desert?" He pointed with his finger while he stuttered, as if the motion would help his enunciation. His eyes never left mine.

"No, I don't trust my car. I took a plane."

"G-g-good idea. You don't want to break d-down in that frickin' desert. You gonna eat? We got good food here." He pushed a handwritten menu to me.

I ordered a burger and fries and sipped the stiff drink I'd made myself. Two young women came in and sat at a table. They seemed to be already drunk; one was swaying in her chair while the other poured clear liquor into her glass with an unsteady hand. The bartender came back from the kitchen, and I waved at him to come over.

"Another Seven?"

"Yeah, thanks. I've got a question for you, if you don't mind."

"Ask away, buddy."

"Have you heard of a lady named Beverly Howitt?"

He broke into a smile. "Sure, I know her. She's the b-b-best-looking woman to ever come out of this town."

"No kidding? I've been trying to reach her. Any idea where she might be?"

"What for?"

"Something she wants to keep confidential, I think."

He considered that, then said "Last I heard, she left town. Must have been a couple months ago."

"How about her parents? Are they local?"

"Her mom is. She's very sick," he said, leaning forward. "Cancer, I believe. I think she's at the hospital in Richfield." The phone rang behind the bar and he picked it up.

"R-r, r-r," he stammered, then took the phone from his ear and looked at it. "They frickin' hung up." He hiked himself up and sat on the back bar.

"Does she have a boyfriend in town?"

"Huh," he laughed. "She used to be with Sam the Gum-Out Man. It was only b-b-because of his money. He's twice her age, but now he's singing the broken heart blues. He usually comes in a little later."

I freshened my drink. "You want a taste?" I said, wiggling the whiskey bottle at him.

A half hour later, the pint was gone. The hippie had come over to bum a shot, and the bartender, whose name was Rasmussen, had a drink. I produced a bottle of vodka and poured a round. The dusk turned to night, and my purpose seemed to slip behind me. I tried not to get drunk, and after a while I returned the vodka to my car and started drinking straight soda. At around eight-thirty, a man with sandy hair and a bloated complexion walked in and ordered a drink. The bartender nudged me with his knuckle.

"There's the g-g-g...the Gum-Out Man."

"Who?"

"Sam the Gum-Out Man."

The man sat alone at a table, a highball glass and brown-bagged bottle in front of him.

"Excuse me," I said, walking up and pulling back a chair. "Do you mind?"

He looked up at me, a flicker of surprise passing through his bleary eyes. "Be my guest."

He was a good-sized fellow, thick in the chest and gut, with a neck like a bull. But his shoulders hunched forward as if his head was an unbearable weight, and his face sagged deeply. He looked so melancholy and defeated I said, "You okay?"

He took a breath and sighed heavily. "It ain't anything I haven't been through before. You'd think a man my age would know better."

"Woman problems?"

He nodded, looking at me sadly, looking for someone, anyone, who would listen. I was probably the only one in the joint who hadn't heard his story.

"Yeah. Jesus. You know what kills me about it? I'm almost fifty years old, and I haven't figured it out yet."

"What's that?"

He raised his eyes, not wondering why I cared, just happy to have someone to talk to, even if it was a stranger.

"Dan Reno," I said, and stuck out my hand. He shook my hand with his meaty paw, but his grip had no conviction.

"Sam McMurray." He sipped on his drink, then put it down and hit straight off the bottle.

"I spent fifteen years married to the same woman," he said. "By the time we got divorced, we could barely stand to be in the same room together. It's like our whole relationship, everything we ever felt for each other, had slowly eroded, one day at a time, until there was nothing left." He paused. "So finally I'm free, single, and I'm ready to take control of my life, right?"

I nodded.

"I hire this girl to work in my store. She's young, cheerful, innocent—I didn't even think about how beautiful she was because she was so young. But somehow we connect, and it goes from there, you know how it is—it happens. She makes me feel like a teenager, like I'm alive again. And then it's like I'm addicted, and she's the drug. I can't stop thinking about her, and then the more I want, the less she gives. I feel like such an idiot, a man my age. God!" He took another swig off his bottle.

"Beverly Howitt," I said.

"What, how, how…do you know her?"

"She's in trouble and needs help. Can you tell me where to find her?"

"What kind of trouble?"

"It happened in Reno. I think she witnessed a murder, and the killer wants to keep her quiet."

"How in the world?"

"She was in the wrong place at the wrong time."

"She's probably at the hospital with her mother, Glenda." He looked at his watch. "You leave now, maybe you can catch her."

•   •   •

The hospital was a larger, more modern facility than I expected. My boots echoed off the tile floor as I went through the automatic sliding doors and across the empty admittance area. I asked the duty nurse for Glenda Howitt's room; she gave me the room number and warned that visiting hours ended in five minutes.

The door to the room on the third floor was closed. I waited in the hallway, breathing the sterile hospital air. A nurse walked by, pushing an old man in a wheelchair. His skin was spotted and hung from his bones, his fingers stuck out from his plaid robe like bird claws, and his head bobbed slowly as he went by me. I looked away, but a cold hand shot out and grabbed my wrist with surprising strength.

"I was like you once," he rasped, his voice thin but forceful, as if a lifetime of hard work and battles had forged an inner strength only death could take from him.

"I believe you," I said. The nurse pushed him by without a word.

Beverly Howitt slipped out into the hallway a couple of minutes later. She wore jeans, tennis shoes, and a pink sweatshirt, and it was easy to see why Sam McMurray had fallen for her. She wore little makeup that I could tell, but she didn't need to, for she had perfect skin and the face of a beauty queen. Her hair was red with a hint of blond, and it fell over her ears and onto her neck like a spring waterfall. She looked at me with blue eyes, eyes that were hurt and vulnerable but knowing, and cocked her head.

"Miss Howitt?" I said.

"Yes?"

"My name's Dan Reno. I flew here from Reno because it's important we talk."

"What about?" she said, licking her lips and blinking.

"What happened last Friday night in Tahoe."

"What?"

"Miss Howitt, may I call you Beverly?" She nodded. "With your help, the people responsible for what happened can be arrested. As long as they're still on the streets, you and others are in danger."

Her face looked angelic, her lips parting, her blue eyes searching, and a tear rolled down her cheek.

"Oh god," she said, and covered her face. I put my arm around her and held her awkwardly, my hand feeling like an uninvited weight on her shoulder.

• • •

I followed her to a lounge down the street called The Detour. The bar was dark and narrow, but further in the interior opened to a less dimly lit area with a stage and cocktail tables. There was a handful of customers in the bar area. I ordered us two bottles of 3.2 beer, then we went into the back of the place and took a table against the wall.

She had composed herself, sitting with her arms crossed as if she was cold. Then she took a big swallow off her beer and had a coughing fit.

"I'm sorry. It went down the wrong way. I can't even drink right."

"Try this," I said, offering the half-full pint of vodka.

"Oh." She smiled, her teeth clicking. "Can you get me an orange juice? No, how about pineapple?"

I went to the bar and brought back a mixture of Collins mix and fruit juices and made her a drink.

"Mmm, very good. I bet you've been a bartender."

"At times."

"Really? But you're a detective now. Sounds exciting."

"Just trying to make a living."

"Oh, don't be so modest. I'm sure you have a lot of interesting stories."

I made her another drink and one for myself, and an hour later I still hadn't asked her a question about the case. When I spoke she rested her eyes on mine, laughing at my attempts to be witty, laughing at things I said that most women I dated simply ignored. There was something special about her, and it wasn't just the way she looked. In the hour we'd been there, she had me relaxed and feeling charming and suave. I wondered if she had that effect on every man she met, or maybe there was a certain chemistry between us. Or maybe she just wanted to avoid talking about the events of last week. I decided it was time to steer the conversation to the issue at hand.

"We need to talk about what happened in Tahoe."

"I don't quite know where to start," she said.

"Tell me everything," I said, and she did, and then some.

Beverly Howitt was born in Salina, at a time when America was still hung over from the lingering stages of the hippie era. She remembered her father as a tall, handsome man with long blond hair who never wore a shirt in the summer and worked occasionally as a miner or a laborer. One day when she was around ten years old, he left to look for work, and never came home. Beverly's mother, Glenda, checked with the police, the local hospitals, called everyone who knew him, and then when there was nothing left to do, she waited by her front window, watching the season turn from fall to winter.

Eventually Glenda Howitt made do by working a day shift at the supermarket and waiting tables by night. Beverly was left to fend for herself while her mother worked, and the worst part was fighting off the advances of her uncle, who used to live with her aunt in the green house on Third Street. He was a shiftless, mean drunkard; one morning he was found dead in his car outside a bar.

Beverly waited for her father to return until one night her mother told her flatly, "He's never coming back. It's just you and me." They lived with an unspoken resolve to someday have a better life. But Glenda Howitt never found a suitor worthy of being stepfather to Beverly, and she grew even more selective as time passed. Beverly began attending high school and became promiscuous, looking for comfort and friendship. "I finally found something I was good at, and it was something that gave me control," she said, but by the time she was a senior, at a time when many of her classmates were just beginning to experiment, she'd come full circle and had stopped dating, even if she knew the boy had honorable intentions.

Glenda Howitt was diagnosed with breast cancer when Beverly was nineteen. At first the doctors thought there was a non-malignant growth on her chest, but it became more painful as the tumor grew. The cancer spread, and they removed her left breast and later her right. The medical bills rapidly spiraled beyond her means. Finally the inevitable happened, and Glenda was forced to sell her home. With few options, Beverly and her mother moved in with her aunt, a bitter, frugal widow. The cancer continued to eat away at Glenda Howitt, spreading to her ovaries and lymph nodes. She was spending more time in the hospital than out, and the bills grew as if they were an extension of the cancer itself. The hospital continued to care for her, but sent an aggressive collection agency out of Salt Lake for the payments.

"We were in trouble; we were almost completely broke, and that's when I made the decision," Beverly told me. "I told Mom I got a good job in Reno, that I'd bring money home. I used the last credit on my charge card to buy her a new dress for Christmas, then got on a Greyhound bus. Twelve hours later, on my twenty-second birthday, I was hired by Dana's."

"Were you okay with the work?" I asked.

"Of course not. I'm not that kind of person." Her eyes flashed at me like I'd just crawled out of a sewer.

"I'm sorry. I guess I don't want to make any assumptions about what a professional escort does."

She looked at me, trying to decide whether I was a liar or a fool. But then her eyes softened.

"Oh, you mean did I go out to dinner or business functions with rich men and get paid three hundred dollars? That actually happened—once. But every other time…" her voice tailed off.

"After a while you learn to turn your mind off. Click, just like a light switch. Half of the men are so drunk they can't do it, and then there are ones who just want to talk. It's almost like being a nurse in a way. But I was good, good at my job." She looked away, pride and anger etched across her face. "I did it for my mother, and I don't regret it. But now it's too late, it's all meaningless." I reached over and touched her fingers, and she clenched my wrist tightly with her hands.

"I have twelve thousand in the bank. But I've decided not to pay the hospital another penny. Mom will be gone soon, and she deserves a proper funeral. Screw the hospital and the collectors."

I was quiet for a minute, letting the moment go, feeling helpless to say anything that would ease her pain. I could hear the knocking of pool balls and the faint clinking of bottles and glasses from the bar up front.

"Let's talk about what happened Friday night," I said, and her eyes jumped, as if she just remembered why we were there. She leaned back and shuddered.

"I got a call for a job at the Crown Ambassador Friday around ten-thirty. It was a two-girl party, with a guaranteed three-hundred-fifty rate, plus tips. I was told to meet another girl there, Samantha. I drove myself in my old Plymouth and got there a little before midnight. I met Samantha in the lobby, and she says this guy's supposed to be a big spender. So we go up to the room, and he lets us in."

"Just one guy?"

"Well, yes."

"Would you describe him, please?"

"Oh, about average height, pretty good shape, thinning hair–"

"Did he pay you cash?"

"No. He gave Dana's his credit card number, so it was all prepaid. But I was hoping for a good tip."

I figured it must have been Bascom's credit card, not Osterlund's, since Osterlund's credit would have been revoked after his bankruptcy. Sylvester probably hadn't considered that once he was married, Desiree might have been tempted to take a peek at his credit card statement. A thousand dollar charge to an escort service would be hard to explain. Regardless, the Tahoe police must have a bead on it by now; checking credit card usage would be one of the first things they'd do. Which would lead them to Gloria at Dana's Escorts, and to Samantha and Beverly. Of the two, Beverly would be easier to find.

"Okay. So you go in the room."

"Yeah. And then, we do…what we do."

"Go on."

"We were there for about a half an hour, and suddenly Samantha's standing up, and this strange man is in the room."

"Hold on. Did Samantha let him in?"

"I didn't see her. I wasn't looking at the time."

"Did Samantha seem surprised?"

"No, I don't think so. I remember her putting her clothes on."

"What happened then?"

"Well, I was on top of the trick. We were, well, in the act. The strange man pushed me off the bed and grabbed the trick by the neck and told him to hand over his wallet."

"Did he have a knife?"

"No."

"Or gun?"

"Not that I saw."

"I'd like you to think back and describe him in as much detail as possible," I said.

"Let's see. He was tall and had on a ratty-looking white t-shirt. His arms were covered with tattoos, and he had blond hair and a long mustache and beard. But not on the side of his face, only over his mouth and on his chin."

"A goatee," I said.

"Yes. He wore dark blue Levi's with a thick black belt."

"Did Samantha ever say his name?"

"No."

"What happened next?"

"I was on the ground next to the bed, and the man keeps on saying, 'Give me your fucking wallet,' then the closet door flies open, and this guy jumps out, yelling like Bruce Lee or somebody, and kicks the tattooed guy in the head."

"Out of the closet?"

"Yes. It startled me."

"Did you know someone was in the closet beforehand?"

"No."

"What do you think he was doing there?"

"He was spying on us. That was my original impression. When he came out, he was holding this square thing. It looked like it might have been a camera."

"Was it a cell phone?"

"No, it was bigger."

"Like a video camera?"

"I really don't know what one looks like."

I handed her my notepad. "Draw me a picture."

She drew a rectangle.

"That's it? What color was it? How big was it?"

"God, it all happened so fast, and I didn't get that good a look. It was black and maybe six inches long by three or four inches."

"Describe the guy in the closet."

"Big, muscular, suntanned. He had a crew cut, or a flattop, actually."

"Then what happened?"

"After he jumped out and kicked the tattooed guy, he punched him a couple times—really hard. Then Samantha opens the door, and I thought she was going to run out, but she didn't, and another man comes in. He had dark skin, but he wasn't black or Mexican—he looked Hawaiian, maybe. He was medium height, not as tall as you, but he was very big. His body was shaped like an oak barrel, and his face, I can't even describe it—I've never seen a scarier looking person."

She pressed her fingers to her temples and looked like she might be ill. I started to say something, but she interrupted.

"I'll be okay, just give me a second." She squeezed her eyes tight, took a couple breaths, then started again.

"The ugly, dark-skinned man grabbed the guy with the flattop. Then the naked guy, the trick, he gets up and starts punching at the tattooed guy and the dark one. I was hiding on the other side of the bed, and then, and then, this all happened so fast, but then I heard this terrible sound, and when I looked up I saw the knife come through his back. I wanted to scream, and I tried to, but I was so scared no sound would come. The flattop guy ran out, and the dark one was holding this huge knife, dripping blood. I stayed curled up next to the bed with my hands over my eyes, shaking I was so scared, and then they were gone."

"Did you hear them say anything?"

"They were cussing, but that's about it."

"Did they say anything to you?"

"No, but I was hiding on the floor next to the bed. They just ignored me and left."

"What did you do then?"

"I got up, and when I saw the body, I freaked. There was so much blood, it was pumping out of him. I panicked and threw up on the floor. When I looked at him again, his eyes were open but not moving. I ran out, and I forgot which way the elevators were, so I took the stairs and got to my car. But I was too scared to drive all the way to Reno, so I drove the other way and found a little hotel in Meyers. I stayed there until five A.M., dozed a little, then I drove to my apartment in Reno, threw my stuff in a suitcase, and drove and drove until I got back to Salina."

I wanted to ask her more questions, press for more details, but she didn't look well. I touched her hand, and we sat in the silence of the room for a few minutes until the bartender said, "Closing time, folks."

When we reached her car she still looked shaky, and I asked if she was okay to drive. She paused, then said quietly, "I don't want to be alone tonight. Can I go with you?"

She followed me back up the interstate to Salina, to the hotel where I was staying. It was almost midnight when we parked in front of my room. We went in, and I tossed a pillow on the floor.

"No, you don't have to," she said, but I told her to take the bed. Then I lay down on the floor in my clothes, with my jacket as a blanket, and slept.

Somewhere in the dark dreaminess of night, a voice drifted on the outskirts of my consciousness, calling my name from some distant place. I tried to ignore it, but the voice persisted, pulling me out of my dreamscape and into the fuzzy blackness of the room.

"You're talking in your sleep," she said, kneeling over me. "Come to bed."

•   •   •

The gray dawn seeped into the room through the thin curtains. I felt the warmth of Beverley's body and the steadiness of her breathing. I reached down to check that my jeans were on, and my breath caught in my throat when my hand brushed her bare thigh. I moved away from her and closed my eyes, hoping for deep slumber and pure dreams. But my mind wouldn't shut off, and I had that restless insomnia that often haunts me after drinking. So I lay next to Beverly Howitt, and my thoughts wandered to my past as I waited out the morning.

After losing my first job out of college with Bill Ortega, I swore off the booze and was hired by Ray Lorretta Bail Bonds. I spent the next three years dead sober, until I went to work for Wenger. Thinking back, I remembered that one of my greatest fears of drying out had been boredom. I learned that it takes a while after going sober to figure out how to replace all those hours previously spent on a barstool. But I quickly saw that working for Ray Lorretta was a lifestyle that was anything but boring. Ray was one of about thirty bail bondsmen in the San Jose area, and he lived at a wildly fast pace.

He was tall and handsome and usually had three or four women revolving through his private office on any given month. How he managed to do this while maintaining his relationship with his wife and three kids was beyond me. He ran a full-page ad in the Yellow Pages, and after seducing the young lady who sold him the ad, he gave her a picture of himself from the shoulders up and told her to include it in the layout. The photo looked like it was taken at a modeling agency. His hair was tousled just right, and he had a cavalier, devil-may-care expression on his chiseled mug. I laughed when I saw the ad, but the number of attractive ladies who came through the doors increased to the point that I found myself showing up early, brown bagging my lunch, and not leaving until well into the evening. When it came to womanizing, Ray had incredible energy and charm, but even he couldn't handle the steady volume of good-looking women the ad brought in, and I did fine with the ones he couldn't fit into his schedule.

Despite Ray's preoccupation with bedding down as many women as possible, he approached his work with deadly seriousness. The stream of lowlifes flowing through his office often mistook Ray's movie star looks as a sign of weakness, and that led to some interesting situations. While working for Bill Ortega, I'd dealt with desperate, violent types on a regular basis, but with Ray, dangerous confrontations and altercations were almost a daily event.

During my first day on the job, three local *cholos* came into the office and copped an attitude. They were trying to post bond for a fellow gang member arrested for dealing, and their collateral was bullshit. The ringleader leaned over Ray's desk, started into his intimidation routine, and Ray zapped him with a 300,000-volt jolt from his Panther stun baton.

The second man pulled a switchblade and ran face first into a dose of pepper spray that made his mother's red-hot chili taste like vanilla ice cream. The last guy was a little less tough, or maybe a little smarter. He started waving a knife and screaming a blue streak of Spanish profanity, while trying to back out of range without seeming chicken. When I finally fumbled my Beretta out of my desk drawer, I think the dude was relieved to see a gun instead of another non-lethal enforcement device.

"Hell, boy, I heard you were quick on the draw," Ray said, then came around his desk, gesturing at the uninjured gang member with his stun gun. "Go visit Mendoza Bail Bonds on Seventh and San Antonio. He'll take care of you if you show some manners." The trio limped out and drove off in their lowered Chevy.

"You think they'll be back?" I asked.

"If they do, you better be ready," he said, as a gorgeous black woman walked in and followed Ray to his private back office.

With my first paycheck, I bought the same combination stun baton-pepper spray device that Ray owned. I also decided I needed a bulletproof vest, but the model I wanted was over $500, and I couldn't afford it. There were cheaper models of body armor, but they didn't have threat level IIIA stopping power. I told Ray I'd have to wait a month or so before buying a vest, hoping he would take pity on me and ease up on provoking his criminal clientele into life-threatening situations. He looked at me with an appraising expression, then rose from his desk and motioned for me to follow him to his back office.

On the opposite end of the room, across from the curved bar with padded rail, entertainment center, and king-sized bed, was a large wooden cabinet Ray used to store his weapons and assorted gear. He unlocked it and chose an armored vest from three that were hanging.

"Try it on," he said. The vest was tight on me. I was somewhat broader in the chest and shoulders than Ray and definitely thicker in the gut. "Drop about ten pounds off those love handles and it'll be a perfect fit," he said, helping me adjust the straps.

"Is it level three-A?" I asked. I had become familiar with the safety ratings, and I didn't see any logic in wearing a vest if it couldn't stop a .44 Magnum round.

"You bet, son. It's also saved my ass a few times, so it's got good karma."

I guessed the fact it saved him was good, but the fact he'd been shot was bad. I wasn't sure how karma fit in, but I gladly accepted the vest all the same.

I worked three years for Ray Lorretta, sober as a Mormon bishop, and traveled all over the Western states chasing skips. When business with Ray was slow, I also did some freelance bounty hunting. Ray taught me how to apprehend and secure subjects quickly and efficiently, and I became good at it. I grew to have a great appreciation for Ray's central theme, which was "Do unto others before they do unto you." This was no business for a negotiator, a talker, or someone who needed to be angry in order to use violence.

There were times when I hesitated, and I paid the price. Two brothers in Austin, Texas, once gunned me down in a rock-and-roll club when I lost the element of surprise. I wanted to avoid a situation in a crowded area, but somehow they were on to me and opened fire without warning. I was hit twice, but was able to shoot the younger brother in the ass as he ran out the front door. The older brother sprinted into the street and was crushed underneath a bus. I walked away with two bruises that looked like raised knuckles sticking out of my midsection, but Ray's Kevlar vest saved my life.

The nature of my work required a good level of fitness, and after losing a foot race to a forty-six-year-old man in Las Vegas, I started working out. I had been a wrestler in high school and junior college, and the old habits came back more quickly than I expected. I hit the weights hard, jogged nightly, and rode a mountain bike in the hills above Los Gatos on a regular schedule. I lost twenty pounds, and at the age of thirty, I was stronger and only about five pounds heavier than when I wrestled in college.

Ray was envious of my new physique, and one night he got drunk and challenged me to a wrestling match. We moved the desks, and I pinned him three times in two minutes. He paid me back by getting me into the boxing ring. We put on the headgear and sixteen-ounce gloves, and he soundly whipped me. I had him teach me the fundamentals, how to move and time punches. We boxed once a week, and I spent a couple extra nights a week at the ring. A month later I boxed him to a draw.

Ray's wife finally caught on to his lifestyle and trapped him one afternoon in his office with a blonde in her early twenties. His wife went psycho and chased him around the office with a knife until finally the cops showed up and subdued her. She never said a word to me, but on her way out she slapped me across the face as hard as she could.

In the ensuing divorce settlement, Ray was forced to sell his business. I was disappointed but not surprised, and secretly somewhat relieved. Working for Ray was exciting, but after a while the novelty wore off, and I needed a break from the endless parade of gangbangers, drug addicts, sexual predators, murderers, and miscellaneous douchebags. As I left Ray's office for the last time, I wondered if I was too old to try a different career. Instead, I went to work for Wenger.

• • •

Beverly insisted on taking me out to breakfast when she awoke. She seemed happy and chipper, while I groused about trying to figure out where to get a cup of coffee. She brought me one from the check-in office, then left to change at her hotel down the street. I washed away my hangover with a second cup and four aspirin. The smell of diesel and the heavy sounds of big rigs signaled the beginning of the workday. I waited outside my door, watching the long-haul and local truckers slowly rumble through town. I was still there when Beverly pulled in and parked her beat-up Plymouth.

"You sure look perky," I said, watching her walk toward me. She wore fresh jeans, modest heels, and a purple sweater.

"I feel a lot better after talking last night," she said, then took me by the hand and led me across the street like a mother walking her child to school. We went into the local diner, which looked like it hadn't changed since the 1950s. It was busy; waitresses bustled about in a hurried but efficient manner, juggling plates, glasses, menus, and order tickets, dodging each other in the narrow walkways. A table of miners, looking haggard and blackened even before work, stood to leave, and we sat in their booth while a busboy cleared the table.

Beverly smiled, her face radiant. Her smile was like a burst of sunshine. The restaurant seemed to become brighter.

"I've been coming here since I was a little girl," she said. I looked at her, and it occurred to me this place might be one of the few happy memories from her childhood.

"It's a great old place," I said.

"It sure is." A waitress came by and took our order. Beverly ordered a Belgian waffle with extra whipped cream and chocolate syrup. I had toast.

"You can't imagine what it's been like to hold everything in," she said. "I didn't want to go to the police. I was afraid they'd arrest me for being a call girl, or maybe think I was involved in some way. Thank you for being kind last night. You make me feel safe for some reason, and I really needed that."

"You've been through a lot."

"Most men would try to take advantage."

We were silent for a moment. "Why do they call Sam 'The Gum-Out Man?'" I asked. I didn't mean to startle her. I was asking mostly out of curiosity, but her mouth dropped.

"You really are a private investigator, aren't you?"

"It's not hard to find people when they're not trying to hide. Especially in a small town. I ran into Sam last night at the bar at the end of the road."

"You mean Rasmussen's? That's where he'd be, I guess."

"So why do they call him that? It's an odd name."

"He used to be a big coke head, and he always rubbed it on his gums. He did a little dealing too—it made him feel cool, I think."

"He seems like a decent fellow."

"He was nice to me. But I've learned it's not a good idea to date a man who has more problems than I do."

"I hope things go better for you, Beverly," I said. "You deserve happiness, maybe more than a lot of people."

"That's a sweet thing to say."

"You've had a tough childhood. Some people would let that destroy them. But I think you have a good heart."

"You know, I don't think anyone's ever said something like that to me." She was still smiling, but her eyes filled with tears.

The waitress brought our orders and left the check.

"Are you going back to Reno today?"

"Yeah, I'll need to get to the airport."

"I was hoping you might hang around town for a day or two," she said.

"I can always come back."

Her face said she didn't believe me.

"I mean it," I said.

"Okay." Her mouth tried to smile.

"About Samantha…had you ever talked to her, or do you know anything else about her?"

She didn't. I asked her a number of other questions, but she had never seen any of the men in the room before. I felt convinced she was being honest and forthright. I believed her role was that of an innocent bystander.

We left the diner and went back across the street to my hotel.

"You sure you don't want to stay the night?" she asked me in the parking lot. "It's been a long time since I've had dinner with a gentleman."

"I'd like to. I hope I can wrap this thing up in a couple of days. Here." I wrote my cell phone number on a scrap of paper. "Can you keep the invitation open?"

"You bet," she said, but she already looked alone and deserted.

"Hey," I said, and we came together. She hugged me, her arms under my coat, squeezing hard. Then she put her hand on the back of my head and lifted her face. Her kiss was as soft and warm as the hues of a lazy summer sunset.

"I don't want you to forget me," she said. I couldn't think of anything to say as she walked to her car. I heard the engine start and watched the Plymouth disappear down the road.

"I won't," I said, my words lost in the brittle cold of the morning.

19

I HEADED BACK TO Salt Lake City, driving under clear skies and a rare winter sun that made it seem like a spring day. The dew-covered meadows sparkled in light, and the green peaks rising from the valley floor emerged out of the shadows with stunning clarity. A few random clouds, brilliant white against the sky, drifted over the mountaintops. A solitary hawk flew out of the clouds and glided in a lazy circle, scanning the flatlands for prey.

It would have been easy to pull over, have a beer, and enjoy the sights. It would have been even easier to pitch the Ford into a brake-stand 180 and haul ass back to Salina to get to know Beverly Howitt a lot better. But my boot stayed glued to the pedal as I drove north on Interstate 15, right up the gut of Utah.

I should have called Edward from the terminal at Salt Lake, but a strange listlessness had taken hold in my chest. I wandered around the airport in a fog, unable to focus on any single line of thought long enough to draw a conclusion. I found myself eating a tasteless sandwich and drinking a watery beer in the anonymous airport bar when my cell phone rang.

"Dan. Dan, can you hear me?" It was Edward's voice coming through the scratchy reception.

"Yeah, I'm here."

"Where?"

"Salt Lake."

"Listen, Mr. Bascom got into it with the detectives again today. Raneswich and Iverson want to sit down with you right away. Mr. Bascom told them you've been all over the Western US talking to witnesses, and they're hitting all dead ends."

"That's too bad."

"How did it go in Utah?"

"Pretty good."

"Yeah? Do you know who the killer is?"

"No, but I've got enough that I think I can find him pretty quick. I know what went down in the hotel room."

"What happened? Why was he killed?"

"Edward, I got to assume what I tell you will go direct to John Bascom and then to Raneswich and Iverson. Understand, I've got fifty grand at stake here."

He was silent.

"Those cops are on their own," I said. "They've got ten times the resources I do, so if they're too damn stupid, that's their problem. I have an arrangement with Bascom that he pays me fifty K if I deliver the killer before the police find him. And that's what I intend to do, hopefully in the next forty-eight hours."

"I see your point," he said slowly. "But that doesn't change the fact that Raneswich and Iverson want to talk to you."

"Do me a favor. Tell Bascom I'm agreeable to talk to the detectives. Just leave it at that."

"I guess that'll work. Between you and me, I don't care if you don't talk to them as long as you close the case—and quick. That's Mr. Bascom's bottom line, and that's what I'm looking out for."

"I respect that. Hang loose, and I'll be in touch."

"By the way, I'm still interested in seeing that place in Carson City when you get back. Just out of curiosity, nothing more."

"Okay."

"So you'll take me?"

"Sure. Keep your pants on."

• • •

The conversation with Edward snapped me out of my funk. I reviewed my options as I waited for the plane. My obvious priority was to find the Samoan at Pistol Pete's. If that was a dead end, I could try to track down Mr. 187 through Samantha's address book. Maybe Cody could help out by accessing prison release information. Assuming I could identify and locate the Samoan, I'd secure him and take him to Bascom and collect the bounty. Pretty straightforward. If the detectives caught up to me before I was ready, I'd piss in their ear and tell them it was raining.

The sequence of events in the hotel room suggested a robbery gone bad. Samantha took a break to let Beverly do the dirty work, and opened the door for Mr. 187. The robbery probably would have been quick and easy, if Osterlund hadn't jumped out of the closet. It was likely that Osterlund was there with some sort of specialized camera or video device that could capture images through the peephole. He may have been taking pictures for his own pleasure or possibly for a blackmail scam on Sylvester Bascom. The blackmail angle made good sense. Sylvester was a perfect target, and Osterlund needed money badly.

But what was the Samoan doing there? Was he just backup for Mr. 187? Did he stab Sylvester in the heat of battle? Or was something else going on? The questions would have to wait. They might never be answered, but my job was to identify and deliver the killer to John Bascom, nothing more. After that, Raneswich and the authorities could go figure out who was guilty of what crime.

The flight back to Reno was uneventful, and when the shuttle bus dropped me off near my car, the skies were just turning dark, the weather clear and cold under a brilliant full moon sitting low over the westward ridgeline. It would make for an easy drive to Tahoe. I decided to take Interstate 80, which would take me back to Stateline through Truckee and Tahoe City. It was a slightly longer drive, but there was a great burger place in Tahoe City I wanted to stop at for dinner.

I pulled my keys out of my jacket, but when I went to my door I saw it wasn't locked. My skin tingled and I frowned. It was possible I had left the car unlocked, but I considered it unlikely. I set my bags on the pavement and walked around the Nissan. Nothing looked unusual about the car. It was dirty when I parked it, and it was still dirty. I lay down and peered underneath, but it was too dark to see anything. I didn't like it. I opened the rear passenger door and checked the interior. Everything appeared as I left it. Before starting the motor, I opened the hood and looked over the engine compartment with my flashlight. Satisfied that the car hadn't been tampered with, I fired it up and drove out to the highway.

• • •

Interstate 80, running from Reno to Sacramento, had been built along roughly the same pass the ill-fated Donner party had attempted to cross in the winter of 1846–47. The group of a hundred or so pioneers left from Illinois in April and enjoyed relatively easy traveling until they reached the territory that would later become the state of Wyoming. A trail guide informed them of a shortcut to the south, through Utah, and across the Great Basin desert into Reno. They were told it would take about a week to reach the Great Salt Lake. All went well until they arrived at the base of the Wasatch Mountains, and the trail petered out in the foothills. The energy and time they spent clearing the thick brush and leading their oxen and cattle over the mountains marked the beginning of their troubles.

It took a month to make it to the small settlement that was Salt Lake City, and then the party was faced with eighty miles of featureless salt desert, near what is now the Bonneville Salt Flats Speedway. The sun baked them by day, and the winds turned freezing at nightfall. They lost most of their livestock, horses, and ox teams, as well as a handful of people, to thirst and Indians. Once they made it beyond the salt flats, five hundred miles of high desert remained to be crossed. They set out on foot, down to one wagon, running low on all provisions and now without cattle. A few of the weaker died of thirst and hunger, but the worst was yet to come.

In November the group reached Reno, in poor shape and badly demoralized, but decided to press on westward over the Sierras toward Sacramento. They were within a few miles of the summit near Truckee when winter unleashed its fury upon them. The snow quickly became so deep it was impassable. With little option, the party made camp on the shores of Donner Lake and spent the months of December, January, and February completely snowbound and isolated from civilization. They were a group made up of mostly farmers, with a high percentage of elderly, women, and children. Their ability to hunt, fish, and otherwise live off the land was minimal, and they began to die of starvation and exposure.

A number of attempts were made by the healthiest pioneers to escape the wilderness, but even in the most protected areas the snow was so deep they would sink up to their hips. They fashioned homemade snowshoes, and, in mid-December, a group of ten men and five women, named "Forlorn Hope" by those left behind, set out on a desperate attempt to cross the mountains. A month later, two of the men and the five women reached a cabin a hundred miles away on the Bear River near Sacramento and were rescued, more dead than alive.

It wasn't until early March that rescue parties were able to reach those who remained trapped at Donner Lake. More than half had died, and many of those who survived did so by eating what meager flesh remained on the corpses of their dead comrades.

· · ·

I drove through the night, west on 80 toward Truckee. A local classic rock station announced it was "reality-is-for-people-who-can't-handle-drugs Thursday." I relaxed, grooving on the radio, remembering the stoned visions of my youth. The lazy days and psychedelic nights, the teenage chicks with bellbottoms and flowing hair looking for astral revelations, psychic communion, or maybe just good old wild times. A twelve-pack of discount beer, a baggie of homegrown, and guilt-free sex without head trips. My friends and I had been too late for the hippie era, but I guess we didn't realize it at the time. Those were good days while they lasted, days when the next morning meant nothing more than waking up and waiting for the party to begin again. At least that's how I remembered it. But that was a long time ago, back before AIDS, and before recreational drugs became big business. After that, all the fun had gone out of it. Or maybe I just wasn't young anymore.

The miles fell behind me, and I crossed the state border into California. Scattered pine trees became visible as the desert started its gradual transition to forest.

The road came over a mild crest and fell into a steep downhill curve, sweeping to the left. I pushed on my brakes, and the pedal felt slack and mushy, so I pushed down harder, but the car seemed to accelerate. My foot jammed the brake pedal to the floorboard, and when I let up, the pedal stayed on the floor. *Sonofabitch, no brakes!*

I stabbed my foot repeatedly against the dead pedal and cursed myself for not trusting my instincts back at the airport.

The Nissan was picking up speed as I held it tight into the bend. Swearing through clenched teeth, I eased up the emergency brake, but it had no effect on the car's increasing momentum. The tires were squealing as the turn reached its apex. I dropped the gearshift into second, and the motor revved loudly as a pair of lights came up close in my rearview mirror. I jerked the transmission down into first, and the engine howled like an air-raid siren, the tachometer bouncing off the red line. The Nissan was slowing, the transmission holding off the pull of gravity. Then the motor backfired twice, sputtered, and died.

The wheel jerked in my hand when the power steering cut out, but I held the car steady, seeing the end of the curve where the grade flattened, and I thought I could manage to slow to the point where jumping out the door wouldn't be suicide. And I probably would have, if it weren't for the truck that came up behind me again, its headlamps blazing in my rear window. My head snapped back as the truck's bumper slammed into my trunk, then I was skidding sideways, the tires shrieking on the coarse pavement, my headlights scanning the banks of the canyon walls beyond the edge of the road.

I fishtailed around 180 degrees and looked directly into the truck's headlights for a long moment, long enough to feel the dread and rage boiling in my gut. Then my car crashed violently into the low steel guardrail. The chassis bounced and shuddered as the car leaned on the mangled rail, then it tilted over with a wretched screech, and tipped down into the darkness below.

The Nissan rolled once, crushing in the roof on the passenger side and shattering the windshield into a dense spider web. My head snapped to the side and clipped the edge of a piece of jagged metal. The car came around upright on all four tires, then a stout pine caught the front end and spun the vehicle around backward. The wheels were locked, which was a stroke of luck. I held the steering wheel straight and skidded down the hillside in reverse, thrashing through sagebrush and thistle, bouncing over rocks, until the Nissan fell off a short drop at the bottom of the canyon and was thrown onto its side, coming to a stop with a bone-jarring splash in the Truckee River.

I was still belted in, which kept me from bathing in six inches of icy water that flowed through the passenger side of my car. The Nissan lay on its side, precariously balanced on the river rocks. My head stung, and I reached up and felt the sticky ooze from a minor gash. I was shaken, but I didn't think I had any broken bones. I had left my gear case on the seat beside me, and I pulled it out of the water. My door was jammed, so I kicked the glass out of the windshield, climbed over the high side of the car, and jumped down onto the riverbank.

One of the Nissan's headlights was shining up the river, reflecting off the black water and patches of snow. I looked up the hill to the road, realizing I had somehow survived a fall down at least a 250-foot canyon. A dark pickup truck, American made, was parked on the highway. The truck's interior light flashed on, and I saw a person climb out, then heard the clunk of the door as the light went out. The full moon clearly silhouetted the man as he jumped over the railing, pistol in hand.

A large boulder lay near the river behind my car. I moved behind it with my suitcase, shrugged into my vest, and jacked a hollow-point round into the chamber of the Beretta.

A minute later I saw the man above, sliding down the scree toward the car. Pebbles and rocks slid past me as he continued to move forward. He was perhaps fifty feet away, standing against a snowy background up the hill to my right, when I drew a bead on him.

"Drop your gun!" I yelled over the rush of the river.

There are times in life when people do things that are inexplicably stupid. The kinds of things that make you wonder what they were thinking, if anything, at that moment. This was one of those times, and the man couldn't have picked a worse moment to have a mental breakdown. He fired two blind shots in my direction—I heard one bullet thud into the dirt, and the other ricocheted off some rocks behind me.

I fired low, aiming at his leg, but he took a step downward as I pulled the trigger, and the bullet hit him in the gut. The impact blew him backward, leaving a red smear on the snow, then his body fell forward, skidding and tumbling down to the water's edge. He came to a stop twenty feet from where I stood, his legs strewn in the river like broken sticks, his chest heaving in the glare of my headlight.

I approached him, kneeling once I was sure he no longer held his pistol. He was throwing up and choking on his vomit. I helped him turn his head so he could clear his mouth, then splashed some water on his face to clean him up.

He was in bad shape. The bullet had blown through him, leaving a gaping, sucking wound in his stomach. His guts pulsed, glistening, and blood drained steadily down his side into the dirt.

"Mr. One Eight Seven?" I said.

"I guess the joke's on me," he said, trying to smile.

His eyes were clouding over. He didn't have long.

"You're dying. It's time to confess your sins," I said, hoping I made a convincing priest.

"Gulp yump, motherfucker."

I started to stand. His face was drained of color, his tongue gray in his open mouth.

"Hey," he wheezed, and I knelt down to him again.

"The sheriff…" he whispered.

"What?" I said, but his head fell to the side, and I heard his breath leave him. His eyes were fixed and staring, and his lips were split in a small smile, as if he died laughing at his own joke.

I checked his pockets and pulled out a soggy wallet. The name on his driver's license was Michael Dean Stiles. It listed a Reno address and a birthday three days after mine. His wallet held four dollars, an assortment of cards, and a small baggie of white powder. I looked at his still, bloody corpse. His jeans were soaked through, and water rippled around his legs. The sleeve of his black leather jacket was unsnapped and pulled up to the elbow, revealing his tattooed forearm. The long beard off his chin looked old and brittle, and moved back and forth stiffly with the breeze that whispered through the canyon.

When I stood, a short burst of machine-gun fire shattered the night. I dove behind the Nissan as a series of slugs plowed into Mr. 187's corpse, bouncing it further into the river. I reached in through the busted sunroof and switched the headlights off, searching the hillside for movement. Another burst rang out, and half a dozen bullets punched into the car's undercarriage. Two of the rounds came up through the roof, narrowly missing me. I sprinted through the shallow water back to the boulder where I'd left my suitcase. The machine gun barked again, sending more shots into my ruined car. I saw the muzzle flash about halfway up the hill, and I fired five shots at it as fast as I could pull the Beretta's trigger. The blast was deafening.

My ears rang in the silence. Five minutes later I saw a heavy figure, stark in the moonlight, climb over the guardrail. The truck parked on the roadside pulled away and sped off into the night.

20

B Y THE TIME THE Nevada County sheriff arrived from Truckee, I had cleaned out the Nissan and carried all my stuff up to the highway, save for the tire chains. In the event some crazy mechanic ever got the car back on the road, he could have the chains with my blessing. I'd taken off my soaked boots and socks and was thawing my feet in my sleeping bag when they pulled up.

Sheriff Bill Cooper and his deputies seemed to be an efficient group. Within an hour, a search-and-rescue team arrived and lit up the hillside with portable lights. I waited in the back of a squad car while an electric winch pulled Michael Dean Stiles's body out of the canyon on a gurney. A deputy also found his gun near where I told him to look.

"What about my car, fellas?" I said.

"You better get a hold of your insurance company and get that wreck out of our river," a deputy said as he walked by.

"Thanks," I called out to him.

It was ten o'clock when we left for the sheriff's office. Sheriff Cooper had given me a plastic garbage bag for the miscellaneous junk from my car, which included jumper cables, a stack of papers from my glove box, an old football, and my sleeping bag. I asked him to stop at a 7-Eleven and he obliged, even went in with me and paid for my dinner, a couple of stale chili dogs. At his office we went over everything repeatedly, and I told him the truth, or at least what I figured he was entitled to know. I started with the murder of Sylvester Bascom, told him I tracked down a hooker in Vegas who was involved with what may have been a botched robbery, and added that I suspected she called her boyfriend, and he came after me. He asked me how the boyfriend would know to find me at the airport. I didn't have an answer.

The questioning went on and on. I had a headache and was tired. Finally Cooper finished up around midnight and drove me to a hotel on Main Street in Truckee. He had not impounded my weapon as evidence. Apparently he believed my contention of self-defense, but he told me to expect a call from the Truckee PD detectives in the morning. I checked into the hotel and lugged my gear and the green garbage bag to my room. I thought about going to the bar next door, but I lay down on the bed briefly, just to rest my eyes, and a minute later I was out.

I woke at dawn in the strange room, still immersed in the surreal landscape of my dream. I was in a coffee shop, sitting at a table with Mr. 187 and Sheriff Grier from South Lake Tahoe. Mr. 187's hair and beard were completely white. A birthday cake was brought to the table, and I tried to light the candles, but the flame kept going out. My father appeared and also tried to light the candles, without success. He made some reference to things not always happening as they should, then he and Mr. 187 walked away together. Sheriff Grier laughed and cut himself a piece of cake. In my peripheral vision there were blurry people and muted voices, but I couldn't hear what they were saying.

• • •

While I was contemplating the dream that early morning, there was no way I could have known that two men were having a conversation that would have given my nocturnal visions a different perspective. They were fifty miles west of Truckee in the foothills above Sacramento, meeting in a room barely lit by the gray dawn. One man, with a salt-and-pepper mustache over yellowed teeth, looked at the cigar between his fingers, then broke it in half and dropped it in an ashtray.

"You let this thing get out of control. That's not like you."

"Look at it this way—Stiles was a liability," the other man said, his eyes opaque against his dark face.

"Stiles? *You're* becoming a liability. I hired you to protect my business interests. So you go kill some rich man's son during a pointless robbery, then you and Stiles go fixin' to whack this private eye, without my okay, and Stiles ends up dead. Stupid. I never expected that from you."

"Maybe Stiles is best in a grave. Dead men can't talk."

"Well, now. Ain't that the truth."

The room was quiet, then the man with the dark skin and barrel-shaped body stepped from the shadows, his eyes glowing with a primal luster. He smiled and took another step, and Sheriff Conrad Pace involuntarily leaned back. He blinked, surprised at his own reflex. It was not like Sheriff Pace to be frightened. It was an emotion he hadn't experienced in years. But when he looked at that wet smile, he felt oddly out of his element. It occurred to him that, given the right motivation, the man standing before him would tear him to pieces with his bare hands.

The feeling was gone in an instant, and Conrad Pace walked behind his desk. He sat and stared out his window to the wet, rolling pastures, where spirals of silver mist reached down from the sky and touched the jade hills. Had he made a mistake in enlisting Julo Nafui? As an enforcer, the man had no equal. But Nafui had run amuck; killing Bascom might well get Nafui arrested, even though half the force was on Pace's pad. And Pace harbored no illusions about the eventual outcome once Nafui faced a murder charge. The big sheriff's jaw tightened as he imagined Nafui implicating him in exchange for a plea bargain. That was unacceptable. He would have to do something about it. Pace looked up at Nafui, at the unnatural hulk of his torso, at his ugly, merciless face. Killing him would be easier said than done. Perhaps there were other options. Sheriff Pace raised his finger and pointed at Nafui.

"I'm gonna straighten this shit out, starting with the private eye," Pace said. "You lay low, and I'll call you when I need you."

Nafui smiled widely, his teeth glistening with saliva. "Don't make me wait too long," he said. "I get antsy when I got nothing to do."

· · ·

The main drag of Truckee was deserted at 6:30 A.M. The wind blew through the streets, echoing hollowly against the storefronts, sending bits of paper and trash swirling across the icy pavement. I had never felt it so cold. For a second I looked up and down the street, searching, then with a jolt realized my old faithful Nissan was on its side in the Truckee River. I walked about half a mile to a 7-Eleven, shivering, my hands deep in my coat pockets. The warmth of the store was a relief. I poured myself a large coffee.

"Damn, it's cold," I said to the clerk.

"This is nothing for Truckee. Hit forty-six below one year. It's only about ten below now."

I rubbed my unshaven mug and hiked back to the hotel. At eight-thirty I called my insurance company to report my car was totaled. They took down the information, then gave me the number of a local towing company that would recover the vehicle. My vehicle. Or now my ex-vehicle. The fucking Nissan—the car I had driven through my marriage, my divorce, through countless drunken episodes, and through three years of sobriety. I had owned it for almost my entire adulthood. It seemed unreal I would never drive it again; to my surprise, I felt a twinge of nostalgic sadness. The car and I had been through a lot together.

My cell rang, snapping me out of my despondent reverie. There were more important things to worry about, I told myself. Like finding out who was trying to kill me.

"Dan?" Cody's voice said.

"Hey, Cody."

"I'm all packed up and ready to go, man. Where should I meet you?"

Suddenly, having Cody around didn't seem like such a bad idea. I gave him the name of the hotel in Truckee.

"I thought you were in South Lake," he said.

"Yeah, I was on the way there and had a little car trouble."

"It may be time to get a new car, Dirt."

"I think you're right. The Nissan's totaled."

"What? Were you drunk?"

"Sober, believe it or not. Remember those hookers I was telling you about? I think one of them sent her boyfriend and another dude after me. Somehow they found my car in the airport parking lot and cut the brake lines. Then they rammed me off Highway 80 with their truck. I flipped and ended up at the bottom of a canyon in the Truckee River."

"Holy shit! Are you okay?"

"Yeah, I was lucky. But the guys came after me in the canyon."

"Uh-oh," he said. "What happened?"

"I told the first one to drop his gun—"

"But he didn't," Cody interjected.

"Yeah. And so I—"

"Blew his freaking head off?"

"No, I aimed low, but he moved and took it in the gut."

"Christ, I'd rather get my brains blown out than take one in the gut," Cody said. "I remember when one of our guys on the force had to wear a colostomy bag for six months."

"This guy's not gonna need a colostomy bag."

"Oh." There was a pause. "Well, fuck him. What about the other guy?"

"He opened up on me with an automatic weapon, sounded like an Uzi. I returned his fire and scared him away."

"I guess we ought to go find this man and engage him in philosophical discussion, eh?"

"Sounds like a plan," I said, no longer so reluctant to enlist Cody's buffalo-style ways.

• • •

Before Cody hung up, I asked him to run a report on Michael Dean Stiles. I was hoping something in his police record might be helpful. Cody said he'd try, as the unmistakable voice of an unhappy woman rang out in the background.

The Truckee detectives met me in the lobby, and we went next door to a small coffee and pastry joint. They pushed me quite a bit harder than the Nevada County sheriff, but I didn't give them any names besides Sylvester Bascom. Eventually they left me after I suggested they confer with Detectives Raneswich and Iverson from South Lake Tahoe PD. Surely they'd have more valuable information than I could offer, I said.

The skies were dark and heavy when I called Edward to give him his daily update.

"Tell John Bascom there were three men in the room when Sylvester was murdered. Two are now dead," I said.

"Wait a minute," Edward said. I heard the phone moving around and muffled voices.

"Reno, this is John Bascom." The words boomed through the small speaker. "Tell me what's happening," he barked, as if it were an order. I was tempted to say, "Yes, sir," but I wasn't in the mood for it. "There were two call girls and three men in Sylvester's room when he was stabbed," I said.

"You know this for sure?"

"Yes."

"What were they doing there? Do you have their names?"

"One of them was Sven Osterlund. He was watching through a peephole in the closet. At this point, I think one of the hookers set up Sylvester to be robbed. But he and Osterlund fought back, and that's when Sylvester was stabbed. I think Osterlund was shot the next day because he witnessed Sylvester's murder."

Bascom was silent for a moment. "My son was killed for what, whatever cash was in his wallet?"

"That's possible. But there may be more to it."

"Yes?"

"It's still conjecture at this point, but drugs and blackmail may be involved."

"Blackmail? Who was in the room besides Osterlund?"

"The second man was Michael Dean Stiles. He's the boyfriend of one of the hookers, and he ran me off the road and shot at me last night."

"He did? Is he the one who stabbed Sylvester?"

"No."

"But he was there, so let's bring him to the police as a witness. Where is he?"

"The morgue."

Bascom didn't even pause. "Goddammit! You killed him?"

"I was trying to wound him."

"So what happens now? Do you know who killed my son?"

"No. But I hope to in twenty-four hours."

"Well, that's the first decent news I've heard. I swear, whoever it is will fry in hell."

"One way or another, I suppose."

"Reno, I advise you get a hold of these two incompetents who call themselves detectives. They're looking for you."

"Apparently they're not the only ones," I said.

• • •

The snow had started falling when I left the hotel. It was still an hour before noon, and I wandered into the empty saloon on the corner to wait for Cody. I was watching the snowfall in silence and sipping a beer when he burst through the doorway.

"What, what? Ha, I didn't even try your hotel! I knew you'd be at the nearest bar. You drunk!" His voice echoed off the walls. He came up behind me, massaging my neck and shoulders with his huge hands. I lost my balance and almost fell off the barstool.

"Come on, Dirt, cheer up! Do they serve food here? Where the hell is everybody? This place is like a ghost town."

"You're looking good, Cody."

"What? My ass! Have you gone queer? I'm over three hundred again!"

His frame was so big he could gain or lose thirty pounds and not look any different. He sat down next to me. The barstool groaned but held; I'd seen him collapse smaller chairs.

"Things okay back home?" I asked.

"Sure, wonderful. Debbie's a great wife, as long as I'm not there. I imagine our relationship would be perfect if we got together maybe once a month to screw."

"Marriage is a tough gig."

"I'd say it's a dying institution. You have any luck with the broads lately?"

"Not like the old days," I said. But then I told him about Beverly Howitt and her involvement in the case.

"You gonna see her again?" he asked.

"Maybe. But first I got to find this Samoan, or whatever he is."

"Let's go track him down."

"Right," I said. "He wrecked my damn car."

"So? Your car was a piece of shit anyway."

"No, it wasn't."

"Okay, fine," Cody said.

"Anyway, I want to try to take him alive. Right?"

"Hey, Dan, this prick shot at you. Let's go stomp his shit into the tar."

"Not my job, Cody. I just need to deliver him to collect the bounty."

"Bounty's balls. That's something I could never figure out about you, Dirt. Someone tries to kill you, and you're nonchalant about it. But I've seen guys insult you, and you want to rip them apart with your bare hands."

"I killed a man last night, Cody."

"Like that guy whose skull you fractured down in LA," he said, as if he hadn't heard me. "Or that dude you sent to the hospital outside of that bar in Gilroy. Remember that time?"

"Every time you remind me."

"Well, I think it's time to rack up some more memories," he said, his hand clasped on the back of my neck, his fingers rough as raw leather against my skin.

We had lunch then hit the road in Cody's Dodge truck, driving south on Highway 89, past Squaw Valley and Alpine Meadows ski resorts, through Tahoe City, and around the lake. The snow continued to drift down from above, and Cody shifted his transfer case into four-wheel drive as we went over the grade above Emerald Bay. I pointed out to Cody that Osterlund's body was found in the bay. He shook his head.

"Why would someone dump his body there?" he said, his red beard glowing beneath his hard eyes. "In plain sight? Unless they wanted him to be found. Like they're trying to send a message."

"Could be they wanted to scare me off."

"Maybe it's time you sent a message of your own."

I found myself watching the passing cars carefully, and I adjusted Cody's side-view mirror so I could see behind us. I took my piece out of its holster and balanced its weight in my palm, feeling the cold metal grips against my skin.

My cell rang as we dropped into the valley, driving on 50 toward Stateline.

"Dan Reno, Detective Paul Iverson," the voice said. "What do you say we get together and shoot the breeze this afternoon?"

"I've got a busy schedule."

"Yes, I've heard. You sound like an industrious man."

"That's how it is when you work for yourself," I said, and the line went quiet for a few seconds, then he said, "Can I meet you at the Lakeside at three o'clock?"

"We can meet at The King's Head," I said.

"Good. I'll see you there at three."

We pulled into the King's Head a few minutes early, and the only other car in the parking lot was a blue Ford Explorer with an E-series license plate. I decided to leave my gun in Cody's truck. Wouldn't need it for a meeting with a cop.

A solitary man was shooting pool when we walked in. He didn't look like a policeman—more like a casting reject from a vampire movie. The paleness of his face made me wonder if he was ill, or afflicted with a disease of the skin. When he moved around the table he seemed to glide gracefully, like a ballet dancer. His blond hair was lank and barely covered his scalp, even though he wasn't going bald. He held the pool cue with thin, almost dainty fingers that were a lighter shade than the white pine of the cue itself. Even his clothes struck me as odd; he wore red slacks and a long-sleeved black shirt.

"Ah, you must be Dan Reno," he said, looking up with nearly translucent blue eyes. "Watch this." He had lined up a two-rail bank shot. He missed it by a foot.

"I've seen better shots in a doctor's office," Cody said.

"Or on a bar," I added.

He raised his eyebrows and smiled without parting his lips. "It must be my lucky day, I get a couple comedians. I'm Paul Iverson."

"Where's your partner, Raneswich?" I said.

"He thought it would be best if I met with you."

"That's good thinking on his part. I hear he's quite the asshole," Cody said. But Iverson laughed. "That's not an uncommon opinion," he replied. "Let's talk about the murder of Sylvester Bascom."

"Speak freely, Detective," I said.

"I'd like to know what you've learned in your investigation."

"I'd like to know what you've learned in yours."

"Tit for tat then, is it?"

"However you want to put it."

Iverson didn't look happy with my response. Two men were sitting at the end of the bar, huddled over pints and shots. One of them was slurring and babbling noisily about his gambling losses. The bartender looked to where we stood and said, "What'll it be, mates?"

"Has that guy been here all day?" Iverson said, jerking his thumb at the whining drunk.

The bartender glanced at his watch. "Not yet," he said. Iverson shook his head and led us to a table in the back.

"We identified a hooker we believe was in the hotel room at the Crown," he started. "But we can't find her. The escort service she worked for is closed, and their records have vanished."

"Dana's Escorts?"

"That's right. Tell me what you know about them."

"I talked to them," I said, thinking that Dana's would have been the immediate link to Beverly Howitt. But it sounded like they'd folded up their operation.

"They told me a woman named Samantha was sent to the Crown," I offered.

"Samantha Nunez," Iverson said.

"Right."

"Have you talked to her?"

"Yeah."

"Where?"

"At a whorehouse down near Vegas," I said, without a twinge of regret. I had promised Samantha I'd not turn her in, but since I figured she sent Mr. 187 after me, the deal was null and void.

"The Cat's Meow," he said. "She's no longer there. You have any idea where she might be?"

"None. On second thought, you might find her at the funeral of Michael Dean Stiles."

Iverson looked at me with narrow eyes. "Why?"

"He was Samantha's boyfriend. I suspect that after I talked to Samantha, she called him, and he decided to try to kill me. My assumption is he was involved in Bascom's death."

"And now Stiles is dead," Iverson said. We stared at each other. After a moment he looked down, tracing a figure-eight pattern on the table with his finger.

"What else did Samantha tell you?"

"Not much. She was in the room, and she said a big black man tried to rob Bascom. Bascom resisted and got stabbed."

"A big black man, huh? And how did this supposed big black man get in the room?"

"She wouldn't say."

"Did she let him in? It sounds like she must have."

"She wouldn't say."

"Mr. Reno, I'm getting a strong impression you're being less than forthright."

I shook my head. "Detective, Samantha Nunez is not dumb, nor is she easy to intimidate. She lives on the edge, and she's a survivor. I was lucky to find her and even luckier to get anything out of her. I've told you everything she said."

Iverson wasn't naïve. He knew I was being obtuse, but he had nothing to charge me with, and he hadn't offered any information of value, which meant he had no bargaining chips. His frustration hung over him like a cloud of stale cigarette smoke.

"What about the black guy? Who is he?"

"I don't know. I'm working on it."

"What else do you know?"

"That's about it."

"Hey, Detective," Cody said. "What's the worst-tasting drink you've ever had?"

"What's your point?" Iverson said irritably.

"Come on, think about it. You ever have a really shitty-tasting drink?"

Iverson looked at me. I shrugged.

"I don't have time for games," he said, but then he leaned back in his chair. "All right, you ever have a Slow Comfortable Screw? It's a screwdriver with a shot of sloe gin and Southern Comfort. Tastes like cow piss with sugar. Why?"

"The expression on your face—you look like you just drank one." Cody grinned and raised his beer. Iverson looked offended for a second, then actually smiled. "If you're thinking about a career in stand-up, don't quit your day job," he said.

I listened to the exchange without amusement. Iverson stood and motioned for me to follow him, while Cody headed to the men's room.

"Look," he said, as we walked to the front door, "you and your buddy there are playing with fire. If I were you, I'd consider leaving town."

"Thanks for the advice."

"Just don't do anything foolish."

"Now why would I do that, Detective?" I said, but he looked at me like I already had.

21

WHEN IVERSON PUSHED OPEN the door to leave, two uniformed cops burst in. One was Deputy Fingsten, and the other was a square-shouldered man in a cowboy hat. Fingsten drew his revolver and pointed it at me.

"Assume the position, asshole," he said.

"What the hell is this?" I said to Iverson, who was either surprised or doing a good job acting the part.

"What's going on, Sheriff?" Iverson said.

"Go back to your office, Detective," the older cop said. "This man's being arrested on a number of charges. You're not needed here."

"What charges?" Iverson said, while Fingsten handcuffed me.

"Take your pick. He's an enemy of the people."

"What charges, Sheriff?" Iverson said again.

"Detective, this is county business. I advise you don't interfere." I caught the sheriff's eye, then read the name printed in gold on his shirt: Conrad Pace. He grabbed me behind the arm, Fingsten took my other arm, and they led me outside.

Iverson stepped in front of the sheriff. "I'm in the middle of interrogating him," he said.

"You can have him after he's booked. Try tomorrow," Pace said, and elbowed Iverson aside.

Iverson watched the men walk me across the parking lot. Fingsten pushed me into the backseat of a squad car. As we drove off, I saw Cody burst out through the doors of the bar, his face hot and red, as if he was greatly embarrassed.

We pulled out onto 50. Pace drove and Fingsten sat next to me in the backseat. After a minute I looked at him and said, "I guess you're not gonna read me my rights."

Fingsten's arm shot out and he backhanded me across the face. The same blow from a stronger man would have broken my nose, but his shot just made my eyes water uncontrollably.

"You got the right to shut your fucking mouth," Fingsten said.

"This how you treat the tourists, Sheriff?" I said.

Fingsten hit me across the face again, harder than before, the back of his fist catching me flush in the nose, and this time I thought he might have broken it. My arms flexed impotently behind my back, and a dark rage rose in my throat. I leaned back, bent my right knee to my chest, and slammed my foot into Fingsten's chest as hard as I could. He tried to block the kick, but my boot went through his hands like a jackhammer through dry twigs, and my heel pounded into his torso with enough force to snap ribs and cause internal bleeding. Fingsten's body shot into the door, his eyes rolled back, and his body went limp.

"Goddamn you, that may be the last mistake you'll ever make," the sheriff said, and he stepped on the gas. We turned off the highway, then we were driving through a residential neighborhood and then down a dirt road. The car lurched to a stop, and I caught a glimpse of Conrad Pace, his face torqued with fury, his hand grasping his pistol by the barrel as he got out and opened my door.

• • •

When I came to, the first thing I saw was Louis Perdie's face up close, his complexion rutted and pitted with blackheads. I was sitting in the snow, my hands still cuffed behind me. Perdie held a coffee cup, and he splashed the contents in my face. I blinked the icy water from my eyes. "He's awake," Perdie said.

"Rise and shine, shit for brains," Conrad Pace said. He knelt down in front of me. When I lifted my head to meet his eyes, a sharp pain in the back of my skull made me dizzy, and I had to look back down.

"Here's how it's gonna be, private eye," Pace said. He snatched my head up by the hair. "When we're done with you, you're gonna want to get as far away from Silverado County as quick as you can. You don't stop to eat, piss, get medical attention, nothing. All you're gonna want to do is get your ass out of my county. Because if you don't, I promise the only way you'll leave is in a body bag. Does that make sense to you? I know you're a stupid fuck, so I want to make sure I'm getting through. Hey! Look at me, asshole!"

I raised my eyes to his face and tried to speak, but the words were strangled in my throat. He and Perdie grabbed me by the shoulders and tossed me down a short incline to the edge of a stream. It was iced over, but there was a three-foot hole cut out near the edge. I felt a knee on my back, and then my head was being pushed under the water. I gasped when I went under, and ice water shot into my sinus cavities. My eyes bulged as if they'd burst free from their sockets, and an intense pressure began to grow in my lungs. I strained to lift my head, but the hands gripping my neck felt like iron. My body bucked hard, but someone had all their weight on my back, and I couldn't move. I squeezed my eyes closed as tight as I could and clamped my jaw shut. In a quiet part of my mind, I realized this is what it feels like to drown. I tried with all my strength to roll over and throw the weight from my back, but my legs were being held, and someone must have been sitting on my shoulders. It started going black around the edges of my vision when they jerked my head from the water.

"Get a good drink?" Pace said, smiling. I retched violently, trying to hack the river water out of my lungs. "I think you need another."

They held me under twice more, and the last time I must have blacked out, because when I regained consciousness, I lay a few feet back from the water.

"Hey, private dick," Pace said, grinning above me. "We got your friend here too. Louis said he wanted to be here with you."

I heard a thud and a grunt, and Cody slid down the snow toward the river. The left side of his face was coated with blood, and one of his eyes was swollen shut. His hands were cuffed behind him.

"You cowards," I wheezed, but then Fingsten was next to me. He stuck his revolver against my ear.

"Say another word, I'll blast your brains all over the snow," he said. "Come on, tempt me."

Then a man I'd never seen before walked into view. The first thing I noticed about him was his coat hung off his back at an odd angle because of the massive slope of his trapezoid muscles. His black hair was very oily, and it clung to his dark, deeply pocked face like an overturned basket of snakes. He seemed to move with unusual strength and purpose as he stepped down the embankment toward Cody.

"I hear you're good with a knife," I said.

Fingsten pressed the muzzle of his .38 into my cheek.

The dark-skinned man turned toward me and our eyes locked. "You know nothing," he said, his voice quiet and very even, as if it wasn't him speaking. Then he smiled, and his eyes were suddenly wet and alive, as if a corpse had come to life.

Samantha Nunez had told the truth about the Samoan, I thought. I watched him and Perdie force Cody's head into the water. The Samoan went about his work without expression or any sign of physical effort. They held Cody under, while Fingsten cackled like a hyena and cheered them on.

When they were finished, Pace lit a cigar, and Perdie removed the handcuffs from my hands and Cody's. The Samoan seemed to have vanished.

"This one's for Fingsten," Perdie's voice said behind me, and he kicked me in the kidneys hard enough to send my body tumbling out onto the frozen stream.

"We see you again, this'll seem like a tea party," Pace said. I heard him hike back up the incline, and then they were gone.

· · ·

It became dark as we trudged through the snow back toward the highway. I didn't have my jacket, and my clothes were torn and soaked. Every time I raised my head to a normal position, a stab of pain shot through my skull, as if a steel spike were jabbing a nerve. I could also feel an odd numbness where Perdie had kicked me, as if some internal organ was damaged, but my body didn't realize it yet.

Unfortunately, Cody was in worse shape. He limped along slowly, his eyes dull and stupefied. I asked him what happened after I left the King's Head, and his story of being apprehended by Perdie and the Samoan was disjointed and didn't make sense. When I asked him to explain, his sentences became gibberish. Concussion, I assumed. We needed to get to a hospital quickly.

The wind started blowing, and the cold became unbearable. Our boots were soaked, and my feet had gone numb. Cody was also without a coat and was turning blue. His hands were balled up in fists, and his teeth chattered loudly.

Cody was walking more and more slowly, and finally he fell to the ground. I put his arm around my shoulder and dead-lifted him to his feet. I clenched my teeth and swore in frustration as we moved forward. Stopping would be suicide; we had to reach shelter or we'd freeze to death. The cold wrapped my body in a clutch of pain, and only the adrenalin from my fear and anger kept me going. I kept looking around for any form of shelter, but there was nothing but snow and skeleton trees. Exhaustion, desperation, and then panic began to overtake me. We slogged forward and crested a hill, and then I saw the lights from Highway 50 in the distance.

· · ·

We were in a large domed room of some kind, surrounded by stainless-steel walls. The structure fanned out downward from the center of the ceiling, creating a circular enclosure. Cody was sitting at a table. We were talking about something casual, but I knew the purpose of the conversation was to distract me from some horrible, unmentionable reality we shared. I tried to ignore the dread in my heart, but it hovered inside me like an idling motor.

Cody stood and walked toward the single door in the room. He held his leg over his shoulder like a huge baseball bat. The appendage looked like it had been broken from a statue. A long peg leg was attached to his hip, but he seemed to walk without a limp. He opened the door, and in walked two men I didn't recognize. One was wearing an Abe-Lincoln-style top hat and smoking a mouthful of cigarettes.

The second man was juggling three pieces of bony spine, and he reached up and snapped his ear free of his head and added it to the objects rotating through the air. The smoking man sat down and removed his hat. His head was flat, as if it had been neatly sliced off by a coroner's saw. I went to shake hands with him, but my hand had no fingers. He opened his fist, and two black fingers lay on his palm. A dark, barrel-shaped man stood in the shadows, but I couldn't see his face.

"Hey. Hey! Come on, wake up!" The voice snapped me out of the nightmare and into the generic colors of a hospital room.

"My, you were yelling. Rest easy, there." The doctor was an older man with reading glasses low on his nose.

"Where am I?" I croaked.

"You're at Stateline Emergency Center."

"How?"

"You were brought in last night with another man. You were nearly frozen to death. Lucky for you the paramedics knew how to treat hypothermia. They saved your life."

I tried to sit up. My hands were wrapped in layers of gauze and looked like white boxing gloves.

"Rest easy," he said, as I struggled upright.

"My friend?"

"He's on the other side of the curtain." He nodded at a green divider hanging from a track on the ceiling. I held up my hands.

"What's my condition?"

"Second-degree frostbite, maybe a touch of third degree. Your feet are wrapped as well. You should recover fully."

"How's my friend?"

"He has a moderate concussion, otherwise about the same as you. There was some doubt about his toes last night, but they're past the danger point." I felt a huge weight rise off my chest.

"How in the world did you end up out there with no jacket?"

"I was brought here in an ambulance?" I asked.

"Yes."

"Has a police report been filed?"

"No, not to my knowledge. Should one be?"

"Cody," I said.

"He's sleeping," the doctor said.

"Thanks for everything, Doc," I exhaled. "We'll need to leave as soon as possible."

"You should spend two days here for observation."

"How about the frostbite?"

"We'll keep the bandages on for two days, then it's very important to not let your extremities get cold again. There's been some damage to the flesh, and although it's not permanent, it could become so if exposed to cold in the next couple weeks."

The doctor left and a nurse came by and dropped off an unappetizing breakfast on a tin tray. I pushed the blankets back and carefully pulled my legs up. My feet were wrapped to the point that walking was improbable. "Jesus Christ," I muttered. I swung my legs down and tried putting weight on my feet.

"Hey, Cody," I said, but he didn't answer. I reached over and pulled the curtain aside. He lay on his back, dead asleep. I let him be and took inventory on my battered body. The pain in my head and neck had subsided, and I could think clearly. When I touched my nose, it felt bruised and swollen, the result of being sucker-punched by Fingsten. My back was still sore where Perdie had kicked me, but I didn't think it was serious. My biggest concern was the frostbite.

I rang the buzzer for the nurse. When she showed up, I asked her to dial a phone number for me. Fortunately, I'd memorized Edward's number.

"Edward," I said quietly. "I need your help. Please listen carefully. I'm at the Stateline Emergency Center. It's about a block east of the Lakeside."

"What are you doing there?"

"The men behind Sylvester's death just upped the ante."

"What do you mean?"

"Look, I got to get out of here, and quick. I need you to come pick me up."

"I'll be there in twenty minutes," he said.

"Good man," I said, but he'd already hung up.

"Hey, Dirt," Cody said, leaning up on his elbow. His eyes were both blackened and horribly red. "I feel like I just went twelve rounds with Mike Tyson."

"The good news is it was a draw, and you'll live to fight another day," I said. He smiled, then winced. "Don't make me laugh, man."

"So the elected sheriff of Silverado County wants us out of town," I said.

"Incredible. You'd think the stupid asshole would at least hide his identity."

"Apparently he thinks we can't touch him."

"He figured wrong," Cody said, his eyes narrowed. "It's a mistake he'll regret."

"We're getting picked up in a few minutes," I said. "We can't stay here. The doctor said we just need some rest. It looks like we'll be all right."

"My truck. I don't know where my truck is."

"We'll find it. It's either somewhere between that stream and The King's Head, or in the police impound yard."

"I can't remember how I ended up at the stream. My mind is blank."

"You've got a concussion. It's normal to lose some memory."

"All our clothes and gear are in my truck."

"I know," I said. "But the first thing we got to do is find somewhere safe to chill out. I've got someone coming to pick us up. We're vulnerable here." Cody looked at his bandaged hands.

"How did we get here?" he said.

"Somehow we ended up in an ambulance. Maybe a good Samaritan came to our rescue."

"A good Samaritan?"

"Hell, I don't know. I must have passed out."

"Probably because you drank too much. Wenger's right, you're a drunk."

"What?" I said, and Cody was grinning broadly. "This ain't any worse than a typical hangover, Dirt. Let's get the hell out of here."

Cody tried to stand up, but couldn't find his balance on his wrapped feet and fell back over the bed, his bare ass sticking out of the hospital gown. The sight threw me into a punch-drunk laughing fit. I tried to wipe my eyes, but my hands were completely useless, and I was laughing uncontrollably, my stomach heaving, tears streaming down my face. The nurse came over to see what all the excitement was about.

"We're checking out," Cody told her. "We'll need two wheelchairs." The nurse looked at me with doubt in her eyes. Cody shrugged. "He used to take a lot of acid."

"Post-trauma stress release," the nurse said, in that detached way medical professionals sometimes speak. "It's not uncommon."

Before they let us go, we had to dictate our insurance information to the nurse. She also gave us a handful of free sample packets containing anti-infection pills for the frostbite. I promised we'd return the hospital gowns once we had some dry clothes.

"Don't bother," she said.

When Edward arrived, he made arrangements to rent wheelchairs, which folded and fit neatly into his trunk. I introduced Cody as my friend and associate, and Edward raised a quizzical eyebrow at me. Cody reached out to shake hands, and Edward looked at him like he was crazy, then grasped the ball of gauze and gave it an awkward pump.

"You guys look like you've been to hell and back," he said.

"You might say that, assuming hell has froze over," Cody said.

"Edward, let's drive over to The King's Head, and we'll start from there and try to find Cody's truck."

"What in the good lord's name happened to you guys?"

"Later," I said, as we climbed into Edward's sedan. It didn't take more than a minute after we arrived at The King's Head to find what we were looking for. Cody's truck was parked down the street at an awkward angle to the curb, as if he'd been forced to stop. The truck appeared unmolested, save for being covered with a light coating of snow.

The nurse had stuffed our personal effects, including wet and muddy clothes, in a plastic bag. Cody asked Edward to retrieve the keys from the bag and open the truck. Fortunately, most of our stuff, including the suitcase I used to carry my bounty-hunting gear, was locked under the truck's bed cover, which was still secured. But our vests and firearms, as well as our jackets, were gone. My cell phone was also missing.

"Edward, we need to go to a hotel," I said. "Can you take a cab out here and drive the truck back for us?"

"What? Screw that," Cody said. "I'm not leaving it here. I'll drive it."

Edward pulled his car forward so Cody could stretch from the backseat of the Ford into the truck's driver's seat. He managed to get behind the wheel without falling, which was impressive considering his hands and feet were hardly functional.

"I'll just drive slow," he said. But before we pulled away, a tow truck came up the street and stopped alongside us.

"I was sent out here to tow this truck," the driver said. "They said it was abandoned."

"Who sent you?" I said.

"Sheriff's office."

"Marcus Grier?"

"Grier? No, apparently he doesn't work there anymore."

"Doesn't work there? I was just in his office last week."

"Well, he's gone now."

"Why?" I said.

"Beats me. I'm just a tow truck driver. I don't work for Silverado County."

"Who called it in then?"

He looked down at his clipboard. "Deputy Fingsten."

Edward turned the key, starting the truck for Cody, and got back into his sedan.

"I guess it ain't abandoned," the tow truck driver said.

"Sorry to disappoint you," I said.

"Hell, no skin off my ass. I get paid by the hour." He smiled, turned around, and headed back down the road.

We drove over to Harvey's Casino. I asked Edward to check us into a two-bedroom suite under a phony name. Eventually Pace and his crew would know we were still in town, but I hoped to avoid that until we were able to defend ourselves.

Edward finished at the check-in counter, then wheeled Cody and me through the lobby and over to the elevators. With my hands and feet the size of soccer balls, and wearing the hospital gown, I'm sure I looked like something out of a freak show, but Cody looked downright scary with his black eyes and unruly beard.

"You look like a broken-down Frankenstein going in for repairs," I told him on the elevator.

"Yeah? Well, I've got advice for you—save yourself some grief and don't look in any mirrors."

Once we got into our room, I filled Edward in on the details of the previous afternoon's events.

"What happens now?" he said. "Do you go into hiding, or what?"

"Or what," Cody said.

"Huh?"

"If Pace suspects we're still in town, he'll try to do something about it," I said. "Pace obviously doesn't want Sylvester Bascom's murder solved. He threatened to kill me if he sees me again."

Edward blinked and his eyes grew round. "Was he serious?"

"He nearly killed us last night," Cody said.

"Edward, your involvement potentially puts you in danger," I said. "You need to be careful you're not followed. If you see anything suspicious, call me right away. Keep your car doors locked. If you're in California and a Silverado County squad car tries to pull you over, drive into Nevada and don't stop until you get to the Douglas County Sheriff's building. It's up Highway 50 a few miles."

"Aren't you going to leave town?"

"No."

"Hell, I just got here," Cody added, a thin smile on his battered face.

"Right now I'd like to talk to John Bascom in person to update him on the situation. And also, would you mind bringing our stuff up from the truck?"

"Are we gonna eat today?" Cody said. It was noon.

"Edward, what do you say? How about a large combo pizza and some beers? And after you bring up the stuff, would you move Cody's truck across the street? Park it in back of Harrah's, in that big main lot, the one that's always packed. Try to find a spot where it's not very visible. Remember, call me if you think you're being followed."

Edward didn't protest or hesitate for a moment. "I'll call Mr. Bascom and ask him to be here shortly," he said, then left on his errands.

"The dude's a trooper," Cody said.

"Yeah, he's a good guy," I said. "I hope he's being paid well."

22

CODY AND I WERE finishing the pizza and drinking beer out of straws. The bandages on our hands were smeared with grease and pizza sauce. There was a knock on the door, and Edward let John Bascom in.

"John Bascom, Cody Gibbons," I said, enjoying a beer buzz and trying, unsuccessfully I thought, for a tone of formality. "He's a detective for San Jose PD and a close friend of mine." Cody was sitting in an easy chair with his legs propped up on another chair. He balanced a piece of pizza on his fist and leaned forward to drink out of a straw angling from a can of Coors. We were both still in our hospital gowns since we couldn't fit our clothes over the bandages on our hands and feet.

"I thought it would be best we talk in person," I said. "I met the man who stabbed your son."

"*What?*" Bascom said.

"Take a seat," I said.

"Have a beer, man," Cody said, but Bascom ignored him.

"Yeah, I met him," I said. "I haven't got his name yet, but I think he should be easy enough to find, unless he goes into hiding, and I don't think he will."

"How do you know he's the killer?" Bascom said.

"I've talked to two eyewitnesses who were in the room. They described him in detail. He was in the truck that ran me off the road, and he shot at me. Then last night, Cody and I were ambushed by him and three cops. They damn near drowned us, then we almost froze to death."

"Three cops? What in hell are you talking about?" Bascom said. His face bunched up and he squinted at me, as if I were an inept underling who'd just blown the last of his credibility. He shook his head. "You're telling me three cops did this to you last night?"

"They were trying to scare us out of town. They don't want me investigating your son's murder."

"Why the hell not? What kind of lunacy is this?"

"It may sound crazy, but it ain't bullshit," Cody said, struggling to open the flip top of a beer with a pen. Edward opened two for him and put straws in each.

"What's this all about, Reno?"

"The Silverado County sheriff, Conrad Pace, does not want me trying to find out who killed your son. I think Pace is impeding the police investigation too—that's probably why Raneswich and Iverson haven't made much progress."

"You think Raneswich and Iverson are crooked?" Bascom said.

"Good chance."

"Goddammit! I knew I couldn't trust those two jackasses!" Bascom's eyes were livid. He began pacing back and forth.

"What could possibly be Conrad Pace's motivation?" he said.

"I don't know that yet."

Bascom looked out the window. "This is all wild, just too wild," he mused. "Do you have any idea why my son was murdered?"

"I still think it was a botched robbery. Sylvester had two hookers in his room at the Crown. One of them let Michael Dean Stiles, a known drug dealer, into the room to rob Sylvester. Sven Osterlund was in the closet, watching and probably filming your son and the hookers from a peephole. Osterlund came out of the closet, and he and Sylvester got the best of Stiles. So the hooker let another man in, who was there as backup. This man stabbed your son."

"The hooker, who is the hooker who let the men in?"

"Her name's Samantha Nunez."

"So she knows for certain what happened," Bascom said.

"That's true," I said. "Raneswich and Iverson are supposedly looking for her. She's disappeared."

Bascom paced the room, rubbing his temples. "Cops on the take, murder, drugs, whores," he muttered. "My son…he had so much to live for…" Grief etched his face.

"You need to watch your back," I said. "These cops know you hired me, and they might try to convince you to forget about resolving your son's death. Their methods won't be pleasant. Check into a different hotel, under an assumed name. Or, better yet, leave town."

"What?" Bascom said. "I'm not going anywhere. Our deal was you deliver the killer. To me. Here."

"I know what our deal is."

"Are you going to finish the job?"

I stared at John Bascom. "These men will figure out soon enough I'm still in town. When they do, they may try to find me through you. You want nothing to do with Conrad Pace, believe me. Leave town. Tonight. Take Edward and your family with you."

Bascom ignored me. "I want the names of all the crooked cops, Reno. If they're protecting the son of a bitch who killed my boy, they need to be prosecuted. I know the editor in chief at the *Sacramento Bee*, and if what you say is true, this will be the story of the year."

I shook my head. "You don't seem to be hearing me–"

"I hear you loud and clear, goddammit! I'm paying you to do a job, not shell out chickenshit advice! From what it looks like, you'd be better off looking out for yourself instead of worrying about me."

"Keep your money. I don't need it."

"I didn't take you for a quitter, Reno."

My mouth tightened, and I looked at the floor and took a deep breath. "You remind me of a man I used to know, Mr. Bascom. He never backed down from a situation in his life. And when he died before his time, it left an empty hole in a lot of lives."

"Is dime-store sentimentality included in a package deal with shoddy, unfinished detective work?" he replied.

"I've got enough bodies on my conscience. I don't need yours."

Bascom paced the room with his hands on his hips. I watched him impotently, feeling like a clown in the hospital gown. After a length of time had passed, he looked down at me.

"I understand you're disabled at the moment, but the killer of my son is still free and nameless," he said.

• • •

After Bascom and Edward left, Cody and I sat around like a couple of extras from a mummy movie, watching TV and drinking slow beers. The next day I found Marcus Grier's home phone number in the white pages and managed to dial his number, but there was no answer.

By our second evening at the hotel, Cody proclaimed he had mastered the art of drinking beer through a straw.

"Watch, I can down one almost as fast as if I was chugging it." He set up a beer can on the table and drained it.

I decided we'd remove our bandages and check out the next morning. We had settled in to watch the seven o'clock movie when the room phone rang.

"Dan, it's Edward." His voice was trembling. "Those guys. Those bastards found me."

· · ·

The way Edward told it, they had caught him as he was walking to his car after having dinner at a small burger joint, a quiet place away from the lights and commotion of the casinos.

"Stop right there, boy," a voice said, and Conrad Pace emerged from the dark, his face shadowed by his cowboy hat. "Nice night like tonight, you're not in any hurry, right?"

"Actually, I am," Edward said.

"You'd best slow down, son. It's downright impolite to turn your back on me."

Edward walked faster and nearly reached his car, but Pace was too close. He grabbed Edward's arm and stood over him, then struck him across the mouth with the side of his gloved fist, the coarse leather opening a cut on Edward's lip.

"A couple friends of yours, a private eye and his buddy. I'd like to have a word with them. So why don't we get in your car and you drive me to where they're at?"

A bloody string of spittle fell from Edward's mouth. He looked up at Pace and saw his yellowed teeth and gray mustache in a streak of light from a car passing by on the road.

"I don't know what you're talking about," Edward said.

"Get in the fucking car," Pace said.

A hand suddenly closed around Edward's neck from behind.

"Pay attention, Theo," a different voice said. Edward froze at the sound of his middle name. His mother was the only one who had ever called him Theo. The hand tightened on his neck.

"You lucky," the voice whispered, "maybe I let you live."

As Edward fumbled with his keys, he saw a dark hand reach out, holding a pair of arced garden shears. The steel blades glinted in the moonlight.

"You know what these are for?" the voice said. "I sharpened them myself."

Edward dropped his keys to the gravel, and as he bent to pick them up a carload of drunks careened into the parking lot, the sedan lurching on its springs and skidding sideways over patches of ice and rock. Laughter and jeers spilled from a partially rolled-down window, and a fleshy buttocks, half exposed above lowered jeans, was pressed up against the glass. The car's tail end came around, the tires locked and skidding, and hit the back bumper of Edward's Ford. The Ford jolted on impact, Conrad Pace was knocked to the ground, and then the hand was no longer on Edward's neck.

The driver of the sedan pegged the throttle, roasting the tires in a well-executed fishtail, and bounced down the curb and back out onto the highway.

Edward snatched his keys up and broke for the tree line, scrambling like a cat with a dog on its tail. His rubber soles caught traction, and he caught a terrifying glimpse of a barrel-shaped, dark man behind him. Edward hurdled a low fence, and then he was in the trees, darting and cutting through the moonlit woods.

He ran instinctively, fueled by fear and adrenaline. The garden shears whizzed past him, tumbling through the air like a pinwheel. Edward leaped a shallow stream and followed the water down into the forest, running full out, his feet dancing around snow-covered rocks, branches, and stumps, his hands knocking icy foliage from his face.

Ten minutes later he stopped, panting and soaked with sweat. His pursuers were nowhere in sight. He crouched and waited, hidden in the lee of a fallen pine, and after a few minutes his pulse returned to normal. That's when he pulled his cell phone from his pocket and called me.

. . .

The next morning the room looked like the aftermath of a high-school party. Empty beer cans were strewn about the floor, and a pizza box lay face down on the carpet. I hobbled into the bathroom and tried to brush my teeth.

"I'm done with these bandages," Cody said when I came out. He was gnawing at his hand.

"Let me call the doctor first," I said. After a minute I reached a nurse who said if we removed the wrapping, we should wear gloves and two pairs of socks for another week. I began tearing at the gauze with my teeth and managed to unwrap my right hand. It was pale and stiff, and a collection of small blisters covered the skin on my fingers. Working the muscles, I was able to make a fist after a minute.

We were peeling the wrappings from our feet when Edward arrived.

"You sure that's a good idea?" he said, watching us pull at the bandages.

"No," I said.

"But it beats the hell out of not being able to scratch your balls," Cody said, flexing his hand.

"Or hold a beer can," I said.

"Speaking of which, looks like you guys had a good time last night," Edward commented, glancing around the room. His lower lip was swollen, and there was a broad scrape across his cheek.

"You okay?" I asked.

"Fine, except for a fat lip," Edward said. "Well, there's no question Conrad Pace knows you're still in town."

"He's probably got a lot of eyes out there. You sure you weren't followed here?"

He nodded vigorously. "Yes, I was very careful. After I lost them in the woods, I made my way out and walked back to the Nevada side. I spent the night at one of the cheap hotels behind the casinos, and picked up my car once it was light. What are you going to do now?" His eyes were round and full of anxiety and expectation.

I stretched my fingers and squeezed them into a fist. "Go back to work," I said.

"Here you go," Edward said, his expression uncertain and a bit incredulous. He had picked up our freshly washed clothes from the hotel laundry. He set the neat stack in my hands. My fingers didn't feel normal; the joints ached, and the pads seemed a little numb. But at least now I could change out of the ridiculous hospital getup.

"Mr. Bascom called his friend at the newspaper," Edward said. "The guy wants to talk to you. From what I gather, this is the type of story that can make a career for a journalist. Here's his number."

Once Cody had his hands and feet free, he called room service for breakfast. "You want anything?" he asked Edward, who politely declined, then left for his hotel.

"Hey," I said, as Cody lumbered off toward the shower, "I promised Edward I'd take him to the cathouse while we're here. I owe him that."

"I'd say we have more important things to do," he replied.

I picked up the phone book and found a listing for a gun shop and shooting range in Stateline. We had breakfast, then walked outside into a thin sunlight that provided little warmth. Cody set out across the street over to Harrah's, while I hung back, watching for a tail. I waited a minute, then followed him. I saw Cody reach his truck, parked under a tree in the middle of Harrah's parking lot. I was still without a jacket, and I put my hands in my jean pockets and hurried to get out of the cold.

"Looks clear," Cody said from the cab as I walked up.

"Yeah, I didn't see anyone suspicious."

We drove around town, running errands, taking care of business. I stopped at the bank and took out three grand in cash. When we drove off the iced-over curb onto the road, my cell phone tumbled out from under Cody's passenger seat. I hadn't seen it since being abducted by Pace, and I had assumed it was gone. The display said I had two messages. The first was from Iverson. He had called that morning, asking I call him back. The second message was from Beverly Howitt. I heard her say her name and leave a number. I jotted it down and folded it carefully away in my pocket.

On the way back into Nevada, we did what we should have done first, which was to find a sporting goods store and buy gloves for our blistered hands. I also picked up a fancy blue ski jacket, one of the expensive brands I had never been able to afford. Cody chose a heavy-duty green parka, size XXL. Before leaving, I found us some thick wool socks and bought both of us new boots.

Our next stop was a shooting range and survival shop on the outskirts of Stateline. I had never seen a store carrying such a huge selection of military gear.

"Hellfire, you could arm a small country," Cody said as we looked around in awe.

"What, are the tanks out back?" I asked the guy behind the counter.

"No, you have to order them through the catalog," he said with a straight face.

An hour later we were outfitted with new top-of-the-line flak jackets and firearms. Cody had given me a ration of shit over my preference for the Italian-made Beretta automatic—he was partial to a Smith & Wesson .44 Magnum revolver—but he quieted down after I outshot him at the store's indoor range. We each picked up three boxes of hollow-point ammunition.

"Payback's a bitch," Cody said, weighing a box of bullets in his hand.

"What's Pace's game?" I said as we climbed into Cody's truck. "Why's he so hell-bent on preventing me from investigating Bascom's murder? What's his relationship with the Samoan?"

Cody gave me a hard glance. "Don't underestimate crooked cops. Once they go down that road, there's no turning back."

"Pace must be involved in something pretty heavy."

"Weird for him to have actually taken part in putting the muscle on us. His kind usually don't like to get their hands dirty."

"Pace is different. He enjoyed it," I said.

"No shit, huh? I'm gonna enjoy punting my foot up his ass. That's a promise. I still feel bad about being on the crapper when they snatched you."

"Bascom was a rich kid. I wonder what he was involved in."

"It's all just mental masturbation, Dirt. How about a little less talk and a little more action?"

23

WE WERE DRIVING THROUGH a neighborhood a few blocks from Pistol Pete's when I spotted the tail. I told Cody to pull over, and I watched a light-blue Subaru turn into a driveway a hundred yards behind us. When we started again, I saw the car back out and slowly follow us.

"Could be anyone of them, Pace, Perdie, or the Samoan," I said, feeling my stomach tighten.

We turned onto Highway 50 and drove east through the tourist traffic. Once we passed the state line, I jumped out at a light and ducked into Harvey's Casino. I watched the street from behind the dark glass doors as Cody drove on, followed by the blue Subaru three cars later. The driver peered toward Harvey's as he went by, but he couldn't see me through the mirrored glass. I looked at him in surprise. "Hello, asshole," I muttered. It was Raneswich.

I went out Harvey's back door, hiking through the ice and mud. I ducked into The Horizon and came out their side exit into the parking lot, then slipped through the double doors of Pistol Pete's. I took a seat in a comfortable chair in the spacious hotel lobby. Pistol Pete's was decorated in an exaggerated Old West motif—gunfight murals dominated the walls, and various cowboy paraphernalia—saddles, bullwhips, rifles, and the like—were on display in large glass cases. A life-size bronze sculpture of a cowboy on a rearing mustang overlooked the lobby from a large pedestal.

I read a local entertainment paper, watching the passersby like a husband waiting for his perpetually late wife. About ten minutes later, Cody walked in, his thick thatch of straw-like hair visible above the masses.

"You lose him?" I said.

"Yeah," he chuckled. "Medium height, stocky, light hair, right?"

"That's Raneswich."

"I parked behind Harrah's and sprinted in the back door. I saw him trying to keep up, but he hit an ice slick and did a header into a parked car. I came across on the pedestrian underpass."

"Nice work," I said. "Let's go."

We split up. My goal was to find the Samoan—Samantha Nunez, for what it was worth, said he could be found at Pistol Pete's. If I saw him, I would try to get him alone and subdue him with my stun gun, then take him to Bascom. As far as plans go, it was thin, but left a lot of room to improvise.

Cody took the keno area, the sports book, and the surrounding slot floors, while I searched the main card floor, including the adjoining bars and slot machine rows. The casino was crowded, even though it was before noon. The masses were a diverse mixture of old folks, kids, white trash and white collar, rowdy drunks, and intently serious gamblers, with a heavy representation of Asians, blacks, Mexicans, and some people who looked like a mixture of all three. I didn't find that to be a curiosity; California had become so racially diverse that people with blended ethnicity were commonplace.

By the end of an hour, I must have looked into a thousand faces. A man in his sixties sitting next to me at a blackjack table lost eight straight ten-dollar hands and finally quit, red faced and muttering "fuck," "shit," and "goddamn" in all their possible combinations. Two dudes who looked barely out of their teens caught fire at the craps table; one rolled the dice for twenty minutes before crapping out. He said he was up $900, then he doubled his bets and walked away broke five minutes later. At the roulette wheel a stunning platinum blonde in a low-cut red dress stood next to a short fat man in a black overcoat. He wore sunglasses, a gold derby with a pink feather in the band, and his blond hair went past his shoulders. His hands stayed busy moving three-inch-high stacks of chips around the board.

Cody and I met at the casino's Mexican restaurant. Neither of us had had any luck spotting the Samoan. But Cody hit a $200-dollar jackpot on the slots and was anxious to try his luck again. We had lunch and headed back to the casino, trading sections. By midafternoon I was bored stiff and doubting Samantha Nunez's tip that the Samoan would be at Pistol Pete's. She'd have every reason to lie; I couldn't think of a good reason for her to tell the truth.

I walked across the casino to find Cody, and was passing the show ticket window when the man I knew as the Samoan stepped out from a door marked "EMPLOYEES ONLY." I froze and watched him speak briefly to a cocktail waitress, who seemed anxious to be on her way. He wore black slacks, a black sports coat, and a gold turtleneck stretched tight across his wide chest. Our eyes met, and I took a step in his direction, my hand reaching inside my coat for my stun gun. He blinked, as if irritated, and his thick lips flattened.

I could see his muscles flexing under his coat from ten feet away. I instinctively moved laterally, getting in better position to strike. His knees were bent, his hands moving away from his body, and I felt sure he'd come at me—he looked like a coiled cobra. But instead he turned and calmly went back through the door from which he'd come.

Within a minute I found Cody wandering the floor. He had lost most of the money he'd won at slots and was grumpy. "I should have quit when I was ahead," he said.

"Famous last words. Come on, I found our man."

"Where?"

"This way." We walked around the casino to the door next to the ticket window. "He came out from here."

"He's an employee, huh? How do you want to play it?"

"Let's stake out the parking lot and take him down when he leaves the building."

"I got a better idea," Cody said. "Let's go knock his dick in the dirt."

"No, wait," I said, but Cody was already opening the door.

"Goddammit," I said, and followed him in.

The hallway was dingy and cramped. It was so narrow Cody almost had to turn sideways to accommodate the width of his shoulders. The walls were once white, but had faded to a dirty gray and were streaked with black in places.

We turned the corner into an area where three women were counting money, filling out slips of paper, and handing them through one of a series of teller-style windows. Behind the window a dozen people sat recounting the money and signing slips. At the end of the row a man was banding stacks of cash and placing the bills in a metal rack.

"So this is where the money goes," Cody said.

"The bowels of gambling," I said. "This is the ass end."

We continued through the room to a wider hallway, past a wall of lockers, a lunchroom, and some closed doors. The hallway turned, and at the end of the corridor I could see a glass door leading outside.

"Hold on," I said, turning around. We walked back and almost ran into the Samoan as he came around the corner.

Later, I would remember a particular odor that emanated from his body. He smelled of char and smoke, as if he'd been tending a garbage fire.

"You work here, where's your name tag?" Cody said.

"You're trespassing," the Samoan said.

My hand was on my stun gun, but at that moment the door from the parking lot opened, and Raneswich and Deputy Fingsten walked in.

I unzipped my jacket to give me access to the Beretta.

"What are you gonna do, tough guy, draw on us here?" Fingsten said, sneering around a plug of chewing tobacco in his lip.

"You know, Fingsten, I think you're in the wrong business," I said. "I think you're going to learn that the hard way, very soon."

Fingsten glared at me, but his hand went to his ribs and he grimaced.

Raneswich hadn't yet acknowledged Cody or me. He stood with his lips pressed and his eyes averted. "These men your guests?" Raneswich finally said to the Samoan. The Samoan shook his head, and Fingsten grabbed Cody by the elbow. "Let's go," he said.

Cody pulled away as if a child were playing with him. "Have you been drinking chocolate milk?" Cody said. "It looks like you got a little mustache. Here, I'll clean it up." Cody grabbed Fingsten by the head and roughly ran his finger over Fingsten's mustache in a scrubbing motion. Fingsten flailed like mad, his feet skittering, his fists hitting Cody ineffectually on the forearms.

I laughed out loud, and even Raneswich smiled.

The Samoan watched impassively, his eyes never leaving me.

Cody finally let Fingsten go, and he immediately drew his service revolver. "Hands on top of your head, now!" Fingsten screamed, his face reddened and his hair a mess. His cap was on the floor—Cody had smashed it flat with his size-thirteen shoe. "Assault on an officer, motherfucker. You are going down!"

A few feet from us, a door opened and a man stuck his head out. "What the hell is going on out here?"

"A trespassing and drunk-in-public violation," Raneswich said.

"These fucking assholes are looking at serious time!" Fingsten yelled, waving his pistol. A group of casino employees had heard the commotion and were gathering down the hall and watching.

"Jesus Christ," the man said. "Let's resolve this in my office."

"Who are you?" I said.

"I'm Salvador Tuma, manager of this casino."

I looked at Cody, who shrugged, and we walked into a big office with paneled walls, tan carpet, a large oak desk, and a number of padded chairs. On the desk was a name stand that read "SALVADOR TUMA, PRESIDENT."

The Samoan walked behind the desk and stood to the side. He continued to stare at me, his pupils small, the whites of his eyes opaque and fractured by a network of tiny veins that looked like electrical current. The rest of us sat, except for Fingsten, who paced back and forth, his face a mask of fury and humiliation.

Salvador Tuma looked about fifty. His hair was graying and his complexion was like coarse sand. He had thick shoulders and good posture. A thin scar ran from the corner of his eye down a cheek.

"Take a seat, Deputy," he sighed. Fingsten scowled and sat down.

"What do we have here?" he said, a man used to dealing with problems, with confrontations.

"A couple drunks trespassing," Raneswich replied.

"How about assault on an officer?" Fingsten yelled, standing and pointing at Cody.

"Junior, if you point at me again, I'm gonna take your arm off and stick it up your ass," Cody said.

Tuma's eyes flickered impatiently. "What's your name?" he asked me.

"I took a wrong turn on my way out. I was gambling at your casino, and I was on my way home."

"His name's Dan Reno," Fingsten said. "He's a private eye."

"You mean the one who–"

"That's right," Fingsten said. "That's the asshole."

Tuma stared at me with eyes that were almost black, and it wasn't until then I made the connection between him and Jake Tuma, the whacked-out dude I had fought at the Midnight Tavern.

"Jake's your son?" I asked.

"You're the one who beat him up?" Tuma said, his voice thick and rising.

"He was blasted out of his gourd on drugs and booze, harassing women at a bar, and he took a swing at me. He brought it on himself."

"That's not how I heard it," Tuma said. He started out of his chair but quickly composed himself and sat back down. His expression went blank as stone, and he stared past me at a point on the wall.

I had no idea if my incident with Jake Tuma could be related to the Samoan stabbing Sylvester Bascom. For that matter, I didn't know if the fact the Samoan worked for Salvador Tuma had anything to do with the murder. But I had no doubt it was not coincidental that we were all in this room together. Regardless, my goal was to get the Samoan alone and take him down, and it wasn't going to happen here and now.

"Well, sorry for the imposition. I'll watch where I'm going next time." I rose from my chair. "By the way," I said, looking at the Samoan, "I enjoyed meeting you the other day, out by that stream. But you forgot to properly introduce yourself."

The Samoan stared back at me, not moving, his ugly face watching, his eyes dead and cold, like a shark's eyes.

"I don't think he's interested in conversing with you," Tuma said.

As we left the office, Fingsten jumped up and protested, but Raneswich pulled him back. We went out the back door into the snowy parking lot.

"Tuma is paying off those cops, no doubt," Cody said as we walked to his truck. "You see how they acted? It's obvious. They work for Tuma big time. You can see it in the way he talks to them."

"That would explain why Marcus Grier wasn't interested in busting Jake Tuma," I mumbled.

"Huh?"

I gave Cody a quick run-down on the fight at Zeke's. "Marcus Grier mentioned Jake was the son of a Pistol Pete's executive, and it was obvious Jake wasn't going to be charged."

"The whole department's probably on the take."

"Grier doesn't strike me as corrupt," I said, then I thought of Mr. 187's final words: "The sheriff…"

"Let's hope not," Cody said. "It'd be nice to know if there's a cop or two in this county we can trust."

"A casino paying off the police," I mused. "What's the point? Aren't they getting rich enough off gambling?"

"Get real. It smells like the mob. The goal is always to make more money."

"I find it hard to believe any law enforcement agency could let someone get away with murder," I said. "I can see them allowing smaller stuff, drugs, prostitution, the usual vices, but not violent crimes."

"Greed's a powerful thing, Dirt. The Samoan didn't shy away from ramming you off the interstate and blasting away at you with an Uzi. Since he's working for Tuma, the cops won't touch him. There's no telling what he might do."

I looked at Cody in silence. Snowflakes were gathering on his head and beard. The creases on his forehead forced his eyebrows into a V, and his mouth was set in a scowl.

• • •

We decided to stake out the rear employees' exit at Pistol Pete's, hoping the Samoan would eventually leave by that door. Cody drove us around the employee parking area first, searching for a dark, full-size American-made truck, but there were at least two hundred vehicles there, and probably a dozen trucks that fit the description.

It became a moot point fifteen minutes later, when the Samoan, Raneswich, and Fingsten all came out of the casino's back door and left together in Raneswich's Subaru. We followed them to a liquor store, and then south, past the city limits and into Meyers. When they went by the last gas station in town, I slowed and hung a U-turn.

"What are you doing?" Cody said.

"They're headed over the pass," I said. "We're going to have to wait to get the Samoan alone. But I've got a hunch. Hang with me." Cody glanced at me sharply, then shrugged. "It's your party."

I pulled a crumpled telephone book page out of my back pocket, and in twenty minutes we parked in front of the address for Marcus Grier's residence. The house was in a quiet neighborhood, about a mile off the main drag. A silver Jeep Cherokee was parked in the plowed driveway under the shadow of a huge old-growth pine, its needles stretching high into the darkening afternoon. Three feet of snow buried the yard, but a neat walkway was carved up to the front door.

We parked on the icy curb and walked to the door, vests on, weapons loaded. I didn't think Grier was part of Conrad Pace's gang, but I wasn't in the mood to take chances.

Near the front door, hidden from plain sight by the shadows, was a broad red discoloration in the snow. The stain was fresh. Cody and I stared at it grimly, and I eased my gun out of its holster. Cody motioned to me and stood on the small, covered porch aside the door, holding his .44. I stood opposite him, my back against the wall, and reached out and rapped on the door. It swung open after a moment, and Marcus Grier took a step onto the porch. He wore a green, long-sleeved shirt and a pair of pleated khaki pants. He saw Cody first and froze.

"Afternoon, Sheriff," I said. "That's Cody Gibbons."

Grier turned in my direction. "What is the meaning of this, Mr. Reno?"

"What happened?" I said, nodding at the spot.

"None of your business," he said, his eyes locked on my gun hand.

"I asked you a question, Sheriff."

"I'm no longer sheriff, Reno, but as a citizen I don't take kindly to two armed men trespassing on my property. What do you want?"

"I'd like to talk to you about a couple people—Jake Tuma and Conrad Pace."

He shook his head. "Sounds like police business. I'm out of it now."

"I don't think so," Cody said.

"Why did you lose your job?" I said.

He raised his head. "Why do you assume it's any of your business?" His voice was a course baritone.

"Cody and I had a run-in two nights ago with Deputies Fingsten and Perdie, along with Conrad Pace and an assassin who works for Salvador Tuma. We were fortunate to survive."

His thumbs hooked in his belt loops, Grier stared us down.

"Pace is going down big time," I said. "Nothing can stop that now."

Grier's face creased in doubt, but I saw a glimmer of hope flicker in his eyes. He looked down for a long moment, then raised his head.

"This morning I found our family dog, dead," he said. "Someone cut him from his throat to belly. I tried to remove the animal before my daughter saw it. But I was too late."

"You know who did it?" I said.

Grier's eyes, bulging and bloodshot, locked onto mine. Then he turned and gestured for us to follow him inside. Cody and I re-holstered our pieces and did so.

We stood at his kitchen table. The area was well heated by a wood-burning stove in the adjoining family room.

"Coffee?" he asked.

"Sure," I said.

"No, thank you," Cody said. But when Marcus Grier set a bottle of bourbon on the table, Cody's eyes lit up. "Whiskey will do," he said.

"You say you've met Conrad Pace," Grier said.

"Yeah, I've had the pleasure," I said, then I told him about Pace's attempt to scare us out of town.

"The Samoan," Grier said. "His name is Julo Nafui. Ex-mercenary, spent time in El Salvador, Libya, Afghanistan—he's not particular. He works wherever there's a paycheck to be had. Apparently, he found an opportunity here."

"He works for Salvador Tuma."

"That's right," Grier said. "Which means he also works for Conrad Pace."

"Nafui's the man who stabbed Sylvester Bascom to death."

"That I didn't know, but I can't say I'm shocked."

"Why is Salvador Tuma paying off Pace? What's their deal?"

Grier poured a jolt of whiskey into his coffee cup. "You ever been to New Mexico, Mr. Reno?"

"I spent a week in Albuquerque one night. Why?"

"There's a small town out there looking for a sheriff. I hear it's not a bad place to live. Maybe I'll drive down there, see the sights, check it out."

"Or maybe you'll stay here and help fry Pace's grits," Cody said, helping himself to the whiskey. "That is, unless you got something to hide."

"What the hell do you know about it?" Grier rose to his feet, his voice booming. He snatched the bottle out of Cody's hands.

"I'm a detective with San Jose PD," Cody said, standing in turn. "I've been on the job for six years. I was right in the middle of the big shakeout a few years ago, when eleven patrolmen were indicted for taking bribes, stealing drugs, and falsifying evidence. One of the patrolmen was my partner. I hear they still keep him in solitary confinement at San Quentin for his own safety."

"I never ratted out another cop," Grier said. "What about you?"

"Let me tell you this, I never took a damn dime, and I watched the guys around me buying new cars and fancy clothes, going out to dinner all the time at expensive joints, divorcing their wives and screwing bimbos, and acting like their shit don't stink. I didn't say a word, but when they put me on the stand, put my hand on the goddamned Bible and said, 'Tell the truth or risk perjury,' you know what?" Cody slammed his hand down on the table, rattling the plates in the cabinet behind him. "I told the truth. Because those patrolmen weren't cops anymore. They were crooks, just like the everyday scumbags we busted on the streets. My loyalty to them went out the window when they started living the fucking highlife with dirty money."

Grier rolled the whiskey bottle back and forth in his hands. Cody sat back down, and Grier reached over and poured a splash into his cup. He placed his hands flat on the table, looking at the two of us.

"So you guys think you can put away Conrad Pace."

"He's going down, Sheriff," I said.

"Talk is cheap," Grier said.

"We'll finish him…with your help."

Grier's eyes seemed intent on bulging out of his skull, and his skin shone as if a coat of oil lay on the surface. Finally he looked away and took a quick pull straight from the bottle.

"Pace," he snorted, his voice edged with disgust. "When he was elected, I'd been deputy sheriff in South Lake Tahoe for four years. I own this home free and clear, and it's a nice life for my wife and daughters. Clean air, slow pace, nice scenery. Not a bad place to raise a family, right?"

I nodded.

"Pace had been a county sheriff in Louisiana," he continued, "and even though there were rumors of trouble from down South, he won the election here easily because there was little opposition. The previous sheriff had retired, and Pace came into town and ran a slick campaign. When Pace took office, he started weeding out the minorities and bringing in his own people. Perdie? Supposedly he's Pace's cousin. And Fingsten is his nephew. I had been somewhat removed from his workings since the county office is down in Placerville. But when he forced me to hire Perdie and Fingsten, I started to understand what he was up to. Those clowns don't do much to hide it.

"Pace somehow got hooked up with Salvador Tuma, a mobster originally from New York. The Tuma family is heavily involved in casino interests in Vegas and Atlantic City. Once Tuma and Pace got in bed together, Tuma set up a drug dealing hub in Placerville that supplies the Central Valley, Sacramento, Stockton, down to Modesto, and also the Tahoe and Reno area. They run everything; coke, meth, ecstasy, pot, you name it. Tuma put his son Jake in charge of the operation. I imagine under Pace's protection, they've made boatloads of money. Pace is getting a healthy cut—you ought to see the mansion he lives in out at Granite Bay. Anyway, Michael Dean Stiles, the man you shot? He worked for Jake Tuma. And so does Julo Nafui. He handles collections and discourages competitors."

"So that's why you let Jake Tuma skate that night at Zeke's."

"Yes. He gets a free pass, thanks to Pace."

"What about the local police departments? Aren't they on to Pace by now?"

"Pace is an extremely effective manipulator, and he's also cunning and ruthless. Somehow nothing ever sticks to him. He's slicker than owl shit."

"How about Raneswich and Iverson?"

"Raneswich is dirty. Iverson, I don't know."

"Did you quit your job?" I asked.

"No. Although I considered it every day for the last six months. What happened was Perdie and Fingsten were both incompetent and spending a lot of time tending to Tuma's drug business. I chewed them out the other day, and twenty-four hours later Pace fired me for misconduct."

I picked up a piece of paper and wrote the phone number of the Sacramento journalist that John Bascom gave me.

"Call this guy, Marcus," I said, handing him the phone number. "He's from the *Sacramento Bee*, and he's familiar with some of the recent events involving Pace and his crew. With your input, he'll be able get a running start on hanging Pace out to dry."

We stood to leave. Grier stared at the piece of paper in his hand.

"Who did that to your dog?" I said.

"It was Perdie. Had to be. It's his style. There was a note pinned to the body saying I'm next unless I keep my mouth shut."

When we drove away, Grier was still on his porch, studying the piece of paper I'd given him.

24

"WE GOT A PROBLEM now, Cuz," Louis Perdie said to Conrad Pace, the phone sweaty against his cheek. "Reno and his buddy were at Pistol Pete's earlier today and ended up in Sal Tuma's office."

Pace's eyes jumped under his furrowed brow. "They talked to Tuma? This some kind of joke, Louis?"

"No, sir, and there's more. They just left Marcus Grier's house."

Pace squeezed his eyes shut and felt his ears reddening. "Louis, you need to make goddamn sure you know what you're talking about."

"One of our guys is following them now."

Pace exhaled, and calmness slowly replaced his anger, an emotional response he attached to the inevitability of what must be done.

"Tell him not to lose them. I'll call Julo Nafui."

• • •

"Now I know what Michael Dean Stiles meant by his last words," I said, as we drove away from Grier's house.

"What's that?"

"He said, 'The sheriff.' I thought he meant Marcus Grier. But he was talking about Conrad Pace."

Cody grunted. "You know what I don't get?" he said. "You got a casino guy paying off a sheriff so he can run a drug ring. You got Michael Dean Stiles, AKA Mr. One Eight Seven, and Julo whatever the fuck helping run the show. But how does that tie in to Bascom's murder? What's the connection between the drugs and Bascom?"

"Julo Nafui knows the answer to that. So does Samantha Nunez. I also told Edward to get Sylvester Bascom's bank records for the last six months. That might tell us something."

"Why don't you ask him to meet us at a bar?"

"All right," I said. "Just do me a favor and try to stay reasonably sober."

"Sometimes I do my best work with a buzz," he said, winking.

It was one of his lines I would remember.

• • •

We took a table at a neighborhood lounge off 50, and I called Edward.

"Julo Nafui," I said, spelling it for him. "Like I said yesterday, he's Salvador Tuma's henchman. He works at Pistol Pete's, or at least has access to the back rooms."

"What are you going to do now?" Edward said.

"My job."

"Oh, right, I meant—anyway, I've got Sylvester's bank records, if you're still interested."

"I am. We're at this dive…hold on. Hey, man," I yelled at the kid tending bar, "what's the name of this joint?"

"The Chatter Box," he said.

"Why don't I meet you there at eight?" Edward said.

After we hung up, I turned to Cody. "I'm gonna try something." I dialed the number Iverson left for me.

"Afternoon, Detective," I said. "Have you arrested Julo Nafui yet?"

"Who?"

"Salvador Tuma's henchman. The one who murdered Sylvester Bascom and probably also Sven Osterlund."

"I see," Iverson said.

"Quit wasting time, Iverson. Arrest Julo Nafui. He's the one who stabbed Sylvester Bascom to death."

"Where'd you find this out?"

"It doesn't matter. He also almost killed my friend and me. Put out an APB on him."

"You don't need to tell me how to do my job," he said. "Hey, John Bascom called my boss and told your story of being dunked and left to freeze in the hills. By Conrad Pace!" He chuckled.

"You find that farfetched? You were there when he abducted us."

"I was there when he arrested you. If Conrad Pace wanted you out of the picture, you'd be sitting in a cell right now, not walking the streets."

"Detective, I'm going to tell you something for your own personal protection. I'm not sure if you're on the take or not, but even if you're not, I don't sense you're going to play any role in taking down the bad guys, other than maybe filing some paperwork. So this is just information hopefully you can use to keep yourself out of trouble. Okay?"

"Continue, please. I can't wait to hear this."

"Conrad Pace is taking money from Tuma to allow him to deal drugs out of Placerville. Two deputies, Perdie and Fingsten, are relatives of Pace, and they're part of the deal. So is your partner, Raneswich. Pace has a vested interest in protecting Tuma, and that includes Julo Nafui. Hopefully you can draw your own conclusions."

"My, my, don't we have an active imagination," he chortled.

"Maybe I'm not telling you anything you don't already know, huh?"

"Listen to me," a different voice said.

I felt a sudden violation at having an unexpected party on the line. My throat tightened, and I could feel the heat rise in my face.

"Who is this?"

"Shut up and listen to me. You come into my town and trample all over my turf, preventing this police department from conducting a proper investigation, and then you start spraying around these ludicrous accusations—"

"How's it going, Raneswich?"

"I should have thrown you in jail last week. Obstruction of justice, breaking and entering, drunk in public, murder—you're a prosecutor's dream. I want you out of town. And not just South Lake Tahoe—that means Reno, Truckee, the whole damn region."

"You're pissing in the wind," I said. "Why don't you go back to drinking from the toilet, or whatever it is you spend your working hours doing?"

I heard Raneswich suck in his breath through his teeth.

"I like your attitude. On second thought, hang around a while. It will make for a real nice day when I lock you up. I know some inmates down at Folsom who would love to meet you."

"Give it up, Raneswich. I know you're sucking off Conrad Pace and Salvador Tuma for chump change. You think they'll give a shit when you're indicted along with them?"

"I find it incredible a person like you is on the streets in this city. But that'll be a temporary situation," he said, and the line went dead.

"Don't you hate it when they get in the last word?" Cody said, as I set my phone down.

"The Tahoe PD has no interest in Nafui," I said.

He raised his beer mug to me. "At least you don't have to compete with them for the bounty." He had a point, but at that moment the money was the last thing on my mind. The exchange with Raneswich had confirmed that the morally insane were running the show, and both the criminals and the dirty cops would stop at nothing to preserve their cozy little arrangement. I was both angry and disheartened, and felt a strong urge to just leave the cesspool to those who inhabited it.

"You know why we're still here?" Cody said, his eyes boring into mine. "Packing this new iron, wearing these vests, hanging around town? You know why? It's because those guys caught us with our dicks out and our pants around our ankles, and it was *easy*. We barely put up a fight, and they took us out to that river and had a good laugh while we nearly drown and froze to death. They treated us like a couple of amateurs."

Cody took a long hit off his beer. "And neither of us wants to leave until that score is settled. We're gonna find those assholes, or, if they find us first, we'll be ready. Then we'll settle the fucking score."

I looked at Cody. Even though his words sounded like boozy, macho, bar-rail boasting, I couldn't argue his conclusion. But my reasoning was a little different. Yes, the criminals and corrupt cops had to be put out of commission. They all needed to go down, because any one of them might gladly kill us, given the opportunity. And that included the whole band: Nafui, Pace, Louis Perdie, and the dipshit cop Fingsten. And Raneswich, and maybe Iverson too, if he got in the way.

When I went out to the back patio to have a smoke, the skies had turned dark. Gray and white clouds were moving slowly over the lake with the wind, from the west. It looked like another goddamned storm.

While we waited for Edward, I took a seat at a cocktail table in the back of the place and called the number for the *Sacramento Bee*. I spent an hour on the phone with a journalist, giving him a detailed account of what had happened during the last three days. I gave him names, dates, everything I could think of. He said there had been vague rumors of corruption in Silverado County for months, but no one ever got a handle on it. "This is big," he said.

"How'd it go?" Cody asked when I came back to the bar.

"I think I just poured a shitload of grief into Conrad Pace's life. We'll see how he and his buddies deal with that."

We had dinner and watched TV, drinking slow beers, staying away from the hard stuff. By the time Edward showed up, I had switched to coffee.

"You look comfortable," I said. Edward was wearing jeans, boots, and a t-shirt. It was the first time I'd seen him wear anything but his business clothes. "Are those the bank records?"

"Yes." He handed me the thick folder. "Give me a margarita on the rocks with a shot of Herradura on the side," Edward told the bartender. Cody raised his eyes and nodded in approval.

The copies of Sylvester Bascom's canceled checks from the last six months covered thirty pages. I flipped through the sheets, looking for large amounts, scanning the payees for Osterlund or Tuma. Out of the dozens of checks, accounting for over $40,000 of expenditures, not one looked like it may have been used to buy or otherwise finance drugs.

"Well, Edward," I said finally. "You ready to head out to the cathouse?"

"Sure, just for the experience—I mean, just to see what's going on."

"Hey, whatever you do is your own business," I said.

"Yeah, monkey business," Cody said, his bulletproof vest tight and bulky across his torso.

We piled into Edward's Crown Victoria and eased our way through the traffic lights on 50, rolling slowly past the casinos, heading out of town. A blanket of whiteness covered the dirt and grit of the city, and snowflakes drifted lazily from the heavy sky. It seemed unusually quiet for Stateline, as if the town was muted by the weight of the snow.

Once the road turned east the forest thinned out, and was gradually replaced by the lonely landscape of the desert. We climbed over Spooner Summit, the Ford's big motor pulling us up the grade. The pass was nearly deserted.

"Edward, I called Iverson and told him it's Julo Nafui he's looking for," I said.

"What is it with Raneswich and Iverson?" Edward glanced at me as he drove. "Are you sure they're in league with these bad cops? Or maybe they're just really incompetent? It doesn't seem like they ever made much progress on the murder."

"That was by design," I said.

"What do you think, Cody?" Edward said. Cody was sitting in the back, leaning against the door with his legs stretched out across the seat.

"They're getting paid off. But their free ride is coming to an end."

As we came off the mountain and glided onto the desert floor outside of Carson City, a jackrabbit darted in front of the car so quickly that Edward didn't have time to react. We ran straight over it.

"Jesus!" he exclaimed.

"Lookit that," Cody said, his head turned to the back window. "Lucky bunny made it. Probably just singed his ears on the oil pan."

I wondered if it was an omen.

•   •   •

The Tumbleweeds Ranch was doing what I assumed was brisk business for a Monday night. We sat at the bar, watching the action. The girls rotated steadily in and out of the parlor, and every few minutes new ones appeared. Edward's head turned like it was on a swivel. He kept tapping his fingers on the bar, and finally I said to him, "Hey, man, why don't you pick one you like?"

"Huh? No, no, that's not why I'm here, you know that. I'm just looking."

"If you say so."

"Maybe you should just buy a souvenir cap," Cody said, pointing at the caps, shirts, and assorted promotional items behind the bar.

"Well," Edward said a minute later, "if I was to partake, who do you think I should pick?"

"What, I'm the expert?" I said.

"Hey, go tear off a piece if you want. They won't bite," Cody said.

Edward tried to smile his way through it, but his face was turning red.

"You're man enough, ain't you?" Cody said.

"Take it easy, Cody," I said.

Eventually a bleached blonde with cantaloupe-sized breasts sat next to Edward, and after a while she led him down a hallway.

While he was gone, I spotted the Asian prostitute who had told me where to find Samantha Nunez. I doubted she would recognize me, but she caught me looking at her and sauntered over.

"My favorite position's doggie style," she said, flashing her million-dollar smile.

"Woof, woof," Cody said between sips off his beer.

"Hey, you. I remember you." She slapped me lightly on the arm with the backs of her fingers. "Did you ever find Samantha?"

"Nope," I said.

"Yeah, she didn't stay in Vegas for long. You didn't get to tell her about her sick family member, huh?"

"Never had the chance."

"You still looking for her?"

"Why?"

"She called me the other day, said she can't reach her boyfriend. Is he the one who's sick?"

"Yeah," I said. "Unfortunately he didn't make it."

"He died?"

"That's right."

"Oh, my god, Samantha doesn't know." She put her finger on her chin and looked down and then looked back at me. "What did he die of?"

I thought of Michael Dean Stiles, lying with his legs in the Truckee River, his beard glistening with vomit, his face bloodless, his last breath leaving his body. What did he die of? Greed probably, and certainly fool-ishness. A career criminal, a drug dealer and a killer, dying like a fool on a winter night in a cold desert canyon. I had a bizarre notion that if I went back there, I would find his clothed skeleton, grinning at me as if he'd had the last laugh.

"Tell Samantha to leave me a message at this number if she wants to know." I scribbled my office number on a cocktail napkin, then excused myself and went to the head. When I returned she was gone, but Edward was back at the bar with an ear-to-ear grin.

"You didn't fall in love, did you?" I asked.

"Other way around," he said, laughing, punching me on the shoulder.

"Way to go, Casanova." Cody reached out and mussed Edward's hair.

I bought the boys a round, and we toasted the good times, fun and laughter that could be had for the price of a few drinks, and free love, or at least love that didn't cost any more than money.

• • •

We left around midnight. The gravel crunched under our boots as we walked to Edward's Ford. I saw something move out of the corner of my eye, and in that dark instant my mind flickered with a vision of my father's death. Then a man holding a shotgun burst from behind the truck parked next to us. When I recognized the identity of the man, the synapses in my brain exploded with alarm. It was Julo Nafui.

He pounced like a cat, his shotgun aimed at Cody. He wasn't more than two feet away when he pulled the trigger. I could see the mucus in the corners of his eyes when the gun went off, the blast erupting into the still night like an angry curse. Cody had been standing next to me, and the next instant he was gone, his body flying back over the hood of Edward's Ford as if he'd been hit by a bus.

I jumped forward and grabbed the hot barrel of the shotgun with my left hand. Nafui yanked it back, but I stepped up and got my right hand around his wrist. He jerked the barrel upward, trying to wrench it from my grip. I ran at him, pushing, locking my forearm around the stock as he kicked out at my shins. He started whipping his powerful arms back and forth in a frenzy, trying to break my grip and throw me off. I held on with everything I had, squeezing desperately with my frostbitten hands.

Then from out of nowhere Edward leapt on to Nafui's back, growling and snapping like a rabid dog. We whirled around the parking lot, gravel spitting beneath our feet. Edward wrapped his hands over Nafui's face, and gouged at Nafui's eyes as if trying to reach the brain. Nafui wrenched his head to the side, and I pushed forward, slamming him into the cab of a yellow pickup truck. The stock of the gun shattered the side window, and Edward's head cracked hard against the window frame. I lashed out at Nafui's face with my right hand, catching an eye, and pushed with my thumb as hard as I could. Nafui roared in pain and dropped the shotgun so he could swat my hand off his face, then the heels of his hands hit my shoulders, and I stumbled back. The shotgun had dropped to the ground next to the truck, and Edward lay collapsed on top of it.

For a split second Nafui and I faced each other, gasping for air, our chests heaving. We were no more than five feet apart. I went for the Beretta, but he pulled his backup piece a fraction faster. I felt the twenty-five-caliber round splat against my vest, and I returned fire as I was falling back. At that range there was no need to aim. The hollow-point bullet tore through his chest like an auger bit from hell and sent a bloody fountain out his back, streaking the door of the yellow pickup. Amazingly Nafui remained standing, his lips curled in a sneer, staring at me with eyes that had turned blood red. He raised his pistol again, and my finger tightened on the Beretta's trigger.

A thunderous shot exploded behind me. I felt a hiss of air, then the right half of Nafui's face vanished into a red mist, slivers of bone and brains spraying into the air like a sudden geyser. His legs kicked out and he fell on his back, the pulp of his head slapping the gravel with a liquid crunch.

Cody walked past me, his .44 Magnum smoking in his hand. His face was white as bleached stone in the moonlight, his eyes coal black. We stared down at the gore of Julo Nafui in silence. Cody's new green parka had a jagged hole in the center, and his body armor was scored and blackened.

My eyes fell back to Julo Nafui. I swore I saw his corpse shudder, then I had an eerie sense his soul was leaving his body. For a second I felt his presence watching me. I froze, staring into air charged with electricity, then the sky flashed, and I saw his spirit being sucked into the earth, like sand falling through an hourglass in fast motion. I staggered back, the hair on my arms and back of my head standing straight out, my face on fire with needles and pins. A small dust twister appeared, danced around Nafui's body for a few seconds, then vanished.

I didn't notice the door to Tumbleweeds open, didn't see the people spilling out until the crowd had formed around us. But I did notice a dark truck parked in the shadows at the far end of the lot, its engine idling. Cody and I looked at each other. "Pace," I said, and then I was running through the parked cars, crouched low and approaching the idling truck from behind.

I heard the transmission clunk into drive, and the truck started forward. I sprinted full out, the Beretta clenched in my fist, and just as the driver began accelerating toward the exit road, I dove into the truck's bed. The driver turned his head, and I saw Conrad Pace straining to look back. He floored the gas, and I tumbled and shoulder-rolled against the tailgate as the truck fishtailed on the gravel. I pulled myself up, balanced on one knee, and fired a round through the plastic window behind the cab. The slug split through the plastic and spider webbed the windshield.

The truck was catching traction and gaining speed. I crawled up to the cab, yanked the sliding plastic window open, reached in and grabbed Pace by the hair, then heaved with all my strength. He came off the seat and I jerked his head back through the window. His feet could no longer reach the pedals and the truck slowed, left the road, and began bouncing over the terrain of the desert.

I rammed my gun into Pace's cheekbone. "Payback time, motherfucker," I said.

"You know the penalty for killing a cop?" Pace said through gritted teeth. "You'll ride the needle."

"You ain't a cop, Pace. You're a crook." The truck had slowed to just a few miles an hour and was careening over a series of deep ruts. The unmanned steering wheel was spinning back and forth wildly as the truck's suspension twisted in every direction. I saw Pace trying to work his hand toward his holster. I gripped his hair tighter and pushed his neck against the window frame.

"In a day or two, your operation's gonna be fully exposed, Pace. You're done. You're gonna have journalists crawling up your ass, and everyone's gonna want a piece of you, the locals, the feds, the IRS. It'll be a hell of a party."

"You ain't got the balls, punk," Pace said.

"It's too late for your bullshit, Pace. Nafui's dead, and the only reason I don't send you to hell with him right now is so you can spend the rest of your pathetic life in a cage."

"Time for you to die," he rasped, and his hand went for his gun.

"Don't do it!" I jammed the Beretta hard into the flesh of his face.

"Fuck you." He pointed his revolver over his shoulder and pulled the trigger. I dropped down low, and four shots popped over my head, the slugs ricocheting off the steel tailgate and singing out into the night. I was still holding him by the hair, but the truck lurched down a steep bank and almost flipped. I lost my grip on Pace and flew across the truck bed, my fingers clawing for a handhold. Then Pace hit the gas and the truck leapt forward, dropping into a shallow gully. The suspension bottomed out, and when the shocks rebounded I was launched from the bed. I landed sprawled in the dirt, and my gun flew out of my hand and disappeared in the darkness.

Pace swung a wide arc and was heading back toward the road. But the truck's front end washed into deep sand and the back tires came off the ground. The motor revved but the tires couldn't find traction. I pulled myself up and ran toward the truck, high-stepping through the scrub. I caught a glimpse of Cody's silhouette running across the terrain, hundreds of feet away. Then Pace jumped out of the cab and drew down on me with his pistol.

His first shot missed, and I kept running. His next shot winged me in the side, tearing a streak through the outer mesh of my vest. The impact twisted me around and I almost lost my balance, but my legs continued to propel me forward. Then I heard the hammer of his revolver click on an empty cylinder. And then once more. He tried to back away, but I hit him at full speed flush in the chest, my shoulders hammering into him with the satisfying impact of a well-executed tackle. Our feet left the ground, and I body-slammed him to the desert floor. His eyes rolled madly, like a wounded animal's. I swung down on him with a right and drilled him in the mouth. His head snapped back, and I felt the imprints of his teeth on my knuckles. "That's for trying to drown me," I said.

"You're a dead man," he hissed. He spit blood in my face and tried to throw me off, but I held him by the neck and punched him again. Blood burst from his nose and soaked his mustache. "And that's for leaving me without a coat," I said. I could see the fury in his face as I pulled him to his feet and flung him against the truck. He bounced off and came at me swinging. He'd done some boxing in his time. But his time had passed. I blocked a left and a right, then slammed my fist into his gut, and his eyes went round with shock. "And that's for fucking with my friend Edward."

Pace gagged and fell to his knees. Then I heard Cody from behind, and I turned and saw him coming like a freight train, like I remembered him on the football field, eyes crazed, his beard red and wild. He snorted like a bull, grabbed Pace by the neck and crotch, and heaved him over the truck.

"Fly away, shitbird," Cody said. Pace hit the ground with a groan of pain.

I stuffed Pace's revolver in my jeans and backtracked until I found my automatic. When I returned, Pace had pulled himself to his feet and leaned heavily on his truck. Cody grabbed him by the collar and started marching him back to the cathouse. I heard sirens in the distance.

"That's right, dumb-ass," Pace grunted. "The cavalry's coming. Who do you think they're going to believe, me or you?"

"Keep moving," Cody said.

"You'll be arrested before you can spit," Pace said.

The crowd was waiting for us in front of Tumbleweeds. Edward had pushed himself into a sitting position against the front tire of the yellow pickup truck. One of the hookers was kneeling beside him, her eyes wide with concern.

"Edward," I said, but he responded with an incoherent mumble. I bent down to him; the back of his head was matted with blood.

"Someone call a goddamn ambulance!" I yelled at the crowd. I sat down next to Edward, oblivious to the bits of flesh strewn about the gravel. "Take it easy, buddy," I said. "You just got your bell rung." He turned his head toward me, but his eyes were distant and unfocused. Cody kicked Pace's legs out from under him and threw him to the ground. The prostitutes, their customers, the madam, and the bartender all stared at us as if they were watching a movie, waiting to see what would happen next.

"Could one of you people get me a damn beer?" Cody shouted hoarsely.

25

THE CARSON CITY POLICE raced into the parking lot a minute later, sirens blaring, and skidded to a stop in the gravel, raising a huge cloud of dust. One squad car lost control, spun out in a 180, and ended up stuck in a ditch. I counted a total of three sheriff's cruisers, two Carson City PD squad cars, two unmarked cars, and one ambulance. The cops surrounded us, getting in each other's way, arguing, talking over one another. Pace yelled for everybody to shut up, and a plainclothes officer led him aside. Another plainclothesman, a pudgy, middle-aged man, took control, getting Edward loaded into the ambulance, telling another cop to cover the dead body for Christ's sake, and instructing the others to interview witnesses.

Cody and I sat where we were, watching the ambulance leave. The plainclothesman in charge knelt next to the covered corpse of Julo Nafui.

"I sure hope you guys have licenses to carry those weapons," he said.

"The dead man was a hitter hired by Conrad Pace," I said. "I shot him in self-defense."

"Sure you did," the detective said, in that unmistakable tone that comes from being lied to on a regular basis. "Get up. We're going to the station."

At least he had the decency to cuff our hands in front. As we walked with Lieutenant Gordon DeHart to his squad car, I looked out past the commotion and saw Pace easing his truck through the desert. Two uniformed cops with shovels were hiking back toward us. When Pace reached the paved road, his tires screeched and the motor revved loudly as he went through the gears. The sound slowly faded into the darkness, like a long echo that didn't want to die.

•   •   •

It was three A.M. before Lieutenant DeHart gave up trying to sort out my story of the tangled events. I found myself unable to explain what happened in a way any sane person would believe. I finally told him to lock us up so we could get some sleep. They put Cody and me in a clean holding cell, and I immediately fell into a dreamless slumber.

•   •   •

"I think I've got a broken rib," Cody said when we woke the next morning. His jacket and vest lay on the floor. He pulled up his shirt to show me the six-inch round bruise in his flesh the shotgun blast had left. "There's not much a doctor can do," he said, grimacing as he prodded his side with his fingers. "They'll just wrap it."

A deputy showed up a few minutes later and led us to a room with a rectangular table. Lieutenant DeHart sat there, next to a man in a suit and tie.

"This is Jack McGregor, Carson City Chief of Police. Help yourself to the coffee and donuts."

Cody and I sat down. "We've interviewed three witnesses who support your claim of self-defense," McGregor said. He was a tall man with a craggy face and droopy eyes. "Some guys were sitting in their car smoking a joint, and they saw everything." He drummed his thumbs on the table, rapping out a quick rhythm. "Based on that, we won't press charges."

"So we're free to go?" I said.

"Not yet. Tell me what you know about Conrad Pace."

· · ·

Two hours later, Cody and I walked out into the weak sunlight, and DeHart gave us a ride over to the hospital where Edward had been admitted.

"Why's McGregor so interested in Conrad Pace?" Cody asked DeHart.

"Chief McGregor is part of a national anti-corruption council. To say he's interested doesn't quite do it. He's leading our zero-tolerance-on-corruption program."

Cody laughed. "I'd say him and Pace are gonna have a lot to talk about."

We had to wait an hour for Edward to get released. His doctor told us he had a fractured skull and a concussion, had taken fifteen stitches in his head, and needed at least a week's rest. While we waited, Cody charmed a nurse into wrapping his ribs.

When Edward came out of his room, he had a three-inch-wide bandage reaching from the back of his neck to the top of his head. They had shaved the area.

"How you feeling, man?" I asked.

"Not so great," he admitted.

"Wait until you see the cool new haircut you got," Cody said, then put his arm around him and walked him outside like Edward was his little brother.

DeHart dropped us off at Edward's car in the nearly deserted parking lot in front of Tumbleweed's. The brothel complex looked different in the light of day. A large windmill I'd never noticed stood next to one of the whorehouses. Behind the buildings, a series of low hills stretched out until they rose into a steep ridge that in the distance looked painted against the sky. I looked at the ground where the battle with Julo Nafui had taken place. The gravel was uniform and smooth, as if it had never happened.

We didn't talk much as I drove us back to South Lake Tahoe. We were almost over the pass, the lake just coming into view, when Cody looked over at me.

"The only time I ever heard Julo Nafui's voice was when we saw him in the hallway at Pistol Pete's. Remember? He said, 'You're trespassing.' That's it. Never heard him say another thing."

"He was a man of few words, I guess," I said.

"Some dark shit going on inside that dude."

"No doubt."

"Good thing he's dead."

I dropped Cody off at his truck at the Chatter Box, and he followed me to Caesar's. We put Edward in a wheelchair and I called John Bascom's suite from the courtesy phone in the lobby.

"Reno, where the blazes are you? I've been calling you all morning!"

"I'm downstairs in the lobby." I pulled my cell out of my pocket. The battery had died.

"Edward Cutlip is missing," he yelled.

"I've got him right here. We're on the way up."

Bascom's wife answered the door. They looked stunned when Cody wheeled Edward in.

"Give your man a raise," Cody said.

"Good god," Bascom said. "What in hell happened?"

"Julo Nafui, the man who murdered your son, is dead," I said. "Your case is closed. It's done. And if it wasn't for Edward, Nafui might have killed Cody and me. Then he might have come after you."

"He's dead," Bascom said, as if he didn't believe it.

"Nafui's brains are splattered all over Carson City, man," Cody said.

"Reno?"

"My first shot probably killed him," I said. "If it didn't, Cody's shot definitely did."

I gave Bascom the details of what happened, and when he asked what we were doing at a whorehouse, I told him I wanted to talk to the hooker who knew Samantha Nunez. I didn't think it was any of Bascom's business why we were really there.

"Did the bastard suffer before he died?" Bascom asked.

"Not for long enough," Cody replied.

"What Edward did took a great deal of courage and guts," I said, and Bascom stared at me then looked away, his expression blank, as if he was considering something that had never occurred to him.

"He's got *cojones* the size of bowling balls," Cody added.

"My wife is present," Bascom admonished.

"I'll mail you my expense report," I said, and turned to Edward, who looked drowsy. "Have him see a doctor before you leave town, please."

We all stood in the suite silently. Through the window I could see the skies were dark and heavy, and the cold seemed to wait outside patiently, knowing it could outlast any mortal circumstance. Bascom nodded at me grimly. Cody and I turned to leave, but before we could, Nora Bascom stepped in front of the door.

"Thank you for killing him," she whispered, her eyes shiny and wet. "I hope he rots in hell." Then she pressed a folded piece of paper into my hand. I unfolded it with the fingers of one hand. It was a check for $50,000. I accepted it without any philosophical musings. I'd earned it.

"Hope he rots in hell," Nora Bascom whispered again, as if it was an invocation. I nodded and said, "Yes, ma'am."

• • •

It was four o'clock and snowing by the time we were packed and ready to leave. Cody's ribs were hurting, so I found the two-year-old bottle of codeine I'd taken from Samantha Nunez's apartment. He snatched it out of my hand and swallowed enough pills to sedate a horse, then cracked a beer and tried to get comfortable in the passenger seat.

The clouds resting on the granite ridges above the westbound pass were battleship gray when we rolled out of town. I drove slowly, the truck's tires crunching over fresh snow, the pines blurred in the haze, the alpine lake choppy and black. Behind us the lights of the casinos glowed steadily, as if even the fiercest winter storm posed no threat.

Cody fell asleep as we went over Echo Summit, his beer can resting half full between his legs. When I stopped at Placerville an hour later, it was dark and the snow had turned to rain. I called Wenger and left him a voicemail saying I'd be in the office sometime the next day. Then I called Beverly Howitt. Her cell voice mail wasn't working, so I left a message with the clerk at the hotel where she was staying.

Cody's chainsaw snoring mercifully downshifted to occasional snorts, leaving me alone with my thoughts for the long drive. I stared past the rhythmic cadence of the wiper blades, out to a world sectioned in black corridors, white lines, and bursts of red light. When I pulled up to my apartment it was ten o'clock. I woke Cody, and hauled my gear inside as he drove away. "Home sweet home," I muttered, but the apartment seemed empty and lifeless. I went to bed, weary and dead tired, my body aching in a hundred different places.

·   ·   ·

I walked into my office in San Jose the next morning, the office of Wenger and Associates, me being the associate. Or so I thought. A man perhaps sixty sat at my desk.

"Well, hello, Dan," Wenger said. "To what do I owe the honor?"

"Sorry I'm late, Rick. I've been tied up."

"Oh, yes. Late. Of course. Let's see." He ticked the days off his wall calendar. "Yes. You are indeed *a little* late. Seven working days late. But seven hours, seven days, hey, who's counting? They're only numbers, right? It could be seven dollars, seven hundred dollars, seventy thousand dollars, maybe even *a hundred fucking thousand dollars.* Is that what you are, Dan? The Hundred-Thousand-Dollar Man?"

"Are you feeling okay, Rick?"

"Yes, indeedy, I am. Just fine, thank you. By the way, meet Jim Phelps. You see, Jim wants a job. He wants to work. He's used to working hard. Comes in on time. Works hard. Comes in early. Leaves late."

Wenger's eyes were wide, and his manic chatter wasn't normal. If I didn't know better, I'd have assumed he was coked to the gills. Either that or he was suffering some sort of psychotic episode. Jim Phelps looked stunned and uncomfortable. "It's my first day," he said with a shrug.

"Sorry, can't talk, Dan. Money, money, made five grand in the stock market yesterday. Dotcom sector's on fire. Time is money." Wenger held his hands in front of him, flapping them side to side from the wrist joint.

"What's up with my desk?"

"Oh, yes. I almost forgot. How very, very inconsiderate of me. You, Dan, are fired. Terminated. Eighty-sixed. Adiosed. Eighty-osed. You are the weakest link. Bye-bye."

His phone rang, and he picked it up and started chattering like a monkey on a crack binge. A box with my personal effects sat next to my former desk. In the box was my bottle of CC, a Rolodex, two pens with the ends chewed, a stack of Styrofoam cups, and an individually wrapped dose of Alka Seltzer. My final paycheck was taped to the bottle.

"I've never seen him like this," I whispered to Jim Phelps. "He sounds like he's lost his mind."

"What have I got myself into?" he said under his breath.

The phone on the desk rang. Out of habit, I picked it up. "Investigations."

"I was given this number. I'm looking for my boyfriend," a female voice said.

"Hello, Samantha."

"Who is this?"

"I came and visited you at the Cat's Meow last week. We had a nice conversation. Cost me two hundred bucks."

"So it's you," she said.

"Nice to hear from you too."

"Whatever. I'm calling because I hear my boyfriend Dean is dead, and I don't believe it."

"That's too bad."

"Can you tell me where he is?"

"Tell me first what kind of scam you and Michael Dean Stiles and Julo Nafui were running on Sylvester Bascom."

"Who?"

"Sylvester Bascom was the man you watched Julo Nafui murder after you let him in the room."

"Oh," she said. I heard her exhale a hit off a cigarette.

"I know everything that happened in the room. I know you let Stiles in to rob Bascom, and then Sven Osterlund came out of the closet and punched out Stiles. Then you let Nafui in, and he stabbed Bascom to death."

"Okay," she said slowly.

"Nafui's dead, Samantha. You don't have to worry about him. My investigation of Sylvester Bascom's murder is done. I'm not working with any police agency, and I assume South Lake Tahoe PD will close the file on the murder since Nafui's dead. It's probably a good idea for you to stay out of the area, though."

"No shit. What other kind of brilliant free advice do you have for me?"

"You want to know what's up with your boyfriend, you tell me what was going on."

"Fuck that."

"I guess this conversation's over."

"Wait. This is ridiculous. I'm not going to incriminate myself over the phone. You're probably recording this conversation."

"Wrong," I said tiredly. "Let me give you a few other things to consider. The drug ring ran by Jake Tuma? It's going down big time. The crooked cops protecting it, including the sheriff at the top, are going to take a major fall. And I know Michael Dean Stiles was dealing for Tuma."

"Just tell me where he is," she said.

"I'm sorry. I have to go. I can't use this phone."

"Hold on," she said urgently. "Don't hang up. Give me your word, for whatever that's worth, that you won't screw me over."

I laughed out loud. "Haven't we had this conversation before? "This is like *déjà vu*. And what about your word? You owe me a night of sex for killing Nafui."

"*You* killed him?"

"Yes."

"I would have liked to have seen it," she said.

"I doubt that."

"I heard Nafui's dead. But I don't know for sure."

"Call the Carson City Coroner's Office."

"All right, listen," she said. "I let Dean in because I suspected this guy Bascom was a high roller. Every now and then I'd get a john who didn't hesitate to pay a premium price, talked about tipping big, that sort of thing. So I'd have Dean wait outside until the right moment, then let him in to roll the chump."

It was a typical Murphy scam, a crime that probably occurred in every major American city on a regular basis. "What about the drugs?" I said. "What's Stiles's connection with Bascom or Osterlund?"

"Osterlund?"

"He was the guy in the closet."

"I never saw him before. Listen, Dean may have been dealing, but it had nothing to do with what happened that night."

"Tell me why Julo Nafui was there," I said.

"He and Dean had become fast friends. They worked together and hung out. He's probably the only man on the planet tougher than Dean, with all that mercenary shit he's done. Talk about a stone-cold killer. He scared the shit out of me and I hated his fucking guts. I thought he was the devil. You sure he's dead?"

"Very sure. Why did Nafui stab Bascom? What was the reason for that?"

"I told you, Nafui was a natural killer. He enjoyed it. He would whip out his big knife and brag he could stab all the way through a person. I guess he wanted to prove it."

"He stabbed Bascom just to prove that?" I asked. "For no other reason?"

"That's right," she said. "Now, where's Dean?"

I cleared my throat. "He's dead, Samantha."

"I don't believe that. I feel him."

"Call the Truckee Sheriff's Office if you want," I said. "They're probably looking for kin to claim the body."

•   •   •

Wenger was still on the phone when I hung up. I picked up my box and walked out onto the damp sidewalk. Jim Phelps followed me.

"Hey, I didn't know I was taking someone's job. I'm a retired marketing manager from Hewlett Packard. I don't need the money. I took this job so I could live the life of a private investigator for a couple months. Then I want to write a screenplay."

I smiled. "Good luck. I suggest you make it a comedy. Wenger ought to give you plenty of material to work with."

26

THE AFTERNOON AFTER WENGER fired me I rode my bike to the gym and worked out harder than I had in months, pushing my muscles to the limit, trying to sweat the booze, cigarettes, and sordid memories out of my system. My answering machine was blinking when I got back to my apartment, still dripping from the light rain that began to fall as I rode home. I hit the button hopefully, waiting for Beverly Howitt's voice, but it was Jim Phelps from the office. He said Wenger had just been taken to the hospital, apparently suffering an extreme reaction to an overdose of allergy medicine.

I spent the next few days drying out and running various errands. Wenger called me the following Sunday. He said he had recovered and was resting at home.

"What the hell kind of medicine were you taking?" I asked.

"Some pills to help with my allergies to my goddamned cat."

"What did you do, take the whole bottle?"

"Very funny," he said, then spent a half an hour trying to convince me to come back and work for him, and also to let him invest my money in the stock market, since he claimed to be getting rich on dotcom stocks. I answered no to both requests, and when he continued trying to convince me, I gently hung up on him. Then I dialed the number I had for Beverly.

"Hey," I said when she answered.

"Is this…who is this?"

"It's Dan, Dan Reno. How are you?" I felt awkward, feeling a sense that whatever there was between us in Salina may have been a drunken illusion on my part. She had been scared and vulnerable, and I had treated her kindly. Maybe there was no more than that.

"I didn't think you were going to call."

"I left a message at your hotel a couple days ago."

"You did? I never got it. But that's understandable, since the clerk here is a hopeless alcoholic."

"There's always hope," I said. "How's your mom?"

"The doctors give her two weeks."

"I'm sorry."

"Me too," she whispered. "Are you still investigating your case?"

"It's over, for the most part. I was concerned you might have eventually been called to testify, but that won't happen now."

"Why?"

"The man who committed the murder has already been dealt with."

"Is he in jail?"

"No, but he's not going to bother anyone again."

• • •

February turned unseasonably sunny in San Jose. Wenger continued calling, mostly to babble about his obsession with the stock market. The computing sector was red hot, and he stopped paying much attention to his investigation business and poured every penny he had into local technology stocks.

In my abundant free time, I found myself spending a ridiculous amount of hours talking to Beverly Howitt. As we grew closer, I became plagued by a nagging loose end: the possibility that a tape of Sylvester Bascom's murder might eventually surface. Beverly and I had just hung up on a Wednesday afternoon when I decided I needed closure on the tape. I had no way of knowing for certain where Osterlund's supposed video camera and tape might be, but I had a few ideas.

I dialed the number for Jane Osterlund, and a recorded voice said the number was disconnected. I then called the only number I had for Brad Turner, his parents' phone number. His mom answered, and after she got over her surprise from hearing from me—it had been at least ten years since we'd talked—she told me Brad had checked into a drug-and-alcohol rehabilitation center last week. It was his third go at rehab, and this time it was a ten-week in-patient program. Mrs. Turner was embarrassingly candid about her opinions of her son and his habits, but after listening to her lament for ten minutes, I interrupted to ask if she had Whitey's number.

Whitey answered on the first ring.

"This is the San Jose Police Department," I said. "I'm calling to investigate Brad Turner escaping from Trembling Hills Recovery Center."

"Huh? Come on. Who is this, man?"

"It's Dan Reno, Whitey."

"Shit. What, you heard about Brado?"

"I just talked to his mom."

"Yeah, she checked him in after Brad got fired from his job."

"No kidding."

"Yeah. Ten freakin' weeks, no booze, no smoke."

"Maybe it'll be good for him."

"I think he'll probably have a nervous breakdown in there. I know I would," Whitey said.

"Everyone's got to dry out sometime," I philosophized.

"Yeah, but not cold turkey."

"Whitey, did you ever talk to Osterlund's mom when you came back from Tahoe?"

"Yeah, I did. And let me tell you, she is one messed-up lady. Rumor has it she's been using her psychic gig to bilk people out of a lot of dough. She'd have them give her money so she could invest it for them in the stock market. Anyway, she bought into this one company that went from around two dollars a share to thirty bucks in two weeks, but then the NASDAQ suspended trading because they think the company is a fraud. When trading started again, the stock fell to twelve cents. I heard she lost almost everything. The bitch screwed over a lot of people."

"I called her, and her number's disconnected."

"Really? Dude, she's probably on the run. I guess that would explain why there's been no word on a funeral for Sven."

No funeral. No matter how morally void your life, everyone deserved a funeral. On the other hand, it was hard to imagine anyone grieving for Osterlund. Maybe his mom thought it would be a waste of money.

"Why are you trying to reach her?" he asked.

"I'm finishing up my investigation of Bascom's murder and wanted to see if she'd taken possession of her son's belongings."

"Dude, who knows? I think she's history. You know what else I think? Sven was probably involved in his mom's scam. He was probably trying to figure out a way to rip off Sylvester."

"Yeah, could be. But still, the question is, why would a well-to-do guy like Sylvester Bascom be hanging around a fuck-up like Osterlund?"

Whitey didn't know, and I resigned myself to the fact that maybe I would never find out what was behind it.

My finger was poised to dial Cody's number, but the phone rang first. I was caught off guard when I heard the voice. It was Marcus Grier.

"I have some news I think will be of interest to you, Mr. Reno," he said, his tone deep enough to rattle a coffee cup off a table. "Both the Sacramento and Reno papers printed front-page stories on the corruption of Conrad Pace's office. I was interviewed by reporters from both papers. Read the articles—I think they're just the tip of the iceberg."

"That's great news, Sheriff."

"You are correct," he said. "I've been rehired."

"I'm glad to hear that. You think Pace will be indicted soon?"

"We'll see. It'll get real interesting in the next couple days."

"Is Pace still in town?" I asked.

"As far as I know. He hasn't formally resigned, but he's laying low."

"He's got balls, I'll give him that," I said. "Marcus, have Sven Osterlund's next of kin claimed his belongings yet?"

"Funny you should ask. A repo company picked up his truck yesterday. The rest of his stuff is being held by South Lake Tahoe PD. No one from his family has contacted me."

"I heard he owned a fancy video camera. Did you happen to find that?"

"A video camera? No, there was no camera."

After we hung up, I dialed Cody, thinking he wouldn't answer because he was probably back to work at San Jose PD. But he answered the phone, his voice gruff and a little uneven.

"Dirty Double-Crossin'?"

"Hey, Cody."

"Good to hear from you, Dirt," he said. "I appreciate you calling, seeing how you're responsible for breaking up my marriage."

"What?"

"When I got home, Debbie gave me the news. She wants out. She even had the fucking papers prepared. Handed them to me right when I walked in the door."

"Shit, I'm sorry to hear that," I said.

"Don't be—it wasn't much of a surprise. But, being that I was saving your ass at the time she was probably in the sack with her attorney, I think the least you could do is buy your old buddy a meal and a couple drinks."

"Sure," I said. "How about Original Joe's at six?"

"How about we hit their lounge right now?" It was half past three.

"You're not working?"

"That's another thing I'll tell you about," he said. "How does the old saying go? When it rains, it pours?"

"Give me an hour," I said. "I need to pick up a couple newspapers."

It didn't take me long to end my two-week sobriety after meeting Cody at the restaurant. Once he started telling his stories, I wasn't about to let him drink alone. Besides his divorce, the internal affairs division at SJPD was intent on making an example of him, and he was on unpaid leave, which was the final stop before termination. After a few drinks and some less than stellar Italian food, I tried to steer the conversation to a subject I hoped would cheer him.

"Check this out," I said. I pulled the Reno and Sacramento newspapers out and set them on the bar. The headline of the *Sacramento Bee* read "Placerville Sheriff's Mansion Bought With Drug Money." There was a full-color picture of Conrad Pace, his cowboy hat crooked on his head, his face still bruised, trying to fight his way through a group of people with cameras and microphones. The article was long; it took up two columns above the fold and continued for two more pages in the middle of the paper. The reporter I'd talked to in Tahoe had tailed Pace and taken pictures of him in front of Jake Tuma's house. The story claimed the house had a meth lab in the garage and was a highly frequented drug-dealing hub. The journalist had parked down the street from the house for a twelve-hour period and reported twenty-three cars stopping for short periods of time. Next to a picture of Pace in Tuma's driveway was one of him at his fancy home in Granite Bay, the most expensive community between Sacramento and Lake Tahoe.

The Reno paper's story had a slightly different bend. Their front page was dominated by a large headline that blared: "Pistol Pete's Linked to

Corrupt Sheriff." It focused on Pace's relationship with Salvador Tuma, and they had pieced together a financial trail showing large cash transactions by Pace. The story elaborated on Tuma's family ties to organized crime and discussed Jake Tuma's drug ring, as well as mentioning Julo Nafui, claiming he had been a hired enforcer for the Tumas. It said Nafui was recently shot to death while attempting to murder enemies of Tuma.

The newspaper articles gave me a sense of satisfaction, but it wasn't until later that evening, as Cody and I were leaving the restaurant, that it finally occurred to me—if Osterlund hadn't destroyed and thrown away the camera and tape, there was one person who might have it.

Twenty minutes later, we pulled up in front of Mandy's apartment complex in south San Jose. Once I told Cody my theory, he insisted we resolve it immediately. The light was on at Mandy's unit. I knocked and heard muted noises.

"Go away," a female voice said through the door.

"Open up, Mandy," I said.

The door opened the few inches the security chain allowed. A black man's face looked out at us. "Get lost, motherfuckers," he said.

Wrong answer.

Cody brushed past me and body-slammed the door open. The chain popped as if it were dry macaroni. The black man was shirtless, his arms covered with designer tattoos. He looked like he might be a cornerback for the local college team. He took a karate stance, but Cody simply barreled him over. They tumbled into the kitchenette, the man's head bounced hard off a tile counter, and then he lay still on the linoleum. "Next time don't cuss at me, *motherfucker*," Cody said.

Mandy watched impassively. Her low-cut blouse was slipping off her shoulder and her bra lay on the floor. The CD case on the coffee table was smeared with cocaine.

"Sorry to disturb your evening," I said. "I'll make it quick."

"Looks like you'll be spending the night in jail," she said, and picked up her telephone.

I reached down and yanked the cord from the wall. "Osterlund's video camera. Where is it?"

"What are you talking about? Are you high?"

"Here's how it works, Mandy. I tie your hands behind your back and duct tape your mouth, while Cody and I wreck your place looking for it. Or you do it the easy way and hand it over."

Her eyes blazed at me. "Gee, Dan, I guess it doesn't matter to you that you're breaking the law right now. Go ahead—tie me up, trash my place. And when you leave, you can look forward to being arrested. How's that?"

"The camera is evidence in a murder investigation, Mandy. The fact you have it means you're withholding evidence. That's mandatory jail time."

"You better just leave."

"Not yet," Cody's voice came from the kitchen. "I'm making myself a sandwich. Where the hell's the mayo?"

A groan followed Cody's voice. "Don't worry about this guy," Cody said. "I'll keep him occupied."

Mandy sat down on the couch and began chopping herself a line on the CD case.

"So if I get you the camera, what happens then?"

"Then you're free and clear."

"As if it never happened?"

"As if what never happened?"

"Well, whatever's on the tape."

"Hand it over and you got nothing to worry about."

She held her hair behind her ear and snorted a rail. Then she leaned back and studied me with glassy eyes. After a moment she shrugged and walked down the hall. When she came back, she held a black camera.

"The tape's still in it," she said.

"What was Osterlund's deal, Mandy? Why was Sylvester hanging out with him?"

"They were both hardcore voyeurs," she said, chopping another line. "Sylvester could barely get it up unless he was watching somebody fuck, or unless he knew somebody was watching him. Sven was the same way, but not quite as bad."

"And Osterlund's angle? Blackmail?"

"Pretty obvious, isn't it? He was going to make Sylvester pay him off, or he'd show the tape of Sylvester making it with a couple of whores to Desiree. It was my idea, but I never thought Sven would go through with it, the crazy son of a bitch."

Cody walked out of the kitchen with a submarine sandwich in his paw. "Got what you need, Dirt?"

"Yeah," I said.

"Sylvester was a perverted weirdo, Dan," Mandy said. "Desiree told me he set up a camera and videoed them every time they got it on."

"Did you watch this tape?" I said, holding up the camera.

"No, I–"

"Good. Forget it ever existed."

"Consider it done," she said.

"Hey," Cody said. "Sorry about your door, and raiding your fridge. I could come back and fix it and maybe take you out to lunch."

"How sweet of you," Mandy said.

As we left, Mandy's date struggled woozily to his feet. "Hey, asshole," he said and started toward Cody. Some guys have a steep learning curve. Cody backhanded him across the jaw with his fist and knocked him out cold again.

"You ought to pick smarter boyfriends," I said to Mandy, but she'd gone back to the couch to take another snort off the CD case. She didn't look up when we walked out.

"Christ, Dirt, get a load of the rack on Mandy," Cody said once we were in my truck. "She looks like she'd be one hell of a good time. You got her number?"

"My advice would be to stay away from her," I said. "She eats guys like you and me for lunch."

Cody laughed as if I were kidding.

27

OVER THE NEXT FEW days, the Federal Anti-Corruption Task Force, the FBI, and then the IRS all flocked to South Lake Tahoe, turning the city into a media circus. Jake Tuma was arrested, and his house was sealed off while the cops went through it. They charged him with twenty-six separate drug-related offenses. The DA's office, armed with a mountain of evidence and amid major public pressure, brought the case to trial promptly and convicted him of most of the charges. The drug-crazed bully who pushed women around when he didn't get his way was sentenced to thirty years in prison. I saw him on TV the day he was sentenced. He stared the camera down, his face furious and bitter, then spat at the lens. He was quoted as saying he had a powerful family and intended to be free on appeal shortly.

The Nevada Gaming Commission sent a team of accountants to scour the books at Pistol Pete's. I heard later that Salvador Tuma left unexpectedly in the night and was rumored to have fled the country. I wondered if Jake thought about his father as he sat on a lumpy, thin mattress, smelling the open toilet in his cell, or when he showered next to men who were fully capable of punching a homemade shank through his liver for any perceived slight.

Marcus Grier had been granted full back-pay for the work he had missed and was now running his department without impediment from

Conrad Pace, who was still county sheriff, but had stopped coming into his office. Shortly after Grier was rehired, Detective Iverson found Raneswich comatose in his apartment, after an apparent overdose of sleeping pills. Raneswich recovered, and he and Iverson both quit the force and vanished. Louis Perdie, Ronald Fingsten, and Conrad Pace all tried to leave town shortly afterward. The Nevada Highway Patrol caught up with Perdie and Fingsten outside of Ely, Nevada. But Conrad Pace was a mystery, for the time being. Somehow, he had slipped through the cracks.

I called Edward Cutlip at Bascom Headquarters and was pleased to find out John Bascom had promoted him to VP of operations, the position Sylvester would have had.

"You know, it was weird," Edward said. "After you and Cody brought me into the suite in the wheelchair and told Bascom what happened at the cathouse, he started treating me differently. It was like I was a different person."

"Maybe he appreciates you risked your life for his cause."

He was quiet for a moment. "Maybe you're right," he said.

•   •   •

The district attorney from South Lake Tahoe contacted Cody and me in early April and said we would be called to testify in the trials of Louis Perdie and Ronald Fingsten. The charges ranged from kidnapping to drug and corruption offenses. We spent six nights at the Lakeside on the city's tab, sitting in court during the day and keeping our nighttime activities to a low roar. The court sessions were tedious, but left me with a couple of enduring images. One was of Louis Perdie in a dark blue suit and yellow necktie. He looked completely different from the violent hillbilly deputy I had known. But when we locked eyes, he gave me the same irreverent, cockeyed smile, as if he were back at the Lakeside's diner, wiping scrambled eggs from the corner of his mouth. The other image was of Deputy Fingsten on the stand, so nervous and scared I could see him shaking, as if he couldn't believe he'd be held responsible for his actions.

On the same day both men were convicted on a series of capital offenses, an abrupt news bulletin interrupted the proceedings: Conrad Pace had been found.

Two peckerwood fishermen stumbled upon his corpse in a shack built on stilts out in the deep bayou in southern Louisiana. They had stopped there when the motor on their skiff gave out. As they climbed the decaying ladder, they knew from the smell something was dead in the old wood slat structure. They thought it was probably an alligator that had been skinned and left behind. But when they walked through the humid air into the ramshackle, creaky room, they found the rapidly decomposing body of Conrad Pace. He was tied upright in a metal chair, his ankles fastened to the chair legs, his arms pinned behind him, his chest and shoulders tightly bound with bailing wire. The wire was buried deep in his flesh, as if his skin had grown around it. His mouth was sealed with duct tape, and two dime-sized holes were in the center of his forehead, like a second set of eyes.

EPILOGUE

Shortly after Conrad Pace's assassination, a leading men's magazine published an account of his criminality and his demise. Cody brought the article to my attention, and although some of it is fictionalized, it struck me as authentic, and I feel it bears repeating. The following is the section of the text I remember most vividly:

Conrad Pace smiled to himself as he drove his new Cadillac across the low bridge over the swamplands. On the other side of the water was New Orleans, and he was deciding what to have for dinner. Maybe seafood gumbo. Or hell, why not the best steak money could buy? And then how about going down to the French Quarter and picking up a black whore for dessert? He laughed out loud. His old friend Louis was probably facing serious time, but so were the rest of those dago gumballs back in Nevada. Meanwhile, he had a new name and Social Security number and a briefcase with $3 million cash in his trunk. It was the way of the world—the simple-minded would always be sacrificed for the elite.

His mind wandered to the home the realtor had just shown him—a large, white-columned, antebellum spread with a front lawn half the size of a football field. Maybe he'd sign the papers tomorrow and then hire an interior decorator. The mess in Tahoe already seemed a million miles away, and he had no doubt his future promised a continuance of the wealth and luxury he had earned.

After dinner, he checked out a couple of strip joints in the Quarter, places he'd been to years before. They hadn't changed much, and half an hour later he followed a woman up a flight of stairs to her apartment. She was just what he had in mind: tall and sultry, with one of those swinging asses that just wouldn't quit, the kind only nigger bitches have. He'd crack her like a shotgun and ram her with his horse cock first thing, he decided. Give that ass a good working over. He followed her inside, his eyes glazed in anticipation, and then out of nowhere a fist slammed into his face.

Pace reeled across the room and grabbed a heavy ceramic lamp. He swung it with all his strength at the shadowy figure coming at him and felt a satisfying crack as the lamp shattered against bone. But a second man seized him from behind and put him in a chokehold, and the man's arms felt like iron girders. Pace couldn't break free from the grip, and his lungs roared in pain. The last thing he saw before he passed out was the hooker's red fingernails clawing at his face.

When Pace opened his eyes, he heard water lapping at the side of the boat, and he could feel the dampness in the air. It must be dawn, it occurred to him, as his eyes stained to see through the thick fog. He lay on the bottom of a pirogue, and it reeked of rotting fish. Two men paddled the boat, their faces obscured behind rain hoods. Pace struggled upright, his head aching violently. His hands were tied behind him, and he felt like he'd been beaten with a baseball bat.

"Do you have any idea who I am?" Pace said.

The men were silent, hunched forward and paddling.

"I'm talking to you. Whoever's paying you, I'll double it."

No response.

"Listen to me, goddammit! I can make you both rich."

The man on the right turned his head slowly, and through the gloom Pace could make out his heavy mustache and thick jowls.

"*Salvador Tuma has a message for you. He wants you to know his son's in prison, and you stole three million from him.*"

"*Fuck Tuma! He went off the radar and left me and his son to clean up!*"

The men kept paddling silently. The fog was dense, and Pace knew he was out on the bayou, but he had no idea where. He peered out into the mist, seeing nothing, and felt an overwhelming sense that he and these two men were the last people on earth.

"*Name your price,*" *Pace said.*

They stopped rowing, and one man stood and tossed a rope around a wood piling that rose from the gray water.

"*The money you stole is already on the way back to Mr. Tuma,*" *the man said.*

"*Yeah,*" *said the other one, speaking for the first time, in a heavy Cajun accent. "But I get to keep your car, me.*"

Pace's mouth moved silently as the men lifted him by the arms. He nearly collapsed from dizziness, then vomited what was left of his supper into the murky water. Pace watched the contents of his stomach rolling with the weak current. He looked around desperately, trying not to panic, his hands straining behind his back against the tightly wound rope. Out of the corner of his eye, he caught a glimpse of a revolver in one of the men's hands. In a detached place in his mind, Pace mused that he'd just heaved up the last dinner he'd ever have, and it was floating away in the bayou, his life floating away, his body reduced to a slick of rancid and steaming human waste.

•   •   •

Beverly Howitt's mother passed away in late April. I flew to Salt Lake City and drove down to Salina to attend the service. Glenda Howitt was laid to rest on a perfect spring day, a day all wrong for a funeral. The sky was a deep cloudless blue, the air smelled clean and pure, and the colors of the trees and flowers were so bright that no painting or photograph would do them justice.

When I got on the plane back to San Jose, Beverly was with me. She hadn't said anything about it; there was no discussion—she just had her suitcase packed and came with me to the airport. Funny the way things work out sometimes. When we walked into my apartment, she looked around, clicked her teeth, and went to work, cleaning, rearranging the cupboards, buying flowers and plants, lending the proverbial woman's touch. She tried to throw out one of my favorite old sweatshirts and actually bought a can of silver spray paint and painted the rusty iron weight set I'd left outdoors for years in the rain and sun.

The stock market had taken a dramatic dive earlier in April and continued to erode as investors started bailing out. Horror stories of day traders and margin investors losing their life savings dominated the local and then the national news. Dotcom companies in the Silicon Valley began going belly up, and hordes of common folk saw their stock portfolios shed value like a dog shaking water out of its fur. Wenger grew increasingly depressed and bitter until he confessed to me that he was many thousands in the red and was closing up his business. In May he moved from San Jose because he felt living here was a daily reminder of how much money he'd lost.

My bank account was still flush with the checks from Bascom Lumber. Beverly and I decided to drive up to Tahoe to see the lake in the springtime, while the peaks were still covered with snow, looking down like content parents at the green meadows and blossoming flowers of the valley. While Beverly packed our clothes, I cleared some miscellaneous junk from the cab of my new Nissan four-by-four truck. I opened the glove box, and there sat Osterlund's camera, like a diary that possessed a morbid secret. I hefted the camera in my palm, feeling its weight, knowing my fingers were obscuring the prints of Osterlund and Mandy. But it didn't matter anymore. Osterlund was dead, and so were Michael Dean Stiles, Julo Nafui, and Conrad Pace. For some reason fate dictated I be the instrument of their downfall. Maybe it was my destiny, or maybe I just happened to be in the wrong place at the right time. Regardless, it didn't matter; it was a chapter in my life I was ready to put behind me. I ejected the tape and stuck it in my pocket.

Beverly had finished packing our bags, and when I walked in, she showed me the picnic lunch she had made.

"I even packed a couple beers for you," she said. "I was thinking we could stop somewhere pretty on the way up to Tahoe."

I kissed her cheek and walked out to the back patio, to my barbecue. I doused some half-burned coals in lighter fluid, then crumpled up the sports section from the morning newspaper and threw it on top.

"Is everything okay?" Beverly called, coming out to join me.

"It will be," I said, tossing a match on the paper. Beverly put her hand on mine, which held the Sony video camera. She looked up at me, sudden realization flashing in her eyes. I pulled the tape out of my pocket and dropped it into the flames, but the fire burned out too quickly. "Wait a sec," I said, and got my bottle of 151-proof rum down from above the refrigerator. I came back and doused the tape with enough booze to keep a man drunk for two days. When I flipped another match into the barbecue, it went up like a Roman candle. Beverly stood in front of me, her head under my chin, her body warm against mine, her face glowing in the heat of the flames. She held my arms tightly around her waist as we watched the tape burn into an unrecognizable scrap of melted plastic.

"It's over?" she asked, leaning into my chest, her hair against my neck.

"Yes," I said. "It's over."

ABOUT THE AUTHOR

Born in Detroit, Michigan, in 1960, Dave Stanton moved to Northern California in 1961. He attended San Jose State University and received a BA in journalism in 1983. Over the years, he worked as a bartender, newspaper advertising salesman, furniture mover, pizza cook, debt collector, and technology salesman. He has two children, Austin and Haley. He and his wife, Heidi, live in San Jose, California.

Stanton is the author of five novels, all featuring private investigator Dan Reno and his ex-cop buddy, Cody Gibbons.

To learn more, visit the author's website at **DanRenoNovels.com.**

If you enjoyed *Stateline*, please don't hesitate to leave a review at

http://bit.ly/amazonStateline

To contact Dave Stanton or subscribe to his newsletter, go to:

http://danrenonovels.com/contact/

More Dan Reno Novels:

Dying for the Highlife

Jimmy Homestead's glory days as a high school stud were a distant memory. His adulthood had amounted to little more than temporary jobs, cheap boarding houses, and discount whiskey. But he always felt he was special, and winning a $43 million lottery proved it.

With all that money, everything is great for Jimmy—until people from his past start coming out of the woodwork. First, his sexy stepmother, who seduced him as a teenager. Then his uncle, just released from Folsom after a five-year jolt for securities fraud, a crime that bankrupted Jimmy's father. Mix in a broke ex-stripper and a down-on-his luck drug dealer, both seeking payback over transgressions Jimmy thought were long forgotten.

Caught in the middle are investigator Dan Reno and his good buddy Cody Gibbons, two guys just trying to make an honest paycheck. Reno, straining to keep his home out of foreclosure, thinks that's his biggest problem. But his priorities change when Gibbons and Jimmy are kidnapped by a gang of cartel thugs out for a big score. Fighting to save his friend's life, Reno is drawn into a mess that leaves dead bodies scattered all over northern Nevada.

Speed Metal Blues

Bounty hunter Dan Reno never thought he'd be the prey.

It's a two-for-one deal when a pair of accused rapists from a New Jersey-based gang surface in South Lake Tahoe. The first is easy to catch, but the second, a Satanist suspected of a string of murders, is an adversary unlike any Reno has faced. After escaping Reno's clutches in the desert outside of Carson City, the target vanishes. That is, until he makes it clear he intends to settle the score.

To make matters worse, the criminal takes an interest in a teenage boy and his talented sister, both friends of Reno's. Wading through a drug-dealing turf war and a deadly feud between mobsters running a local casino, Reno can't figure out how his target fits in with the new outlaws in town. He only knows he's hunting for a ghost-like adversary calling all the shots.

The more Reno learns more about his target, the more he's convinced that mayhem is inevitable unless he can capture him quickly. He'd prefer to do it clean, without further bloodshed. But sometimes that ain't in the cards, especially when Reno's partner Cody Gibbons decides it's time for payback.

Coming in 2015:

DARK ICE

HARD PREJUDICE

Made in the USA
Columbia, SC
20 January 2022